Where Life

Will Lead Me

Book 2 of the Past Times Series

~~~

NANCY MOSER

Overland Park, Kansas

WHERE LIFE WILL LEAD ME

ISBN: 978-1-7339830-4-4

Published by:
Mustard Seed Press
10605 W. 165 Street
Overland Park, KS 66221

This story is a work of fiction. Any resemblances to actual people, places, or events are purely coincidental.

All Scripture quotations are taken from The Holy Bible, King James Version.

Cover design by Mustard Seed Press

Printed and bound in the United States of America

The Books of Nancy Moser: www.nancymoser.com

Historical Novels

Where Time Will Take Me (Book 1 of the Past Times Series)
Where Life Will Lead Me (Book 2 of the Past Times Series)
The Pattern Artist (Book 1 of the Pattern Artist Series)
The Fashion Designer (Book 2 of the Pattern Artist Series)
The Shop Keepers (Book 3 of the Pattern Artist Series)
Love of the Summerfields (Book 1 of Manor House Series)
Bride of the Summerfields (Book 2 of Manor House Series)
Rise of the Summerfields (Book 3 of Manor House Series)
Mozart's Sister (biographical novel of Nannerl Mozart)
Just Jane (biographical novel of Jane Austen)
Washington's Lady (bio-novel of Martha Washington)
How Do I Love Thee? (bio-novel of Elizabeth Barrett Browning)
Masquerade (Book 1 of the Gilded Age Series)
An Unlikely Suitor (Book 2 of the Gilded Age Series)
The Journey of Josephine Cain
A Patchwork Christmas (novella collection)
A Basket Brigade Christmas (novella collection)
Regency Brides (novella collection)
Christmas Stitches (novella collection)

Contemporary Books

The Invitation (Book 1 of Mustard Seed Series)
The Quest (Book 2 of Mustard Seed Series)
The Temptation (Book 3 of Mustard Seed Series)
Crossroads
*The Seat Beside Me (*Book 1 of Steadfast Series)
A Steadfast Surrender (Book 2 of Steadfast Series)
The Ultimatum (Book 3 of Steadfast Series)
The Sister Circle (Book 1 of Sister Circle Series)
Round the Corner (Book 2 of Sister Circle Series)
An Undivided Heart (Book 3 of Sister Circle Series)
A Place to Belong (Book 4 of Sister Circle Series)
The Sister Circle Handbook (Book 5 of Sister Circle Series)
Time Lottery (Book 1 of Time Lottery Series)
Second Time Around (Book 2 of Time Lottery Series)
John 3:16
The Good Nearby
Solemnly Swear
Save Me, God! I Fell in the Carpool (inspirational humor)

Children's Books

Maybe Later (Book 1 of the Doodle Art Series)
I Feel Amazing: the ABCs of Emotion (Book 2 of the Doodle Art Series)

DEDICATION

To those brave men, women, and children

Who left behind what was

To discover what could be.

Hail Kansas, my Kansas.

PROLOGUE

Spring 1879
Piedmont, New Hampshire

"As the mayor of Piedmont, New Hampshire I now officially recognize our new town motto." Frank Moore — new mayor and town butcher — revealed a sign that had "Piedmont" in large letters, and beneath it, "Where Justice Prevails." With difficulty he pounded the stake of the sign into the frozen ground. Two men rushed forward to take a whack at it.

Finally planted, the crowd of onlookers applauded.

Justine Braden slipped her hand around her fiancé's arm. "Finally."

Harland put his hand on hers. "A new mayor, a new motto, and a new beginning, all because of you. And the Almighty, of course."

Justine wouldn't argue with him. If she had stayed in New York City where she had grown up, Piedmont would still be under the tyrannical rule of the bully, Quinn Piedmont. And if God hadn't given her the gift of time travel, the sins of the past would have remained hidden and unrectified. God gave the orders and she did the legwork. They were a team: an all-knowing, powerful Master and His willing-but-flawed servant.

Pastor Huggins stepped forward. "Everyone is invited to the meeting house for pies, cakes, and other confections."

His announcement elicited more cheers than the sign had, and people headed to the building behind the church.

Justine and Harland turned to join the others.

So much had happened in the past year. Because of Justine's travels through time, the town bully, Quinn Piedmont, had been convicted of a long list of offenses, including the attempted murder of his own brother, Thomas. Free of Quinn's oppressive influence, a weight had been lifted from the town, a veil pulled aside, a slate wiped clean.

Speaking of Thomas . . . he joined them as they walked down the road. "A fine ceremony, don't you think?"

Justine smiled. "In truth I think the good citizens of Piedmont enjoy any event that will let them eat pie and cake."

"Me included," Harland said.

"You two are jaded," Thomas said. "The new motto commemorates the justice you helped bring about, Justine."

"You were a large part of that," she said. "Quinn thought he'd killed you. To have you return to Piedmont and prove him wrong—and guilty—after twenty years . . ." She linked her hand around his arm. "To discover that you are my father . . . *that* is cause for celebration."

He put a hand on hers. "Nothing has made me happier than to come out of the shadows and take my place by your side."

Justine felt a fresh wave of gratitude for their remarkable reunion. Being an only child, and with her mother gone, and her other father—Noel Braden, the man who had raised her—passed, she had a newfound appreciation of family. That her ability to travel through time had helped make that happen was a blessing she didn't take lightly.

"People seem to be leaving you alone today," Harland said.

She wished he hadn't brought up her one personal frustration since the truth about her gift had come out. "Actually, they're not leaving me alone."

"What's happened?" Thomas asked.

She told them about the newest invasions of her privacy: the two notes that had been slid under her door during the night, and finding Mrs. Newcomb waiting outside this morning, ready to pounce. "I'm not sure what to do to stop them."

"You've explained you're not traveling back to visit their relatives. You've made that clear."

"Very. Repeatedly. But they won't—"

Someone tapped Justine on the shoulder from behind. She turned around to see Mrs. Beemish, the wife of the stationmaster. The frenzy in the woman's eyes let Justine know what would come next.

She cut her off before it began. "I'm not time-traveling for people, Sarah."

Her frenzy was replaced with disappointment. "But Rachel said —"

"I'm saying no to everyone."

It was almost comical to watch a seventy-year-old woman pout.

"You're not being fair, Justine. God gave you a gift. Aren't you supposed to use it?"

"I am. But at His command, not my own. At the moment God wants me to stay in 1879."

"He does?"

"He does." *Try arguing with that.*

Mrs. Beemish didn't argue, she huffed. "You're being greedy, Justine Braden." She stormed away.

Justine sighed. "They always feel the need to make me feel guilty. I'm not being greedy, am I?"

"You are not." Thomas got them walking again.

But Justine suddenly found the idea of spending time at the celebration abhorrent — pie or no pie. In fact, being anywhere in Piedmont riled her.

"Harland, let's go up the mountain."

"Now?"

"Please. I need to get away. Be away." She looked up at her father. "If you'll excuse us?"

He nodded, as usual, accepting her eccentricities. "I'll save you some pie."

She and Harland turned around, walking against the crowd. Justine let silence fall between them because she wanted to hold her thoughts until after they were at Harland's special spot on the mountain.

Harland let her forge the way up the wooded trail at her own speed, reaching the top behind her. "You are driven today."

She stood up straight, taking deep breaths. "I am."

When her breathing calmed, she led him to the sitting rock they often shared. She gazed across the treetops, seeing the Connecticut River beyond, and Vermont beyond that. "This view always calms me. It's utterly beautiful."

"As are you."

She skimmed over the compliment. "Remember our time on the mountain last autumn when I talked about how much I've changed since moving here from New York?" She looked at him. "You changed me. This whole experience changed me. I have a purpose now. God made good come from bad – for the town, but also for me."

He wove his fingers through hers. "You also changed me because – "

"I have to leave."

He angled to look at her. "What?"

"My work is done here."

"People will leave you alone. Eventually."

"Can you be sure about that? They think of me as this 'being' with magical powers.'"

"Your gift *is* rather remarkable."

"But it's not magic. And to be clear, it's not mine to use as *I* wish."

"So God *is* saying no? You weren't just saying that to fend off Mrs. Beemish?"

Justine had to be honest about it. "Put it this way: God isn't saying yes." She tilted her head back, taking comfort in the warmth of the spring sun after a hard winter. "Things feel different now. Though I innocently happened onto that first foray into the past, after that, I was drawn to it – directed to go, if you will."

"He spoke to you?"

"Nothing like that." She put a hand to her midsection. "I felt a nudge, an inner 'go now' that I had to follow."

"You didn't have to," he said. "Other women in your family said no."

"But I needed to say yes."

"You *chose* to say yes."

She shrugged. "I want to say yes again."

He cocked his head. "But you said —"

"I know." She stood to face him. "I feel no compunction to stay here and use my gift. But I do feel compelled to use it again."

"Where?"

She knew he would be shocked by her answer. "Out west."

"Where out west?"

"Kansas."

He blinked. "My mother and sisters live —"

"I know." She let him fill in the blanks.

He rose and began to pace. She gave him time to do so.

Finally he stopped. "My family would be thrilled."

"Would *you* be thrilled?"

"I don't know. Mother and my sisters haven't lived as a family for nearly nine years. I've never even been to Kansas."

"Actually, we wouldn't have to live with *them*. . ." She waited, hoping he would get the gist of her words.

He grinned. "Are you asking me to marry you? Again?"

She knew it wasn't the proper way to do such a thing. And yet . . . "I *am* asking. We've talked about it. Many times. But this time I ask because I like the idea of getting married in Kansas. With your family present."

He pulled her close, kissed her, and said yes.

In that order.

**

"You can't move away. You belong here." Goosie, the Tyler family housekeeper, maid, and loyal friend, frowned in a pitiful manner. Her deep wrinkles grew even more pronounced.

Justine took her hands. "My work is done here."

Goosie's eyes grew large. "So you have more time-traveling to do in Kansas, thousands of miles away?"

"I don't know." *I hope so?* "Moving there will also give Harland a chance to be with his mother and sisters."

"Nice girls they are — or at least they were when I knew them," she said.

9

"Thank you," Harland said. "But there's one thing Justine has neglected to tell you."

"Actually, two things," Justine said.

He waved a hand, giving her permission to break the news.

"Harland and I are going to get married out in Kansas."

"Finally." Goosie embraced Justine first, then Harland. "I am so pleased."

"I'd like my family to be a part of it," he said.

"As they should be." Goosie's face grew sad. "I wish I could be there."

This was the news Justine had anticipated the most. "You *can* be there." She led Goosie to the settee and sat down beside her. "Harland and I are in agreement. We want you to join us."

"Me, out west?"

"You, out west, with us. We'll have the adventure together."

"You don't want me there."

"We most certainly do," Harland said.

"We need you there," Justine added. "You're a part of us."

Goosie looked around the room. "But the Tyler home . . ."

"You've taken care of it all by yourself since Granny died eleven years ago. You've carried out your duty—and then some."

Goosie nodded. "I've lived here since I was ten."

Which could work for or against our plan. "Wouldn't you like to see a new part of the country?"

She considered this a minute, fingering the tatting on her cuff. "I'm eighty-nine years old. I don't want to be a burden to you."

Justine put an arm around her shoulders. "You could never be a burden. You are like a grandmother to me. I love you dearly and I want you to be with us."

"I do too," Harland said.

Goosie's eyes filled with tears. "When do we leave?"

CHAPTER ONE

A month later, Justine stood in the house that had been in the Tyler family for seventy-nine years. Four generations had lived there. Loved there.

Am I crazy for leaving?

She heard a different word enter her thoughts. *Brave. You're brave.*

She didn't feel brave.

Goosie came in the front door and handed her a letter. "Only one today. I told them to forward all mail to Dorthea's address in Lawrence, Kansas."

Harland nodded at the letter. "Who's it from?"

Justine looked at the return address and felt a twinge of anxiety. "It's from my lawyer in New York."

"Uh-oh," Goosie said.

"It doesn't have to be bad news," Harland said.

She hoped not. Justine and her lawyer had been exchanging letters and telegrams for the past two weeks. She'd given him instructions to sell the family mansion, give the servants generous severance and glowing references, and have her lady's maid, Franny, donate most of her clothes to charity. Justine had assured them all she would be home shortly to oversee the process.

The only possession she'd specifically wanted to keep was a cigar humidor that had been her father's, and her mother's jewelry. Any proceeds from the sale of the house and furnishings were to be divided fifty-fifty: fifty percent would be sent to an account she had opened in a Kansas bank, with the other fifty-percent was to be divided between her parent's favorite charities. She'd thought everything was taken care of.

She ripped open the letter, hoping it wouldn't reveal some hitch in their plans. She read the short note and laughed.

"What's so funny?" Harland asked.

She handed him the letter and he read it aloud, "'I thought you might be interested to know that Morris Abernathy and Faye Coskins are betrothed. They plan an autumn wedding.'"

"Morris? The man you were engaged to before me?" Harland said. "That makes you laugh?"

She remembered a particular evening at the opera—a lifetime ago. "Faye was the victim of a previous broken engagement and everyone from my set spurned her—including Morris. I saw her crying at the opera and purposely spoke with her, mentioning that she and her mother should come for a visit the next week. But . . ." The rest of the night's events forced themselves front and center.

"But?" Harland asked.

"That was the night Mother died." She spread her arms to encompass the room, the house, and the town of Piedmont. "Yet, here I am among loving family. Betrothed to the most wonderful man in the world." She kissed his cheek to confirm it.

"But your laugh?" Goosie asked.

"I laugh when I remember what Morris said about Faye's sad situation. He told me that Faye's father was too rich for her to remain single."

"Ah," Goosie said with a nod.

There was nothing more to say about that.

Except good riddance.

**

Justine stood in front of Granny's headstone. She wasn't sure if God would allow her this one last bit of travel through time in Piedmont, but she hoped He would indulge her. Righting the wrongs of the past wasn't her motive, love was. Wasn't God all about love?

She was wasting time pondering what God would or wouldn't do. She could *know*. Now.

She knelt before the headstone and traced her fingers over Granny's name.

The winds of time took her away. *Thank You!*

She found herself in the cemetery, but Granny's headstone wasn't there.

"Jussie."

Justine turned around and found Granny standing there, the elderly Granny she'd known and loved before losing her when she was ten.

She fell into her arms and Granny rocked her back and forth. The scent of honeysuckle wove its way around them.

"You're here."

Granny stood erect. "Of course I'm here. Where else would I be?" There was a knowing twinkle in her eyes.

Justine held her hands, not wanting to let go. "I'm moving away from Piedmont."

Granny nodded. "Out west."

"You know?"

She shrugged. "I know what the Almighty lets me know. He shared that bit of it. And that you accomplished what I could not."

"Quinn is in jail. The town is thriving now that it is free of his oppressive ways."

"Praise God. 'He preserveth the souls of his saints; he delivereth them out of the hand of the wicked.'"

Indeed. "I'm so glad to see you again. I prayed God would allow it."

"He encourages love. 'I love them that love me; and those that seek me early shall find me.'"

Justine smiled. "You didn't used to speak in Bible verses."

"Where I am now they are life verses, constant reminders of all He is and does. They are life-lines. Speaking of life-lines, I hope you keep adding the wisdom you collect to the Ledger."

Justine had carefully packed this precious family book. "I will. I promise."

"Good. Because the wisdom of hundreds of years needs to be kept alive—and increased." Granny shook her head, smiling. "The wisdom up here astounds me."

"I like hearing your view of heaven."

"It's not just my *view*. It is my reality. My eternity." She stroked Justine's cheek. "I've known Harland since he was a boy. I approve of him. I know you'll be very happy together."

To find out Granny knew about their betrothal gave Justine much joy.

"But . . ." Granny said.

"But what?"

"Your time out west will not be without incident."

"Do you know something?"

"I know no details. Only that you are not through using your gift."

"So there *is* more to do?"

Granny gave her the look she deserved. "There is always more to do. God's gifts can't be returned."

"That's on your headstone."

"Hmm. Good place for it."

"So I'm going to be traveling back in time while I'm in Kansas?"

"Let Him lead you. There's work to be done. His work. Now that He knows He can trust you . . . 'For unto whomsoever much is given, of him shall be much required: and to whom men have committed much, of him they will ask the more.'"

Justine felt the wave of the responsibility. "I hope I'm up to the task."

"He doesn't give us more than we can handle."

Justine was suddenly aware of time passing. Though God had been gracious in allowing her this visit, she needed to say what needed to be said.

"I love you, Granny. I always have and always will. Our time together in the past has been special, very precious to me, but—"

"But you're moving west, away from *here*." She spread her arms to encompass the cemetery.

Tears welled up in Justine's eyes. "To find you again, only to have to say goodbye . . ."

Granny took hold of Justine's hands and held them close between them. She looked into her eyes. "What did I just tell you? God has shared with me bits and pieces about you, letting me know how you are, what you're doing. I trust Him to continue the blessing as He sees fit."

"I like the idea of that."

"It's more than an idea, it's how He works. He 'is able to do exceeding abundantly above all that we ask or think, according to the power that worketh in us.'" She solidified the verse with a nod. "Who can argue with that?"

Justine chuckled. "Surely not me."

She pulled Granny into her arms one last time and closed her eyes, soaking in the moment, embedding it in her memories forever.

And then . . . time took her away.

**

Justine, Harland, and Goosie stood in the cemetery — each in their separate areas.

They were leaving for Kansas today. It was time to pay their respects to those they were leaving behind. Justine looked to her left and saw Harland stooped beside his father's grave. And to her right, Goosie lay flowers on the grave of *her* father.

Justine sank to her knees in front of the graves of her mother and grandmother with her other relatives buried close by.

There was a thud. She looked over her shoulder toward her house and saw Thomas putting the last of their luggage in the back of a wagon to take to the train. She waved a hand, indicating they'd be done in a minute.

On impulse, Justine turned to her mother's grave. "Thomas loved you, Mamma. If only you 'd loved him back. He's gracious in every way. He's even told me to call him Thomas, giving homage to Father for bringing me up as his own. That's the kind of man he is. You missed out on so much . . ."

She looked across the cemetery that had been the starting point of her time travel. There was a feeling of comfort here.

Of *knowing*. She was traveling to Kansas, a land as foreign as Piedmont had been to New York City. But she was stronger now. She felt confident she could adapt and thrive. Though she'd been alone in her first move, now she was surrounded by people who loved her.

She finished what she had to say. "I'm leaving Piedmont today but I'm not moving back to New York. I've instructed the lawyers to sell the house. I expect you'll be disappointed with my decision, but it can't be helped. My life has changed beyond anything either of us could have imagined. I am not meant to be a socialite. I am meant to use our gift to help people find justice. My work here is done. After a visit to New York to wrap things up, I'm moving to Kansas with Harland Jennings—the son of Jesse and Dorthea? Dorthea and his sisters live there. And . . . we're getting married."

She remembered all the grand plans her parents had envisioned for a fancy society wedding. Perhaps it was best they weren't around to see the simple ceremony that would probably occur in the far off *west*.

She glanced over her shoulder. Thomas stood nearby. She motioned him close and put an arm around his waist. "Thomas is going out west with us, Mother. As is Goosie. I will be with family old, and family new."

Harland and Goosie approached. Thomas opened his arms, letting them into their group. "May God bless us and keep us safe."

"Amen to that."

Justine turned toward the road. "Come now. A new adventure awaits."

**

The adventure to Lawrence, Kansas involved one detour to New York City to tie up loose ends.

The carriage from the train station pulled in front of the Braden residence on West 34th and Fifth Avenue. Harland was used to the big city, having received his medical schooling in Boston. Thomas had lived here most of his adult life, watching

Justine grow up from the shadows. But Goosie? She'd never lived anywhere but Piedmont, and her only traveling experience had been to nearby Haverhill. New York City was a strange, perplexing place.

"Here we are," Justine said.

Goosie peered out the window. "Is this city hall?"

"It's my family home."

Goosie pressed a hand to her chest, staring at the marble-faced mansion. "I feel embarrassed that you stayed in the house in Piedmont. It's a shack compared to this."

"Nonsense, it was perfect," Justine said, as Harland helped them out of the carriage. "Come everyone."

The butler opened the door before they reached the top of the steps. He smiled. "Miss Braden. How nice to have you home again."

"Thank you, Watson."

The others trailed in, their gaze moving up the walnut staircase, traveling over the coffered ceiling, running down the portrait-covered wall, and landing on the mosaic floor.

"Gracious, Justine," Thomas said. "I've been in the kitchen of this place to secretly check on you when you were growing up but had no idea it was this . . ."

"Grand," Harland said. "Mightily grand."

The housekeeper appeared from the back. "Miss Braden. Your lawyer told us you were coming."

Her lawyer. "I hope he's told you my plans for the house and . . ."

"And for the staff," she said. "The severance pay is very generous."

"We wish you much happiness," Watson added.

"Thank you. I would like to introduce you to our guests." She began with Goosie, drawing her forward. "This is Augusta Anders, the wonderful woman who has been overseeing the Tyler home in Piedmont for seventy-nine years."

Mrs. Bain's eyebrows rose. "Gracious. You have more stamina than me, Mrs. Anders."

"Miss." Goosie bobbed a curtsy.

"And this is Thomas Piedmont." She desperately wanted to add, *my father,* but thought it best — in this house that was built by the man who raised her — to leave such delicate matters unspoken.

"And finally . . ." she drew Harland close. "This is my fiancé, Dr. Harland Jennings."

Mrs. Bain beamed. "A doctor? Oh. Well then."

There was a hint of disdain in her voice. Being a doctor meant Harland was held a slice below the captains of industry that populated New York society. His was a needed profession, but not necessarily lauded. "Thank you for your best wishes," Justine said.

"Yes, miss. Of course. Best wishes."

"And congratulations to you, Doctor," Watson added.

"It's nice to meet both of you," Harland said. "We appreciate your hospitality."

At the word, Mrs. Bain nodded once. "You are surely tired. Let me show you to your rooms."

"Our luggage," Thomas said, turning toward the door.

"It will be brought to you, sir," Watson said.

Thomas helped Goosie negotiate the stairs.

"Mrs. Bain, would you please put Miss Anders in the room next to mine?" Justine asked.

"Of course, miss." She nodded toward the guests and spoke to Justine. "After settling in would you like to come down for a light supper?"

Justine glanced at the others, who looked weary. She felt confident in speaking for them. "I think not. But we would appreciate a tray of bread, cheese, and fruit brought to each room. Along with some tea perhaps?"

Harland and Thomas nodded.

She thought about sending the men a valet to assist with a bath but thought that would be too awkward to those who were used to fending for themselves.

With a wave good night she let the men be led to their rooms. Harland blew her a kiss.

Justine walked past her own room to see that Goosie got settled into hers next door.

Goosie took two steps inside the door and stopped. "This is *my* room?"

"It is."

She leaned close. "I don't feel right being here. I'll go sleep with the servants."

Justine put a hand around her shoulders. "Your servant days are over. At age eighty-nine you are officially retired from service."

"But what will I do?"

"You'll be my friend. And I will be yours."

Goosie touched Justine's hand that lay upon her shoulder. She gazed across the room at the canopied bed, the rose-colored curtains with tassels, the velvet-upholstered settee, and two chairs set near the blazing fireplace. "I'm not sure what to do in such a room."

"How about I stay for a bit, until you feel more at ease?"

"That would be nice, Jussie."

Mrs. Bain appeared in the doorway, having seen the men to their rooms. "Do you need anything else, miss?"

"Would you send Franny in, please?"

"In here?"

"Yes. And I believe Miss Anders and I will enjoy our cheese plates together."

"As you wish." She closed the door behind her.

"She doesn't know what to do with us—the rest of us," Goosie said.

"I've learned that the issues of status and hierarchy are not exclusive to high society but extend to the servants." Justine motioned toward the chairs. "Shall we?"

Goosie eased herself into the cushions. "You'd think because I've been sitting most of the day I would long to stand, but more and more this old body prefers sitting."

Justine sat on the settee. "Don't mind if I do."

"Are you sure about selling this place? I don't know anything about Kansas, but I do expect our home there will be nothing compared to this."

"I don't need this."

"But you *have* this. It's yours."

Even Justine was surprised by her new attitude. "I never, ever thought I would say this, but I much prefer the simple, cozy house in Piedmont to this massive monument."

Goosie looked over her shoulder at the bed. "We could fit all the quilting ladies in that bed."

"And even their children." There was a knock on the door. "Come in."

Franny entered, her face beaming. "You're home!"

"Hello, Franny. I am home — for a short time." Justine introduced Goosie.

Franny bobbed a curtsy. "Nice to meet you, Miss Anders. Would you like help getting ready to retire?"

Goosie put a hand to her chest. "Me?" She chuckled.

"Not yet," Justine said. "Actually, I wanted to ask you some questions. Would you join us?" She motioned to the other chair.

"Sit?"

"I know it's not proper, but please."

Franny perched herself on the edge of the settee. "What can I help you with, miss?"

"You've worked here since I was born, yes?"

"Before that. Since your mother and father married and moved in here. Actually, I worked in Mr. Braden's household before that, as an undermaid. When we moved here, I became Mrs. Braden's lady's maid. And then I helped with you and became your lady's."

Goosie nodded her appreciation. "I was with the Tyler family for nearly eighty years."

Franny's eyes grew large. "You were in service, ma'am?"

"I was."

"Eighty years . . ." she shook her head. "That's a lifetime."

Goosie chuckled. "Yes, it was."

Justine returned to her question. "My parents weren't betrothed long, were they?"

"Not at all. Mr. Braden was immediately smitten. They were betrothed and married very quickly. A month or so. Quick it was."

Now, it would get dicey. "Because it had to be?"

Franny fingered the pocket of her apron.

Justine leaned toward her. "I'm the woman of the house now, Franny. There have been too many secrets. Let me know the truth. It's all right."

Franny pulled at the folds of her apron.

"Is my biological father named Thomas?"

Franny stood and took a step back. "You know about that?"

"I do." Justine said, motioning toward the door. "He's here. Now."

Franny looked toward the hall. "He's one of the guests?"

"He is. My fiancé is here too, Dr. Jennings."

Franny began to pace at the foot of the bed. "Oh my. I'd heard that Mr. Abernathy got himself engaged to someone else, but I didn't know that you . . ." She stopped pacing. "Is the doctor from Piedmont?"

"He is. But now the four of us are moving to Kansas. Dr. Jennings has family there."

The news was obviously too much for her and she sat again. "How did you find . . . how did you discover your father?"

Justine waved that story away. "God arranged it." She got to the core of her questions. "Were my parents happy?"

Franny looked as though she wanted to pace again but remained seated. "Your father—Mr. Braden—tried to make everyone happy."

That sounded like him. "But Mother didn't." This was not a question.

"When the missus got word that Mr. Thomas died . . ." Franny bit her lip. "You said he's here?"

"He is. He didn't die."

Franny pressed a hand to her forehead, her head shaking. "She never said it aloud, but I knew she loved him."

"Oh," Goosie said.

"Is something wrong?"

"He never knew," Justine said. "How incredibly sad." She had a second thought. "Should we tell him?"

"I don't know," Goosie said. "Will knowing fill him with regrets for staying in the shadows?"

She was right. "I don't want to hurt him."

"Then we should remain quiet about it."

"Agreed." *At least for now.* Justine returned to her questions. "Continue, Franny. You were explaining how my parents felt about each other?"

"It comes down to this. Your mother almost left."

"Left my father, Noel?" This was unbelievable.

Franny nodded. "She was planning to leave when you were about three. Though Mr. Braden was a good man, they were not a good match. Your mother was headstrong and he was quiet and didn't enjoy society much."

"No, he didn't."

"When she heard that Mr. Thomas had died, her wanting to leave got worse. She was so distraught, and couldn't tell your father why. He didn't know what to do. In the hope that she would be happy, he took all three of you to Bedford Springs, a spa in Pennsylvania, to rest and recuperate. I went along, of course. A lovely place. Wonderful food."

"Did it help her mood?"

Franny cocked her head, as though the question was difficult. "When the mister went back to the city early for some business something-or-other, your mother changed. She was happier at the spa, more jovial. I think she found a few friends who took her mind off her troubles. I spent most of my time with you. You loved feeding the ducks."

Justine had a vague memory of ducks. A pond. "Did that happiness last when we went home?"

Franny stared into the fire. "At first. Your mother was still sad about Mr. Thomas, but there was something else driving her. She made me mend all her clothes and bought some new ones for you in a larger size — you were growing like a weed. She checked the mail every day, clearly waiting for a letter from someone. When nothing ever came she grew despondent again. Took to her room. For the longest time even you couldn't make her smile."

"I wonder who she was waiting to hear from."

"I asked her, but she wouldn't say. I assume she'd made a new friend at the spa and was looking forward to a correspondence." Franny sighed. "The mister tried very hard to make her happy. He bought her whatever she wanted — and then some. But then the war started and he left to fight. I will never forget his face when he said goodbye to you two. He looked twenty years older."

"The reality of war will do that," Goosie said.

"I think your mother loved the mister some," Franny said. "They could *seem* happy."

Justine thought back to her childhood. "I hate to admit it, but I was oblivious to any issues they were having. I loved both of them and they loved me. I just assumed they loved each other."

"Children are like that," Goosie said.

"With Father gone . . ." Justine said. "It was her chance to leave."

"Almost did." Franny took a handkerchief from a pocket and blew her nose. "I remember one day when I helped her pack to leave for good."

"Where was she going?"

"To Kansas, I believe. A place with a man's name . . . "

What? "Was it . . . Lawrence?"

"That's it."

Justine shivered. "Why Kansas?"

Franny ignored her question a moment. "You're going to Kansas. Just like the missus."

"It appears so." Justine got back to her question. "Why was she going to Kansas?"

"That was my reaction. I asked her why there, and she had no real reason. Didn't know anyone there but had some feeling that was the place she should go."

Justine felt a shiver course up and down her arms. "Mother was going to Kansas and now I'm going there? And not just to the state, but to the same city?"

"That *is* an odd coincidence, isn't it?" Franny said.

No coincidence at all.

Goosie lifted a finger to make a point. "Our moving there is meant to be, Jussie."

"Apparently so." She felt strengthened by the affirmation. "So Mother was packed?"

"Had the train tickets bought. You were going with her, of course. So was I. But then she got the telegram that the mister had been badly injured and was coming home."

"She couldn't leave."

"I suppose she could have, but she didn't." Franny continued. "When he got home he needed extra care. Your mother stopped looking for the letters and did right by him."

"She did a good thing," Goosie said. "She put his needs above her own."

"That, she did," Franny said. "Mr. Braden needed her, and so did you, Miss Braden."

My seemingly selfish mother sacrificed herself for her family. For me. "I hate to say this aloud," Justine said, "but that doesn't sound like her. Self-sacrifice wasn't one of her strongest qualities."

"Jussie!" Goosie said. "Don't be so hard on her. She lost the man she loved, then stayed with a man she didn't love. That's the essence of self-sacrifice."

She stayed with Father. She didn't run off to Kansas.

"You certainly would have had a different life if you'd been brought up out west," Goosie said. "Without a father."

Justine's thoughts turned to the could-have-beens. "I wouldn't have known you."

"Or Harland. Or found your real father. Or discovered your gift."

"What gift, miss?" Franny asked.

Justine changed the subject. "Thank you for telling me the truth, Franny. I appreciate your candor."

She leaned her head back and looked at the painting that hung above the mantel. It was a portrait of her mother in her twenties wearing a ruffled white dress with a five-stone ruby necklace. She pointed at it. "Isn't there a miniature of this portrait?"

"There is."

"I'd like to take that with me."

"I'll find it, miss."

"And the necklace . . . it's very lovely but I don't remember Mother wearing it."

"That's because it was lost—during that trip to the spa."

"Lost?"

"That's what she said. I wish I could give it to you, but I can't."

So be it.

When Justine stood, Franny did the same. "Will there be anything else, miss?"

"Nothing tonight."

Franny left, leaving Goosie and Justine in front of the fire.

"Are you all right?" Goosie finally asked.

Justine shrugged. "I wish I would have known about this before Mother died. It would have helped me understand her."

"She *could* have told you."

"Perhaps. But I find it disconcerting to discover the man I knew as 'father' was not the man my mother loved."

"And now you're making a new life with that man."

"In Lawrence, the place Mother was going to start her new life." Justine looked at the portrait. She could see Granny in her mother's eyes. "I went into the past one last time," she said. "To say goodbye to Granny."

"When did you do this?"

"This morning."

"You have had a long day."

Justine smiled. "She said I'm not through using my gift."

"There's more to do?"

"That's exactly what I asked."

"And she said?"

"There is always more to do. God's gifts can't be returned."

"Just what it says on her headstone."

Justine nodded.

"Are you going to be traveling back in time while we're in Kansas? Righting some other wrong?"

"It seems so."

Goosie shook her head. "More adventure to come."

Justine stared into the fire, wishing it had the answers she craved. "It scares me a little."

"You came through it back in Piedmont. God will watch over you again. He doesn't give us more than we can handle."

Justine chuckled. "Granny said that too."

"She often said that."

Justine stood and wandered the room, pausing at a pastoral scene that looked very much like the low mountains around Piedmont. "Do you realize when I left New York I knew nothing about my gift and now I'm going to live it out in a new land?"

"Perhaps your mother was supposed to use *her* gift in Kansas," Goosie said.

Justine froze. "Do you think so?"

"You're being sent there. . . maybe there's work left undone."

Justine let the weight of the responsibility fall upon her shoulders—and then slip away. God had helped her do the work once, He would help her do it again.

There was a knock, and a maid came in with their food and drink. It was time to refuel. To be renewed and refreshed.

Their new life was about to begin.

CHAPTER TWO

They were beyond exhausted when they reached Lawrence—a town forty miles west of Kansas City.

Six days on the train had made their bodies tired, their minds numb, and their patience thin. During that time Justine rediscovered something about herself, something she'd always known but had learned to press down while living the quiet life she had established in Piedmont. She was prone to complaining and had to fight the impulse to express every grouchy grumble out loud.

There was much to annoy her: the jostling of the train, the sound of the train, the food on the train, the sleeping on the train . . . yet those were bodily inconveniences. Mentally she was anxious, being challenged by the new life *and* the time travel that lay ahead. Emotionally, she was grateful to be sharing it all with her dear family. More than once she thanked God for them, for giving her these exact people. There were none better.

Goosie provided the soft comfort of a grandmother's care, putting everyone else's needs above her own. Thomas was the wise and generous father who shared stories of his life in New York that involved watching her grow up from afar while he ministered to the poor of body and soul. Harland was her rock, her intuitive, loving fiancé, who shared a joke when she needed to laugh, a shoulder when she needed consolation, inspiration when they imagined their new life together, and a strong presence at all times, even when they sat in silence and watched the world rush by.

This new world was very different. New England was defined by hills, with tight winding roads lined by towering trees that covered the sight of any building set back more than twenty feet. But Pennsylvania, Ohio, Indiana, Illinois, Iowa, Missouri, and now Kansas? There was so much space, so much sky. It was like they'd thrown off the tight and cozy covers of

New England and were stretching their limbs on the bed of the world, unencumbered. It was freeing yet also rather frightening. They were vulnerable now. More than once Justine fought the urge to make herself small and warm like she felt back home with a quilt pulled over her head. It took courage to sit tall and face what was coming with her shoulders back and her chin held high.

The most unexpected gifts were the clouds. She knew with full certainty that God was in the clouds, and He was quite a show-off. From wisps to puffy billows to looming towers He created cloud panoramas that were white, yellow, pink, purple, and blue. There were grand sunrises that trumpeted the day and vivid sunsets that sang a lullaby at night. In Piedmont they'd never seen either end of the day in all its glory. But now, with the horizon visible in a full circle? It was glorious.

Kansas City was a bustling town, rippling and surging with a myriad of people. There were cowboys with wide-brimmed hats and leather vests, guns slung low on their hips. Sleek businessmen with the chain of their watch hanging from their vest pocket, looking for the next deal. There were men plying their trade with shouts of "the very best" this and that, from hotel rooms to steak dinners to gambling opportunities. There were Negros selling newspapers and hot coffee, carrying luggage and selling tickets, finding a new way of life after obtaining their freedom. And families, so many families, wearing simple clothing that focused on function over fashion, parents herding their children forward, ever forward to the promised land just beyond the horizon.

Justine had seen diverse people before, with one exception: Indians. She'd read accounts of the Wild West and Indian fights, teepees and war cries. But beyond the drama she sensed a deeper truth. They were a people overcome by an undulating and demanding mass of newcomers wanting what *they* had. Some were dressed like everyone else, though they wore their black, straight hair long beneath their hats. But some wore leather tunics and leggings secured with leather ties, with the occasional ornament of feathers or beads. Their soft shoes looked extremely comfortable. They seemed to be a people caught between two worlds.

Goosie summed it up best. "Kansas is the world on a plate."

Yes it was. It was their world. And Justine was hungry.

On the last leg of their journey from Kansas City to Lawrence they took an enclosed carriage. Although they were excited to be close to their destination everyone looked older. A bit beaten down.

The carriage went over a bump.

"That's one," Justine said.

"One what?" Harland asked.

"One bump." She made a pained face. "Once we got in this carriage I figured my body could only tolerate three more bumps."

Thomas smiled. "What happens if there are four?"

"You don't want to know."

Harland looked out the window at the last vestiges of Kansas City. "A city, but so rustic."

It was that. "It's new," Thomas said. "Piedmont was founded in 1790. All of this has come about in the last thirty years."

Harland nodded. "I heard that before the railroad pioneers came up the Missouri on riverboats. They stopped in Kansas City to load up with supplies to begin their overland trek west on the Oregon Trail." He sighed deeply. "I admire their courage to leave everything they knew to start over in a land they'd never seen."

"Like us," Goosie said.

Justine smiled. "Like us."

"I can't imagine riding and sleeping in a covered wagon," Thomas said. "Sleeping outside where it's always too hot or too cold."

Justine nodded. "I've heard it could take them six months to get out west. Our six days is nothing compared to that."

Leaving the city behind they traveled west on a dirt road through rich farmland. An occasional white clapboard house marked a farm.

Thomas pointed out the window. "To have so much space to farm, unencumbered by trees and rocks and hills . . . If I were a farmer, I'd want to move here. It's a chance to succeed in ways people can never succeed back East."

"May *we* succeed," Harland said. "I'm heartened to know doctors are always needed."

"As are preachers," Thomas said.

"As are women who can make fresh bread and pies," Goosie said.

Their list was so practical. Justine's offering was less . . . touchable. "I guess I can say that people always need justice."

"That, they do," Harland pulled her hand around his arm. "And you're just the woman to give it to them."

Maybe. Hopefully.

After an hour they turned up a residential street lined with large clapboard houses with wide porches. "Is this your mother's neighborhood?" she asked Harland.

"We'll find out. I hope so. These houses are very nice."

"The style isn't that much different than the houses in Piedmont," Goosie said.

"They're newer. And a bit further apart," Harland said.

Thomas took a deep breath and let it out. "That's what Kansas is all about: breathing room. I like it very much."

The carriage slowed and stopped in front of a large white house with a blue door and trim. Daffodils lined the edge of the porch. A moment later, a woman came outside, rushing down the steps to greet them.

Although Justine and Dorthea had only met in the past when Harland was a child, she easily recognized her by her white-blond hair. Harland's had been that color when she'd first met him, but had darkened in adulthood. But Dorthea's had not. Although nineteen years older now, she was still a striking woman. She'd obviously conquered the stresses of widowhood, farming near Piedmont, bringing up three children alone, then moving to Lawrence to start new. Those trials showcased her strength and courage. Justine was happy to finally be able to meet her.

Harland exited the carriage and ran into his mother's arms. They had not seen each other since she had moved west with his sisters nine years before.

She squealed when he lifted her off her feet and spun her around. Her cheeks blushed rosy red with happiness.

Harland returned to the carriage where the driver was helping Goosie alight. Then came Justine and Thomas A wagon carrying their luggage pulled up behind.

"My, my," Dorthea said, staring at Justine. "I've wanted to meet you for so long. I can't believe that day is finally here."

Harland handled the introductions, starting with Justine. "Mother, this is Justine, my bride-to-be."

Dorthea took her hands and peered into her eyes. "My dear girl." She drew Justine into an embrace. Then she pulled back. "Mmm. Lavender. You wear my favorite scent."

Justine glanced at Harland. "He says I smell like a meadow."

Harland blushed. "A lovely meadow."

"I agree," his mother said. She turned to the others. "The rest of you I know though it has been far too many years." She went to Goosie and took her hand. "Was your trip a good one, Goosie?"

"Exciting. I've never been away from Piedmont."

"You chose an ambitious journey for your first time."

"It's now or never," Goosie said. "But I will say I'm ready to stay put again."

Thomas was next. They stood and appraised each other. Yet there was a stirring in the air between them that was very interesting.

"Nice to see you again, Dorthea."

She studied him a moment. "Pastor Piedmont . . . I haven't seen you since . . ."

"The year was 1857. I believe I may have changed a bit in twenty-two years."

She put a hand to her hair. "As have I."

"Not a whit," he said.

Dorthea blushed. "We all thought you were dead."

"My brother tried to kill me, but God had other plans." He smiled at Justine. "Plans to reunite me with my daughter."

"Harland wrote to me with the details. How extraordinary. And marvelous."

"We agree," Justine said.

Dorthea slipped her hand around her son's. "There is nothing like a family reunion to make one count their blessings."

Harland pointed to the house. "Speaking of family reunions? Where are Beebee and Ellie?"

Justine nodded. "I'm eager to meet them."

For the first time, Dorthea's face lost its cheery glow. "There's a story in that. Let's go inside."

"Sir?" The man bringing the luggage stood nearby. "Where do you want it?"

Harland looked to his mother. "Will you give him the directions to the hotel?"

"I will not," she said. "Because you are all staying here."

Justine looked at the house. It didn't look large enough for so many people. "We don't want to impose," Justine said.

"I guarantee, you are not," Dorthea said. "Come inside."

The next half-hour was spent getting the luggage to their rooms. Harland, Justine, and Thomas took the three small bedrooms on the second floor next to Dorthea's. Goosie was assigned a small room on the ground floor, off the kitchen — which was a relief. "No stairs!" she said happily.

Once again Harland asked about his sisters, and once again was put off until they had time to settle in and freshen up from their travels. Dorthea was kept busy filling the wash stands in each room, providing towels, and showing them the location of the privy. She offered to help them unpack, but they said they'd do it themselves.

By the time Justine got her things put in the bureau and armoire, she was exhausted. She sat on the bed and let herself fully acknowledge that she was sitting in Lawrence, Kansas, 1400 miles from New Hampshire. The entire journey seemed surreal, a blur. Looking back, it had presented itself as a series of tasks-to-do that they'd accomplished with dogged purpose, with little mishap.

"I'm *here.*" Hearing the words said aloud made them real, and she smiled and repeated them for good measure. "I'm here."

Thank You, God.

**

Justine crossed the hall and knocked on the jamb of Harland's open door. "All settled in?"

He was working in rolled-up shirt-sleeves. His brow glistened as he shoved a trunk into the corner. He set a pile of books on top, moving one an inch to the right. "There."

"Very homey."

He ran a hand through his wheat-colored hair. "How is your room?"

"It will do nicely." She picked up one of Harland's books, then set it back. "But I have a question for you. Where are your sisters going to stay? We must be taking their rooms."

"I agree it's odd." He unrolled his shirt sleeves and buttoned the cuffs. He tugged his vest down an inch, then offered Justine his arm. "Shall we go downstairs and get some answers?"

They met Thomas on the stairs and together went down to a well-appointed parlor conducive to conversation with a settee and six chairs facing inward. The fireplace mantel was draped with a length of red velvet topped with matching candlesticks on each end, a blue vase, a small bronze bust of someone that Justine did not recognize, and a daguerreotype of a man in a Union uniform. "I recognize your father," she said.

"That's right," Harland said, "you met him when you visited him in . . . what year was — ?"

"Shh!" Justine saw Dorthea and put a finger to her lips.

Dorthea came in the room. "You've found my little nest."

"It's a delightful, cozy room," Justine said.

"Very inviting," Thomas said.

Goosie joined them. "The kitchen is very well-appointed."

"I'm glad you approve," Dorthea said. She glanced toward the photograph. "That's my husband, Jesse. He lost an arm at Gettysburg and died soon after coming home." She looked at Justine. "I overheard Harland say you met him?"

Uh-oh. They hadn't told Dorthea about Justine's ability to travel into the past. She looked at Harland. Was now the time?

Harland stepped between his mother and the picture. "I'm sure she met him when she visited her grandmother in Piedmont."

Justine took her cue from him. Now was *not* the time. She changed the subject, nodding toward a rocking chair near the window. "I am guessing that is your seat of choice?"

"How perceptive, my dear." Dorthea motioned for them to sit, then sat in the rocker, backed to the window. "I can't tell you the number of hems I have tacked up and buttons I have sewn on while seated in this chair."

"Harland told me you are a skilled seamstress?"

"Just a seamstress," she corrected. "After we moved here I found it necessary to sew dresses for myself and the girls, and ended up starting a dressmaking business. Ladies like being able to choose their own fabrics and style rather than ordering from a sketch in the Montgomery Ward catalog." She made a face. "Besides, those clothes never fit right."

"The girls . . ." Harland said. "I'd like to see them. Is Ellie starting classes at Kansas University in the fall?"

Dorthea sighed deeply, letting her hands fall into her lap. "Alas no."

"Why not? She'd seemed excited about it."

"She was," Dorthea said. "For a time. I even had Flora Richardson come and speak with her about her studies." She seemed to realize no one knew who that was. "Flora was in the first graduating class in seventy-three, was the first woman graduate, and the valedictorian."

"That's impressive," Justine said.

"It is. But it wasn't enough to sway Ellie from her new goal."

"Which is?"

Dorthea sighed again. "Different and far away. You sisters are not here at all. They went to the Montana Territory."

"I don't even know where that is," Justine said.

"West. And north, abutting Canada."

"What are they doing there?" Harland asked.

Dorthea fingered a crease in her skirt. "Beebee is married."

"What?"

Her hand stopped and she took a deep breath as if to fuel her answer. "She fell in love with a riverboat captain and announced they were marrying—after far too short a time by anyone's standards, except hers. They got married two weeks ago and have taken the riverboat called the Far West up the Missouri and the Yellowstone rivers." She removed a handkerchief from her sleeve and wiped her eyes. "I didn't want her to go—I didn't want her to marry him. He's much older and she barely knows him." She sighed deeply. "But you know your sister."

"Actually, I don't. I'm nine years removed. I've been at school and then in Piedmont."

Harland was missing one very important point. "Where is Ellie?" Justine asked.

"She went with them."

Harland burst out of his chair. "She's far too young to make such a decision."

"She's nearly nineteen."

Justine couldn't give an opinion regarding Ellie's age. She'd been a very naïve twenty-year-old when she'd left her life in New York City to come to Piedmont. She was only twenty-one now.

"Fine," Harland said, beginning to look defeated. "Let's say she's old enough. Why would she want to go along? Surely riverboat life is difficult."

"Aren't they heading into Indian territory?" Thomas asked.

"The Battle of the Little Big Horn was only a few years ago," Harland said. "It was in all the papers."

Dorthea nodded. "Actually . . . the Far West steamed up there right after the battle and collected the wounded. Those on the ship were the ones who brought the first news of Custer's defeat to the rest of the world."

"Mother, you should have stopped them from going!" he said. "It's not safe. They need to be protected."

Dorthea stood and faced him. Her petite frame only reached his chin, but her proximity caused him to take a step back. "It's true you don't know your sisters — or me. We came out here — three females alone. We came on faith and have dealt with everything that's been thrown at us ever since."

When she put it that way . . .

Dorthea continued. "There is one overwhelming influence out here in the West — one that you haven't experienced yet: our independent spirit." She pointed outside. "Where New England has existed for 150 years, this town has existed but a few decades. Everyone who's come here has left their known lives behind and has chosen the unknown and the chance to be a part of something new and exciting."

"And dangerous?" Thomas asked.

"Sometimes." Dorthea walked to the window and moved the lace curtain aside to peer out. "I dragged the girls here to fulfill *my* dream and desire for a new beginning. Although I offered my opinion about their recent plans, I couldn't do anything to stop them. I've left them in God's hands."

What could any of them say? They had just trekked halfway across the county on their own quest to start over. To begrudge Beebee and Ellie their choice of traveling across the second half would have marked themselves hypocrites.

"Why did you choose Lawrence?" Thomas asked.

Dorthea let the curtain drop back in place. "My aunt and uncle owned this house. Their son was the cousin who helped me farm in Piedmont after Jesse died. When Uncle Peter got sick, I took the girls and moved out here to help — and start over. Sadly, he died soon after, and Aunt Jan died last year. They bequeathed this house to me. My cousin moved on to Oregon." It had all come out in one breath. "And so, here I am."

"I would have liked to meet your daughters," Justine said. "I never had siblings and was looking forward to getting to know them."

"Why didn't they wait for us?" Harland asked.

Dorthea shrugged. "Riverboats have schedules. It was time to go." She dusted the top of a chair with a finger, then turned it under. "Their departure reinforces my utter joy in having you come." She looked at each in turn. "Your letters never really explained your reasons."

God sent us?

"Our reasons are complicated," Harland said.

Justine nodded, then stifled a yawn. "Excuse me."

"We'll have plenty of time to talk." Dorthea walked toward the dining room. "Come help me set the table. Goosie has been kind enough to help me with dinner. First we eat, then you sleep, and tomorrow we'll go to church. Some friends have invited us all to noon meal. *Then* your new lives begin."

She made it sound so simple.

Dorthea got six plates out of a sideboard and handed them to Justine. She pointed at glasses, then opened a drawer to reveal flatware. "I'll leave you three to the chore and go check on dinner."

When she left, Harland said, "I wish Mother would have written to me, telling me what was going on. Perhaps I could have dissuaded the girls from going."

Thomas shook his head. "You heard her speak of their independent nature. They're grown up, Harland. Your influence is limited."

"If I ever had any."

"I'm proud of them," Justine said. "It takes courage to set out into the unknown." She touched his hand. "As we did."

He set a fork in place. "I have the feeling *our* first bite of courage is only the first of many."

But would their courage taste bitter or sweet?

CHAPTER THREE

"…for thine is the kingdom and the power and the glory forever. Amen."

The congregation of God's Mercy Church filed out of the sanctuary — if you could call it that. Justine had grown up attending Trinity Church in New York City, a grand, Gothic cathedral that elicited a feeling that God lived among its lofty rafters. Its grandiosity implied that the worship that occurred there had some chance of reaching the God of the universe.

There was nothing grandiose about God's Mercy. It was comprised of four walls, a roof, mismatched chairs, and some widows with cracked panes. Pitiful was the word that came to mind.

Justine immediately felt a check to her system. *It's not where you worship, it's that you worship.*

As she had judged the church, so others had judged her — or rather, judged her dress. Although the fashion in Piedmont had been more casual than New York City, Lawrence was a further step away from what was — what Justine used to consider — fashionable. The women here wore simple dresses made of printed cotton, with white collars or lace pinned at their neck and cuffs. The bustle, which was such an important — though silly — accoutrement of city fashion, was totally absent.

Good riddance.

Justine was rather surprised that she didn't disparage the simpler fashion. The old Justine would have looked down at it and even gossiped about it. But the new Justine . . . she vowed to speak with Dorthea about altering her own clothes to suit the more casual west. Or maybe Dorthea could make her some new dresses. This was her home now. She wanted to fit in and relished not having to show off and impress.

She took her turn shaking the hand of the ancient pastor. Dorthea was ahead of her and made the introductions.

The pastor's phlegmy eyes perked up when Thomas was introduced.

"You're a pastor?"

"I am."

"Could you wait a few minutes after the line has gone through, so I can speak to you?"

"Of course."

Justine easily put two and two together. The pastor had to be in his eighties. He wanted a replacement. Once through the line they all stepped aside to wait. "It appears you're going to find a new flock," she told Thomas.

He shrugged. "What will be will be. I *would* like to feel useful."

"At least you'll have a job," Harland said.

"Lawrence needs doctors of the flesh as well as doctors of the soul," Thomas said.

Justine knew that a huge part of Harland's identify was using his skills. She also knew that he'd find a way to settle in and start serving those in need. It was his nature. Actually both men in her life were givers, always looking for ways to help others. Sometimes their goodness shamed her.

The sound of children's laughter caught her attention. She glanced toward the noise and saw them playing tag among the headstones of a cemetery.

How odd that *her* place of business was a cemetery.

She whispered to Harland as she nodded toward the headstones, "I'm going to take a stroll."

He saw the direction of her gaze and gave her a knowing look. "When will you be back?"

"I'm not planning to *go* anywhere other than taking a stroll to see how it feels."

She slipped into the cemetery and walked up and down the rows, praying quietly. "If there's something You want me to do, some place You want me to visit, lead me there."

She noted the recent history revealed in the dates. There was no one who'd died before 1850, with most passing away in the last decade. Unlike Piedmont, which had a Colonial history, any time-travel in Lawrence would probably take her back to the less distant past.

Justine was disappointed not to feel a call-to-action. Perhaps her instinct was faulty because she was still recovering from their trip. Perhaps today was not the day. Perhaps she wasn't supposed to go back in time at all.

"Justine?"

Harland beckoned her over. A man stood nearby: tall, middle-aged, and completely bald. His strong features looked Scandinavian or Dutch.

"Uriah," Dorthea said to the man, "this is Justine Braden from New York City."

The man did a double-take and stared long enough to make her feel uncomfortable. As though he recognized her.

But they hadn't met.

Had they?

"Good morning." Even with only two words spoken, his voice resounded with powerful bass tones.

"Justine," Dorthea continued, "This is Uriah Benedict and his wife, Alva. We're going to their home for the noon meal."

"We appreciate the hospitality," she said.

Oddly, Alva looked to her husband as if needing his permission to respond. She was much younger than he and seemed a mouse to his cat.

"You are always welcome at our home," the woman said.

When Uriah nodded, she seemed relieved.

Something wasn't right between them. Justine's curiosity was piqued. Hopefully, dinner would provide some insight.

**

The Benedicts lived four blocks from church. Thomas rode one of Dorthea's horses, and the rest rode in her surrey. In tiny Piedmont there had been no need to own a buggy, or even horses. With a population of only a few hundred the entire town could be traversed on foot in five minutes or less. But Lawrence was home to over 8000 people and was spread out. A carriage was not a luxury but a necessity.

The Benedict home was a mansion built of brick, its porch flanked by white columns. Inside there were intricate moldings at the ceilings and edging the wide stairs to the second floor. If Dorthea's modest home could have four bedrooms on the second floor, the Benedict home had to have double that number. Which led Justine to ask a question she immediately wished she could retract.

"This is such a fine, large house. Do you have any children, Mrs. Benedict?"

Her expression clouded. She looked to the floor. She shook her head. "None. I'm sad to say, God has not blessed us."

"There, there," her husband said, almost jovially. "We are perfectly happy just the two of us, right, wife?"

The tone of the wife-designation—that could have been spoken as an endearment—seemed harsh, as if equating her to a possession. Not Alva. But Wife. Alva looked to the floor and nodded.

They were shown into a lovely drawing room. It wasn't as nice as the one Justine grew up in in New York, but for the west where artisans and supplies were more limited? She was impressed. And yet there was something forced about it. The gilt-edged frames of the paintings, the five-stick candelabra with crystals hanging from each stem, the painted vases that seemed to scream *look at me, I came all the way from the Orient.* Justine wasn't sure if she was reacting out of snobbery or insight. But again, there was something off as if the Benedicts were trying too hard to be . . . whatever they were trying to be.

When seated, Justine sat near Alva and noticed her necklace. There was something familiar about it. Then she figured it out. "You have a lovely necklace, Mrs. Benedict. Rubies?"

Alva put a hand to the jewelry. "I believe so. Uriah gave it to me."

"It's beautiful. My mother wore a similar necklace in a small painting I have of her. You share good taste."

"Thank you."

A Negro butler with silver hair brought in a tray of aperitifs. He started with the ladies. The liquid was a pale green color.

Mr. Benedict held up his glass. "I serve to you some absinthe, all the way from France. It will stimulate our appetites." He lifted his glass. "*Prost!*"

Justine wasn't sure about drinking the liquid at all. She'd heard strange things about the spirit, that it created hallucinations and was poison. She looked to Harland. He was a doctor. Would he drink it?

His face was serious, as if he was having the same thoughts.

"Come now, guests. I promise you it's perfectly safe." Mr. Benedict's voice hardened just a bit. "Do not insult me by abstaining."

Mrs. Benedict drank hers first, downing the glass. She closed her eyes and lifted her chin a bit, as if savoring the effect. Dorthea did the same.

"Cheers!" Harland said.

Goosie followed suit. Then Thomas. And finally Justine.

She only took a sip and was surprised by the taste. A bit earthy, fruity. A tinge of anise in it? She felt the warmth flow through her chest.

"So?" Mr. Benedict asked, looking directly at her.

"It is not unpleasant." She glanced at the butler. He was staring at her, as though studying her in much the same way Mr. Benedict had done at church. She looked away.

"So," Mr. Benedict said. "You are here in our mighty Lawrence. What next?"

What a weighted question.

Harland answered. "As my mother may have told you, I am a physician and wish to find a position, helping where I can. Eventually I'd like to open my own practice." He pulled out a piece of paper. "Perhaps you could guide me? I made inquiries, but only have three possibilities on my list."

"Let me see."

Harland handed the list to Mr. Benedict, whose left eyebrow rose. "The first, Dr. Bean? He mostly treats horses."

"I didn't know."

"And definitely *not* the second. Not at all."

Harland took the list back. "Not Ravenwood Hospital? Why not?"

"It is a lunatic asylum."

"I . . . I hadn't heard that."

"Certainly your talents could be better spent helping real people."

Justine took offense. "You don't consider people with mental ailments *real?*"

"I consider them beyond help." Mr. Benedict pointed toward the list. "Contact Dr. Gregory. I'm sure he'll welcome your help." He set his glass on the butler's tray. "As an expert in real estate and development, I know many people in Lawrence — everyone, actually. So please come to me with any needs or questions — I'd hate for you to make a wrong step."

There was a hint of menace in his voice which was heightened by Alva furiously bobbing her head as she agreed with her husband's every word.

**

"What is wrong with Mr. Benedict?" Justine asked once they reached home.

"There's nothing wrong with him," Dorthea said, hanging her drawstring purse on a hat rack by the door. "He's simply a powerful personality."

"A domineering, controlling, and dangerous personality," Justine said.

Dorthea looked at her. "That's harsh. You've only just met him."

She *had* overstated. "I don't mean to offend, but generally I am known for my keen intuition about people."

"She does have that," Harland said with a smile. "She knew I was an amazing, captivating, and exceptionally intelligent man the moment she met me."

Justine was going to play his game, but decided to use his teasing to her advantage. "I did instinctively see Harland's attributes. Who's to say I'm not right about Mr. Benedict?"

"I'm to say," Dorthea said. "Alva is my very best friend. He is her husband. I won't have you speaking ill of him."

Even if it's true?

Justine looked to Goosie. "You have good instincts about people. What did you think?"

Goosie looked hesitant to take sides.

Justine had a moment of clarity. *Dorthea is our hostess and my future mother-in-law.* "Never mind," she said.

But then Goosie blurted out, "He makes my wary-bells chime."

Thomas chuckled. "That's a unique way to put it. Even apt." He slipped his hands in his pockets and looked around the parlor. "Dorthea, do you have a deck of cards?"

"I do," Dorthea said.

"Would you like to play Old Maid?"

"I beg your pardon?"

"Beg mine too," Goosie said.

"Don't get your dander flying, ladies," Thomas said. "It's a card game. Would you like to give it a go?"

"I suppose so," Dorthea said.

Goosie nodded.

"Justine?" her father asked.

She needed time alone with Harland. "Maybe later. I thought Harland and I would take the surrey and go exploring. Would that be all right, Dorthea?"

"Of course." She looked through a table drawer. "Now, where are those cards . . ."

Justine and Harland went outside and got in the surrey. "You seem to have a plan," he said.

"Not really. I just wanted to get you alone to talk with you. I hope you don't mind."

He chucked the reins and they started moving. "I never mind a chance to spend time with you—alone."

They stopped at the first intersection. "Which way shall we go?" she asked.

"May I choose?"

"Absolutely." They turned west. "Do you have a destination in mind?"

"Ravenwood," he said.

She was surprised. "But Mr. Benedict talked disparagingly about it."

"Too disparagingly," Harland said. "It's like he was desperate to keep me away. My curiosity was piqued."

"But the insane . . ." She felt guilty for her thoughts. "Do you really want to work with them?"

"I don't know. I may not be able to help their mental deficiencies, but I could help with their bodily ailments." He shrugged. "I have no idea whether it's a good idea or bad. But I'd like to explore the options. Let's call it's an adventure."

It was a good word for what she was feeling. "This is all so new."

"Only thirty years' old."

"That's true, but it's not the *new* that I was referring to. This is all so new to all of *us*." They drove through a mud puddle. "I thought God sent me here."

"You've given up so soon?"

"I walked through the cemetery and felt nothing. No nudge or inkling to stop at a particular headstone." She needed to say it. "What if coming here was a mistake?"

He took his pocket watch from his vest pocket and looked at it. "We have been here approximately twenty hours and you've already given up?"

"Not given up exactly, but—"

"God's not working as fast as you'd like?"

Ouch. She took his arm. "I know I'm too impatient. Forget I said anything."

"Nice try," he said. "But I know you *are* impatient."

She didn't like her faults being so exposed and changed the subject. "Do you agree with my intuition about Mr. Benedict?"

"I do. I've seen men like him before, those who are used to getting their own way, and usually stop at nothing to get it."

"Alva is cowed by him."

"We don't know her well enough to know if her acquiescence is merely her personality or the result of his control over her."

"I imagine both. I doubt that a man like Mr. Benedict would choose a wife who had an independent nature. He'd choose a woman who'd follow him."

"Who'd bow to him."

They reached the west edge of Lawrence, driving into the countryside. "Just so you know, I'm not going to bow to you when we're married."

"I'd never want you to." He stopped the surrey and got down.

"What are you doing?"

He picked a cluster of wildflowers, then bowed to *her,* presenting her the blooms. "Milady."

Her heart swelled to accommodate the love she felt for him. "How did I ever get a man like you?"

"Providence." He got back in the surrey.

They rode a bit in silence, enjoying the billowy clouds and the spring air. But Justine's thoughts returned to Mr. Benedict. "Why did he serve us absinthe, a drink which has such a sordid reputation? Why not some sherry?"

"It certainly was odd."

"He must serve it to Alva quite often. She downed it, and closed her eyes like she relished its affects."

"I noticed that."

"Perhaps it makes him easier to tolerate?"

"If she's depending on drink to make it through, then I feel sorry for her."

"She's so much younger than he is," Justine said. "A good twenty years, I think."

"Older men often marry younger women." He grinned down at her. "After all, I'm twenty-four and you are but twenty-one."

"Nearly the same."

"Nearly."

Again her thoughts returned to Benedict. "Did you notice he had to tell us the absinthe came from France? And then he used a German toast, even though Benedict isn't a German name."

"To your first point, yes, I noticed. I think Mr. Benedict likes to show off his wealth. Regarding the toast? You're being too sensitive. I've been known to say 'Prost' on occasion and I'm not German."

She agreed with his assessment. "Obviously he's found a way to ruffle my feathers."

"Judge not, lest ye be judged."

"I hate it when you're right. I'm too quick to come to conclusions about him."

"That's generous of you, but don't discount everything you feel about him. As Goosie said, Mr. Benedict makes her wary-bells chime."

She spotted a sign up ahead. "There's Ravenwood."

He pulled the horse to a stop. "Having come this far, I'm not sure what to do. I can't just show up on a Sunday and apply for a position."

"You don't even know if you want a position there." She looked up the long drive to a very wide, two-story building. She noticed there was a fence and a gate. She nodded toward the fence. "To keep patients in?"

"It makes me a little nervous."

She agreed. But then she heard a woman singing and saw her working in a garden off to the left of the building. "Maybe we could just stroll up to that lady and have a chat. Informally."

"Say we're new to the area. Introduce ourselves."

"There's no harm in that." Then why did her stomach tie up in knots?

They parked the surrey outside the gate — which wasn't locked — and walked toward the woman who appeared to be in her forties. She was planting seeds in a carefully prepared row, singing.

"'Mid pleasures and palaces, though I may roam, be it ever so humble, there's no place like home . . .'"

I know that one. They walked closer and Justine joined on the refrain. "'Home! Home! There's no place like home. There's no place like home!'"

The woman stood erect, her face glowing with delight. "Well done, miss. Well sung."

"I return the compliment. I'm Justine Braden." She turned to Harland. "And this is Harland Jennings. We've just moved here from New Hampshire."

"Well, well now," the woman said. "That's a long ways."

"It is. And you are?"

"Virginia Meade. Please call me Virginia. I'd shake your hand, but . . ." She wiped her dirt-stained hands on her apron.

"And please call me Justine." She surveyed the plot. "The garden is so well-tilled and fine. You definitely have a talent for it."

Virginia brushed some stray strands of black hair off her face with the back of her sleeve. "The patients like the fresh vegetables. I work the garden for them."

Justine stepped into the opening. "Harland is a doctor."

Virginia looked him over. "Are ya now?"

Justine noticed a man approaching. Virginia glanced over her shoulder. "Eddie. Come here. Meet these nice people."

The man was about the same age as Virginia and had the muscles of someone who did physical work, plus an engaging smile. He didn't offer his hand, but removed his hat. "Nice to meet you."

"Eddie is the caretaker and fixer of all things that need fixing," Virginia said.

He looked away. "I like to keep busy."

"Eddie's got a heart as big as the sky," Virginia said. "He'll do anything for anyone who needs it."

"I try."

The two exchanged a look, and Justine had the feeling that Eddie enjoyed being at Virginia's beck and call.

"Eddie, this is Justine Braden and *Doctor* Harland Jennings."

A bushy eyebrow rose. "Doctor, you say?"

"I might be interested in a position. Is there someone I can speak with?"

"The director is Mr. Sutton, but he isn't around on Sundays," Virginia said. "We could give you a tour though. Would you like that?"

"That would be very nice. Thank you."

Eddie hurried ahead to the front door which was centered on a wide porch with rocking chairs set in a line. Three of the six were filled. One man rocked furiously, his face intent on the task. A second mumbled to himself. Only the woman looked up.

"Maddie, shouldn't you be taking a nap?" Virginia asked.

The woman nodded and Eddie held the door for her. Maddie scurried inside. "People 'round here like to keep to a schedule," Virginia explained. "Makes 'em feel safe. Keeps 'em calm."

"I believe everyone prefers that," Harland said.

Virginia smiled. "A schedule or feeling safe and calm?"

"Both."

Eddie held the door and they went inside. A wide foyer led to a large parlor. Perpendicular hallways extended in opposite directions. Many doors could be seen down their lengths. The patient's rooms?

Unlike any hospital Justine had ever seen, there were flowers and plants painted on the walls of the living area, vining around the mantel, framing a sideboard, and overflowing to the corner of the ceiling.

"The paintings are lovely," Justine said.

"They certainly brighten up the place," Harland added.

"Ginny did 'em," Eddie said, nodding at Virginia. "She's an artist."

"You exaggerate, Eddie, but yes, I did paint them." She ran a hand along the curve of a Hosta leaf. "I like to dabble. It's my hobby."

"It could be more than a hobby," Justine said.

"You have real talent," Harland said.

Eddie leaned toward Virginia. "I told ya."

She shrugged. "I've always had an interest in things that grow. I grew up on a farm and actually wanted to study botany, but my husband thought that was crazy." She chuckled. "Said it was an excessive application of body and mind for a woman.'"

"Learning is excessive?"

"Spencer thought so. At least that's what he put on the papers when he had me committed."

Justine gawked. "Committed? You're a patient here?"

"Did I say otherwise?"

"Well no, but you're so . . ." Justine didn't know how to say it.

"So normal?" Virginia chuckled again. "Didn't mean to misrepresent myself, but everyone you see here is committed. Except Eddie. Though *he* probably should be."

Eddie grinned. "I have my days."

Justine exchanged a glance with Harland. Things were very curious.

"How I miss my book," Virginia said.

"Your book?"

"*British Wild Flowers,* illustrated by John Sowerby." Virginia sighed. "I used to study that book, and drew my own illustrations from that book."

"You don't have it anymore?"

She shook her head. "When Spencer brought me here it was left behind." With a shake of her head and a flip of her hand she dismissed the memory. "But I showed him. I painted my own versions of the plants. Not as good as Sowerby, but it makes me happy."

"Makes everybody happy," Eddie said. He moved to point at some sprigs of purple asters. "I especially like these. I got Ginny some seeds to plant her own out in the garden."

"Yes, you did. You are very kind."

"Does your husband come to visit often?" Harland asked. "If you'd like, I could talk to him about getting your book back."

She touched Harland's arm. "You are such a dear man. Spencer is long gone. Left Lawrence for parts unknown."

"Leaving you here?"

Her face suddenly grew sad. "It was for the best."

Justine wasn't sure she should pry, but her curiosity got the best of her. "Why do you say that?"

A man came into the parlor, dressed to the nines. His eyes widened when he saw Justine, and he immediately took her hand and drew it to his lips. "Mademoiselle. *Enchanté*."

"Behave yourself, Leo, Miss Braden isn't used to your charm."

He winked at Virginia, then suddenly took Justine into his arms, waltzing around the furniture as he hummed a tune.

"Stop that, Leo!" Virginia said. "It's not time to dance."

"It is always time to dance!" He twirled Justine under his arm, then let her go, bowing. "Until next time, mademoiselle." He took a book from the mantel and left the room.

"He does love to waltz," Virginia said.

"He's very good at it."

"Don't tell him that or he'll sweep you away every time you come to visit."

Visit? Justine hadn't thought about coming to visit Virginia — whether Harland got a doctor position or not. Yet she did find the idea intriguing.

Virginia pointed to the righthand wing and said, "On with our tour. That is the men's wing, and this wing to the left, is for us womenfolk."

They walked down one of the long halls that had small bedrooms on either side. One woman was in bed, and another was sitting in a chair looking out the window.

"How many patients are here?"

"Thirteen, last count," Eddie said.

"But a few come and go as they feel the need," Virginia added.

"The need?" Justine asked.

She stopped walking and drew them in confidentially. "Many people know they aren't quite right, and when they feel a spell coming on, they show up and stay until they feel right again. Then they go back to their other home."

"Do you have a doctor on staff?"

"Used to. Used to have a lot of things. But now . . ." she sighed. "We're down to just us thirteen. We're at ease with each other and help each other."

"We're like family," Eddie said.

"That's nice," Justine said.

Virginia continued walking. "Medicine-wise, I've learned a bit about nursing general sickness and such, and we take people into Lawrence when they need special care, but Dr. Bean is a hack. When Robert broke his wrist he wrapped his wrist with a dirty bandage. Actually, he knows more about horses than humans — likes 'em better too. That's one reason we generally keep to ourselves. The townspeople prefer it that way. They have their families. We have ours."

Virginia waved at a middle-aged woman who stood before a mirror in her room, trying to pin her hair into a bun. "Let me help you, Sissy." Virginia smoothed the strays and pinned them in place. She put her hands on Sissy's shoulders and looked in the mirror with her. "There you are. Pretty as a picture."

Sissy smiled at herself and touched Virginia's hand. She looked to the hall and saw Justine and Harland and suddenly looked worried.

"It's all right," Virginia said. "No need to worry. They're friends, come to visit."

Sissy looked relieved. She bobbed a curtsy.

"Nice to meet you," Justine said.

Virginia rejoined them and they moved further down the hall. "Sissy doesn't talk much but we know what she means — most of the time."

Justine thought of Goosie, and how for years she had feigned an inability to talk out of fear. Was there a similar reason that Sissy kept quiet?

"And this here is my room. I got my pick since I've been here the longest. I like being at the end so I get two windows with two views."

"She gets to look at her garden whenever she wants," Eddie added.

"How long have you been here?" Harland asked.

"Eight years now." She looked to the ceiling. "I was committed in seventy-one."

"Forgive me, but you being here is hard to fathom," Justine said. "When we saw you in the garden we thought you worked here."

"That, I do. Gotta earn my keep."

"That's very commendable," Harland said. They returned down the hall. He addressed Eddie. "Mr. Sutton is in charge, and you fix things that need fixing. Who else works here?"

Eddie looked to Virginia.

She cocked her head as if not understanding the question. "Everyone who can, works. Sally and Sadie do most of the cooking. Sally makes the best rye bread in a two-state area. A store in Lawrence even sells it for her."

"That's very resourceful," Harland said. He exchanged a look with Justine. Everything was oddly done.

"We are nothing if not resourceful," Virginia said. "The Lord helps those who help themselves."

Suddenly, they heard a blood-curdling scream. Virginia and Eddie ran down the hall toward the parlor and were greeted by a thirty-something woman, running from the other hall. "Sally cut herself! Come quick!"

Harland followed them into a kitchen where a woman held a bleeding hand wrapped in a cloth.

Sally looked at the strangers. Virginia rushed to explain. "Dr. Harland can help you."

Indeed, he could. Harland sat nearby and set to work examining the cut in the palm of her hand.

"This is all so stupid," Sally said. "I was busy talking with Sadie and wasn't looking at what I was doing and the knife slipped and . . ." She shrugged.

"Being in the fold of your palm is a bad place as far as pain," Harland said. "But it doesn't look like it will need stitching."

"Glad for that," Sally said. "I hates needles."

"Everyone hates needles," Eddie said.

A clean towel was torn apart and made into a bandage. Minutes later, it was done.

"It's going to throb some," Harland said.

"It's already doing that," Sally said.

"I have some aspirin powder in my bag," he said, "but I didn't bring it with me."

"We have some here," Virginia said. "I'll get it."

Sally looked pale.

"I think you should lie down," Harland said.

"I think I should." Sadie helped her up and they headed for the doorway. But then Sally turned back and pointed. "Take one of those loaves of bread as payment, doctor. I made plenty."

"Thank you. I will."

Virginia returned with the headache powder and left it with Sadie to dispense. "Well now," she said to Justine and Harland. "I'm sure you didn't come here today planning to use your doctoring."

"I'm glad I could help."

Virginia exchanged a look with Eddie, then eyed Harland with a mischievous smile on her lips. "Would you be interested in stopping by every now and again and helping out with all things medical?"

Harland looked at Justine. She thought it was a wonderful idea so gave her a smile.

"I would love to — if it's all right with Mr. Sutton."

Virginia clapped her hands. "It will be. So there you go. You come and say hello and end up with a job."

"And perhaps we ended up with new friends too," he said graciously.

Justine heard the chime on a grandfather clock in the foyer. "We need to get home."

Virginia wrapped a loaf of bread in a napkin and saw them out. "See you soon," she said.

"Nice to meet you," Eddie said.

"And you." Justine and Harland walked down the drive and through the gate to the surrey. "What a surprise that was," he said.

"On so many accounts," Justine said. "Virginia is a talented woman. She doesn't seem insane in any way."

"Who knows for sure," he said. "She may be able to act perfectly normal when she needs to."

"Eddie is sweet on her."

"What?"

"Can't you tell? He dotes on her."

"He helps everyone."

Justine chuckled. "Men. You see what you want to see, but not what's right there in front of you."

CHAPTER FOUR

The next week went by quickly with each newcomer finding their place.

Goosie found purpose helping Dorthea with the cooking. Justine often saw them sitting together at the kitchen table, comparing recipes.

Thomas spent his days with Pastor Karvins. And yes, he was being groomed to take over the duties at the church which included visiting parishioners in need of counsel and care.

After a visit with Dr. Gregory—Uriah's recommendation—and finding the man gruff and dismissive, Harland decided to hang up his own shingle. Surprisingly, Uriah helped him find a small space to rent. Harland got busy setting up his private practice, with a commitment to go to Ravenwood a few times a week. He was as happy as butter on bread.

Which left Justine to . . . to . . .

Be confused.

She was rather shocked at how easily each member of her family had found new friends, a place to spend their time, and a new purpose.

Other than Alva Benedict and Virginia Meade, Justine had met no one who spurred her to move beyond a polite greeting. Her only friends were an odd duo: the wife of a powerful man, and a patient in an asylum.

She and Dorthea had been invited to Alva's that afternoon for tea. Chitchat and cake. An enjoyable occasion, but Justine was bothered by the assurance that God hadn't brought her all the way from New Hampshire to attend a tea party.

Both Harland and Goosie had responded to her impatience with the same verse from First Timothy: "Follow after righteousness, godliness, faith, love, patience, meekness." She didn't particularly like the verse as she didn't think her job was to be meek. Righteous and godly seemed beyond her ken, though her faith was strong, and her love unfailing. Two out of six did not speak well of her character.

She and Dorthea walked to the Benedicts, their heads bowed and a hand upon their hats against a spring wind. Justine felt her hat pins threaten to give way. Her hair was going to be a mess.

"Now do you see why I tie my hat under my chin?" Dorthea asked. "It really helps."

"Could you add some ties for me?. And perhaps take a few flowers off the brim. I think I lost a daisy a block back."

Dorthea laughed. "You can keep the flowers, I'll just sew them on more securely when I add some ties. It's a simple fix."

"For you."

"I'll teach you. We can fix your hats while we simplify your dresses for life in Kansas."

"Don't expect too much from me sewing-wise. I went to a quilting bee in Piedmont and they gave me the job of threading needles, *not* sewing."

"You have your talents and I have mine. You don't have to be good at everything."

"Hmm."

Dorthea stopped walking. "Don't say *hmm*. You're very talented."

"You are too gracious. I can't sew, can't cook, can't paint, can't garden, can't play a piano or sing. I can needlepoint chair cushions, but that doesn't count for much."

Dorthea resumed walking and Justine noticed she didn't argue with her list.

"You were brought up very differently from most people I know," Dorthea said. "You've seen many far-off places and been to the opera and theatre. You've rubbed shoulders with people of power. My family were poor farmers and came over from Ireland. They remained poor farmers. We had to learn to *do* to survive."

Justine was well aware of how little she'd struggled. "I admire you for your strength and determination."

"By coming here you've shown your own measure of both," Dorthea said. "You're on the cusp of a brand new life. The rest will come."

Justine appreciated her encouragement. She knew God would show her His plan in *His* time.

Dorthea changed the subject. "Alva has the most delightful porch for tea-taking, but this wind . . ."

"I'd like to see more of their house. She has skill with decorating."

"I'm sure it seems modest compared to what you're used to in New York."

Justine couldn't argue with that. "New York was my old life. I'm selling that home."

"You really are starting over. Cutting ties."

"I am." It made her feel good to say it. Justine added to her defense. "In Piedmont I stayed in my grandmother's home which was very humble of decoration and size."

"I know the place," Dorthea said.

Of course. She knew the place.

Justine wanted to tell Dorthea that she was familiar with the Jennings' home in Piedmont—circa 1860. As she was familiar with the younger Dorthea, the mother of three small children, and a husband still alive before losing his life in the Civil War.

But she couldn't tell her any of that. Dorthea didn't know about Justine's gift. And as such, Justine couldn't talk with her about her frustration about not being definitively called to go back in time here in Lawrence.

They had all agreed not to let others know of her gift if they didn't have to. Common knowledge in Piedmont had led to a celebrity status and the pressure of performing on demand. Justine wanted to do God's work and get His desired results without causing a commotion. Was that possible?

They reached the Benedict's. The butler greeted them at the door. "Come in, ladies. Get out of that wind."

"Thank you, Caesar," Dorthea said.

He led them into the drawing room and they sat down.

"How are you enjoying Lawrence, Miss Braden?" he asked.

Justine was rather surprised he spoke to her directly. The Braden servants would never think of such familiarity.

But this is the West. Things must be more informal here.

She answered his question. "I am enjoying Lawrence very much," she said. "Though I'm still finding my footing."

He chuckled. "Don't trip now."

She enjoyed sharing the joke with him. "I'll do my best."

"Caesar!"

At the sound of Uriah's voice, the butler's smile immediately faded and with a nod he left them.

Uriah's voice changed from gruff to fawning. "Welcome, lovely ladies," he said. "Alva will be down momentarily. She wasn't feeling well this morning."

"I'm so sorry," Dorthea said.

"We could come another day," Justine said.

"No, no," he said. "She needs some womanly support right now."

Why?

He looked up the stairs. "Here she is now." He went to take his wife's hand as she reached the foyer. He accompanied her into the parlor as though graciously sharing his possession.

"Forgive my tardiness," Alva said.

"I told them you weren't feeling well," her husband said.

"Come sit down." Dorthea took Alva's arm and led her to a soft chair. The woman sank into it as if she had little choice but to do so.

"I will leave you then," Uriah said. "Darling, do be mindful of your health. I'm sure the ladies wouldn't mind if your teatime is shortened."

"Of course not," Justine said.

As soon as he left, Dorthea and Justine removed their hats and straightened their hair as best they could without a mirror. Then they moved their chairs closer to Alva. Dorthea took her hand. "You're pale," she said.

"Should I tell Caesar we are ready for tea?" Justine asked.

"Please."

Justine walked down the hall beside the stairs, toward the back of the house. She heard the sounds of a kitchen and entered. A cook was placing teacakes on a serving plate while Caesar poured hot water from a copper pot into a silver tea service.

"Miss Braden," he said. "Is everything all right?"

"I believe Mrs. Benedict could benefit from some of that tea."

Both servants looked toward the front of the house. "I told the missus not to have visitors today," Caesar said.

"What's ailing her?" Justine asked. "If I may be so nosy?"

The cook answered. "Stomach issues. I have some soup on the stove. I'm hoping she can keep that down."

"Perhaps we should leave?"

Caesar bit his lip. "I . . ." He glanced at the cook, who went back to stirring the soup. "Never mind."

Not so fast. "If we may have a moment?" she asked him.

He hesitated but led Justine into the butler's pantry. "Yes, miss?"

"Forgive me for being presumptuous. I know I'm new here, but I'm concerned that something is seriously wrong."

Caesar's dark eyes flit from left to right, then seemed to see a place far removed from the here and now. "I commend you for your intuition and concern. The missus has been feeling poorly for some time, and I . . . I'm worried."

"About her health?"

There was a moment's hesitation.

Justine realized there was no reason for him to trust her. She lowered her voice. "My intuition is well-tuned. My fiancé is a doctor. We both want what's best for Mrs. Benedict, so if there is something we should know that would help her, please share."

He studied Justine's eyes a moment, and she felt as though a connection was made. She had the odd notion that she would look back on this slice of time as a bellwether moment between them.

But then he blinked. "Thank you, Miss Braden. I will keep that in mind." He looked to the kitchen. "Let me serve the tea. Perhaps that will help."

He had more to say. Much more.

Justine went back to the parlor. "Tea is coming presently."

"Thank you," Alva said weakly.

Dorthea gently waved a feather fan near Alva's face. "After you left her complexion went from pale to flushed." She lowered her voice. "She says it's not due to her monthly. Or the *change.*"

"Regarding the latter, I sincerely hope not," Alva said. "Uriah and I long for children. We've been married nearly five years."

That was a long time to be childless.

Caesar brought the tea, gave Alva a worried look, but didn't say anything. Dorthea offered to serve.

After taking a bite of cake Dorthea said, "This is delicious. Mrs. Russo is such an excellent cook."

But Alva didn't eat anything.

"How long have you been feeling ill?" Justine asked.

"Nearly a week." She offered a weak smile. "At first I though I might be expecting, but . . ." she sighed. "I'm sure it's just the grippe. It will pass."

"Do you have a fever?"

"None that I notice." She looked away, toward the stairs. "Uriah has been utterly kind and caring. I could not ask for a more solicitous husband."

Justine was confused by this description, for despite his fawning flattery, there was something demanding about Mr. Benedict that belied any sort of loving care. Or perhaps she was being too quick to judge.

But then she remembered her short conversation with Caesar. Though nothing damning had been said, much was implied.

**

"I know you didn't like it when I spoke badly about Uriah yesterday," Justine said to Dorthea as they walked home. "But there *is* something wrong in that house."

"I shouldn't have snapped at you. I defended him even though I agreed with your concerns," Dorthea sighed deeply. "There is something wrong. Alva was as helpless as a babe. We had to help her back to bed."

"I'm not just talking about her feeling ill." She wanted Dorthea to confirm her feelings without saying more.

"I know. Uriah is . . . "

Justine prodded her. "Is . . .? Please tell me what you know."

"That's the trouble," Dorthea said, stepping around some horse droppings on the street. "I have known Alva since before she and Uriah married, yet he is an enigma to me."

"In what ways?"

"He is very strong-minded but he is also . . . it's hard to explain."

"Try."

She stopped walking, as if needing to be still for her thoughts to gel. "There's a desperation to him. As if he's so afraid of losing control of every situation that he presses himself forward too much, too fervently. Is that what you felt?"

"Not exactly." *Not at all.* "I didn't sense desperation but manipulation. A conniving nature that always looks for ways to get what it wants. It's as though he's always thinking ahead, beyond the moment."

"You make him sound evil."

It's what I feel. But Justine didn't want to share that thought until she had proof. "I'm usually good at reading people, sensing who they are beyond what they portray to the world — almost in spite of what they portray to the world."

"That's a heady gift."

Or a heady curse. "In Uriah's case, if I can't pinpoint exactly what seems off with him, it doesn't negate the fact that there *might* be something off with him." She was surprised when Dorthea didn't come to his defense. "Do you feel the same?"

She didn't nod or shake her head and they walked a block in silence. Then Dorthea said, "A year ago I stopped by the Benedict's unannounced to see if Alva wanted to go to the farmer's market. It wasn't like me to just show up, but the autumn day was so crisp after a very hot summer. It was such a relief to have a cool day that I went on impulse." She looked toward the street, her face drawn with concern.

"What happened?"

"I had just reached the porch steps when I heard Uriah's voice through the open windows."

Justine caught the implication. "Was he yelling?"

She held up a hand, wanting time to finish the story. "Very loudly. I was concerned, and naturally rather embarrassed. I nearly turned back when I spotted Caesar on the far side of the porch, hiding near the parlor windows. He was spying."

Justine felt her eyebrows rise. "Did he see you?"

"He did and immediately put a finger to his lips. Then he beckoned me to join him."

"Really."

Dorthea nodded. "I didn't want to, and yet . . . I wanted to know what was going on. So when he pointed, I went around to some side steps that led up to the porch and stood with him, pressed against the house. He pointed inside, wanting me to look and so I did. That's when I saw Alva sitting on a chair in the parlor in her nightgown. Barefoot. Uriah stood over her, pressing a cup of something toward her. She kept shaking her head. She said, 'I don't want to drink it.'"

"Did she drink it?"

"After he threatened her."

"How did he threaten her?"

Dorthea stopped walking and stepped to the side of the street, turning her back to a couple walking by.

Justine stood beside her and lowered her voice. "What did he say to her?"

"He said she would drink it or he would never share her bed again." She glanced up. "I don't think Alva is necessarily a passionate woman, but she does long for a child."

"He's despicable to use that against her."

Dorthea nodded. "She drank it."

"What was it?"

"I don't know. But as soon as she drank it, we saw Uriah help her upstairs to bed." Her face pulled to show her scorn. "He was so solicitous. Oozing with kindness as if he truly cared about her."

"Did Caesar know what she drank?"

"He said it was tea, but also said that something had been added to it 'for her own good.' He made it clear it wasn't good at all."

Justine knew her next words might be an overreaction, but said them anyway. "Was it poison?"

Justine expected Dorthea to say something like "Absolutely not", but she only shrugged.

"Is that why she was sick today? Is he doing it again?"

"I don't know. She *did* get better last fall. They even had a Christmas party and I saw her on his arm at some town events—he's a bigwig, you know. Quite the real estate developer."

"It's still suspicious."

"Yet she *could* just be sick. The change in seasons makes many people suffer one brief illness or another."

Justine didn't believe this was the reason.

Dorthea took her arm and resumed their walk. "I'm glad I told you. At least I'm not standing alone in my concern."

"Thank you for trusting me. I will always be on your side—and hers. And we two are not alone. Caesar is aware."

"He may be aware—and probably knows much more than we ever will—but that doesn't mean he will do anything about it. Uriah is his employer and has been for years before Uriah came to Lawrence. There's history between them. Loyalty."

"Blind loyalty? Or fear?"

Dorthea shrugged. "*I'm* afraid of Uriah. And I'm afraid *for* Alva."

"Would you like me to send Harland to check on her?"

Her face brightened. "That would be much appreciated. He could simply say he'd heard she wasn't feeling well. A courtesy call."

And perhaps so much more.

**

The ladies detoured from their homeward route to go to Harland's new medical office in downtown Lawrence. He was inside, meticulously painting the letters on a sign: *Harland Jennings, Physician and Surgeon.* As he was painting the last "e" Justine and Dorthea waited in the doorway, not wanting to cause him to err.

He finished the lettering and stood upright, expelling the breath he had been saving. Only then did he see them. He nodded toward the sign. "What do you think?"

"I think you having your own practice is long overdue." Justine admired the sign. "You worked under Dr. Bevin so long, it's exciting for you to be on your own."

"Is that the word for it?"

"You aren't excited?" his mother asked.

"'Terrified' is a better one."

"Nonsense. Lawrence is lucky to have you."

He kissed her cheek. "My biggest supporter. Now then. What has brought you ladies here?"

Justine thought about saying the polite thing but Alva's struggles took precedence. "We have a patient for you to see. Alva Benedict."

"She's ill?"

"Again," said Dorthea.

His right eyebrow rose.

The Alva-situation was explained – as much as it could be.

"When you saw Uriah forcing her to drink something, perhaps it was simply some tea with medicine in it. Patients often balk at taking their medicine. It never tastes good."

Justine hadn't thought about that and was about to back down, when Dorthea put a new point on it.

"What about Caesar spying on them? Being concerned?"

"Concerned then, and concerned today," Justine added.

"Caesar came here with Uriah in the sixties," Dorthea said. "Logically his loyalty would be with his employer more than his employer's wife."

Justine sighed. "So would you go check on her?"

Harland hesitated. "It's not as simple as you think. If what you suspect is true — that Uriah is causing his wife's illnesses — he won't appreciate my interference. And if she's innocently ill, then she's probably under the care of Dr. Gregory. There are certain professional ethics to me barging in and taking over for another doctor."

"We can't do nothing," his mother said.

Justine wiped a dot of paint from Harland's cheek. "Can we blame your concern on our newness to the town? I was visiting, saw Alva wasn't feeling well, and asked you to go?"

"That *is* the truth," he said.

"The truth is, you need to try," Dorthea said.

When the ladies didn't move he said, "Now? You want me to go now?"

"If you would."

He dipped his paintbrush in a cup of turpentine and rolled his shirtsleeves down. Justine held his coat for him.

"My bag?"

Dorthea handed it to him.

"Let us know how it goes," Justine said.

"You'll know firsthand. For you are going with me."

She balked.

"You *are* the source of me knowing about her illness."

They went outside and Harland hung a newly painted "Back Soon" sign on the door.

"I'll be at home," Dorthea said. "Let me know what happens."

As Justine and Harland walked toward the Benedict's, she had second thoughts. "Do you think we're overreacting?"

"Better safe than sorry." He drew her hand around his arm. "You just wanted to spend time with me, didn't you?"

"Very much so."

"I thought living in the same house would give us more time together, but it isn't so."

"We're together but *with* other people most of the time," she said. "If not for the front porch, we'd have no time alone."

He gently nudged Justine a bit further to the right as a wagon drove past. "I was going out to Ravenwood tomorrow. Would you like to come with me?"

"Three times this week. That's an odd way to get time alone, but yes. I would like to see Virginia again. Last time she told me how much she enjoys our visits."

As they neared the Benedicts, Justine's stomach tightened. "I hope Uriah isn't at home."

"Keep in mind he's an important man in Lawrence. He's not evil. Men generally aren't evil."

"Are you forgetting Thomas's brother? Quinn was the mayor of Piedmont and was the essence of evil."

"Good point. But let's not judge Mr. Benedict until we have more evidence."

"I hope there's *no* evidence," she said. "I hope it's all our imagination."

They walked up the steps to the porch and Harland knocked. Caesar answered, his face a little confused at seeing her back. "Miss Braden? Dr. Jennings."

Harland spoke up. "Justine told me that Mrs. Benedict is under the weather. I thought I'd stop by and see if I could be of any assistance."

Caesar's face softened. "That's very kind of you, doctor. Come in. I'll let her know you're here."

Caesar started upstairs, but paused when Uriah came into the foyer. He announced the visitors. "Dr. Jennings has come to check on the missus," he said.

"Whatever for?"

Justine spoke up. "When Dorthea and I were here for tea, she was feeling poorly." *You, yourself said she was under the weather.*

Harland took over. "I don't mean to intrude. I know we're new in town, but as you know I am opening my own practice and am eager to put my skills to good use."

With a flip of his hand Uriah motioned Caesar to return downstairs and retreat to the back of the house. "That's commendable, Dr. Jennings, but I assure you Alva does not need another doctor. She has a weak constitution and is highly susceptible to the changing of the seasons. She has a cold. Nothing more." He took a step toward the door, opening it. "We do appreciate your kind care and take comfort knowing that a gifted physician like yourself has graced our fair city. Good day to you."

The door was shut behind them. As they began to walk down the street, Justine looked back and noticed someone at a second floor window. "Look!"

Alva stood with the lace curtains pulled to the side. She raised a hand in a weak wave.

Justine waved back and waited for Alva to do something more. Instead, she retreated into the room.

Justine hurried Harland along so she could speak freely. "Did you see that? She needs us. She wanted us to come back."

"You are overstating," Harland said. "She merely waved. She did not beckon us inside by gesture or words."

He was right, of course. "But didn't you see a wistfulness in her expression? A resignation in her wave?"

Harland chuckled. "All that? No, I did *not* see *all that.*"

Justine stopped walking. She pointed to the house. "Something sinister is going on there. I know it." She put a fist to her chest. "I feel it."

She was relieved when he didn't argue. He looked back to the house, then to her. "I've learned not to go against your intuition, but I can't see any recourse — for the moment. I can't force my way into the house. We can only make ourselves available and see what happens."

She huffed and started walking again. "I hate when you're right."

"Don't worry. It doesn't happen that often."

**

Clothes. Justine needed help with clothes.

It seemed frivolous in the midst of Alva's problems and yet . . .

Dorthea happily agreed to help.

Justine opened her armoire and took out a bustled dress with frills at the neck and cuff.

"That's stunning," Dorthea said with a voice full of appreciation.

"Isn't it too fancy for Lawrence?"

Dorthea fingered the fine lace. "We're not averse to fashion here, you know."

"I don't mean to offend. It's just that I've noticed a simpler way of being fashionable. Perhaps less ornamentation? Fewer layers and draping?"

Dorthea lifted up the back of the dress that seemed lifeless with no undergarments beneath it. "Gracious. It's so complicated. What do you wear as support?"

Justine went to her trunk and pulled out a tie-on bustle made of strips of mohair. Then one created with ruffles, and another made of wire with intricate ties. "There's this one. Or this one. And this. And finally . . ." She tossed a fourth one onto the bed. "That one's stuffed with wood shavings. Not a favorite."

Dorthea picked them up warily. "As a dressmaker I've seen variations of these but to have so many . . ."

"You should see the ones I left behind. Not to mention the crinolettes and tiered petticoats. Or the ridiculous crawfish contraptions for ball gowns with trains that made me feel like I was wearing a fish tail."

Dorthea chuckled. "All in the name of fashion."

Justine held the dress in question at arm's length. The intricate lace came from Belgium, the striped overskirt was hand-embroidered. The pleated back and peplum culminated in an enormous emerald green bow, over another full-length cascade of satin pleats hanging over a two-foot train. "If I put this on without its bustle, can you adjust the back so the skirt won't drag in the muck?"

"Of course."

Justine put on the dress—sans support beyond a normal petticoat. "It feels so light."

"It will feel lighter still once I shorten all the layers in the back," Dorthea said. "I'll have to cut fabric. Is that all right?"

"Cut away. And get rid of the bow entirely."

"Are you sure?"

"I am." Though she really wasn't. As Dorthea measured and marked things with pins, Justine looked at herself in the full-length mirror. "I'd like the bodice to be simplified too," she said. "Taking the bows off the cuffs would be a good start."

"Don't do too much there," Dorthea said. "The changes in length and in the back will be sufficient."

Dorthea applied her skills to the other six dresses and skirts Justine had brought along. "Since most of your clothes are on the fancier side, I'd be happy to make you a few simpler ensembles."

"I would appreciate that. And make Goosie something new too."

"We could go shopping at the general store for fabric. They have a decent selection of yard goods."

Justine didn't mention that her New York dressmaker ordered fabrics in from Paris. "That sounds perfect."

Dorthea held the last dress in front of herself, looking in the full length mirror. "This is exquisite."

"You can borrow any of them," Justine said.

"Maybe if we're both wearing these styles we'll start a new trend. We could make Lawrence, Kansas the new fashion capital of the west."

Justine chuckled. Then she thought of something Dorthea would enjoy. "I have something to show you." She took out her fashion scrapbook and they sat on the window seat. "I've always been fascinated with clothes and have compiled this book of sketches and clippings as a sort of history of fashion."

Dorthea flipped through the pages. "You drew these?"

"Some of them. I spent most of my allowance buying examples of dresses." She pointed at a dress from the early 1800s. "I had a few from the Regency era that have this narrow silhouette and high waist." She turned the pages to another sketch. "And this one with huge sleeves is from the 1830s." More pages. "This was drawn from a favorite of Mother's from my childhood with its huge hoop skirt. I have the sketches, but left the actual dresses behind in New York."

Dorthea slowly perused the pages. "You are quite an expert."

"It's meaningless knowledge," she said. *Though not completely meaningless.* Her fashion knowledge had come in handy as she'd traveled into the past.

"Not everything has to have a deep purpose in it," Dorthea said. "Can I take this book with me? I'd like to take time to enjoy all the drawings."

"Of course."

Dorthea pointed to Justine's dresses. "Which one would you like me to alter first?"

"The green one, I think."

Dorthea took the book with her and paused at the bedroom door. "You know I am capable of making wedding dresses too."

"In due time."

"Just let me know."

**

"You were quiet at dinner tonight, Justine," Goosie said as they washed the dishes. "Is something wrong?"

Everything. Nothing. She needed to put the Uriah-Alva issue aside. She'd had a lovely afternoon with Dorthea and needed to focus on that.

She forced herself to change the subject. "How are you liking it here?"

"Very much," Goosie said.

"You've been put to work, cooking and cleaning. We did not travel halfway across the country for you to still be a servant."

Goosie handed her a wet plate to dry. "I have been a servant for your family since I was ten. I don't know how to be anything else."

"You could find some lady friends and have tea and . . . you used to be in a quilting group back in Piedmont."

She shook her head. "My eyesight isn't good enough for that anymore. And truth be, I never enjoyed it much." She gave Justine another plate. "I like to cook. I like to clean. I like to serve people and make them happy. It's what I'm here for."

"You have a servant's heart."

"Nothing wrong with that."

"I'm not saying there is. It's just that your goodness is so far above mine . . ." Justine chuckled. "I do *not* have a servant's heart."

"I know."

She scoffed and stopped drying. "That's not very nice."

"You said it. And it's biblical. I may have the gift of serving, but you have the gift of perception. You see beyond what's before you and can put all the clues together into a larger whole. I don't have that gift. That one is yours. It's special and—"

They heard laughter and turned toward the dining room. They exchanged a glance and as one, tiptoed to the kitchen doorway, listening.

They heard Thomas and Dorthea chatting happily. Dorthea's giggles made her sound far younger than her forty-five years.

Goosie and Justine smiled at each other. "Isn't that interesting?" Justine said.

Goosie grinned. "Very."

Justine was happy for them.

CHAPTER FIVE

Harland and Justine stepped onto the wide porch of Ravenwood. This was their fourth visit. Last time the head man, Mr. Sutton, had told them to always go right in. No need to knock.

And so they did. A few patients waved shyly. Justine and Harland were beginning to know the residents by name — and eccentricity.

Sissy scampered down the hall toward her room. Leo, the most eccentric of all, spotted them and waltzed over to Justine, sweeping her into his dance. "Good morning, mademoiselle." He hummed a few bars. "You dance divine!"

She indulged him with a few spins before he let her go.

A very shy girl, Maddie, came into the foyer, hugging the wall, giving Leo a wide berth. After he had swept himself away, she smiled at them.

"How are you today, Maddie?" Justine said.

She nodded once.

"We've come to see Virginia. Is she here?" Justine immediately realized it was a stupid question

Maddie pointed toward the hall of the women's wing. "She's paintin'."

They found Virginia standing on a chair, wearing a worn man's shirt, her hair tied under a scarf. She held a paint palette and was in the midst of painting a maple leaf. She gave them a glance, smiled, and moved to step off the chair.

"Don't stop on our account," Justine said.

"Let me finish this leaf."

They watched as she swept some umber-colored paint into three lobes of the leaf, then turned the flat brush on end and added sharper edges, then a stem. She took a deep orange on a new brush, and retraced her steps, leaving a bit of the umber on the edges. She held that brush in her teeth and took another one of dark brown, and with a flit-flit-flit drew the stem and veins. "There."

"That's amazing," Justine said. "Even though I watched you, I still couldn't do it myself."

"Nonsense." Virginia held out her hand and Harland helped her step down from the chair. "As with everything, it just takes practice." She pointed the brushes at the two of them. "You are the reason I'm painting again."

"How so?"

She looked down the hall at the flowers. "You know how you see a thing too often that you don't really see it at all?"

"I do," Harland said.

"Before you came to visit, the paintings had become invisible. Seeing them through your eyes made me want to add more." She pointed at the tree branches that grew from the ceiling, stretching toward the flowers below. "I chose a maple in honor of your New England roots."

"How sweet of you," Justine said. "Are there maple trees in Kansas?"

"A few. More oaks and cedars. Cottonwoods." She set her palette on the floor. "But you didn't come here today to talk about painting—or trees."

"I came to speak with Mr. Sutton," Harland said. "He's told me he would like to set up a specified area that I could use to see patients."

Virginia beamed. "He told me about that. Your presence is so very welcome." She smiled at Justine. "As are your visits."

Harland bowed. "If you'll excuse me, ladies?"

He left them, and Justine nodded toward the paint palette. "Why don't you paint as we talk?"

"I do hate to waste the colors." She stepped into a room, spoke with someone there, and returned carrying a chair, placing it in the hallway. "For you." She retrieved her brushes and stepped onto her chair, returning to the maple tree. "You've been in town nearly two weeks. How are you liking Lawrence?"

"It is a fine town. The streets are so wide, the sky so . . ."

"Limitless?" Virginia suggested.

"That's an apt word that implies much."

"When I lived on the family farm my brother and I used to lay down in a field when the night was clear. We'd find the constellations and see who could spot a shooting star." She peered down at Justine. "Cole said they were good luck. But Mama said it could mean the opposite too, a foreboding sign." She pointed her brush as an extension of her finger. "Mama was right. Too right."

"What happened?"

Virginia hesitated, and her forehead furrowed as she made a decision. "I don't share this with many people — very few in fact. But since you've made such an effort to visit me these many times . . ."

Justine's curiosity was piqued. "You can trust me with your story. I promise."

Virginia nodded. "I know I can. And so . . . have you ever heard of Quantrill's Raid? The Lawrence Massacre?"

"I'm afraid not."

"Living in Lawrence, you will hear of it, even though it was sixteen years ago. Ever heard of Bleeding Kansas?"

Justine was embarrassed. "No. Sorry."

Mercifully, Virginia went back to painting. "The bleeding part started in 1854 before Kansas was even a state. Congress said we could choose whether to be slave or free. Missouri had a lot of slave owners so many of them would ride over the border to pressure the free-state people on the Kansas side to choose slavery."

"I can imagine there were a lot of heated discussions."

Virginia scoffed. "Discussions? No. Violence, yes. They didn't talk, they attacked. A lot of blood was shed. Butchery even. On both sides."

Justine cringed. "Your family were free-staters?"

"Avidly. We were abolitionists. We traveled here from Boston and were members of the New England Emigrant Aid Company. Our sole purpose was to make sure Kansas was declared a free state."

"Was it?"

"It was, in 1861. We thought things were settled. Mama and Pa got some land east of here and started working it. But then the real war started."

"The War Between the States." *At least I know about that.* "My father was wounded in the war. And Harland's father died."

"They fought for the Union?"

"They did."

"Good." Virginia moved her chair a few inches to the right and began to add more leaves growing out of the joint of wall and ceiling. "The war ended fourteen years ago but people's memories run deep. It's good to know we were on the same side."

"You mentioned some sort of raid?"

"Quantrill's Raid happened in sixty-three." She stopped in the middle of a brush stroke as if her memories overwhelmed. "My world changed that day." Virginia stepped off the chair and sat on it, her shoulders slumped, her brush and palette held, but forgotten.

Whatever she was going to say wasn't going to be good. Justine didn't know whether to ask questions or remain silent. Finally, she asked softly, "What happened?"

"My parents died that day."

Justine drew in a breath. "I'm so sorry."

Virginia nodded once. "My father was murdered by those evil slavers, those Bushwhackers."

Justine waited for her to mention her mother, then asked, "Was your mother murdered too?"

Virginia shook her head. "Might as well have been. They came thundering up to our farm in the wee hours of the morning, waking all of us with shouting and yelling. They barged into the house. They yanked Pa outside with Mama screaming at them, pulling at them. They tried to get her to let go of Pa, but she wouldn't. Pa was trying to talk sense to them, saying he wasn't a Jayhawker, he hadn't hurt any of their kind over in Missouri. But it didn't matter to them. A man pushed Mama back a few inches." Her chin quivered. "Then he shot Pa."

"I'm so sorry." Justine wished there was more she could say.

"Mama and Pa fell to the ground, and the man shot Pa some more. Right there, with Mama a few inches away from him."

"That's barbaric."

She stared into the air between them. "We found out later who they were. William Quantrill ran a group of pro-slavery thugs based in Missouri. They planned a raid on Lawrence. On the way there they killed any man or boy who could hold a gun and who might have abolitionist leanings. But like with Pa, they didn't much care if the man was guilty or not. They had the devil in their hearts and killed to kill."

"What about you and your brother?"

"When we heard the thunder of the horses, Pa told Cole and I to run out the back way, into the fields. Told Mama too, but she stayed with him." Virginia moved her hands toward her ears. "I will never forget the sound of the gunshots and Mama's screams."

Father, how can You allow such evil?

"When the men rode off, I stupidly stepped out of my hiding place in the corn and yelled at them, dumb and defiant. They laughed at me. The man who killed Pa even tipped his hat at me." She shuddered. "Soon as they were gone we ran to Pa. Mama held him in her arms, wailing and rocking. Pa's face . . . what was left of it . . ." She shook her head. "He had such a pretty smile."

Justine let tears flor.

"Even though Cole was just fifteen, he wanted to ride after them and 'kill them all' — which made Mama wail all the more. I tried to talk sense into him. There were hundreds of 'em. One boy couldn't stop 'em." She set her paint supplies on the floor and clasped her hands in her lap. "He probably would have gone, but for Mama clutching her chest and dying, right there in the yard."

Justine gasped and went to her side, wrapping an arm around her. Virginia stood and let Justine encompass her in a full embrace. "I'm so sorry, so sorry. So-so sorry . . ."

After a minute, Virginia pulled away. She wiped her eyes with the tail of her overshirt. "What we suffered is bad enough, but it was just the beginning of the bloodbath. Nearly 200 men and boys were killed in Lawrence that morning."

"Two hundred?" It was shocking.

Virginia nodded. "Plus, before riding back to Missouri the hoard set the downtown on fire. Most of the businesses burned to the ground. We were totally unprepared. Like I said, there'd been ugly acts committed on both sides for years, with free-staters rushing into Missouri and killing innocents because they thought they had slaves, and slavers coming here to Kansas and killing those who were against slavery. Revenge beget more revenge. I didn't think it would ever stop."

"Were these raiders soldiers?"

Virginia shrugged. "I don't know. They weren't wearing uniforms, and were a rough-looking bunch. Heard later they only lost one man."

That was surprising. "Didn't the men in Lawrence fight back?"

"Didn't have a chance to. They were surprised at five in the morning. Lawrence *had* built battlements and had soldiers on guard since the war started in sixty-one. We'd heard plenty of rumors about how this or that was going to happen. But when nothing came of the rumors, people got complacent and thought they were safe. No one was safe. Tit for tat. An eye for an eye . . ."

"How is Cole? Does he come to visit you here?"

"He died too."

What? "That night?"

Virginia sighed the sigh of someone who'd suffered too much. "He died from a farm accident soon after Spencer put me in here. Right after the children died."

Justine let her jaw go slack. "You had children? And they died?"

Virginia sighed a wistful smile. "Anna and Luke. They were just wee ones. Anna was four and Luke was three."

Justine sought the support of the chair. "They died?"

"They got sick while I was in here. If I'd been home, I know I could have saved them." Her expression grew hard. "I didn't belong in here."

Justine noticed she didn't say: *I don't belong in here*. "You said you were committed because of your interest in botany?"

"That was a lie," she said. "Or a partial lie. I apologize for that. It's true Spencer thought my interest in botany was excessive and unnecessary for a woman, but it was only one excuse, one so-called proof that I was insane."

"Pardon me, but you are *not* insane."

"No, I'm not." She sighed. "The thing was, after the children were born so close together I was overwhelmed with two in nappies, plus running the farm. Cole and I were still reeling from my parents' death and I was still angry at the men who murdered Pa. I wasn't an easy woman to live with."

"That's no reason to call you insane."

"I had changed from the willing young woman Spencer courted. I was only fifteen when the war started and had lived through the constant violence of Bleeding Kansas since I was nine. Even though I was twenty-one when we got married I had no experience with love and beaus. I was very naïve." She smiled at some memory.

"He swept you off your feet?"

Virginia's face softened. "Nah. That's not his way. But he was attentive and made me think a normal life was possible. Looking back, it's like he conquered me, like soldiers overtaking a hill." She shook her head. "When Spencer wanted something he got it. And he wanted me."

Something didn't jibe. "If he wanted you so much, why did he commit you — unfairly?"

She looked at the mural and touched a ladybug she'd painted there. "We were happy for a while. I was so thrilled when we had the children. But then, afterwards . . . I felt down and blue after each birth. Such an odd thing." She looked up. "I loved each baby, but didn't? Wanted to be around them, but didn't?"

Naïve. Overwhelmed. Conquered. Such strong words. "You were exhausted."

She nodded. "I don't know why I'm telling you all this. I guess it's obvious I haven't had many visitors over the years. You ask a few questions and I go off, boring you with stories about my life. If you need to go find your husband . . ."

Justine reached forward and touched her hand. "I'm here because I want to be. You are not boring me. I want to know about your life. Please continue."

"You're very kind. From the moment we met I knew we could be close."

Another patient walked past them to her room and pointed at the new leaves. "I like autumn."

"Me too, Sarah Ann."

Justine hoped Virginia could get back to her story. She had a deep feeling that it might be linked to why she had come to Lawrence. As soon as Sarah Ann went into her room, Justine tried to get Virginia to resume the story. "You were overwhelmed by the children?"

She nodded. "The more I focused on myself, the madder Spencer got, especially because I wasn't helping on the farm at all, barely getting out of bed some days, and *he* was never a good farmer. He always said he came from farming but that had to be a lie. He didn't know sorghum from corn."

"I wouldn't know that."

"Most people don't. But farmers do—need to. Plus, he and Cole didn't get on well, and . . ." She sighed deeply. "The tension around the farm was like a spring pulled across a creek. It was bound to snap back at somebody, or pull someone in."

"What made it snap?"

Virginia scraped a fingernail against some dried paint on her hand. "One day I had an episode. Looking back I can see I was acting crazy. Both babies had the runs and I didn't feel good and just wanted to sleep, and *they* wouldn't sleep and the house smelled like poo." She scrunched up her face as though smelling it now. "Then Spencer came in and yelled at me for not having dinner ready. I exploded and threw things. Shattered my mother's best soup tureen, denting the wall with it." She closed her eyes as if wanting to stop the memories. "He grabbed my arm and dragged me out of the house and into the wagon. We fought. Cole came running and tried to help, but he'd been upset with me too. I wasn't acting rational. All my frustrations from the war and death and children and too much work . . ."

"One temporary breakdown does not justify commitment."

She raised a finger. "But it *is* an excuse for one. That's the day he took me here. A Mr. Roswell ran the place at the time, not a nice man like Mr. Sutton at all. When we got here I was sobbing like I would never stop. Wailing. I'd heard about Ravenwood. I didn't want to go here. I clawed at Spencer and fell to the ground. I wouldn't walk on my own. They had to carry me in. I kept screaming, "Why? Why?""

Justine's heart broke for her. "It wasn't fair."

"No, it wasn't. They locked me in a room. I pounded on the door and screamed until I collapsed from exhaustion."

"You poor thing."

"When I woke up and remembered where I was, I pounded again, screaming for my babies. Who was going to take care of my babies?" Virginia looked at Justine, her face pulled and pitiful. "I had to get home to them."

"Of course."

She took a ragged breath. "I got my thoughts in order and realized the only way I was getting out was to stop having a fit and start acting like a mother, act like a sane woman. So I fixed my hair and smoothed my clothes. And I waited until I heard someone in the hall. Then I rapped on the door and said, "If you please? Could I have a cup of water?""

"Did someone bring it?"

"Mrs. Roswell came. She brought water and some bread. Her being a woman, I thought she would understand my predicament. I calmly explained my actions, apologized for my behavior, and asked to go home. But she shook her head and said that Spencer had signed the papers to have me committed. I wasn't going anywhere. And I didn't go anywhere. Didn't ever see Spencer again. Or the children."

Justine was taken aback. "He just left you?"

"He did. I was crazy with worry and longing for Anna and Luke. I tried to act rational and calm even though I wanted to scream and yell. I played to Mrs. Roswell's female nature, needing one friend. But they wouldn't let me out."

Justine remembered there wasn't much of a fence. "Couldn't you just run away? Run home?"

"I tried. Twice. But they caught me and brought me back and often kept me tied to my bed."

"That's inhuman."

"I prayed and prayed God would save me. I prayed and prayed for my children. I asked God to forgive me for resenting them and for causing trouble. If only I'd been a better mother, a better wife."

Justine thought of her own flaws. "Even if you were going through a hard time and acted badly, you did not deserve to be held prisoner."

"Thank you for that. But fair or not, it's where I was. A while later I got a letter from Spencer saying the children, my babies, had been sick and were dead and buried. And Cole had died . . . —I didn't even get to go to their funerals. I begged and begged but they wouldn't let me. Said it was for my own good."

"I don't know what to say." Justine pressed a hand to her chest. "It's too much for anyone to bear."

"Spencer's letter said he'd sold the farm and was heading west. It was *my* family's farm!

Justine's throat was tight. "He didn't tell you any of this in person?"

She shook her head.

"You lost everyone."

She sighed deeply. "I did. And Spencer did. I suppose he was overwhelmed too. "

"You're too generous." Justine's heart broke for her. "He took no pity on you. None."

Virginia scoffed. "Pity and empathy have no place in Spencer's heart. At least he had the heart to bury the children in the family plot."

Justine fought back tears of rage. "Where is Spencer now? We'll find him for you. I'll get some men to come with me: there's Harland and Thomas, Pastor Karvins, and even the police if need be. We'll talk to him and get you out—"

Virginia shook her head. "It's been too long. He's long gone."

"The coward."

She shrugged. "The only merciful thing he did was pay for me to stay here."

"He paid your captors to keep you prisoner."

She nodded. "That's when I resigned myself to having Ravenwood be my home—I didn't have any other home to go to. No family home, no parents, no brother, no children, and no husband." She looked down the hall and waved at Sarah Ann as she came out of her room. "These people are my family now. And things got better around here after Mr. Sutton came. He's as kind as the Roswells were wicked."

Justine remembered the conversation during their first meeting. "You've been here eight years?"

"I have."

"Have you gone out at all?"

Virginia looked toward the foyer. "No reason to, other than I might like to visit the graves of my family."

Graves . . .

Suddenly, Justine knew what her future held. "Why don't you go to the graves? With me? Maybe we could get Mr. Sutton to let you have an outing."

Virginia looked down the hall. "I may not have belonged here when Spencer brought me, but I do now. I wouldn't feel comfortable being out in the world—I've tried a few times, but didn't stay out long. This is my world."

"Then perhaps I can go for you? Be your eyes?"

Virginia's eyes brightened. "That would be very kind of you. And maybe you could bring some flowers for the graves?"

"I would be happy to."

They both looked toward the head of the hall and saw Harland coming toward them. He was smiling.

"So?" she asked him.

"I now have an official office for patients. Next time I come I'll stock it with some common medicines and bandages for the times I'm not here."

Virginia clapped. "That will be a relief to everyone."

" I'm glad to help." He nodded down the hall. "I checked on Sally's hand and gave her a fresh bandage. It's healing well." He looked at the leaves. "You've made some progress."

Virginia chuckled. "It's not progressing much at the moment."

Justine explained. "We got side-tracked."

"Telling stories."

Oh, the stories. "Virginia was just telling me about her family's farm. I'm going to visit and put some flowers on her family's graves."

At the word 'graves' Harland's eyebrows rose. Justine gave him a slight nod.

Virginia gave directions. "The farm is east of town, between here and Eudora. Take the main road and head east about three miles. When you get to the three oak trees on your right, turn left. Our farmhouse is the next driveway on the right."

Justine wasn't interested in the house. "Where is your family buried?"

"There's a plot behind the house, down by a grove." She sighed wistfully. "Started with two, grew to five."

Justine drew her into a final embrace. "I will visit them tomorrow." She thought of a detail that might come in handy. "What was your maiden name?"

"Dawson," Virginia said. "Thank you for doing this. You're a dear woman. I look forward to our next visit."

Justine and Harland left Ravenwood and headed home.

"You found graves to visit," he said.

"Her family's. Her children's."

"She lost children?"

"To illness. She also lost her brother. And her parents during a Bushwhacker massacre that killed two hundred in Lawrence."

Harland stopped walking. "I had no idea. The grief she has suffered . . ."

"She never should have been committed, but that's another story."

"One I'd like to know. I think you need to start at the beginning."

Harland listened intently and was just as appalled as Justine had been. "How could one woman endure so much?"

"She should be hard and bitter," Justine said. "I would be."

"Her life story stirs up many questions."

Justine began counting them on her hands. "Where is Spencer? Why did he commit Virginia to Ravenwood? Who are the men who killed her parents, and have they been brought to justice?"

"Regarding the raid . . . it was 1863, Jussie. It was wartime. As Virginia said, there were atrocities on both sides."

"I'd still like to know the truth of it."

"But would Virginia? *Your* curiosity is aroused, but what's the purpose in Virginia knowing?"

Justine felt her fervor wane—but only the smallest bit. "I've been searching for a reason we were brought here. I've explored the church cemetery and felt nothing. God gave me the gift of time travel to facilitate justice. Only He knows what kind of justice. I can't just sit by and not try."

Harland draped his arm around her shoulders. "I wouldn't expect you to."

Good.

"Which family member do you want to visit?" he asked.

"Probably all of them. In Piedmont it took many visits to get the full story. I expect the same here. But I'd like to start with the children. I think their fate is the hardest for Virginia to bear."

"But they weren't murdered. It's horrible they died, but there was no crime."

She sighed with the weight of it. "I wish I knew where Spencer was now. All Virginia knows is that he went west."

"*West* is a big place."

She sighed. "One step at a time. I'll start with the children and go from there."

They rode a short way in silence. Then Harland asked, "I think you should tell my mother about your gift. She's the only one in the household who doesn't know about it."

Justine had been thinking about this. "I agree. I'd like to be able to discuss my journeys with Thomas and Goosie. I can't do that without being secretive. I don't want to be secretive."

"Or put the burden of your secrets on another. With Mother and Thomas getting close . . ."

She smiled. "I heard her giggling like a girl with him."

"She deserves happiness. She's been alone too long."

"Now that your sisters have moved away, she has to be lonely."

"Even with us here?"

Justine glanced at him and could tell he was only half-serious. "Loneliness takes many forms."

"When do you want to tell her?" he asked.

"If I'm going tomorrow . . . "

"At dinner tonight?"

She nodded. "I wonder how she'll react."

"You'll have Goosie and Thomas to give their testimony."

"And I did see *her* twice in the past . . ."

He chuckled. "This will be an interesting evening."

**

The dinner prayer was said in concert, with Justine adding a silent prayer for the right words to explain time travel to her future mother-in-law. They spent the bulk of dinner talking about Virginia's crisis-strewn life. All were suitably appalled and Thomas offered to go see her — as well as all the patients at Ravenwood. Not surprisingly, Dorthea asked to go along. Goosie offered too, if they wanted the company.

Justine's plan was to set up the *need* for time travel and get to the actual explanation just before dessert.

All three of her co-conspirators — for she had told her father and Goosie that she was going to reveal her secret — kept giving her pointed glances, with many raised eyebrows that asked, *"When are you going to say it?"*

She helped remove the dinner dishes and returned to the dining room with slices of rhubarb pie. Once everyone was settled, she said, "Tomorrow I am going to visit the graves of Virginia's family."

"That's very sweet of you," Dorthea said. "You can cut some flowers from my garden."

"Thank you, I will." She glanced at Harland. "While I'm there I plan on traveling back into their lives to get more details about how they died."

There was a moment of silence as they all exchanged glances. Dorthea put down her fork.

"That's one way to broach the subject," Harland said under his breath

"I thought stating it plain was best," she said.

"A little preamble might have been advisable," Thomas said.

"Tact, Jussie," Goosie said.

Now, you give me advice? Justine shoved her pie toward the center of the table and looked at Dorthea. "I'm sorry to blurt it out like that."

Dorthea just sat there, her brow furrowed. "Blurt out . . .? What did you say again?"

Her look of total confusion caused Justine to adapt her presentation. She clasped her hands on the table. "God has given me the gift of being able to travel through time."

Harland snickered. "I didn't think you could be any more direct, but I was wrong."

"You could help," Justine said.

Harland, who was sitting cattycorner from his mother at the table's head, angled his body toward her. "I know it sounds bizarre and fantastical."

"Because it is," Thomas added.

"But it's true, Mother. Justine does have the gift of time travel."

"Time travel? What does that mean?"

"It means I bodily visit the past."

Dorthea blinked. "But why?"

The rest of them exchanged a look, then shared a nervous laugh.

"This is the question you ask?" Harland asked. "I expected a *how*-question."

"Justine said God gave her the gift, so I believe her. There are many things in this world I don't understand. That doesn't change the fact they exist."

Justine was inspired by her faith, and stood to give her a kiss on the cheek. "Thank you for your trust."

"You're welcome. But please answer my question. Why have you been given this gift?"

Justine returned to her seat. "To facilitate justice for past wrongs."

"Like what?"

Thomas raised a hand, and Justine deferred. Who better to explain it?

"I've started to tell you a bit about my life back east, but there's much you don't know. Namely, that my brother tried to kill me—he thought he *had* killed me and would have tried again if I hadn't stayed in New York." He looked lovingly at Justine. "I always knew Justine was my daughter but couldn't step forward until the past had been set right." He smiled. "She only found out last year."

Dorthea looked at Justine. "So recently?"

Justine nodded. "I spent the first twenty years of my life thinking that Noel Braden—who raised me—was my biological father."

Dorthea looked from Justine to Thomas. "Thank God you two found each other."

"Exactly," Thomas said. "And we *do* praise God."

Goosie spoke up. "Quinn tried to kill Thomas, but he wasn't the first in his family to be so evil. His grandfather killed *my* father, and killed the real founder of Piedmont, taking his name, assuming his life."

"Gracious," Dorthea said.

Harland got back to the time travel point. "Justine discovered all these crimes and truths by going back in time."

Dorthea cocked her head. "For God. You brought about justice for God."

Justine let out a sigh. "Yes. That's exactly right."

"He must trust you very much."

"I hope so. I try to follow His lead. His will." Murders, fraud, and mysterious parentage. Justine thought of something more personal to add. "I met you in the past. Twice."

Dorthea jerked her head back. "Me? When?"

Justine chuckled. "Again, you accept what I say so easily. I appreciate that."

"You've given me no reason to doubt anything you say."

Justine felt lucky to become a part of Dorthea's family. "I met you the first time on New Years' Day, 1857. There was a potluck in Piedmont's meeting hall, and you were in line getting food with Bee-Bee and Harland." She looked at him. "He was just two and not cooperating at all. You had your hands overly full."

Dorthea shook her head. "I don't remember that day with any specifics, but we always enjoyed the New Year's dinner at the church. And Harland *was* a handful."

"Still am," he said, winking.

"When was the other time we met?"

"In 1860. I met Harland at Dr. Bevin's where he was helping out. I was visiting that year looking for Thomas, and Harland offered to take me to him." She looked fondly at Harland. "Such a talkative, precocious five-year-old, who already had a talent for medicine."

Dorthea nodded. "One time my husband fell and cut his head and Harland took care of it."

"*That* was the day I'm talking about," Justine said. "You were boiling laundry in a pot in the yard. Ellie was just a baby. It was autumn."

Dorthea gawked. "Every detail you mention is true. As if you were there."

"I *was* there."

Dorthea stared into the air, thinking back. "I vaguely remember a woman coming by for a short bit. But her name wasn't Justine. I would have remembered that name."

"I said my name was Susan. I said I was a friend—"

"Of the Tylers!" Dorthea took a cleansing breath. "Oh my. You really can go back in time."

Thomas spoke up. "As we've said, because of Justine's travels my brother Quinn was brought to justice and we were reunited as father and daughter."

Dorthea let this soak in a minute. "So you want to use your gift to give Virginia justice?"

Justine felt a wave of relief. "That's exactly what I want to do."

Dorthea slapped the table. "Then you should do it. Let me know how I can help."

Justine shook her head, incredulous. "Don't you want to know *how* I travel back?"

"No need. That's a story for another time." She pointed at the desserts. "Eat your pie, family. And no need for you to help with dishes, Justine. You need to get to bed early. Tomorrow you're going to have a busy day."

They dutifully ate their pie. *Praise the Lord!*

**

Harland stood in the doorway to Justine's room to say goodnight.

"It's barely nine," she said. "I feel silly going to sleep so early."

"Mother's orders," he said with a flick to her nose.

They listened to the happy chatter coming from the parlor as Dorthea and Thomas played cards. "Your mother is an amazing woman. Completely trusting even though she barely knows me. I don't know if *I* would believe me."

Harland ran a finger along her cheek. "Mother is a unique blend of faith and facts. Since father died and she was left with a farm and three small children she's had to set her emotions aside and do the work. She used to quote a verse from First Chronicles to me: 'Be strong, and do it.'"

"That's a good verse."

Harland linked his hand with hers. "Coming out here took faith, and since then Mother has tackled this new life with dogged pragmatism." He leaned forward and kissed her gently. "She has the same independent intelligence and courage as another woman I know."

She appreciated the compliment. "What if I go to the cemetery and nothing happens?"

"If you don't go to the cemetery nothing *can* happen."

True.

He gave her a proper kiss. "Good night, my brave darling." Justine got ready for bed and was just about to blow out the lamp, when she remembered something very important she had to do. She slipped out of bed and knelt beside it, bowing her head. She prayed to the One who'd given her the gift, to the only One who knew the past, the present, and the future.

CHAPTER SIX

The next morning, Goosie came into Justine's bedroom as she was dressing. She closed the door.

"Good morning," Justine said, buttoning her blouse. "Is something wrong?"

Goosie shook her head and picked up Justine's nightgown, hanging it on the back of the door. "You're going back today?"

"Hopefully." *Is she going to try to talk me out of it?* "I'll be fine, Goosie. God's in charge of my traveling. He's with me every step of the way."

"I know He is. It's not that."

"What then?"

Goosie looked around the room. "I just thought you might need my help getting ready."

Was she feeling left out? "I always appreciate your help."

Goosie looked around the room, as if searching for something. "In Piedmont you usually took your travel bag along, filled with clothes you might need in order to fit in. I used to help you. Remember the old clothes of Granny's we found in the trunk?"

"I do remember. It was very helpful — as were you. But I think I'll leave the bag behind — at least this first time."

"What if you end up in a place where it's winter?"

It was a possibility. But Justine didn't want to haul a carpetbag into the past. She'd discovered that whatever she was wearing or holding traveled with her — both ways. If she *wasn't* holding the bag, it would be left behind. "I think I'll risk it."

Goosie eyed Justine's white blouse and the brown skirt draped on the bed, then pointed at her single petticoat. "Your ensemble seems overly simple."

Justine smoothed her slip. "I think it's safer this way. Luckily, the everyday styles of the past few decades haven't changed that much. And you know I can't wear a bustle that would connect my clothes to the eighteen-seventies."

"But hoop skirts were popular in the sixties. Perhaps you should wear a hoop."

Justine shook her head. "Talk about cumbersome. I think a simple skirt with a petticoat will suffice. At least I hope it will. Settlers didn't populate Kansas until the 1850s, and they dressed practically. I don't think fashion was foremost on their minds."

"*If* you stay in this area. You could end up in some other far-away place. Couldn't you?"

Justine had *not* thought about this. "In Piedmont, I stayed in the vicinity of Piedmont. I guess I assumed any traveling from Kansas would stay in Kansas."

"God may have other plans."

Justine slipped the skirt over her head and let Goosie hook it in the back. "You've certainly made my mind spin."

Goosie pat Justine once to indicate the skirt was hooked, then came around to face her. "I didn't mean to confuse you. I just want you to be prepared."

"I appreciate that."

Goosie plucked a stray piece of lint from Justine's shoulder. There was something else on her mind.

"What else is bothering you?"

Goosie put the lint in a pocket of her apron. "It's not a bothering, but . . . the other night you asked me how I liked it here. But how about you? How are you liking it?"

"It's certainly different than New Hampshire, a little rough around the edges, but I like the potential here. There's a constant sense of expectancy as if anything can happen. Good things."

Goosie nodded vigorously. "Personally, I think it's the best thing that's ever happened to me."

Justine was taken aback. "You do?"

"I lived in your family's home from 1800 to coming here. Same town. Same views. Same people."

Justine chuckled. "That, you did."

Goosie took a deep breath, as if inhaling fresh air for the first time. "Lawrence is everything you say and so much more. It's the chance to be a new me." She put a hand on Justine's. "I know that sounds silly, considering I'm nearly ninety. Maybe it's because I *am* nearly ninety that it's pulled at a place in my heart, but I love it here."

Justine touched her cheek. "You amaze me."

Goosie touched the hand that touched her cheek. "See? Something else new."

"You've always amazed me."

Goosie squeezed her hand. "We're two amazing women, that's what we are."

Justine wouldn't think of arguing with her.

**

It was eerie.

Walking east, away from Lawrence, walking into the Kansas countryside, walking alone . . .

Walking to a cemetery. Hopefully walking into the past . . .

The situation made Justine realize how few times she had ever been fully alone. In New York City and even tiny Piedmont there were always people nearby. Even when she'd traveled into the past — into the dense woods around Colonial Piedmont — she'd come upon people almost immediately.

Lead me, Lord . . . wherever and whenever . . .

In the here and now there were no people nearby. In their absence, she took note of her surroundings. Fields stretched north and south, the brown earth tilled, ready for seeds of wheat and soybeans. Dorthea had told her about a grasshopper plague that had devastated thousands of square miles, with the insects blocking out the sun for hours, eating plants, wool off sheep, and even fabric and wood. All evidence of that devastation was gone and the farmers were planting. She admired their determination and stamina.

Groves of trees with new spring growth spotted the land here and there, marking rivers and streams or softening the edges of the occasional farmstead.

She looked overhead and marveled at the expanse of sky that stretched horizon to horizon like an inverted blue bowl with dabs of white clouds pulled and feathered with God's brush.

A yellow-breasted bird landed a branch of white blooms in a plum thicket nearby and sang to her. She stopped and listened as the bird started each phrase with three notes like an introduction, then let loose with a fluttering of sixteenth notes. He repeated the process but the latter notes were never quite the same. When its song was complete, the bird flew away. She happily applauded.

See? You are not alone, Justine. I am all around you. Although she carried a bouquet of flowers from Dorthea's garden, she was spurred to gather some of the wildflowers into a second bouquet for the graves. As she continued her walk she marveled at how God had taken the time to ease her anxiety. "You are a God of details, aren't You?"

Some butterflies dallied on nearby wildflowers, as if God had sent them as a finale. Justine walked with more confidence. She felt with her entire being she was supposed to go to the grave of Virginia's children. What she wasn't so certain about is whether anything would happen.

It's not up to you.

"I know, I know," Justine told the voice in her head.

She saw three oak trees on the right side of the road and turned left. Virginia had said her family's farm was the first driveway on the right. She spotted it in the distance and walked toward the house to introduce herself rather than be caught trespassing.

She stepped onto the porch and was ready to knock when the door suddenly opened. A woman wiped her hands on her apron. "Yes?"

"I'm sorry to bother you. My name is Justine Braden. I came here from Lawrence and —"

The woman looked past her. "I don't see a wagon. Or a horse."

"I walked."

The woman tilted her head. Was she impressed? "What can I do for you, Mrs. Braden?"

"Miss."

"The question stands."

"I am a friend of Virginia Meade Dawson? Her family used to live here."

The woman nodded. At least they had a connection now. "Is she the crazy one they locked away?"

Justine wanted to argue, but let it go. "She asked me to visit the graves of her family and put these flowers there. Apparently, there's a spot down by a grove?"

The woman pointed to the north. "Down there a piece. You're welcome to it."

Justine thought ahead. "I may want to return on another day. Would that be all right?"

The woman thought a moment. "I suppose. But when you do, take the narrow lane that goes from the road right to the graves."

Perfect. "I will do that. Thank you."

Justine walked down a gentle hill toward the small grouping of trees. She spotted five headstones peeking out from tall grasses. Obviously, the current owners didn't care to keep it tended. She spent the next half-hour pulling weeds and grass as best she could. She spotted some columbine flowers growing nearby and found comfort in knowing these same flowers grew in New Hampshire. She added some to her bouquets and placed some flowers on each grave.

The area cleared, she knelt before the small headstones of the children. Anna was born in 1867 and Luke in 1868. "You would be twelve and eleven now. I'm so sorry your young lives ended too soon."

Before she traced Anna's name on the stone, Justine prayed the prayer that had become part of her time-traveling ritual. "Father, protect me from harm as I travel back in time to right the wrongs of the past. Give me wisdom and strength to accomplish this task You have set before me. Amen."

She took a cleansing breath, bracing herself for the inner tightening and *whoosh* that would take her away. Then she reached for the headstone and let her fingers trace Anna's name.

Nothing happened.

She tried again to the same results.

She reached over to trace Luke's name.

Nothing happened.

"What's going on?" She sat on her haunches, trying to think. She didn't always go back. She'd proved that at the church cemetery.

Yet she couldn't shake the *knowing* that today was the day she was going back in time.

Justine looked at the other three headstones. Suzanna, Josiah, and Cole. She moved to Suzanna's grave, but hesitated. Would she be taken back to 1863, to Quantrill's Raid? She didn't want to experience such violence.

It's not your choice, it's Mine.

She nodded. "Thy will be done." She traced Suzanna's name and was pulled away.

Pulled back in time.

**

Justine opened her eyes and found herself in darkness.

The moonlight revealed a small grove that looked as if it could have been the same location as the cemetery. The trees were younger and there were no gravestones at all. The leaves of the trees were fully formed and the nearby fields were heavy with mature plants. The air was stifling and sticky even though it was night. She was glad she hadn't dressed for winter, nor brought along her carpetbag.

She looked around to get her bearings. Through the dim she could make out the silhouette of the Dawson's home a hundred yards away. All was quiet. She heard an owl hooting in a tree. *Who, who. Who are you?*

I'm here, Lord. Now what? She didn't want to go to the house and knock at this time of night. Yet during her other journeys into the past, she always saw someone who led her into the moment.

This time she was alone.

Justine sat down amid the grasses to wait until a light came on inside the house. Then perhaps she could knock, or approach someone who came out to do chores.

But as soon as she got comfortable she felt a rumbling. She pressed a hand to the earth. Was it an earthquake?

And then she heard it. Horses. Galloping. Lots of them. *Quantrill's Raid?*

Justine stood, unsure what to do. She wanted to run to the house to warn the Dawsons but there was a rule she'd learned in her travels: she was forbidden from trying to change what happened. She was there as an observer. Unfortunately, she was about to witness unspeakable atrocities, murder, and death—deaths that would change the course of Virginia's life—and she could do nothing to stop them.

Lord, please help! Help them. Help me. I don't know what to do!

Suddenly some lights came on in the second floor of the house. Had they heard the horses?

The thundering grew louder; evil riding through the darkness.

Justine's heart beat double time. She couldn't just stand there.

She hurried toward the house, staying in the shadows.

A light was lit in a back room on the first floor. Justine slipped behind a shed to hide and watch. Suddenly an older boy and girl rushed outside in their nightclothes. Virginia and Cole? At the back of the house Mrs. Dawson called out softly but vehemently to her children, "Run into the fields. Hide! And don't come out!"

They ran toward the fields.

"You too, Suzanna," Mr. Dawson said.

"No. I'm staying here with you, Josiah."

"No one rides like that in the middle of the night with good purposes," he said. "It's got to be Bushwhackers. They're coming. You need to—"

Just then a troupe of six men rode toward the house, stirring up a flurry of dust in the moonlight. Suzanna pushed her husband back through the door and the two of them disappeared inside.

Three of the riders dismounted. They strode toward the door as if to conquer it. They pounded and yelled. "Open up! Now!" They didn't wait, but forced their way inside.

Justine jolted at the sounds of banging, breakage, slaps, and cries of pain. To her right she heard the low voices of the siblings, and saw them hunkered down at the edge of the field, tensely watching. She could read their minds. They wanting to obey their mother and stay safe, but also wanted to rush to the house to defend their parents.

There was a violent commotion and Justine heard heavy footfalls on the front porch. A man came out, dragging Mr. Dawson. Another man held Mrs. Dawson around her waist as she clung to her husband. They stopped not twenty yards from Justine. The other men sat on their horses, observing the violence as if it had nothing to do with them.

Mrs. Dawson begged and pleaded for their lives. Mr. Dawson told them they were innocent farmers, they weren't Jayhawkers. They'd never hurt anyone.

Their pleas fell on deaf ears.

Then Mr. Dawson stopped pleading, as if he knew what would happen. "Please Suzanna. Let go of me. Let me go."

It was pitiful and horrible to watch.

The man who held his wife forcibly tried to yank her away from her husband. But she held onto him.

Just like Virginia told me.

"Please stop!" Mrs. Dawson cried. "There's no reason to hurt us. We've never hurt anyone. We're living peaceful lives."

"There's gonna be no peace tonight," one of them said with a laugh. "Shoot 'em, Wat."

Another egged the tall man on. "Get it over with. We got places to go, people to kill."

Wat pushed Mrs. Dawson back a few inches, then shot her husband. Right there with her arms around his legs.

Justine stifled a gasp. The couple fell as one.

Once again, Mrs. Dawson was pulled to the side as the tall man shot her husband again. And again. And again. Justine clapped her hands over her mouth, needing to scream.

"That should do it," Wat said smugly, as he stood erect. When he turned into the moonlight his face was visible. He had long hair and a straggly beard. Somehow he looked familiar.

"Onward, men!" he called out.

The voice and the face — even with the beard and hair . . .

It clicked. Wat was Uriah Benedict!

As if called to confirm it, the man paused and looked toward the field. His smirk sealed it.

The man who killed Virginia's father was Uriah.

The men rushed back to their horses and rode off toward their next victims.

Virginia stepped out of the field and shouted after them, shaking her fist. "You cowards! You murderers! Damn you! Damn you to hell!"

Justine saw Uriah glance at Virginia and was fearful he would shoot her, but instead, he tipped his hat and rode on. "Tally ho, boys!"

Cole rushed out of the field to his father's side. Virginia went to their mother, taking her into her arms, both of them sobbing at the horror before them.

Mrs. Dawson pushed Virginia away and moved to hold her husband, wailing in a way that made Justine's nerves cry. Then she let out a blood-curdling and clutched her chest. She moaned. And slumped to the side.

Virginia rushed to her. "Mama?"

Virginia and Cole called out, "No! No! Don't leave us! You can't."

But she could. And did.

Justine was relieved when she felt a stirring. God took her away from the horrific scene.

When she opened her eyes she was in the cemetery again, standing before the headstones of the Dawsons who had died at the hands of evil men.

She fell to her knees and cried.

If only I could fly.

After witnessing Quantrill's Raid, Justine was spent physically, mentally, and emotionally, yet she had no choice but to walk back to Lawrence.

There was too much to think about. No thought remained front and center long enough for her to deliberately consider what it meant, who it would affect, and what she should do about it. It was like trying to catch a fish in a whirlpool.

She didn't notice the sky or the land, didn't listen to the song of a bird, or appreciate the flowers of spring. She walked forward step after step, seeing nothing but the road leading her home. She was even too exhausted to pray and in truth was in no frame of mind to do so. She was angry at God. How could He allow such evil in the world?

"Miss? Miss?"

A man touched her shoulder and she turned. There was a driverless wagon behind her.

Justine had no idea how many times he'd called to her. She had not heard the wagon or the horses at all. She stared at him blankly, momentarily forgetting where she was.

"Are you all right?" he asked.

No. Not at all.

"Let's get you in the wagon and I'll take you wherever you need to go."

She let herself be led to the wagon, and with the last of her energy stepped up to the seat.

The man climbed in beside her and took the reins. "Where to?"

"Home."

"Where's that?"

She shook her head, at first not remembering. She blinked twice, slid back to the present. She gave him the address.

The wagon began to move and she let herself be rocked back and forth. She didn't dare close her eyes for fear she would slip into oblivion and fall off.

"Can I ask what you were doing out here so far from your home?" he asked.

Witnessing an execution.

Thankfully, he accepted her silence, saying, "That's all right. You don't need to tell me. Sometimes silence reveals wisdom."

Good. Because at the moment it was all she could manage.

**

The man had to support Justine as they climbed the steps of the porch.

"Hello?" he called out. "Help please?"

Harland came running out of the house and rushed to help, taking over for the man. "What happened?"

"I found her staggering on the road into town, out east. She's done in."

"Thank you for bringing her home, Mister . . .?"

"Seth Dobbins. And you're welcome." He tipped his hat and left.

Harland helped Justine inside, leading her to the settee in the parlor.

Goosie rushed out from the kitchen. "What happened?"

"She nearly collapsed on the road coming home from the Dawson's."

"I'll get you some water," Goosie said. "Or tea? I could warm up lunch?"

Justine didn't know what she wanted. Or needed.

"I should have gone with you," Harland said.

"No," she managed. "It was a journey I needed to make alone."

He studied her face. "Did your journey involve going . . . back?"

"It did." She pressed her fingers to her eyes, wishing she could blot out what she'd seen.

Goosie sat nearby. "Do you want to talk about it?"

No, she didn't. Yet, maybe it would help.

"You don't have to tell us right now," Harland said. "Maybe you should rest."

Rest sounded wonderful, but Justine needed it said. "I will rest—I need to rest. But I also need to tell you. It's too important to wait." She told them the entire story of the deaths of Mr. and Mrs. Dawson. She ended her story with the cry of defiance by Virginia, shouting after the murderers who'd just destroyed her family. She felt stronger for sharing it.

"I feel so bad for her," Goosie said. "To lose both parents in one night in such a horrible way? Such an event sticks with you forever."

Justine closed her eyes and sighed "Why did God allow such evil to happen? Why did He let good people die?"

Her questions were met with silence. Then Harland said the only thing that could be said, "I don't know."

There was one last part of the story she needed to add. "I saw the face of the man who did the killing." She looked from one to the other, feeling sick to her stomach. "We know him. We've had dinner at his house."

"You can't mean . . . ? "

"I do. It was Uriah Benedict."

Harland's face was incredulous.

"Are you sure?" Goosie added.

"You have to be sure," Harland said. "He's a respected member of the community."

"Who is poisoning his wife," she said.

Another round of silence.

"What should we do?" Goosie asked.

Justine shook her head. "I need to know more."

"Which means more trips to the past," Harland said.

She nodded.

Goosie looked confused. "More traveling won't change the fact that he's guilty. He should be arrested and tried for murder."

Harland raised a finger. "As bad as it was, it happened during wartime."

"They weren't acting like soldiers," Justine said. "They weren't dressed in any uniforms. They were ruffians and marauders, taking part in a guerilla raid against innocent civilians. They killed nearly two hundred in Lawrence."

"Can justice be satisfied for such crimes?" Goosie asked.

Justine pressed her fingers to her temples. "I can't accuse Uriah of a war crime. What proof can I give? That I was there? That I saw him?"

"You're right. You have to keep digging," Harland said.

Justine shuddered. "I am very willing to do God's work and will obviously go where He sends me, but I fervently pray I don't see another crime like I did today."

"Whatever journey is yours, it will have to be postponed for another day." Harland helped her to standing. "Right now you're going to rest. I insist."

"I'll bring you some tea, bread and soup—no arguing," Goosie said.

Justine didn't have the strength.

Once upstairs, she let Harland remove her shoes and fluff her pillow. He placed a quilt over her. "Sleep," he said.

It was odd to be in bed in the middle of the day, but she let her body sink into the softness.

Yet she had one more question before he left her. "Should I tell Virginia I know who killed her parents?"

Harland stroked her face. "You'd have to tell her about your gift. Are you ready to do that?"

Of this she could be certain. "I'm not."

"Then you wait. You'll know when the time is right."

She took his hand and kissed it. "Thank you for being here. I have the feeling I'm going to need your support many times in the coming days and weeks."

"I'm not going anywhere."

With that assurance she let herself sleep.

CHAPTER SEVEN

Justine felt like she was swimming to the surface. Upon reaching the top, she gasped. She opened her eyes.

She wasn't under water. She was asleep.

It was still daytime. She'd had a good nap.

But then she realized she was dressed in her nightgown. The light streaming in the window was morning light, not the light of afternoon when she'd gone to rest. She looked at the mantel clock, which read eight.

Eight?

She dangled her legs from the side of the bed. Her stomach growled. On the bedside table was a tray of soup, a cup of tea, and some bread and butter. She picked up the bread and found it hard. She took a bite anyway.

The door to her bedroom opened a crack, and then more. Goosie came in. "You're awake."

"Is it . . . tomorrow?"

"It is."

"I can't believe I slept so long." She began to undo the buttons on the yoke of her nightgown. "I don't even remember you getting me in my gown."

"We tried to wake you for supper, but you were in a daze so we got you comfortable." Goosie glanced at the meal tray. "You must be famished. You missed supper and breakfast too. Thomas and Harland have left for the day. Harland hopes to officially open his practice in a few days."

Justine took her blue day dress from the armoire. "I feel guilty. I should be there to help him."

"Do you need help dressing?" Goosie asked.

She felt embarrassed that they'd had to baby her. "I can manage. I've been a burden long enough. I'll be right down."

"I'll make you some eggs."

"I'm the one who's tardy. I'll eat whatever is left over. Is Dorthea here?"

Goosie took up the tray. "She is."

"I need to speak with her."

"As you wish." Goosie sighed. "I must say I'm concerned about you, Jussie. It's not like you to sleep even to eight, and definitely not like you to sleep half the day away on both ends of the night."

I'm concerned about me too. "Perhaps it was the physical exertion. I'm not used to walking miles at a time. And then the raid, all that I saw . . . the experience left me drained." Images of the death of Mr. and Mrs. Dawson flashed and left her grieving anew. No foray into the past had stuck with her like this one. Not even witnessing the death of Goosie's father in 1800. That was one man's violence against another. This was a mob.

"I'll be down presently."

She got ready in record time. Her mission today was to find out more about Uriah Benedict.

Why did the thought make her shiver?

**

Justine entered the kitchen and found Dorthea sitting at the table. "Good morning. How are you feeling?"

"Better. Thank you."

"You wanted to speak with me?"

"I did."

Goosie pointed to the table where a fresh piece of buttered bread and jam was next to a steaming cup of tea.

"I said don't fuss."

"That's not fussing."

Justine sat down and ate. "Firstly," she said after her first sip of tea. "I want to apologize for sleeping an extravagant length of time. It's not like me."

"Like you, or not, you must have needed it," Dorthea said. "Harland told Thomas and I what you witnessed. I'm sorry for everyone involved. I don't know Virginia, but living through such a tragedy makes me feel for her. And finding out that Uriah was their killer?" She swallowed. "It's hard to fathom."

Goosie set a cup of tea before Dorthea and placed one for herself before joining them. "What are you going to do next?"

Justine shook her head. "I can't accuse Uriah until I have proof."

"If what you've said is true, then Alva is in danger. We can't let her stay with him."

"Did you speak with her yesterday?"

"I stopped by to check on her. She was out of bed, acting normal."

Justine chastised herself for feeling disappointment. Did she want Uriah to be guilty of the present crime so she could accuse him of the crime from the past? "Did Uriah act suspiciously in any way?"

"He was the perfect gentleman."

"Who is a murderer," Goosie said.

"And a poisoner," Dorthea said.

The problems in the present took precedent over the problems in the past. "We need to get her out of the house," Justine said "Away. At least until I find out more about Uriah and can prove his offenses."

"But like Harland said, a crime of war . . .?" Goosie asked. "Is that a convictable offense?"

Justine wasn't sure. "Soldier killing soldier is the way of war. Killing defenseless civilians is not."

Goosie stirred sugar in her tea. "How do we find out more about him?"

"How do we keep Alva safe?" Dorthea asked.

Justine pondered the questions while she ate some bread. Then it came to her. "Toward keeping her safe . . . we need to get her away from Uriah. Does Alva have any relatives living close by?"

"None that I know of."

Another bite. Some tea.

"Do *you* have any relatives close by, Dorthea?" Goosie asked.

"After my aunt and uncle died, their son moved away. So I *did* have relatives here, but not anymore." After a pause, Dorthea nodded to herself. "I do have a friend in Topeka. I could invite Alva to join me for a visit, as a respite from being ill perhaps?"

"That might work." Justine wiped her mouth with a napkin. It felt good to have a plan. "Can you send your friend a telegram?"

"I will. I'm sure she'd love to have us visit. Every time I get a letter from her she extends an invitation."

"Do you think Alva will be happy to have a few days away?"

"I think she will be relieved," Dorthea said. "She argued with Uriah about the medicine he wanted her to take. She's a smart woman. She's got to know something is amiss, but he exerts such total control over her I doubt she knows how to escape."

"Will Uriah let her go?" Goosie asked.

Justine pushed away from the table. "There's only one way to find out. Let's go."

**

After Justine's trip to 1863, seeing Uriah Benedict calmly sitting in his parlor was unsettling. To all who saw him, he was a man of status and manners, not a crazed marauder who dragged people from their beds to kill them.

"Is something wrong, Miss Braden?" Uriah asked.

Justine realized she'd been staring. She stifled her desire to pepper him with a dozen questions about his past. Now was not the time. Now was the time to get Alva to safety. "I'm sorry. My mind is elsewhere." *In another time, another place.* She smiled at Alva. "I'm so glad you are feeling well again."

Alva glanced at her husband, then away. "As am I."

Dorthea chimed in. "I do hope you'll accept my invitation. I think you'll feel even better after a few days at my friend's house."

"Who are these people?" Uriah asked.

"Ben and Mary Bates. He works for the railroad."

"Hmm."

Dorthea turned to Alva. "You'll be doing me a favor by being my companion. I don't like traveling alone. We would leave tomorrow morning. Perhaps staying three nights?"

They all looked to Uriah, who took the time to cross his legs. Justine could tell he loved owning the power of yes or no. With the smug smile of a master throwing a crumb to a slave, he said, "You may go. The day after tomorrow. You will stay two nights and return on Sunday."

Justine didn't like the day's delay or one fewer night away. Who knew what Uriah could do in that one day between fear and freedom?

But Alva took what she could get. She exclaimed happily, ran to his side, and kissed his cheek. All the while, Uriah's eyes were on Justine as if he knew she was behind it all. He didn't quite understand what was going on, but knew he didn't like it. At all.

One of these days, Uriah Benedict would get what was coming to him. God had set Justine on a journey that would make certain of it.

**

Justine sat on the porch swing waiting for Harland to come home for lunch. She had so much on her mind she didn't realize when the swing stilled. She'd get it going again, but then it would stop. Go. And stop. Again and again.

She stood when she saw Harland approach. "Glad to see you up and about," he said. "How are you feeling?"

"Fine. But . . ." She realized her tone would seem petty, but couldn't stop herself. "Where have you been? I needed you and you weren't here."

He paused on the top step. "Well now. Here I am, concerned about your well-being . . . I'm sorry if Mr. Greene's broken leg inconvenienced you."

Oops.

He ran a hand through his sandy hair. "What about you being gone, Jussie? I go out of my way to support you and your gift because I know how important it is. I need the same respect when I use *my* gift."

Her face softened and she ran to him, wrapping her arms around his waist. "I'm so sorry. I know I've been utterly focused on my travels and —"

He gently peeled her arms away. "Perhaps it's good we talk about this — and something else, Jussie. What about our wedding? You proposed before we left Piedmont and I accepted. Yet you never speak of it. You seem content for us to live in rooms across the hall from each other. I want to live as man and wife — even in this house if need be. I long for the bond of marriage. The question is, do you?"

She felt completely wretched and covered her face with her hands. "I'm so, so sorry." She looked between her fingers, then let her hands fall away. She touched his cheek. "I thank God for you, Harland. And I *have* taken you for granted."

"Yes, you have." Then he took her hand and kissed it. "You're taking your gift for granted too."

"How so?"

"I never hear you thanking God for the gift. You often treat it like a burden."

If only she could go back to bed and hide her shame under the covers. "I can't seem to do anything right."

He put a finger beneath her chin. "That's enough of that. It is not a time to seek pity, but a time to be grateful and humble."

I've been neither.

He put his arm around her and led her back to the swing. "When I got here you looked troubled."

She patted the swing.

He sat beside her. "If you were smiling I would take this as a romantic invitation, but considering the crease between your brows . . ."

Justine pressed a finger to the crease, willing her face to relax. It was an impossible task. "I'm going to get wrinkles before my time."

He took her hand and rested it upon his leg.

"How is Mr. Greene?" She knew the question would sound solicitous, but needed to make an effort.

"He's hurting. And the injury will affect his ability to work."

She was relieved to feel genuine compassion. "How can we help?"

"He's not married, so he doesn't have a family to feed, but I told him I'd pay him to do some less physical tasks around my office."

"We could also make him some meals?"

"That would be nice." His face seemed relaxed again. "Now . . . your turn. How can I help you?"

"I'm not sure you can."

"Ye of little faith."

"There *are* a few things on my mind."

"I'm all ears."

She angled toward him. "Dorthea and I went to the Benedicts and invited Alva to go on a short trip with your mother to Topeka, to visit a friend. We want to get Alva out of the house. We are afraid for her."

"Is she still sick?"

"She seems better."

"Then our concerns may be unfounded."

Justine didn't want to hear it. "There's not just the poisoning, there's the fact that Uriah is the man who murdered Virginia's father." Which led to her second concern. "I need to find out more about him."

"When are you going back again?"

"Soon. But first I'm going to speak with a few people around town. See what kind of man he is."

"And if they all speak highly of him? What then?"

She shrugged.

"You're hoping they revile him. You're hoping to find evidence against him."

"Well . . . yes."

"You need to be careful, Jussie. If you criticize him or imply wrong-doing. . ."

"I'll have to choose my words carefully."

Harland got the swing rocking again and drew her close.

She leaned her head against his. "I want to do what's right, what God wants me to do. But I'm not sure what's my idea and what's His. I'm here for a reason and everything that's happening is for a reason. I'm just trying to figure out what that is."

"You *will* figure it out. Just don't let your zeal get ahead of God's revelations."

"Does that mean I can't ask people about Uriah, even if I'm subtle?"

He chuckled. "You. Subtle?"

"I *can* be—when needed." *Sometimes.*

"Ask God to give you the right words. Use His words, not yours."

Justine knew she had a tendency to speak first and think later.

"You can do it. 'Be swift to hear, slow to speak . . .'"

"I'll do my best."

**

The desire to get some fabric for a new dress was the perfect excuse for Justine and Dorthea to go to Talbot's General Store, the largest store in Lawrence. Surely they knew Uriah and could tell her something about him.

But as Harland had warned, she needed to choose her words carefully. What better way to do that than to pray. *Lord, help me only say what You want me to say.* He'd helped in such a way before. She trusted Him far more than she trusted herself.

As usual, downtown Lawrence was bustling. It was a marvel. "Look at the people," Justine said to Dorthea. "I noticed this in Kansas City, and its repeated here. Each one wears a uniform."

"What do you mean?" Dorthea asked. "I don't see uniforms at all."

"Sure you do," Justine said. "Look. The jeans, vests, and wide-brimmed hats mark the cowboys. The Indians wear their uniform of long black hair, headwraps, and plaid blankets around their waists. Businessmen wear dark suits with narrow bow ties. And—"

"Farmers wear tan sack-coats and boots."

"Ex-slaves wear cotton shirts and vests."

"The women wear uniforms of pastel day-dresses," Dorthea said. "And every single one wears a hat and has a shawl."

"Almost all." She pointed to two women who strolled nearby. She lowered her voice. "They're showing their upper class status by wearing gloves and a jaunty feather in their hats."

Dorthea chuckled. "You have the eyes of a newcomer. But I know New York is very diverse."

"In different ways. Perhaps more ethnicities, and far more people, but it's different."

"No cowboys. And no Indians."

"None of those." She sighed. "Actually, in the city, my world was very small. I rarely ventured beyond the homes and entertainments of my small circle of friends."

"Very wealthy friends."

She nodded, trying not to feel guilty about it. "I didn't see . . ." She waved a hand to encompass the distinctive people in front of her. "Variety."

"I like variety," Dorthea said.

"I do too. In New York . . . as Shakespeare said, 'We are almost as like as eggs.' Yet in many ways my personal community was as small as that in Piedmont."

"How interesting," Dorthea said. "Perhaps you'll enjoy the interaction with all kinds of people in Kansas." She slipped her hand around Justine's arm. "I know meeting you has been very enjoyable."

Justine felt extremely blessed. "I have high hopes for the future. But . . ."

"But?"

"To enjoy the future I need to deal with the past."

"Uriah Benedict."

They reached the store and entered Talbot's with a nod to fellow shoppers. Dorthea received many greetings and made introductions. As she chatted about some friend's wedding, Justine strolled over to the bolts of fabric. A middle-aged woman behind the counter asked, "May I help you, miss?"

"Yes. Please." She offered her friendliest smile. "My name is Justine Braden. I'm new in town and am staying at Dorthea Jennings' home?" She nodded toward Dorthea.

The woman nodded. "You're engaged to her son."

News traveled fast. "I am."

"Glad to have you here," she said. "Dorthea's a peach, that's what she is. And a talented seamstress. And those daughters of hers . . ." She shook her head. "Bitten by the pioneer bug. All the way to Montana too. Now there's a new frontier."

"I wish I could have met them before they left."

The clerk shook her head. "I've been here thirty years. When the west-bug bites, there's no waiting around to scratch. Life's too short."

Justine welcomed the opening of a new subject. "You've been here so long. I'm just now learning about the history of the place. Such strong people surviving such a violent past..."

The woman's face grew pensive. "Lost my husband to Quantrill's Raid."

Justine's pulse quickened. *Had she seen Uriah?* "He was shot in Lawrence?"

"No. Wasn't shot at all but died just the same."

Dorthea joined them. Bad timing. "Good morning, Sadie. How are you today?"

"Fine, Dorthea. I just met Miss Braden here."

"Call me Justine. And please, continue with your story about your husband dying in the Raid." Justine gave Dorthea a pointed look, hoping she'd withhold any further pleasantries.

The woman hesitated, but Dorthea nodded at her. "Please, Sadie. I'd like to hear too."

Sadie wrapped some stray hanks of lace around her hand as she talked. "My husband and I lived in Eudora. That's out east a bit," she added for Justine's benefit. "We heard gunshots all around, and got word from a Negro who'd run all the way from Hesper, that Quantrill was on the move, heading to Lawrence in a murdering mood. The man, Henry, was exhausted, so my husband Jerry left with two others to go warn the town. They were riding so fast and reckless that one got thrown from his horse and knocked unconscious. Hurt his arm bad too. He came to and told the others to keep going. But then Jerry's mare stumbled and fell on him. The horse died and Jerry was hurt something awful. His friend took him to a nearby farm where my Jerry died the next day." She swallowed hard, her face a mask of misery. "We heard later that no one got to Lawrence with a warning. If only they had."

A man came out from the back, looked at the woman and asked, "You all right, Sadie?"

Sadie nodded and introduced Justine to her current husband.

"I'm sorry for bringing up bad memories," Justine said.

The husband put a protective arm around his wife. "We like to leave the past where it belongs. Lawrence is thriving. We focus on that."

Sadie nodded. "After the war, I moved to St. Louis." She smiled at her husband. "That's where we got hitched. Just moved back here last year. Lawrence is a different place now than it was then."

Justine tried another tack. "I've met some good people here. Mr. and Mrs. Benedict have been very hospitable to us."

"They are good people," the husband said. "Uriah is a shrewd businessman, but I don't necessarily hold that against him. He was savvy and bought up land when it was cheap. Wish I'd done the same."

A man came in the front door and both husband and wife looked up to greet him. "Mayor Usher. Come meet a new resident of our town."

A distinguished-looking man with a ready smile came in and removed his hat, revealing a receding hairline. "Only *just* mayor," he said with a smile. "Nine days mayor." He bowed to Justine. "The City Commission elected me last week."

"Congratulations. It is a fine town."

"I am humbled to serve."

"He's too humble," the store owner said. "Mr. Usher was the Secretary of the Interior under President Lincoln. He heard the Gettysburg address from the platform and was in the room when Lincoln died."

The mayor held up a hand. "The latter is something I'd rather forget. Lincoln was a great man, a kind and generous man."

Justine was duly impressed and liked the mayor's self-deprecating nature. He would be the perfect person to give an honest opinion of Uriah. "I enjoy meeting new people. We've already had dinner at the Benedict's. Mr. Benedict seems . . ." she left it open.

Mayor Usher chuckled. "Uriah is a force of nature," he said. "He's sharp and savvy. We bought land over on Tennessee Street from him and built our home there."

Shrewd, sharp, and savvy. But is he capable of murder? And poisoning?

Unfortunately, the mayor changed the subject. "What brings you to Lawrence, Miss Braden?"

God and justice. "My fiancé's family lives here." She smiled at Dorthea.

"Good morning, Mrs. Jennings," the mayor said.

"Morning, Mayor."

"I hear your son moved here too?" the mayor asked. "Harold?"

"Harland. He's a doctor and is opening a new practice down the street. Plus, he's volunteering out at Ravenwood."

"How commendable," Mayor Usher said. "Let me know if there's anything I can do to make your transition to the West more pleasurable, Miss Braden." He looked to the owners. "Speaking of things to do, Margaret asked me to check if that new set of dishes has come in."

"Not yet," the missus said. "But we expect it any day."

"Very well then," he said. "I must go to work. I have much to learn, being a mayor. Nice to meet you, Miss Braden. Mrs. Jennings. Good day to you all."

"He's a good one," the shopkeeper said. "We got sidetracked. How can I help you ladies?"

**

Justine sat at the kitchen table and cut the rhubarb into small pieces. She didn't even notice Goosie standing beside her.

"You trying to be a surgeon like your husband?" Goosie asked.

Justine didn't understand.

"I've never seen such precise cuts."

She looked down at her work. "I like to do a good job."

"Nonsense," Goosie said, scooping the rhubarb into a bowl. "Something's on your mind. Out with it."

Justine set the knife down and wiped her hands. "I tried to find dirt on Uriah, but came up empty. Apparently to the world he's a talented businessman."

"Wouldn't be the first time a man was a butterfly in public and a wasp at home. The most frightening evil comes with a smile and good manners."

Justine shivered.

"Oh dear, you poor girl," Goosie said, running a hand up her back. "The weight of the ages is on your shoulders."

It was nice to have someone understand. "It's like one of Virginia's wall paintings. Going back to 1863 let me paint a single leaf. But I still don't know what kind of plant it's going to be. A tree? Or a flower?"

"Which means?"

Justine drew in a new breath then let it out. "I'm going back again. Tomorrow."

"Then you're doubly in need of a piece of fresh-baked pie. Or two."

It couldn't hurt.

CHAPTER EIGHT

The next day after the noon meal, Justine kissed Harland goodbye. He helped her into the surrey and held onto her hand. "You do know we're the only couple in the world who shares a goodbye that involves one of them going back in time."

"Do you mind that I'm going?" she asked.

He tucked the edge of her skirt into the seat area. "From the first moment I met you I knew you were unique. I just didn't know how unique."

How strange? How bizarre?

"Be safe," he said. "*That's* what I worry about. You have no idea what year you're going to visit." He looked around and lowered his voice. "If Uriah was evil once, he was evil twice."

"And he might be evil *now*," she said. "Be aware of Alva for me. She and Dorthea are leaving tomorrow and I won't feel she's safe until she gets away."

"Will do." He stepped back and blew her a kiss.

Justine headed east, out of town. She was glad Dorthea had let her take the surrey. If her travel left her as exhausted this time as it had the last, she would welcome having her own ride home.

The day was cloudy, leaving no happy sun or puffy clouds as an sign of good travels. Even the birds and butterflies were absent. She tried not to let the somber atmosphere affect her mood. On impulse she decided to sing. She was rather surprised when the Doxology came out: "'Glory be to the Father and to the Son and to the Holy Ghost; as it was in the beginning is now and ever shall be, world without end. Amen.'" She laughed. "How appropriate. It speaks of time." The song lightened her mood and she found herself humming the melody the rest of the way to the turnoff.

She was glad the current owner of the Dawson place had given her permission to use the back way to get to the family cemetery. She loosely tied the horse to a branch, giving him leeway to nibble at the grass.

Justine looked at the five gravestones before her. She'd already decided she wasn't going to try to use the parents' stones to go back this second time. She hoped to visit a more recent time, after Quantrill's Raid. And so she knelt beside

Cole Dawson's headstone. "Lord? If you will?" She repeated her traveling prayer and traced her fingers on his name.

God willed.

**

Justine opened her eyes. At first, she wasn't positive that anything had happened because she was still in the family cemetery. The canopy of the summer trees was spotty as the grove was newer, the trees smaller than the grove in 1879, yet taller than the grove of 1863. She had traveled sometime in between.

She noted there were only two headstones.

She looked toward the house. Everything was quiet except for the drone of the cicadas. Although she'd only just arrived, the heat of the day was like a cloak and made her unbutton the cuffs of her dress and roll them to her elbows. She certainly didn't need Granny's shawl, so tied it around her waist.

Suddenly she heard a woman's scream. And children crying.

"No! Spencer, no! What are you doing? Let me go!"

She recognized the voice. It was Virginia!

Justine raced toward the house, standing along its side, listening.

"You will do what I want you to do, wife!"

The way he called her "wife." *As if she's a possession.*

Justine's memories flooded back to the first time she'd met another man who used the same tone with *his* wife.

That other man was Uriah Benedict.

Justine had to *see*. She moved to the window and peeked in. She gasped. The husband had short hair and a cropped beard, but despite the altered looks, he made Justine remember another time. Another place.

On this very farm. The man called Wat who killed Virginia's father.

Her mind scrambled to put the pieces together. Wat, the murderer, looked like Uriah. The husband yelling at his wife looked like Uriah. But Virginia's husband was named Spencer.

Spencer was Uriah?

Her moment of revelation was diverted by the struggle inside. Spencer dragged Virginia away from her children as they cried and clung to her. A boy and girl, three or four years' old. Luke and Anna.

Virginia yelled at her brother. "Cole! Pull them back. Keep them safe!"

He gently pulled the children to safety as Spencer wrapped an arm around Virginia's waist and carried her against his hip, sideways out the front door. She yelped in pain when her arm slammed hard against the jamb, but he didn't stop.

Justine left the window and hid at the side of the porch. Virginia did her best to kick and claw at her husband, but she was as ineffectual as a pesky fly biting a horse. He hauled her down the porch steps and pushed her to the ground. He pointed at a horse and wagon. "Get up there! Now!"

Virginia sobbed, shaking her head. "I'm not crazy, Spence. Don't take me there! I'll be fine. I'll be better. I promise."

He grabbed her upper arm, leaning close to yell in her face. "You can't go half a day without crying about something. You're unstable. You're not fit to be a mother. Or a wife."

"I'm just tired. I had two children in a year. The farm chores, the heat, I'm not sleeping . . ."

He thrust a finger in her face. "You're worthless. *I* could take care of the kids better than you."

"But you *don't* help, you — "

He slapped her face, making her fall to her side. "Don't you ever criticize me!"

Cole came out to the porch. "Stop it! Don't hurt her!"

Spencer pointed at him. "Stay out of this. It's none of your business."

The children came outside and hid behind his legs. Their cries of Mama were plaintive, so Cole knelt down and held them close.

This had to be the day of Virginia's commitment at Ravenwood. Even though Justine's heart ached and her muscles twitched with anger she could not interfere.

"Get up!" Spencer yelled.

A sobbing Virginia sat up, dirt clinging to the tears on her cheek. With a yank to her arm, he yanked her to standing. "Get up there!"

She shook her head.

In one massive movement he lifted her up and tossed her onto the wagon's seat where she fell onto the bench.

When she started to climb down, he rushed to the porch and grabbed the little girl. "You want me to hurt her?"

Anna screamed and tried to pry herself free. "No, Papa! No!"

Virginia held up her hands. "Stop! Leave her alone!"

Spencer stood at the edge of the steps. "You will go with no more nonsense. All this carrying on only proves you're a lunatic."

Virginia's expression collapsed as if her high emotions had been drowned by no emotions at all. "I'll go," she whispered. "Let her down."

Spencer set the girl on the porch, where she ran back to Cole. Then he strode to the wagon, climbed in, and they pulled away.

Virginia mournfully peered back at the house. The children ran down the drive after her. Anna tripped and sprawled, and Luke rushed to her side.

Cole ran to kneel beside them, drawing them into his arms. "It will be all right. Shhh. Don't cry now. Uncle Cole is here."

"But Mama . . ."

"I know, I know."

"Papa hurt me," Anna whimpered.

"I know he did." He dried their eyes with a handkerchief, then stood and offered each a hand. "Let's go inside and get a slice of bread and some buttermilk."

"No!" Anna put her hands behind her back. "I want Mama!"

Luke followed his sister's lead. "Me too! Mama!"

Cole put a hand on each of their shoulders. "You can't have Mama. I'll see what I can do, but right now we have to stay here. All right?"

Justine's heart melted at seeing the two cherubic faces stare up at him.

"All right?" he repeated.

"All right," Anna said.

Luke nodded.

He gave them each a hug, then led them inside. "Let's get that bread now."

"With strawberry jelly on it?" Luke asked.

"With strawberry jelly —"

Justine stepped into view, walking toward the front of the porch. "Hello."

"Who are you?"

"Justine. A friend of Virginia's. I came to visit, then heard the commotion and hid. I'm so sorry."

He nudged the children up the steps, then pointed to the road. "Did you see everything?"

"I did. I felt for her. He's so . . . "

"Mean and evil. That, he is."

"Will she be all right? Should we go after her?"

Cole looked in the direction that the wagon had gone. "There's no stopping Spencer. Not when he's mad like this. I know where he's going."

"Where?"

"A hospital place west of Lawrence."

"Ravenwood?"

"That's the one. You know of it?"

"Slightly." Justine pretended ignorance. "Is Virginia . . . why is he bringing her there?"

He peered down the road. "I wish things could be like they used to be."

"How so?"

He shook his head, his shoulders slumped from the weight of the situation. "You came here to visit my sister?"

"I did."

"Then you know she's been struggling?"

"I'm aware. But that doesn't mean she needs to go to Ravenwood."

Cole ran a hand through his dark hair. "I'm so confused. She hasn't been acting normal, and all I want is for her to feel better, but this?"

She scoffed. "*This* is not better."

"Uncle Cole?"

He blinked at the sound of Anna's voice. "I'm coming." He turned to Justine. "You want to come inside?"

"I would. Thank you."

She followed them into a simple parlor with one red upholstered chair, a rocker, and two wood chairs. The curtains at the open windows billowed like flags of surrender. There were a few paintings of flowers on the wall that looked like Virginia's work.

He led her to the back of the house, to the kitchen. There was a sink with a pump, a wood stove with four burners, an oak icebox, and a much-used table with six chairs and a stool. Pots hung from the ceiling near the stove, and cooking utensils dotted a wall, each on their own hook or nail.

The children stood by a wood counter. Justine spotted a loaf of bread peeking out from beneath a towel. Cole sliced two pieces, then looked to Justine. "Want one?"

It was best to eat when she could. "Yes. Please."

He sliced two more and brought them to the table. The children sat in a chair and on the stool. "Have a seat," he said to Justine.

She sat nearest the girl. "Do you like jelly, Anna?"

She nodded enthusiastically. "I hepped Mama make it."

"I did too," Luke said peevishly.

"They'll be none of that tone," Cole said. He brought over a jar of jelly and slathered each piece, edge to edge. He cut the children's pieces in half and passed them around. They ate greedily.

"We never did have our midday meal," Cole said, taking a seat. He nodded toward the front of the house. "Instead, *that* happened."

Justine chose to act ignorant. "So it was a surprise?"

He hesitated.

"It wasn't a surprise?"

He got up and poured the children a drink. "Buttermilk?" he asked her.

She'd never tried it. "That would be nice."

He completed the task and returned to his seat with an admonition to the children, "Don't spill." He glanced at them, then stood again. "Let's take your bread on the porch. Then you can go play." He took their food outside.

Justine spread jelly on her bread, took a bite, then a sip of the buttermilk. Both were delicious.

Cole returned. "Sorry. They've seen enough. I don't want to add to their worry."

"You're a good man."

He shook his head. "If I was a good man I would've been able to keep Spencer from taking her away. I would have loaded Virginia and the kids into the wagon a long time ago and left."

"And leave your family's farm?"

He took a bite and shrugged. "Nothing but bad memories here."

"Why don't you sell?"

"Virginia won't let me. She loves this place — bad memories and all."

Justine had so many questions, it was difficult to set them in order. "What made Spencer do this? She's not crazy. Yet you said it wasn't a surprise."

Cole studied his buttermilk, turning the glass around and around. "She's always been prone to moods. She can be the sweetest thing, happy and funny, and then she'll dive into a funk. She'd recognize what was happening and would say, 'I'm sliding down the hill.' Or when she was feeling better, 'I'm climbing the hill.'"

It was an apt description of moods. "Did she ever reach the top?"

"Once in a blue moon. I often told her that we learn endurance through pain. You have to go through the pain to learn how to overcome."

"I suppose that's right."

Cole pushed his bread toward the center of the table. "With the little ones coming right after the other, and the hardship of trying to make a living here . . ." He gave Justine a second look. "You know all this. You being her friend and all."

She felt a stitch in her stomach. "I know some of it. But you're with her all the time, seeing it all firsthand. She loves you very much and appreciates you." Justine knew she could say that much.

"I love her too. When our parents died, it was just us two. I wasn't a kid. I was fifteen but she took to being the leader and kept the farm going."

"She's a very strong woman."

"She is. Usually." He sighed. "I hate to admit it but it felt like a blessing when Spencer came along." He looked at Justine from under dark lashes. "Virginia was aching to have someone love her and take care of her for a change. Spencer was that someone." He paused. "For a while."

Justine didn't know details but had to pretend she did. "When do you think things changed?"

Cole didn't hesitate. "When the kids were born." He looked toward the porch and the sounds of kids playing. "Virginia reached the top of the hill when those two came, until the to-dos of mothering overwhelmed and Spencer . . ." Cole shook his head.

"The children don't take him to a hilltop moment?"

"He resents them, maybe even hates them."

"Those are strong words."

"Can't think of none better. He's never said it in so many words, but I don't think he ever wanted children. He may have thought he did, or liked the idea of them, but he is a horrible father." He nodded toward the porch. "They're used to making themselves scarce."

"He grabbed Anna . . . does he hurt them?"

"Not too often, and worse than that? He ignores them." Cole scoffed. "Sometimes I wonder if he knows their names. When he does speak to them it's a bark: 'You! Go do this' or 'You! Don't do that.' He treats them like they're bugs he'd like to squash."

"Poor things," she said.

"On bad days I regret my part in Virginia's and Spencer's courtship. If it weren't for me, they might never have met."

"How so?"

He drank the rest of his buttermilk and wiped his mouth with the back of his hand. "I was driving the wagon to Eudora for my weekly trip for supplies when I came upon a tree blocking the road. I stopped, and Spencer came up on his horse and helped me move it aside. We got to talking and I ended up asking him back for dinner." He shrugged. "If not for me . . ."

"They had happy times, didn't they?" Justine said. "And she has the children." *For a while.*

"Nothing's all bad or all good. But I often think about that day, bringing Spencer to the farm." He chuckled. "I had no idea he couldn't be a farmer, shouldn't be a farmer. It's not in him. Caesar and me do most of the work because Spencer is pretty worthless."

Caesar? "Caesar?"

"A Negro who came with Spencer. Traveled from Pennsylvania with him. He's been working with Spencer since before the war. Used to work at some fancy resort—that's where they met."

Caesar at a fancy spa?

Yet beyond her musings of Caesar's history being intertwined with Uriah's was confirmation that Spencer *was* Uriah Benedict.

"I hope Virginia gets to come home soon." He looked toward the front of the house. "I should have known something was going to happen. Last week a man came to the house. I was outside doing chores, but I saw him. He was dressed in a suit and he and Spencer went off on their own, thick as thieves. I saw Spencer signing some paper."

Commitment papers? "Did it have something to do with Ravenwood?"

His face lit up with revelation. "Like papers putting her in there? Do you really think that's what it was?"

"It's just a thought . . ."

He slapped a hand on the table, making the buttermilk in her glass quiver. "Here I am again, one step behind whatever scheme Spencer has up his sleeve."

"Scheme?"

He shook his head. "I don't trust him. It's like he's always thinking of a new way to sway things in his favor. He's kind of . . . slippery."

His assessment matched Justine's escalating view of Uriah's ways.

"How do you think Virginia is doing?" Cole asked.

She ignored the question. "Should you go after them?" she asked. "Stop him?"

Cole pointed at the children. "How can I do that? They took the wagon. I can't leave the children alone. Caesar's here, but he has chores to do."

I could watch them. But she couldn't. Justine never knew how long she'd be in the past. If she disappeared before Cole got back . . . Plus, as far as she knew, Cole *hadn't* gone after his sister in 1871 which meant Justine couldn't encourage him to go now. The situation spurred her to stand. It was time to say her goodbyes. "I'm very sorry for your situation, Mr. Dawson. I pray it works out well for all of you."

Only it wouldn't. Virginia would remain in Ravenwood, and Cole and the children would die.

She looked at him with a wistful heart. "I need to be going."

He stood. "I'm sorry for jabbering at you like this. You came to see Virginia and I've burdened you with our troubles."

The normal response would be, "It's no burden," only it *was* a burden. More than he could imagine.

He walked her out and she saw the children chasing some chickens near the barn. "Where's your horse?" he asked.

"I walked."

"I'd give you a ride but . . ."

They saw a man coming out of the barn. A short Negro man. "Caesar, would you get Queen saddled for our guest? She needs a ride home."

She stared at him. Their eyes met.

He removed his hat and nodded. "I'd be happy to do that."

She forced herself to snap out of it. "No need. Thank you. I'll enjoy the walk." She couldn't leave without asking him at least one question. "I've met Mr. Meade a few times, but Cole says you've been with him for many years?"

His eyes turned from friendly to nervous. "I'm slow at learning from my mistakes."

"Excuse me?"

His face grew serious. "Watch yourself around Mr. Meade, miss."

A child cried out and they saw Anna on the ground, holding her shin.

"I'll get 'er," Caesar said. He gave Justine a nod. "Nice to meet you, Miss Braden."

Don't leave! I have so many questions!

"Uncle Cole!"

"I need to go," Cole said. "Very nice talking with you. I'm sure Virginia would like for you to visit her at . . . you know."

"I will do that." *Eight years from now.*

Reluctantly, Justine walked down the drive toward the road. As soon as she was out of sight, she felt a tingling inside. With a yank and a pull, she was taken from the past to the present.

Now *that* was a ride.

She'd been returned to the cemetery, her horse and surrey close by. As expected, she was exhausted, not just physically, but emotionally.

Uriah Benedict killed Virginia's father when he was using the name Wat, and then married her under the name of Spencer Meade?

Justine's anger pushed through her fatigue. She climbed into the surrey and set off for home.

But then Caesar's words forced their way into her thoughts: *Nice to meet you, Miss Braden.*

Miss Braden? How did Caesar know her name?

God's ways were mysterious indeed.

**

The surrey made quick work of the road between the farm and Lawrence, but as Justine neared home she slowed the horses. Should she go to Ravenwood and speak to Virginia? What would she say?

Virginia didn't know Uriah at all. Spencer had committed her and headed west. He'd come back to Lawrence under a different name. His actions were despicable, but they weren't criminal.

Plus, from Cole's comments, Virginia's moods *were* erratic. That her husband had put her in Ravenwood seemed unfair, yet partially understandable. Justine might not think Virginia needed to be at such a place, but the fact was, Virginia *was* still there eight years later. How had she put it? She was *resigned* to being there.

Virginia was the victim of a bad marriage and emotional distress. She'd endured inconsolable loss. But where was the crime from her past that demanded justice?

Justine stopped the surrey at a Lawrence intersection, immersed in her thoughts. Then . . .

In a flash of a black suit and the violent jiggle of the surrey, Uriah climbed in beside her.

She scooted out of the way, as he sat next to her. He brought with him the smells of cigars and a spicy cologne. He took the reins.

"What are you doing?" she asked.

He didn't answer, but turned the surrey onto a side street where he stopped the horses. Only then did he look at her. "Miss Braden."

Just a short while ago she'd seen him do awful things in the past. Now, he was beside her. Her stomach knotted and she tried to gain control of her emotions. "Mr. Benedict. What is the meaning of this?"

"You've been asking about me around town."

The knots grew tighter. "I believe your name came up in conversation when I was buying some dress fabric." She forced a smile. "You should be used to that. As an important man, it is not unexpected." His dark eyes bore into hers, making her look away. She continued. "I'm sorry if it seems presumptuous. I meant no offense. We're simply new in town, and you and Mrs. Benedict were the first to show us hospitality by inviting you into your home. I was just making small talk."

His gaze softened—a bit. "If you have questions about my family, come to me."

"Thank you, I will." *After this morning my questions have increased tenfold.* She felt a surge of boldness. "Dorthea is looking forward to Alva's companionship tomorrow. Such a close friendship is something to be cherished." *So don't do anything to disrupt it.*

He looked forward. "I regret giving my permission."

"Why?"

"Alva is delicate. I fear a change of scenery and schedule will test her constitution."

It will make her feel better.

He got out of the surrey as quickly as he'd gotten in. He tipped his hat. "Good day, Miss Braden."

It took a full three minutes for Justine's heartbeat to find a normal rhythm. Cole had called Spencer slippery and a schemer. That, he was. If his intent had been to frighten her, he had succeeded. If it had been to stop her?

"You don't know me very well, Mr. Benedict."

She chucked at the horse and headed home.

**

"Hello? Anybody here?"

There was no answer.

Justine was hit with a sobering thought: *While I travel through time, their lives go on as usual. Without me.*

She tossed Granny's shawl on the back of a chair and slumped onto the cushions. "Welcome back, Justine. How was your trip? What year did you visit? Who did you see? What do you think it means?"

The silence remained so. She closed her eyes. And slept.

**

"Jussie?"

It took Justine a moment to grasp where she was. She didn't remember moving from a chair to the settee, or using Granny's shawl as a pillow.

She put her feet on the floor. "I must have fallen asleep."

"So it appears." Harland sat down beside her, putting his arm around her shoulders. "What time did you get back?"

She arched her back which rebelled against her awkward sleeping position. "Two or three maybe?" She wasn't really sure. Ironic that time was her business and she hadn't noticed the time. She looked at the mantel. "Is it really five now?"

"It is. We all got home an hour ago but let you sleep."

Dorthea appeared in the doorway to the kitchen. "Dinner is served."

Justine went to the table as if moving around in a dream. *This* is real. *This* is now.

"Are you all right?" Harland asked as he held out her chair.

All she could do was nod.

Thomas said grace, then carrots, potatoes, pork chops and buttermilk biscuits were served. Justine let the conversation flow, as everyone shared their daily doings: Thomas and Goosie had helped a family-in-need with Pastor Karvins, giving them a good meal and finding them a place to stay. They loved Goosie's pie. Dorthea spent time with her quilting group. And Harland had seen his first child-patient in his new office, a little boy with a cough. Justine tried to listen intently but found an odd emotion stirring.

Anger. They weren't asking about *her* day. She'd traveled through time. Didn't that deserve some attention? Her breathing turned heavy as the *want* moved to *need*. When it was clear they weren't going to ask, she pointed at her biscuit and said, "This is the second time today I've had buttermilk."

At her awkward transition everyone stopped eating. "How so?" Goosie asked.

Finally, I get to talk. "I had a glass of buttermilk back in 1871. With Virginia's brother and her children."

Her family jumped in to repair their negligence. "We're so sorry we didn't ask" met "I forgot" and was followed by, "How was it?"

She enjoyed their chagrin and words of appeasement. "May I share a complaint?" she asked.

They looked worried, but Thomas said, "Of course."

"I know the world doesn't revolve around me. I also am aware that everyone has busy lives, but . . . it's like traveling through time is equivalent to me going to work as a clerk at Talbot's or spending the afternoon having tea with Alva. I traveled through *time*." She stroked the last word for emphasis.

Once again, they offered assurances that they did *not* take her gift for granted.

Dorthea offered the most understandable excuse. "Since your gift is so extraordinary, I have a hard time comprehending it."

Others nodded.

Thomas spoke next. "I thought making too much of it would make you uncomfortable. I know when someone praises my preaching too much, I get embarrassed by their fussing. It's not that my words come easily, but I feel guilty for accepting praise for something that's just what I do."

Justine was chastened. Thankfully her common sense overrode any more expressions of her selfishness. "I am sorry to complain. I never should have said anything. You each have your own special talents. Truth is, I don't go around showing interest in your activities. It was selfish for me to expect . . ." She couldn't find the word.

Harland touched her hand. "What do you need from us, Jussie? Honestly."

Justine looked at each well-intentioned face. So accepting. So loving. She could—she should—accept their current interest as enough. And yet, Harland had asked her to be honest. "To be fully truthful . . . unlike Father, I need you to fuss. At least a little?"

Laughter filled the room and Justine joined in. "I don't really mean that." *Do I?*

Goosie gave her a wink. "Of course you do. And I agree with you. You deserve to be fussed over. And so . . . what happened on your journey today?"

Justine felt silly for causing so much trouble. Next time she'd act more mature. But for now, she told them about Virginia being hauled away by her husband to be committed at Ravenwood.

"What an awful thing for him to do," Dorthea said.

"It was made more awful because of who her husband Spencer actually is," Justine said.

"Who he is?"

She paused for effect. "Spencer Meade is Uriah Benedict."

Harland dropped his fork to the floor. "How can you be sure?"

"I saw him clear as I'm seeing you. Uriah is tall, slim, and bald. This man was tall, stocky and had a trimmed beard and short hair, but it was him. His voice was the clincher. He had Uriah's deep, gravelly voice. And . . ." She paused for effect. "We need to remember that Uriah is also the man who killed Virginia's father during Quantrill's Raid."

Her audience was still.

Dorthea broke the silence. "I wish I was taking Alva away today. I don't like the idea of her being in his house another minute."

Justine lifted a hand, having something more to add. "On the way home, when I was stopped at an intersection, Uriah climbed into the surrey beside me."

"What for?" Harland asked.

"He was unhappy that I'd asked about him at Talbot's. And he said he regrets giving his permission for Alva to join you on your trip."

She put a hand to her chest. "He's not reneging, is he?"

"Not yet."

"I repeat, I wish we were leaving today."

"That wasn't all he said," Justine added. "He issued a warning."

Harland looked alarmed. "Did he threaten you?"

Justine didn't want him storming over to the Benedict's. "Subtly. Not directly. He said if I wanted to know about his family, ask him."

"As if he'd tell you."

"Did his warning intimidate you?" Thomas asked. "Do you want to stop probing into his past?"

"Not a bit." She pushed her plate forward and leaned against the table. "Wat, Spencer, Uriah, or whatever name he goes by, is a murderer, a horrible father —"

"What did he do to his children?" Dorthea asked.

"At the very least ignore and despise them," she said. "I had a long talk with their Uncle Cole and —"

"Didn't Cole die in an accident?" Harland asked.

"And the children got sick and died?" Goosie added.

So you were listening.

"Yes, on both accounts," Justine said. "My conundrum is that I don't know what to do next."

"So much revolves around Virginia," Harland said. "Someone we met by chance."

She gave him the look he deserved.

"I stand corrected," he said. "Not by chance."

"You need to tell her that Spencer is Uriah," Dorthea said.

Justine shook her head. "What will that matter? There's no crime in taking a new name. America is full of people who've started over."

"But now he's poisoning his second wife," Dorthea said.

"We suspect he's poisoning her," Harland said. "There is no proof."

They each were silent, pondering the complexities of the situation.

Suddenly, a word came into Justine's head. "Caesar!"

"What about him?" Harland asked.

"During my trip I saw him at the farm. He helped me into the surrey. He worked there. Cole said he came from Pennsylvania to the farm *with* Spencer."

"And obviously continued to work for him when Spencer became Uriah," Goosie said.

"If anyone knows the truth about Uriah, it's Caesar," Thomas said.

Justine pushed back from the table. "I need to talk to him."

"No." Harland pressed his hands in the air, indicating she should sit. "Not this evening."

"And not without thinking things through," Thomas said. "Uriah can't know about your revelations, or any conversation you might have with Caesar."

"There's a lot going on that we don't understand yet," Dorthea said. "For one thing, people don't change their name for no reason."

Harland nodded. "What made Spencer change his name *from* Wat and *to* Spencer, and then *to* Uriah?"

"He didn't want people to know he committed his wife to Ravenwood?" Goosie asked.

"That's not enough reason."

"It's clear there's more to learn," Justine said.

Harland reached out to her. "You'll need to be very careful, Jussie."

"I know." The stakes were so high. Justine had one more thing to share with them. "When I first met Caesar at the

Benedicts, he said a few things that made me wary about Uriah, and today, in the past, he told me to watch myself around Spencer."

"Who is one in the same. He's given you two warnings." Goosie visibly shivered.

One more thing. "Also, today, when I was leaving the farm Caesar called me by name—and we hadn't been introduced. Miss Braden. He called me Miss Braden."

"How can that be?" Dorthea asked.

"He overheard you talking to Cole?" Thomas suggested.

"No. He didn't. There's no explaining it."

"It happened when you visited my life too," Harland turned toward the others to tell his story. "I was only five but I remember a woman singing in Dr. Bevin's office as a distraction while he was setting a broken arm. — — Justine was that woman. And yet she only sang during her visit into the past, not in the actual past."

"How do you know that?" Thomas asked. "If it's in your memory, then perhaps she's always been a part of that memory. Maybe her past is *the* past."

They all stared at the air between them.

"There is so much I don't understand and that can't be explained," Justine said.

Dorthea nodded. "As I said earlier, I have a hard time comprehending what you do."

Justine pressed her hands against her face. "God does keep me guessing."

**

Sleep did not come easily to Justine. She tossed left, then right, her thoughts tossed along with her body.

I'm tossed between two worlds, between what was and what is.

She sat upright, looking to heaven. "What am I supposed to do with this knowledge You're giving me? A man named Wat killed Virginia's father. He changed his name to Spencer and committed Virginia to a life in an asylum. Their children died. He ran away and came back as Uriah. And now Uriah is trying to poison Alva. How can I stop him?" The problem was painful, almost too much to bear.

We learn endurance through pain.

She blinked. Those were Cole's words—his wise words. Timeless words that needed to be written down for the ages.

Justine got out of bed and retrieved the family Ledger from a drawer. She lit a lamp at the desk and sat. She flipped through the pages of life-lines that had been immortalized by the women of her family for over three hundred years.

She dipped a pen in ink and turned to the most recent entry, one from her grandmother: *God's gifts can't be returned.*

She smiled, hearing Granny's voice share that very personal piece of wisdom. "No, they can't," she whispered. Meaning that she *had* to keep going into the past as many times as God allowed.

Until then . . . she added two new life-lines to the Ledger. Seth Dobbins, the man who'd given her a ride back to Lawrence after returning from Quantrill's Raid had said, *Sometimes silence reveals wisdom.*

Silence. "I'll have to remember that whenever I'm with Uriah. I need to heed Caesar's warning. I can't say too much."

Then she wrote down the life-line from Cole: *We learn endurance through pain.*

She cringed at the thought of Virginia's pain. Her new friend had lost so much and yet she'd found happiness through the act of enduring. Each trip into the past increased Justine's opinion: Virginia was an inspiration.

Which increased Justine's determination. She would endure whatever might come to bring justice out of Virginia's pain.

CHAPTER NINE

"How about packing this?" Justine held up Dorthea's best skirt.

Dorthea carefully folded a bodice. "I think I have enough with two. It's only a few days. My friend Mary has an easy-going nature. There will be no need to dress up in Topeka."

Dorthea finished by packing undergarments and toiletries. There really wasn't much for Justine to do but keep her company, so she sat on a chair by the window.

She noticed Dorthea's forehead was furrowed. "Are you nervous about the trip?"

Dorthea placed her silver brush and mirror on top of her clothes and latched her valise. She sat on the bed. "Extremely. Not about the time Alva and I will have together or the journey itself, but about the repercussions that may follow from Uriah. We thought he was dangerous before, but now we know he's capable of anything. And the way he intimidated you . . ." She shuddered.

Justine wanted to reassure her but felt the same trepidation.

"Do you want me to get any specific information from Alva?" Dorthea asked.

"Don't press but find out what her life with Uriah is really like. Find out anything about his past. Find out if she really thinks he's poisoning her."

Dorthea nodded. "That's a lot."

"It is." Justine sat beside her on the bed. "Please remember that you can't tell her what we know about Uriah, can't mention Quantrill's or Virginia, or that we know two of his other identities."

"I wish we could tell her what sort of man he is."

"I expect she already knows."

Dorthea picked at a spot of dried food on her skirt. "Did others back in Piedmont know about your gift?"

Justine thought of the day when her secret came out — and the repercussions. "Eventually they all did. It wasn't planned. I simply got caught appearing when I wasn't there before."

"That would require some explanation."

"Not surprisingly, it changed people's view of me. They were curious and wary. And then came the request for favors. Many of them wanted me to go back into the lives of their families. I became a novelty act. A circus performer asked to do tricks."

"No wonder you left."

Justine squeezed her hand. "I'm very glad we did. It feels good to start fresh."

"Like Spencer did when he became Uriah?"

Justine didn't want to give the man any respectable motivations.

"I have a question for you about time travel," Dorthea said.

"Ask anything."

"Does the amount of time you live out while you're in the past coincide with the amount of time passing here? Or when you come back have you been gone just a few minutes?"

"The latter." Justine thought of an example. "When I went back to 1857 — before I was born, before my mother ran off to New York — I stayed overnight but when I came back to the present, only a few minutes had passed. I stayed overnight another time in 1800 when Goosie's father was murdered."

"Gracious."

"I know. I've seen a lot of horrible things."

"God must trust you a lot."

"I hope not too much." She looked out the window across from them, but saw nothing but her own worry. "My biggest fear is letting Him down."

Dorthea touched her shoulder. "You won't."

"I appreciate your confidence."

"To my first question I add another: how long can you stay in the past?"

"I don't know. I have no control over when I'm brought back."

"That must be frustrating."

"A little perhaps, and yet I'm glad I don't have the responsibility of choosing *when*. God has a purpose for me in the past, something for me to see and discover. Once that purpose is served, He brings me home again."

"Your faith is strong."

Justine sighed. "It's stronger now than it was, but I need it to grow even stronger."

Dorthea nodded. "Faith is like love; it has no limit."

If that isn't a life-line . . . "I like that."

Dorthea put her arm around Justine's shoulders. "You are so special to me. I loved you before I met you, but now . . ."

Justine leaned her head toward Dorthea's until they touched. "Me too."

They sat a minute, sharing the moment. Then Dorthea asked, "How old was your mother when you met her in the past?"

"Twenty, the same age as I was at the time."

"How strange that must have been."

"Strange, but also fascinating. She took me under her wing as a peer. I even shared her bedroom overnight. She confided in me and we chatted like two friends."

"That must have been enjoyable."

"Very much so. If only everyone could meet their parents as peers, not parents. The generations would understand each other better."

Dorthea picked up a hair ribbon that had fallen to the floor. "I wish I'd understood my parents. We came to America from Ireland when I was nine, during the potato famine that left us starving. I was so concerned with *me*. As an adult I've often wondered what their lives were like before they married and had children. Before we were starving."

"I didn't know you were from Ireland. That's where I'm from too."

"Really? What part?"

"County Mayo. Around Cong."

Dorthea's eyes grew wide. "That's where we lived! What your mother's maiden name?"

"Tyler. But her parents were Hollorans." She pointed to the cameo she wore at her neck. "This is my great-grandmother, Abigail Holloran."

Dorthea studied it a moment. "I've noticed that pin before. It looks like you."

"That's what Goosie said when she gave it to me."

Dorthea beamed. "My oh my. — We may have some connections in the past. Our family name was Fitzmorris. We knew some Hollorans in Ireland."

Justine loved the idea that their families might be linked. "Perhaps they were my relatives, left behind. My immediate family came to Piedmont in the 1790s."

"Long before ours." Dorthea looked a bit disappointed, yet made the best of it. "Still, to have our families linked by an area in Ireland? What a coincidence."

Justine chuckled. "There's no such thing. Knowing how God works I've seen great life-puzzles put together out of nothing. I know He brought me to Piedmont after my mother's death to meet Harland and to find my father, and now He's brought us here, to you. There are no coincidences involved. Just God's amazing plan."

Dorthea smiled a smile of satisfaction. "Believing His plans . . .who knows what the Almighty has in store for us?"

Justine spread her hands. "I can't wait to find out."

Dorthea retrieved some earrings from a footed box on the dresser. "Speaking of family history . . . these were passed down through many generations. I wore these earrings on our wedding day."

Justine admired the green circular stones in a silver setting. "What kind of stone is this?"

"Connemara marble. They mine the stone near the west coast. Not too very far from Cong." She sighed deeply. "I still miss my Jesse."

"The war created many widows."

"He was such a good husband and father — though he was a little impatient with Harland."

Justine thought of something that might interest her. "I'll be right back." She returned, carrying the Ledger. "Would you like to see the life-line I got from Jesse?"

"Life line?"

Justine showed her the Ledger and explained its history. She turned to a recent page and pointed at a specific entry.

Dorthea read: "September 1, 1860: Jesse Jennings, "'Take time.'"

"Short but wise," Justine said.

"I wonder why he said it."

"I know exactly why. He wanted Harland to farm and didn't approve of him spending so much time helping Dr. Bevin. He was impatient with him."

"That's very true."

"After he cut himself and the Harland came to his aid, your husband realized the best thing he could do for his son was to take some time with him, show him how to be a farmer, but also let him develop his own gifts."

"All that, summed up in two words."

"Wise words."

Dorthea smiled, clearly immersed in happy memories. "Jesse did try to take time, though he never fully accepted Harland's medical interests. He died when Harland was eight, so he didn't see how the children blossomed. But I did. Harland wanted to move out here with me and the girls, but I wouldn't let him."

Justine knew this part of the story. "You let him go to school to be a doctor. He appreciates that—we all do."

"As a parent, one of the hardest things to do is letting our children become people in their own right." She got a mischievous glint in her eye. "You'll understand once you have your own."

"Someday."

"When's the wedding?"

Justine laughed. "I have no idea."

"Don't wait too long. Life is short. If you're going to marry, marry."

It wasn't that simple. "I'd marry Harland today if not for my travels. Right now I'm immersed in two worlds. I don't feel as though I can marry Harland until the Uriah situation is settled."

"But then there will be another journey for justice. There may never be a good time to marry. You might simply have to make time." She smiled. "As Jesse said . . . take time."

Justine let this truth sink in. She needed *time* to think it through. With a grin she turned the tables. "What about the sparks flying between you and my father?"

Dorthea blushed prettily. "It's true. We *are* courting."

How wonderful she admitted it. "I know it's new, but is marriage a possibility?"

"I wouldn't discount it." She cocked her head. "What would you think about that?"

Justine was surprised when tears threatened. She stood and held out her arms, letting Dorthea fill them. It was nice to think some happy thoughts about the future.

Not the past.

**

Dorthea had offered to pick Alva up on the way to the train depot but they'd received a note from Uriah saying he would meet them there. Justine wondered if his choice had little to do with convenience or logic, and much to do with his need for control. No matter the reason, Thomas, Dorthea, and Justine drove to the Kansas Pacific depot to meet their friend.

"Do you think Uriah will be there first, or make us wait?" Justine asked.

"Does it matter?" Thomas asked.

She shrugged. "The first would show his exacting nature — being early — and the second, his haughty pride, making an entrance."

Thomas looked surprised at her assessment. "I know you've learned deplorable things about the man's past, but —"

"And present," Justine said. "Which *is* the reason we're taking Alva out of his reach."

He gave a reluctant nod. "I hate to think that anyone can be as evil as you think him to be. People *do* get ill. And maybe he's left the sins of his past behind and has started fresh."

Justine knew he was wrong on both accounts but admired his quest to see good in people. "You are very generous," she told him.

"God is merciful and forgives. He tells us that we who are without sin should not throw stones at other sinners."

His goodness partially quenched her fire against Uriah yet ignited a question. "If Uriah has repented and is living a good life now, then why is God allowing me to go into the past—more than once—to show me his awful deeds? My gift is to be used to facilitate justice. If Uriah has turned his life around then why is God uncovering his past sins?"

Dorthea nodded emphatically. "You're going back because he's still doing evil and needs to be stopped. Don't you agree, Thomas?"

"It appears I am surrounded." He sighed deeply. "I'll leave it to God to show us what's what."

They reached the depot and he helped them out of the surrey, setting Dorthea's valise beside a bench. They scanned the area.

"They're not here," Dorthea said.

Justine checked the depot clock. They only had fifteen minutes until it was time to board.

With five minutes to go, Uriah and Alva arrived. Justine was surprised to find he drove his own buggy, then chastised herself for the thought. Apparently, she *did* have a chip on her shoulder regarding all things Uriah, which led her to a silent prayer. *Help me see the truth, and only the truth, Father.*

Uriah carried her bag toward the group. Alva immediately embraced Dorthea. "I'm so excited for our trip," she said quietly.

"As am I."

"Wife," Uriah said, with a tone that implied she'd done something wrong.

She immediately stood upright and returned to his side. Apparently, *he* would control when she could be excited.

Uriah glanced at the depot clock then took out his pocket watch. "Their clock is a minute fast."

Yours couldn't be slow?

He tucked his watch away. "I must leave. I have business with the mayor."

You can't wait a few minutes to see your wife off?

Alva turned to hug him, but it was awkward, as he was already half-turned to leave.

And then he was gone.

The rest of them shared an uncomfortable moment.

Alva let out a breath she'd obviously been saving. "*Now* I can be excited." She grinned. "Because I am. Very."

They laughed with her. "I promise we'll have a wonderful time with Mary and Ben," Dorthea said.

Alva glanced toward the place where their buggy had stood, as though making sure Uriah was truly gone. It was a pitiful gesture and reinforced Justine's opinions.

The train-whistle blew. A conductor stepped forward. "All aboard!"

Justine wished the ladies a lovely trip. Thomas handed the porter their bags, then pulled Dorthea into a warm embrace.

"I wish Uriah would hug me that way," Alva said, wistfully.

Justine had no words of encouragement, only some advice. "Forget Uriah. Forget Lawrence and home and duties and everything here. For the next few days focus on you. Enjoy yourself."

Alva nodded. "I will try."

The ladies boarded the train. Thomas and Justine waited until they found their seats and waved from the window as the train pulled away.

Thomas peered after them, his brow furrowed. "They'll be fine," Justine said. "It's good for friends to have special times together."

He shook his head once. "I know. I approve of the trip. But seeing Dorthea go . . ." He shook his head again, with more force. "I'm going to miss her."

"It's just a few days."

"I know. It's silly."

Justine slipped her hand around his arm. "I do believe my father is in love."

"I am."

She leaned her head against his shoulder. "She loves you too, you know."

He stopped walking to look at her. "She does?"

Justine laughed. "You act like a smitten schoolboy."

They walked again. "I haven't loved anyone since your mother. And that love was unrequited."

Justine felt bad about that. "I'm not sure Mother was capable of fully loving anyone."

"She loved you."

"Perhaps." She noticed he didn't argue with her.

He helped her into the surrey, then got in himself. "Where would you like to go?"

She sat a moment, then remembered Uriah's words. "Uriah said he was going to speak with the mayor. He'll be gone from the house. Now is the perfect time to speak with Caesar."

"Are you sure about that?"

"He's the only one other than Virginia who knew Uriah when he was Spencer."

Thomas chucked at the horse. "Promise me you'll be careful."

"There's nothing to worry about as long as Uriah isn't there."

"Would you like me to go with you?"

She would, but it wasn't feasible. "I think our two against Caesar's one might overwhelm. But you could drop me off. I'll walk home."

"I can do more than drop you off. I can pray."

"I will never reject that offer. Ever."

**

Justine knocked on the door of the Benedict home. *Father, give me the right words to unlock the truth.*

Caesar opened the door. "Good afternoon, Miss Braden. Mrs. Benedict isn't here." He blinked. "You know she went to Topeka with Mrs. Jennings."

"I do know," she said. "I saw them off at the depot."

He cocked his head. "Then how can I help you?"

"I would like to speak with you, if I might. About Alva, and . . . other issues."

His eyebrows rose. "Me?"

Justine nodded toward the interior of the house. "May I come in?"

He hesitated. "This is highly unusual."

"I know it is. And I apologize, but I assure you it's very important."

He finally nodded. "I think it would be better if I came outside. We could talk out back, by the stable." He glanced behind him. "Let me tell Mrs. Russo where I'll be. Walk on 'round."

Justine walked around the side of the house and saw a small stable. It was empty. She was glad he'd insisted on privacy. One never knew what servants would hear — or share.

Caesar came out the backdoor of the house, and Justine saw the cook peering out the kitchen window. Their conversation would ignite curiosity. Justine vowed to be quick about it.

Caesar motioned to a place under a small overhang, in the shade. "What did you want to talk to me about, Miss Braden?"

She decided to state it plain. "Spencer Meade."

He took a half-step back. "I . . . I don't know the man."

"Of course you do. You've known him from way back, before you two lived at the Dawson place. Before the war? When his name was Wat?"

He lowered his voice even though they were alone. "How do you know all that?"

"I can't say. But I *do* know Uriah is Spencer. I need to find out what kind of man he *was* in order to understand the man he *is*. Where and when did you meet him?"

Caesar moved his weight from one foot to the other as if balancing the truth on a pivot.

"Please, tell me, Caesar. It's crucial I know."

He took a deep breath. "I met him in 'sixty, at the Bedford Springs resort in Pennsylvania."

Which confirmed what Cole had told her. And the name of the resort . . . where had she heard that name before? "What were you doing there?"

"Whatever they wanted me to do. I carried baggage, got the guests towels or food, and moved their chairs so they weren't sitting in the sun."

"What was Spencer doing there?"

Caesar bit his lip. "He wasn't Spencer then. He was Wat. Lionel Watkins."

Justine nodded once. "He's had three names."

"Four. Lionel wasn't his first. He was born Ralph Smith."

Justine pressed a hand to her head. "Why does he keep changing it?"

Caesar looked at the sky for a moment as if finding the answer there. "He's a complicated man. After he lives a life for a while, he gets an itching to change things. He's real good at becoming somebody else."

"Only someone who's done bad things changes their name so often."

Caesar hesitated, then nodded.

"So he *has* done bad things?"

"If you only knew . . ."

"Knew what? Tell me what he's done."

"There's more to tell than time in a day." Caesar glanced to the right and left furtively. "There's a lot to know about Mr. Benedict from *before*."

"I need to know everything. I want to help."

He ran a hand over his short-cropped hair. "Is Miss Alva safe?"

"For the time being."

"Good. Mrs. Jennings taking her away eases my mind."

"Because?" Justine needed him to say it.

"I've seen far too many things I shouldn't have seen. When the mister is through with someone they . . . they just disappear."

"Like Virginia?"

He blinked twice at her knowledge. "Yes'm. I felt so bad when he took her away."

"Virginia is doing well. I met her at Ravenwood."

He stared at her. "She's alive?"

"She is."

"And she's still there?"

"She is."

"The mister told me she died." He sighed, as if this wasn't the first time he'd been lied to. "I'm glad she's all right. She was a sweet woman."

Justine had to get him back to the present. "Is Mr. Benedict through with Alva?"

"Seems so."

"Why?"

"His reasons don't jibe with common sense. I think it's because he doesn't want children. And I don't think he should have children. He—"

"He had two children with Virginia."

"You know about that too?"

"I do."

Caesar shook his head. "The more Miss Alva presses him for a child the more he pulls away. Plus, I think there's some issues in town . . ."

"Such as?"

"Hard saying. I catch a word here and there when one of his business cronies come to call. Something about land and payments?"

"He owes money?"

"I think it's more like he took money." Caesar drew in a new breath. "Him being Uriah is coming up on the longest spell he's had with a name since I've known him."

"Then why not just leave Alva? Why poison her?"

He didn't deny her accusation. Nor did he hesitate. "He wants power."

"What does he gain by her death?"

"That, I don't know. But a lust for power is what drives him."

Justine's mind swam with questions. "When did he change from Lionel Watkins to Spencer Meade?"

Caesar looked down. "There was a bank robbery and he was wanted and—"

"He robbed a bank?"

"The Younger boys and Frank James did the dirty work. But Wat was there. I was there too. In the woods nearby. They killed a man that day."

"When was this?"

"After the war, in sixty-six. Up in Liberty, Missouri."

Justine took a few steps away, trying to sort it all through.

Then Caesar asked, "You related to Mavis Braden?"

He brings up my mother's name, out of the blue? "I'm her daughter."

He nodded. "I met you at the spa when you was little. Your parents were there, but your father went back to New York early, and then Lionel . . . He was a lady-charmer."

"He charmed my mother?"

He fiddled with a button on his vest. "Seeing him now, it may seem hard to believe, but back then he was quite the dashing dandy. Seducing pretty ladies, getting them to buy him things, or conning them out of money, and making promises . . ."

Her throat was dry. "He conned my mother?"

Caesar looked hesitant. "I shouldn't have said anything. Nothing untoward happened between them—but he acted like it *would* happen."

"Such as?"

He looked toward the house. "I need to get back."

She touched his sleeve. "Please, Caesar. This is personal now. My mother . . .?"

"I'll say it quick-like. Lionel made her think they were going west together. Got her to say she was leaving her husband."

"I didn't know my parents had marriage problems."

"They did then. Even before your pa left the resort, Lionel and your ma were in cahoots. She really took to him."

It was an incredible story. "What was she going to do with me?"

"She was taking you with her. After some time with Lionel at the spa she went back to New York to settle things there, then was going to bring you back and take a steamer to Kansas City with him."

"But he hates children."

Caesar shook his head. "He never planned on taking either one of you. He got your ma to give him a necklace for fare money and kept it."

The words of Mother's lady's maid came back to her. Something about a ruby necklace being lost during a trip to a spa—the Bedford Springs spa. Franny was the one who'd mentioned the name of the resort.

"Was it a ruby necklace?"

"Yes'm. It was."

So the necklace Alva was wearing that first day wasn't *like* her mother's necklace, it *was* her mother's necklace.

Caesar continued the story. "Soon as you and your mother went home, Wat went west. And took me with him."

"Why?"

Caesar looked at the ground. "He caught me stealing at the hotel. Said he always wanted a servant, and having one fit in with the la-di-da role he was playing. Getting respect is everything to him. I was part of his image. He gave me the choice of going with him or he'd get me fired. He threatened to send me down South where they'd take me for an escaped slave." He shook his head adamantly. "I was never a slave. Ever. I was born free in Philly."

One large question loomed. "Since you know what kind of man he was—and has continued to be—why have you stayed with him?"

He waved a fly away from his face. "Don't think I haven't asked myself that question a thousand times. I guess part of it is that *I* wasn't a good man. I did my share of stealing and lying. I had no ties, nowhere. Family was long dead before I got the job at the resort. Wat gave me somewhere to be. Someone to be." He sighed. "Truth is, a body gets going on a road and just keeps going. When he married Miss Virginia and had them two children, I thought things would be better. And they were for a time."

The children. "I'm so sorry about the children."

"Me too." He looked heavenwards. "I had a wife once, almost had a child."

"What happened?"

He looked at his feet, moving a pebble with a shoe. "Before Spencer put Miss Virginia away . . ." He hesitated. "I was married two years to Alvira, a real nice lady I met in Eudora. Miss Virginia let us stay in a room off the kitchen. Alvira helped her with the young'uns and cooking. Almost had young-uns of our own, but . . ." His dark eyes misted. "Alvira died. The baby died too."

"I'm so sorry."

She watched him fight against tears. "Alvira was the only woman I ever loved. She and the baby were my chance to have a normal life. When they were gone, I didn't want to go on. I was done. Spent. I didn't have no fight left in me. When Spencer sent Miss Virginia away, I let it happen."

I know. I was there.

"Later, when he said *go,* I went. He said *do,* I did." He shrugged.

Justine didn't blame him. Uriah was a force one didn't cross without pause. "I understand. I'm so sorry."

"Us two went out west for over a year." He shook his head. "A rough year full of gambling and cheating. Came a time when even Spencer had enough of it. "One day he announced he wanted to go back to Lawrence and start over. I was ready. That's when he became Uriah."

"But you kept your name?"

He shrugged. "I am who I am. Such as I am. The mister shaved his head and beard, got some businessman clothes. He *does* have a talent for changing. He started walking different and talking different, using different words. He acted respectable and people were taken in. While we were in Salina he won a plot of land in Lawrence in a poker game. He took that as his new start."

"No one ever recognized him as Spencer?"

He shook his head slow. "Actually, his name . . ." He hesitated. "Before we went west one man said his name too much."

"I don't understand."

"We buried him east of town."

"For saying his name?"

"Too much." Caesar shrugged and made a stabbing motion.

Justine felt the breath leave her.

"There are two things that'll make Uriah do the worst: if he feels disrespected and if he feels his plans are in jeopardy."

"Don't cross him."

"Don't cross him."

Justine thought about the times she'd already had a run-in with Uriah. She'd have to be extremely careful. "You're very loyal."

"Or stupid. Twice I thought the mister had changed — starting over with Miss Virginia on the farm, and starting over with Miss Alva." He shuddered. "I don't want the missus to get hurt. I'm tired of feeling guilty for not doing enough to stop his evil ways."

"Then stop him this time, for Alva's sake."

"Easier said than done."

"You have a history with him and have remained loyal to him no matter what. Maybe it's time you stood up to him. Tell him you won't stand by and see Miss Alva suffer."

Caesar's hand formed fists at his side. His breathing quickened. "I can't. You know I can't."

Justine touched his arm. "Now's the time to do the right thing — *before* he does something to Alva that's irreversible."

"The bad I've seen . . . he ruins everything that's good."

"He has to be stopped."

He blinked. And blinked. Then his eyes steadied. "He has to be—"

They both looked up at the sound of a buggy turning onto the drive, coming toward the stables. It was Uriah. Justine's heart fell to her feet.

Caesar rushed to help Uriah out of the carriage.

But Uriah brushed past his extended hand and glared at Justine. "Miss Braden. What caused you to make a beeline from the depot to my home? You know Alva is gone." He looked at Caesar, who was taking care of the horse. "What's she telling you?"

I *didn't tell* him *anything.*

Thank goodness Caesar thought fast. "She was telling me about Miss Alva and her plans with Mrs. Jennings."

"They're going to have a lovely time together," Justine said.

Uriah glared at Justine, then at Caesar, then back again. "You came to my home to update my servant with details that are none of his business?"

Lord? Words please? "Actually, I came over to speak with Mrs. Russo about a recipe for the tea-cakes she served. Dorthea liked them so much I thought I'd learn how to make them as a surprise when she returns."

His gaze made her cringe. "Mrs. Russo doesn't work in the stables."

It was time to make a getaway. "You're right. If you'll excuse me." Justine walked to the house and entered by the kitchen door.

Her spine tingled under the gaze of Ralph Lionel Spencer Uriah Benedict.

**

Harland and Thomas came into the kitchen after work. "What are you doing?"

"I'm making tea cakes."

Her father peered into the bowl. "I'm not complaining, but… "

"Why?" Harland asked.

She gave the bowl an extra stir, brushing a stray hair away from her face with the back of her sleeve. "Long story."

Goosie greased a pan with lard. "But a good one."

They sat at the table. "We have the time," Harland said.

"And the curiosity," her father added.

Justine told them about her conversation with Caesar, the information about Uriah's three previous identities, his involvement as a shyster, bank robber, gambler, and murderer, as well as the death of Caesar's wife and baby.

Their response was similar. They each shook their head, incredulous.

Justine stopped her story. "You act as if you don't believe me."

"Oh, I believe you," Thomas said. "I sit in awe of you. You have one conversation with Caesar and he tells you Uriah's secrets — and his own?"

Justine was taken aback. "He's worried about Alva. I think he's had enough and is on the verge of helping us."

"Isn't it a little late for him to gain a conscience?" Thomas asked.

"Actually, I had the same thought." Justine stirred the batter. "Caesar said he thought Uriah had set aside his evil ways when he married Virginia and had children. But . . . he hadn't, hasn't."

"Caesar's own story is quite interesting. A Negro finding his way through the Civil War couldn't have been easy," Harland said. "Even if he was from Philadelphia."

"Plus all the violence over slavery between Kansas and Missouri before and after?" Thomas added. "We shouldn't judge him."

Justine was partially appeased and handed the bowl over to Goosie to pour into the pan. "You don't even know the most astounding part of his story."

"Go on."

"Uriah—when he was Lionel—knew my mother at a spa in Bedford Springs in Pennsylvania."

"Uriah. Knew Mavis?" Thomas asked.

She nodded. "When we were in New York before coming here, Mother's lady's maid told Goosie and I about the same trip." Justine filled them in, ending with, "The plan was to head west to Kansas City."

Thomas shook his head. "Your mother, out here? In the wild west? She left Piedmont to go to New York because she longed for life in a big city."

"Was your mother . . . romantically involved with Lionel?" Harland asked.

"Caesar said nothing 'untoward' happened, but I don't know."

Goosie shook her head. "I can't believe Mavis would be so naïve. Until Franny told us that story, I had no idea her marriage to your father was troublesome, or *that* troublesome."

"Neither did I. Of course, I was only two or three then, but even later . . ." Justine tried to think of signs she might have missed. "Mother and Father were never visibly affectionate toward each other, but I just assumed that was the way of most marriages."

Harland took her hand and kissed it. "Not our marriage."

He was adorable. She wished she could throw herself into his arms.

"You were saying something about your parents' relationship?" Thomas asked.

She glanced at Harland. He winked at her. "Last year I learned that my father married my mother because she was expecting me."

"They grew to love each other in their own way," Goosie said.

"I think they did."

"So what happened to change things so your mother *didn't* go west?" Harland asked.

"Didn't go then, and didn't go a second time," Justine said. "Franny told us she had tickets bought to come here, to

Lawrence, but then Father was wounded and came home from the war, so we stayed."

"Lawrence? Not Kansas City, but specifically Lawrence?" Dorthea asked.

Justine nodded. "I asked Franny the whys of it, but she didn't know. But did say Mother was adamant about her choice."

Goosie bit her lip. "Just think: your mother was coming here and now you're here. Do you think God was leading her here to do the job you're doing now?"

The idea was astonishing. "She said no to the gift."

"She said no," Goosie said.

Justine pressed a hand to her forehead. "That trip would have been in 1863. Lionel Watkins was a part of Quantrill's raid that year. Was she supposed to come to stop him?"

"As a part of the time travel, could she—could you—do that?" Harland asked.

"We can't change the past, but could we change the future?" Her thoughts bounced against each other. "If Mother had been able to stop Lionel in 1863, then he might not have robbed a bank, married Virginia and Alva, or killed a man for saying his name too many times."

"What?" Thomas asked.

Justine waved the question away. "Caesar said it."

Harland drummed his fingers on the table. Then stopped. "All these crimes came *after* 1863 when your mother felt the urge to go to Lawrence."

"Felt the urge and rejected it," Goosie added.

"Not as deliberate as all that," Justine said. "She got word that Father was wounded and was coming home. She had to stay."

"She said no, but you've said yes," Harland said.

I've said yes. It was like trying to sort through a scattered stack of alphabet blocks to get them in the right order.

"Sounds like you have another trip in your future," Goosie said.

She accepted that. But there was something about the situation that bothered her deeply.

"You turned quiet. What's wrong?" Harland said.

"If Mother was called to bring justice but said no or couldn't go, and the result was sixteen more years of evil by Lionel, then it means there are repercussions beyond me being called to facilitate justice from the past. Me *not* doing it can cause pain and suffering in the future. The future *can* be affected even if the past cannot be changed." She looked at each one in turn. "I *have* to stop Uriah. I *have* to do what Mother didn't do."

Harland gave her a wistful smile. "We know *you* can do it."

She nodded, but felt overwhelmed. — —

"Are you going to talk to Virginia first?" Goosie asked.

"And tell her what?"

"Shouldn't she know that her husband is living nearby? And he's married," Goosie said.

"That makes him a bigamist," Harland said.

"Bigamy is the least of his troubles," Thomas said.

"His troubles are Alva's troubles," Justine said. "She will suffer under his next move."

Thomas dipped a finger in the batter and licked it. "As such, we need to be careful not to push him." Justine felt a tug in her stomach. "I think it's too late for that. He saw me talking with Caesar."

"Does he know what you were talking about?"

"No." She pointed at the tea cakes. "I said I was getting this recipe."

They shared a moment of silence. Then Thomas extended his hands. "Come now. Let's ask God for direction. Only He knows the full truth."

"Let's also ask for His protection," Justine added.

"And His wisdom," Harland added.

Goosie made a list on her fingers. "And insight and strength and courage and — "

Thomas began. "Holy Father . . ."

CHAPTER TEN

Their surrey turned into Ravenwood.

"Thank you for coming with me to break the news to Virginia," Justine told Harland and Goosie.

"You know someone's always in need of something medical at Ravenwood," he said.

"And I have little to do at home with Dorthea gone." Goosie lifted a single finger. "Besides, Virginia's a survivor. That's the sort of woman I want to meet."

Justine slipped her hand around Goosie's arm. "I'm sure she'll like meeting you too. And I can use the moral support."

The surrey stopped out front and Harland helped the ladies down then offered them his arms. "Shall we?"

Mr. Sutton greeted them and was introduced to Goosie. He told the ladies that Virginia was out in her garden, then led Harland to a patient who was having severe headaches.

On the way toward the garden, Justine showed Goosie Virginia's mural.

"She has true talent," Goosie said. "But . . . it seems wasted here."

"Perhaps." Justine gave Goosie a short tour, saying hello to the residents who sat in the parlor or the ones they met in the hall. As they went out a side door, Goosie commented under her breath, "They don't seem insane."

"I agree. They just seem eccentric. You'll find Virginia as sane as you and I."

Goosie chuckled.

Justine spotted Virginia on her knees, planting in the garden. She helped Goosie walk across the uneven terrain.

Virginia saw them and stood, waving. "Justine! So glad to see you."

They walked between the rows of plants. "Virginia, I'd like you to meet my dear friend, Goosie Anders. Goosie, this is Virginia Meade."

They each bobbed a little curtsy. "Nice to meet you, Mrs. Meade," Goosie said.

"Virginia. Please."

Goosie nodded.

"Goosie . . . how did you get that name?"

"My given name is Augusta but as a child I used to play with the geese."

"Goosie it is, then." Virginia surveyed her garden. "I have the beans in. Cucumbers and squash are next."

"I miss my garden back in New Hampshire," Goosie said. "I especially liked rhubarb."

Virginia made a face. "Never did take to that one. Such a funny-looking plant.

Justine patted Goosie's hand. "Goosie makes delicious rhubarb pie."

"And strawberry-rhubarb."

"Now *that* sounds tasty." Virginia nodded toward two chairs in the shade. "Shall we?"

Justine deferred and let the other women sit. Virginia wiped her dirty hands on her apron and sighed. "I was due to sit a spell. My knees aren't as young as they used to be."

Goosie laughed. "We can talk more about knees when you're nearing ninety."

"Ninety?" Virginia looked impressed. "I wouldn't take you for a day over–"

"Eighty-five?"

They all laughed.

Virginia brushed dirt off her dress. "I agree that being thirty-four does not give me the right to complain about aches. And you didn't come here to talk about them, either. To what do I owe the honor of this visit—though you don't need a special reason."

Justine looked at Goosie, wishing there was a subtle way to do it. "I have some interesting news for you about your husband, Spencer."

She froze a moment. "Spencer. Really?"

Justine decided to say it plain. "He's in Lawrence."

Goosie chimed in. "He returned a few years ago."

Virginia leaned back in the chair and just sat there a few long moments. Then she sat upright. "Why hasn't he come to check on me? Say hello? I'd like to know how he is. Wouldn't you think he'd want to know about his own wife?"

I doubt he's given you a second thought. "There's something else you need to know about him." But before Justine could say more she saw Eddie walking toward them, carrying a chair.

"Eddie, how sweet of you," Virginia said.

He set the chair down and looked to Justine. "Sit a spell."

"Thank you."

Eddie began to leave, but Virginia stopped him. "Stay. Justine says Spencer is back."

His eyebrows rose. He didn't look pleased. "Is he coming to get you?"

How interesting that Eddie was worried about Spencer coming to *get* Virginia, yet Virginia had only mentioned a visit. "Actually, I don't think you'll see him at all."

"Why not?" Virginia asked.

Justine looked to Goosie for support and received a nod. "Spencer lives in Lawrence under a new name and has a new appearance. He's become someone else. His name is now Uriah Benedict."

"I've heard of him!" Eddie said. "I've never met him but I've heard his name around town. He's a big muck-a-muck. He's friends with the mayor."

There's one more detail you need to know . . . "He's married."

Virginia's face struggled with the news. "But he's married to me."

"Which makes him a bigamist." Justine didn't say more. It was Virginia's crisis. She needed a moment to let it sink in.

Finally she spoke. "I'm happy for him."

"Happy for him?" Justine could not have been more surprised if Virginia had danced a jig. "You're not angry with him?"

Virginia shook her head. But then she peered into the canopy of branches above them. She stood. Then she looked to the ground and wrapped her arms around herself.

Eddie put an arm around her shoulders. "It's all right to be mad."

Virginia nodded once. Then her forehead furrowed. She choked. She gulped a breath and released a sob. She collapsed to the ground with Eddie's arms easing her way.

This was the reaction Justine had expected. "I'm so sorry to tell you all that."

Virginia let herself be fully enfolded by Eddie's embrace. She mumbled into his chest expelling eight years' worth of pain and heartache: *Left me . . . abandoned, afraid, confused . . . children . . . Cole . . . alone . . .*

Goosie and Justine stood nearby, their arms linked, wishing they could help, and sorry to have caused the pain.

Then suddenly Virginia sat erect, letting Eddie's arms fall away. "Help me up."

Eddie did so, then handed her his handkerchief. She dried her eyes. She breathed in and out, still not seeing the here and now, but looking within toward an inner struggle.

The three onlookers felt helpless and unsure. They said nothing, just waited. Justine felt as though Virginia was at a crossroads. Choices were being made.

Finally her gaze turned to Eddie, then Justine and Goosie. "Thank you for telling me."

Justine let out a puff of air. *You're welcome?* "I'm sorry to be the one—"

"No, no," Virginia said, "I am glad to know. They say the truth shall set you free." She took a deep breath and smiled as if it was the freshest breath she had ever taken. "I am finally free."

Free? Justine had never thought of that reaction.

Eddie touched her arm. "You're free."

The two exchanged a look that spoke volumes. And then they embraced, deeply and fully, finally at liberty to express their affection.

"Look at that," Goosie whispered as she squeezed Justine's arm.

It was mesmerizing to witness the love between them.

Virginia and Eddie finally released each other, but stood close, an arm around each other's waists. "I can never repay you for telling me the truth, Justine."

It was not the reaction she'd expected. "You're welcome."

"What are you going to do now?" Goosie asked.

Virginia smiled at Eddie. "For now I'm going to bask in the happiness that comes with having options. I've had so few choices in my life."

Goosie nudged Justine and glanced toward the road.

Yes, yes, she was right. "We'll leave you then," Justine said.

Before they left, Virginia rushed toward her, encasing her in a hug. "I don't know how to thank you."

You just did.

**

Harland helped Goosie and Justine into the surrey, took his place on the seat, and drove away from Ravenwood. "So," he said, "was your visit with Virginia dramatic?"

—"In a very unexpected way," Justine said.

"Did you tell her that Spencer had moved back to Lawrence, had a wife, and had changed his name?"

"We did. And it made her happy," Justine said.

Harland gawked. "That's not a normal reaction."

"The news made Eddie happy too," Goosie said. "They embraced."

"It's clear they love each other," Justine said.

Harland turned onto the county road leading home. "You saw an attraction the first time you met them. I didn't see it, but you did."

"And I was right. Virginia said she was finally free."

Harland did a double-take. "Free from Spencer, as in she wants a divorce?"

"Perhaps," Justine said. "Eventually. But I think the freedom she's feeling involves being emotionally free of the hold Spencer had on her."

Goosie nodded. "She's lived with uncertainty for eight years. Finding out he's moved allows *her* to move on."

"That's a happy result," Harland said. "Unexpected and happy."

Justine agreed. She hated to bring up another subject, but it had to be addressed. "Her happiness leaves me wondering what to do next. We know more about Spencer's past. Considering her reaction to the Uriah-news, does she need to know that he was the man who shot her father?"

Neither Goosie nor Harland had an answer.

Justine continued. "I'm hesitant because she has this calm about her now. She has gone through so much loss and pain and she's finally happy."

"She was beaming," Goosie said.

"I fear telling her such an awful truth will destroy that happiness, with little good to come from it."

"Then why were you shown that truth?" Harland asked.

Despite wanting to avoid the telling, Justine knew what had to be done. "I have to tell her everything I find out."

"I agree," Goosie said. "But in that regard . . . perhaps we should have the two of them to dinner. Perhaps such hard truths can be told best in a homey setting."

Harland nodded. "I have to go back to Ravenwood tomorrow. I could ask them then." He looked at Justine. "Yes?"

She nodded.

"Wednesday then," Goosie said.

It was as good a day as any.

**

Justine forced herself to sit on the porch swing. *There's nothing more to do right now. Relax.*

She heard the front door open and Harland came out. "What are you doing?"

She made the swing rock up and back but its path was crooked. When she tried to right it, it swung wildly. "I'm relaxing. Can't you tell?"

"Clearly. Can I come and not-relax with you?"

She stilled the swing with a toe to the porch. "Please do. I'm a flittering flurry."

He sat beside her and gently pushed back. The swing submitted to his command. "See? You just have to be gentle with it."

She tossed her hands in the air. "I'm so agitated I can't even drive a porch swing."

He took one of her hands and rested it upon his leg. "You need to *stop* driving your thoughts. Just let them sit for a while."

She sighed. "I wish I could but I feel such a huge responsibility. I thought it revolved around Uriah and Virginia. But I'm the only one who's upset about it. Why should I pursue this if it will only upset her? I'm not sure she will care if he is brought to justice."

"I admire her peace." He squeezed her hand. "Maybe some of it can rub off on you?"

She stood and faced him. "I'd love to feel peace and calm." She pointed at the house. "I'd love to spend my days having tea with new friends, or help out at church, or learn how to cook or sew or knit, or assist you with patients, or become the Canasta champion of Kansas."

His smile was understanding. "*I* am the Canasta champion of Kansas."

"You can be overthrown."

He laughed. "All those visits to the past . . . remember that's not the woman you are. That's not *all* the woman you are. For you *can* do all those everyday things."

"*And* get justice against Uriah Benedict and right the wrongs of his past?"

"That too. In your spare time." He drew her back to the swing and put his arm around her. "Yours is not an ordinary life, Jussie. Your life is meant to be extraordinary. It already is."

She leaned against him and closed her eyes. "So what do I do next?"

"This," he said, pulling her even closer. "Next, you do this."

**

Justine managed to relax for thirty-five minutes. But then Harland needed to get back to his office. He asked her to join him and she'd been tempted. But during the last thirty seconds of her thirty-five minutes she got an idea.

"Not today," she told him. "I'm going to bring some tea cakes over to the Benedicts today."

"For what purpose?"

"I want to thank their cook and reinforce the story I told Uriah that I'd been at his house to get the recipe."

"And while you're there you can happen to see Caesar?"

"Maybe. Though mostly I will be there as a show for Uriah. As such I'm going to have to ignore Caesar, yet I can't overly ignore him, and . . ." She sighed deeply.

"Or else Uriah will be suspicious of your non-interest?"

She began to doubt her plan. "It seemed more logical in my head."

"It's very logical," he said, putting on his hat. "But Alva and Dorthea are home tomorrow. Why don't you wait? Seeing Alva would be a good reason to visit."

Perhaps. Yet the stirring in her stomach pushed her to go today

They kissed each other goodbye and Harland went back to his office. Justine gathered some teacakes in a basket and walked toward the Benedict's. As she turned onto their street, she had the sudden thought that Uriah might not even be there, which would mean she might be able to speak with Caesar ag—

She stopped short when she saw two men carrying somebody out of the Benedict's house by the feet and under their arms. The person was obviously hurt.

She hurried forward. It was Caesar!

Justine ran. "What happened? Is he going to be okay?"

But even before she received an answer, she saw the mass of blood on his head. Saw his arm hang oddly as though broken.

"He's gone, miss. I'm sorry." They put Caesar into the back of a wagon.

Gone. Dead? Caesar was dead. Caesar, her friend, her source, her—

Two other men came out of the house. One was Uriah. One, carried a medical bag like Harland's.

She ran up the steps. "What happened to him?"

The doctor ignored her and said a quick goodbye before leaving Justine with Uriah. "Come in, Miss Braden."

She went inside and saw a pool of blood at the foot of the stairs.

"As you see, our dear Caesar suffered a tragic fall."

She looked at the blood, then at Uriah. There was a slight smirk in his eyes and she wanted to yell, *he didn't fall! You pushed him!*

"You brought tea cakes," he said. "How nice."

She'd forgotten the basket of sweets but quickly composed herself. "For Mrs. Russo. As a thank you for the recipe."

He took the basket from her and put a hand on her back, turning her toward the door. "I will make sure she gets them."

She pushed against his hand, not ready to leave. "How did he fall? He was an able man. Able men—"

"Die all the time." He had the audacity to shrug. He applied a look of consternation that did not fool Justine. "Alas, I will miss him."

"Alas, you will miss him? That's all you can say? After he's been with you for decades?"

His expression changed. His jaw tightened. "How do you know how long he's worked for me?"

Her throat tightened and she spun on her heels toward the door of her own accord. She had one more thing to say to him. "*He* was a good man."

She was on the sidewalk to the street when she heard his parting words. "Good men often die, Miss Braden. Often."

Shivers coursed up her back as she hurried away.

**

"Uriah killed him," Justine told Harland. "Because of me."

Harland showed Justine to a chair in his office. "We don't know that."

She gave him a look.

"We can't prove that."

Justine had thought about it on her walk to his office. "Perhaps I *can* prove it. Perhaps I'm the only one who can."

He peered out the window, then at her. "You want to go back into Caesar's life?"

"We have to catch Uriah in the act."

"Even if you see him do it in the past, you can't change anything. You're only there to observe."

Justine hated this limitation. "But if I see who else saw Caesar be pushed, then maybe I could get them to turn Uriah in. It's not a coincidence he killed Caesar while Alva was out of town."

Harland scoffed. "The only person who might have seen what happened would be a servant and they aren't going to tell and risk losing their job — or worse."

She sighed, fully frustrated. "The police won't investigate. They'll take Uriah at his word."

"You're right."

She burst from the chair and began pacing. "I don't want to be right! Caesar cared about Alva and worried for her safety. That's why he was telling me about Uriah's past." She remembered their conversation at the stables. "Caesar had many regrets about his life, about staying with Uriah."

Harland strolled to his office window and watched a wagon drive by. Then he turned toward her. "Maybe you can't prove Uriah killed *him*, but maybe Caesar's headstone will provide a way for you to go back and see details about Uriah's other crimes."

"Beyond the raid and Virginia's commitment?"

"He's had four names. Caesar mentioned a bank robbery, right?"

"I don't want to be a witness to that. He mentioned the Younger gang and Jesse James." She shuddered to think about being around such awful men.

"Maybe you wouldn't go back to that," he said. "Your trips have involved someone you know, namely Virginia. Although I can't predict what God has in mind, He seems to send you to events that are more personal."

His words made her feel more at ease about the prospect of another trip. "I guess I'll try to go after Caesar's funeral. He can't talk to me in this time, but maybe he *can* talk to me in past times." She felt tears threaten. "But one fact remains."

"What's that?"

"If Caesar *hadn't* talked to me, he'd still be alive."

Harland pulled her into his arms and she let herself cry.

CHAPTER ELEVEN

Sitting beside her family at church, Justine tried to concentrate on Pastor Karvins's sermon. But she couldn't get her mind off of Caesar's death and the man who was responsible. The man who sat across the aisle in the front pew with the rest of Lawrence's upper crust. She stared at the back of his bald head—his shaved head—and remembered the wild-maned man with the beard who killed Josiah Dawson, and the man with the neatly cropped hair and beard who bodily heaved his screaming wife into a wagon. A man of many faces, many names, many personas. And certainly many crimes.

She didn't relish the days ahead when she would travel back into Caesar's life, a life that was deeply intertwined with the life of this murderer peering up at the preacher, pretending to be pious.

Suddenly, Uriah turned his head. His eyes met hers. Her heart skipped a beat and she nearly turned away. But she didn't. She glared at him, unsmiling. *I know about you, Uriah Benedict. And I will do everything in my power to bring you to justice.*

He blinked once and turned forward again. His sudden fidgeting implied he had gotten her message? *Squirm, you cretin. Squirm.*

Pastor Karvins's voice broke through the moment with a verse. "Heed the word of the Lord! 'Fret not thyself because of evildoers, neither be thou envious against the workers of iniquity. For they shall soon be cut down like the grass, and wither as the green herb. Trust in the Lord, and do good; so shalt thou dwell in the land, and verily thou shalt be fed.'"

Justine smiled. She'd love to be fed a good dose of justice.

Amen to that.

**

Justine stood at the train station with the rest of her family, waiting for Dorthea and Alva's return from Topeka. Uriah was across the depot, standing tall, his hands clasped in front, his gaze fixed on the track.

"He's waiting for his victim to return," she whispered.

"Hopefully not," Goosie said.

"Hopefully not," Harland said. "Surely he won't move against Alva so soon after Caesar."

Might Caesar's death actually save Alva?

Thomas checked his watch. He was visibly eager to have Dorthea back. "Hopefully the two ladies had a relaxing respite from all this drama."

Justine turned to her father. "Drama? This is more than drama. This is life and death."

He caught himself and nodded. "Forgive me. I'm just looking forward to having her home."

"My father, the romantic." She slipped her hand around his arm.

He put a hand to his mid-section. "I know it's silly, but I do feel quite young again."

They heard the wail of a train-whistle, and soon felt the ground vibrate. As the train pulled into the station trailing a cloud of black smoke, they all stepped forward to greet the ladies.

Except Uriah. He didn't move. Didn't flinch. Alva would have to come to him.

The train stopped and steps were put in place. Other passengers were greeted with smiles and hugs, and for a fleeting moment Justine feared the ladies weren't on the train.

But then Dorthea appeared with a wave and a smile. Thomas rushed to meet her with a kiss to her cheek and an embrace. They each got a turn to greet her, but she did not move on, instead waiting until Alva stepped down. Alva received her own welcomes from the group. In Justine's opinion she had never looked better. Her cheeks were rosy, her smile genuine.

Until she saw Uriah. A flash of fear veiled her happiness. But then she stood straighter. "If you'll excuse me. I see my husband."

She strode to Uriah with her head high, her shoulders back.

"That's an Alva I haven't seen before," Justine whispered. She expected Alva to embrace Uriah and perhaps kiss his cheek. Instead, she gave her husband a nod and walked toward their buggy.

For a split second, Uriah faltered. His transition from his statue-stance to movement was awkward, and he walked after her.

Goosie giggled. "I'm betting that's the first time Uriah Benedict has ever walked behind a woman."

Dorthea grinned. "After this trip I think we'll all see a few changes in Alva."

"It was a good respite, then?" Justine asked.

"A trip of revelation, rejuvenation, and resolve."

"All that?"

"All that." She took Thomas's arm. "Let's get home. I'm eager to tell you all about it." She looked at Goosie and Justine. "Any news here?"

"It can wait."

**

Once home, they gave Dorthea a chance to freshen up, then met in the parlor to hear about her trip.

Justine was nervous, though hopeful. Alva's confidence and Dorthea's proclamation that the trip had led to revelation, rejuvenation, and resolve brought a optimism that was sorely needed.

Dorthea took a seat on the settee beside Thomas, immediately taking his hand and resting it on her knee. "I had a marvelous time away—and I thank you for making it possible—but I am very glad to be home again." She smiled up at Thomas.

"We missed you too," he said. "Greatly."

The other three exchanged glances, acknowledging the couple's joy. Justine hated to interrupt—and didn't have to.

"Now then," Dorthea said. "Our trip had a double mission: to get Alva to safety and to obtain information about Uriah."

"And?" Harland asked.

"Both missions were successful."

Justine felt a wave of relief. "I do like her new confidence."

"I liked how it surprised Uriah," Harland said. "He didn't know what to do with her."

"What is the root of that confidence?" Thomas asked.

"Witnessing a happy marriage."

"Your friend?"

"Mary and Ben have been married ten years. They have three children so there was always activity and laughter."

Justine remembered something. "Alva longs for children."

"She does. She will be a wonderful mother. And yet . . ." For the first time a cloud passed over her face.

"What happened?"

"By witnessing the happy family and the strong love between Mary and Ben, Alva realized what her own marriage lacked."

"I'm sure she already knew," Goosie said.

"She knew, but thought it was the norm. She told me the marriage of her own parents was less than happy. Contentious even."

"She's used to tension," Justine said.

Dorthea nodded. "The revelation came in witnessing a marriage that was different. Marriage can be joyful and full of courtesy, respect, and all-out laughter. Alva told me she couldn't remember ever seeing Uriah laugh."

"I believe that," Justine said.

Goosie raised a hand. "Did she tell you why she married him?"

"She did." Dorthea looked at Thomas, then away. "As I said, all she'd ever known was a quarrelsome marriage. Her mother was apathetic to Alva and her siblings, and her father

173

abusive. Uriah was a good catch. Apparently, he *can* be quite charming."

Justine thought of Uriah as Lionel and how he had charmed her own mother.

"What else? You mentioned rejuvenation?" Goosie asked.

"The Bates household is very spontaneous compared to the structure Alva is used to." Dorthea laughed. "Sometimes the children could have used a little *more* structure—they could get quite rowdy—but even when they were naughty, they were disciplined with love, not a whack across the face, which is what Alva was used to."

"Discipline with love . . . that's how I grew up," Harland said. "You were a wonderful mother even though you had to handle most of our growing-up years alone."

"Thank you, dear one. I appreciate that." Dorthea grinned. "You did turn out rather well, if I do say so myself."

Justine loved seeing the camaraderie between them. Although her own childhood had been rich with material things, it had suffered from a lack of warmth and joy.

"And the family meals . . ." Dorthea raised her hands in a sort of surrender and looked at Goosie. "You and Mary should exchange recipes, for you both have a gift for making food that puts taste above fussiness. Mary does all her own cooking and made the most marvelous steak and onion pie." She shook her head and closed her eyes. "I had thirds."

"I would love to get the recipe," Goosie said.

Dorthea patted her pocket. "Actually . . ." She removed a paper. "I took the liberty of getting it for you."

It was nice to share a laugh. "I can see that you were rejuvenated too," Justine said.

"I was. The past few months have been a bit tumultuous, with the girls going west and . . ." She stopped, as though fearing she'd said too much.

"And us moving in."

She looked at each of them in turn and put her hands to her chest. "I love having you here. Don't ever think otherwise. And Goosie, you have eased the burden of meals and the household in a way I never expected. But everything that's happened is life-changing. To get away for a few days and have no responsibility other than to eat and laugh and talk and play Whist . . ."

"What's Whist?" Thomas asked.

"It's a card game I'm going to teach you. You'll enjoy it."

Justine turned to Harland. "Just when I was about to be the Canasta champion of Kansas."

Dorthea looked confused at their inside joke.

"Everything sounds wonderful," Harland said. "I'm glad *you* had a good time."

"But please let us know when there are things you need us to do around here," Justine said. "We never want to be a burden."

"You are not and never will be. I promise."

Justine moved to the last word on Dorthea's list. "Finally, the resolve? What did Alva resolve?"

"To stand up for herself. To not exacerbate and defy Uriah's many moods, but to stop living in fear. To refuse to bow and scrape under his reign. They are man and wife, not master and slave."

"I'm not sure Uriah will take kindly to his new title," Harland said.

"Alva knows her strength will require delicacy."

"What did you learn about the poisoning?" Justine asked.

"She doesn't want to believe it."

"But she's the one who sounded the alarm," Thomas said.

"Actually . . ." Justine moved to the fireplace, trying to capture the sequence of her memories. She turned to face them. "Actually, Caesar was the one who suggested it to me. He saw Uriah forcing her to drink something."

"I asked her about that. It was some tea he often gave her that tasted awful."

"Perhaps the entire incident is innocent," Goosie said.

There had to be something to it, and yet . . . "So we *save* Alva from Uriah by getting her out of town for a few days, for no reason?" Justine said.

"There is a good reason," Dorthea said. "And good results. She came back a changed woman. Poison or no, she has come back stronger and wiser."

"That's something," Harland said.

Dorthea continued. "Alva was going to talk with Caesar about what he thought he saw. She likes him very much and he's very loyal to her, sometimes over-protective, and . . ." She paused as the rest of the party exchanged glances. "What's going on? Suddenly you're all looking at each other as though you share some awful secret."

Thomas put his arm around her. "Unfortunately, we do. Caesar is dead."

She froze a moment, mouthing words but saying none.

"He fell down the stairs yesterday," Thomas said. "I'm so sorry."

Dorthea shook her head back and forth, again and again. "Alva will be devastated. All the strength she garnered on our trip will be wiped away." She stood. "I have to go to her."

Thomas took her hand. "You shouldn't."

"I should! She needs reinforcement and support. Without Caesar she'll fall under Uriah's control again. I know it."

"There's more you need to know about Uriah, more I learned from Caesar." Justine didn't want to say it, but had to. "Uriah caught us talking, which may be the reason he was killed."

"Killed?" She sank back to the chair. "You said he fell."

"Pushed," Justine said. "At least that's what I believe."

"But can't prove," Harland added.

"Yet." She returned to her own chair. "In the few days you were gone we discovered more information about Uriah's past."

"He's Spencer, Virginia's husband. I know that."

"He also had the name Lionel Watkins. He was involved with my mother when I was a child."

"What?"

Justine shared everything she knew.

**

176

Justine kept Dorthea company as she unpacked. She shoved the valise under her bed, then just stood there, looking helpless.

"What's wrong?" Justine asked.

"I really need to see Alva."

"You can't do that. Going over there will put too much importance on Caesar's death."

"You're saying his death isn't important? He was her friend."

"I know he was—which may have been part of the problem. Technically, he was their servant. If Alva acts overly upset she might incite more of Uriah's wrath."

Dorthea sat on the bed. "From what you've said, Caesar's been with Uriah for nineteen years. Shouldn't Uriah be more distraught than anyone?"

"Should be, but . . . he killed Caesar. I know it. That proves how little anyone means to Uriah Benedict."

"That's why I'm so afraid for Alva." She patted the place beside her and waited until Justine sat. "We made a plan."

"A plan?"

"If she needs help, she was going to send Caesar to get us."

"And now he's gone."

Dorthea fell back on the bed, making the mattress jiggle. Justine followed. "Our plan is moot. Do you have another one?"

"As soon as it's possible, I'm going back into Caesar's life."

Dorthea turned her head to look at her. "Aren't you afraid?"

Justine thought of saying that she wasn't afraid because God was with her. But instead she told the full truth. "Yes, I'm very afraid."

"I pray that God protects You."

She was counting on it.

Chapter Twelve

"Ashes to ashes, dust to dust."

Justine looked past the open grave to the simple wooden grave marker that would be her conduit into the past. Soon. She'd travel very soon.

There weren't many people at Caesar's funeral. Five servants from the Benedict residence and a few people from town revealed the narrow scope of his life.

Justine and her family were there, as were Uriah and Alva. Uriah took his usual stance, hands clasped in front, straight, unbending, and cold. Alva stood next to him, fighting tears. Her eyes were red and her face puffy.

At the benediction, Alva gasped once and let the tears come, but when Uriah glared at her, she quickly reined in her emotions. So much for her new resolve to be strong and stand up to him.

Don't judge her. You've never lived with such a domineering person.

Justine wrestled with her own tears, and in doing so realized *she* was also controlled by Uriah's presence. For to grieve for Caesar in public would imply a relationship. Uriah already suspected too much.

The service ended and the mourners filed away. Justine and Dorthea moved forward to give their condolences to Alva but it was impossible to do so privately. Uriah kept her by his side at all times, forcing them to exchange trite words of regret and comfort.

Justine looked at Uriah and said, "I'm sorry for your loss, Mr. Benedict. Caesar's loyalty to you and your family was an inspiration."

Harland added, "He was a good man."

Uriah blinked once. "He will be missed. Won't he, Miss Braden?"

He'd singled her out. *I'm next. He's going to come after me.*

She felt the intensity of his gaze. With difficulty she raised her chin. "Caesar *will* be sorely missed, but never forgotten. Of that, you can be certain."

She took Harland's arm and walked away, her heart pumping, her nerves screaming.

"You purposely goaded him," Harland said. "Is that wise?"

No! Why did I do that? She tried to rationalize it. "I wanted to yell at him, point out the nineteen years of service Caesar gave him even when he was Lionel and Spencer. I wanted to let him know what I know."

"Those are revelations for another time."

She'd come too close to spilling everything. She pulled Harland to the side. "I wish I could tell him that I'm not going to give up. I know who and what he is. He needs to be very afraid."

Harland stepped between Justine and her view of Uriah. "This is not *your* justice to be served, Jussie, but God's. 'Pride goeth before destruction' . . ."

And a haughty spirit before a fall. She suffered a sigh and calmed herself. "You're right. This isn't my plan. It's His."

Harland put a gentle hand on her arm. "He chose you for this, Jussie. Trust Him to help you trust yourself."

She squeezed his hand. He was such a godsend. "I welcome your correction when I stray from the goal. Thank you."

"We all need checks and balances."

"Me, more often than most."

"Not at all." He pulled her arm around his and they walked to the surrey where the others were waiting. They climbed in, the three women making do in the back seat meant for two.

On the way home, Dorthea let *her* frustration loose. "Uriah wouldn't let Alva talk. He was a guard, watching over a prisoner. He's already doused her fire. All her strength and resolve was gone."

Justine agreed. "You should check on her tomorrow. Remind her of your lovely time together. Encourage her to be strong."

Dorthea nodded once, though she looked unconvinced. "We have ladies' circle at church every other Wednesday. I usually pick her up. Hopefully I can get some time alone with her then."

"A perfect opportunity," Thomas said over his shoulder. "Help her get her life back to its normal rhythm."

Dorthea shook her head vehemently. "We want to break that rhythm, get her out more, set her free from that awful man."

He nodded. "Tell her I'd be happy to speak with her any time she needs an ear."

"I appreciate that," Dorthea said. "She'll appreciate that."

The shared apprehension about Alva and Uriah confirmed Justine's plan. "I'm going back tonight."

"You're going to a graveyard at night?" Goosie asked.

Justine was surprised at her hesitance. "I didn't think you were superstitious."

Goosie shrugged. "It's just not a place I'd like to visit in the dark."

Justine looked toward the west. The sun was long past its prime. "I don't have much choice."

"You could go tomorrow," Dorthea said.

"I don't want to wait. Each hour Alva is with that man is an hour too long. The sooner I find out what God wants me to know about Uriah, the better."

"I'll go to the cemetery with you," Harland said.

She was touched. "You will? You'll wait for me?"

"It won't be that long a wait," he said. "You've said that time barely passes in the present, no matter how long you're gone in the past."

She leaned forward and touched his shoulder. "I'd love your company."

"Actually, I'd like to witness what happens when you leave and come back. Feed my curiosity."

"Only one person has seen me. Back in Piedmont, Mabel saw me disappear."

"As long as you reappear . . ."

Goosie gasped. "What if you don't? What if you're stuck in the past? Have you ever thought of that?"

Justine suffered a twinge of fear — for she *had* thought of it. She pushed it aside. "This gift is God's doing. I trust Him to take care of me, no matter where I am."

"No matter *when* you are," Thomas said.

"Can you die in the past?" Goosie asked.

Justine had wondered about this too. "I hope not. Again, I have to trust God to keep me safe and return me safely home."

"I don't think you can die there," Thomas said.

She chuckled at his rare opinion. "Why is that?"

"You're in the past as an observer, to get information that is needed in the present to right some wrong. If you die, the information is lost, and the trip is without worth. God's ways are never worthless."

Justine was comforted by his logic.

**

Justine was thankful for the full moon.

Walking through the cemetery in the dark made her skin tingle. Each headstone created a shadow where goblins could hide. *You're sounding like Goosie.*

"Ouch!" Harland said.

She'd held his arm too tightly. "Sorry," she whispered. "Despite all logic, it is rather spooky."

"It makes me remember every ghost story my sisters used to tell me. They loved making me cower under the covers. They'd laugh and laugh."

"Sounds lovely."

"I did my own share of tormenting them, stealing their hair ribbons, putting frogs in their beds."

"Actually, my comment holds."

"It sounds lovely?"

"I didn't have siblings."

Harland slowed. "How lonely you must have been."

She appreciated his sympathy, but the mention of loneliness made her think of her current situation. "You want lonely? Try traveling back in time, all alone, not knowing where or when you'll end up. Not knowing what you're supposed to do there, and *knowing* that while you're there, you're supposed to uncover some awful deed."

He touched her hand that was linked with his. "Maybe dealing with your childhood loneliness made you stronger for your travels."

"Maybe." She leaned her head against his shoulder as they walked. "You always find the bright side. That's *your* gift."

"Glad to be of service." He looked up as they passed under trees that covered the moonlight. "I'd like anything bright right now. You get to leave. I'm left here in the dark."

"My hero," she said.

They reached Caesar's grave, the ground disturbed from the burial.

"Here we are." She wrapped her arms around him. "I love you, Harland. I appreciate you coming here. Please pray for me."

He held her close, a hand behind her head, tucking it beneath his chin. "Lord, watch over this precious woman as she travels on this journey of Your making. Give her wisdom and great insight and let her see whatever You want her to see to bring about justice."

Justine felt his heart's quick rhythm match her own.

He pushed her back and lifted her chin to give her a kiss. "Safe travels, m'love."

She walked to Caesar's simple grave marker that had *Caesar Johnson b. 1832 d. 1879* carved in the wood. "I never knew his last name. I should have known his last name." She looked at Harland in the moonlight wanting . . . something from him, yet she was unable to pinpoint what it was.

"You know his name now. Go back and find out about Uriah, but also find out about Caesar. You can honor him by being a witness to his life."

"And find out if Uriah killed him."

"That too."

With one last look at Harland, she knelt before the marker and traced his name with her fingers. The familiar force pulled her from within, like she was flying blind.

I was blind and now I see.

**

Justine felt an inner and physical *oomph* that told her she'd arrived. She opened her eyes and found herself in bright sunlight. She stood on a vast lawn that stretched toward a wide white building, three stories tall, with railing along an exterior veranda that led to room after room.

I'm at a resort.

As soon as she thought the thought, she knew exactly where she was: the Bedford Springs Resort in Pennsylvania. And she knew *when* she was: autumn 1860. More importantly, she knew who she would see there: Lionel Watkins, Caesar, her mother, and hopefully her father. The ache of missing her parents was replaced with excitement. *How many people get to see a loved one who's passed?*

She heard a horse whinny and turned in time to see her father walking toward a waiting carriage. "Papa!" she called out before she could stop herself.

He looked at her, paused a brief moment, then touched the brim of his hat before entering the carriage. He looked so young. She felt a wave of longing. She missed him so.

The carriage pulled away and regret assailed her. If only she'd arrived a few minutes earlier she might have had the chance to talk to him. Justine watched the carriage until she couldn't see it anymore. *Goodbye, Papa.*

With a sigh and a shake of her head she set her disappointment aside. There was work to be done.

Justine walked through scatterings of fallen leaves to the porticoed entrance. Once inside, her blue day dress received immediate scrutiny from the female guests in the lobby. She felt offended until she realized it wasn't because her dress wasn't nice enough, but because it was different—nineteen years different. They all wore wide hoop skirts, high necklines, and wide pagoda sleeves over lacy undersleeves. Although Justine appreciated the gentle sway of the skirts when the women walked, she did not envy the task of getting through narrow doorways or sitting. She was glad she wasn't wearing her bustle. Now *that* abomination would have caused a stir.

She pulled Granny's shawl tighter. It was time to find her mother. As she walked to the registration desk, she saw a much younger Caesar carrying the luggage of a couple going to their room. Her stomach tightened knowing that this place, this time, was the beginning of all that was to come.

"May I help you, miss?"

She focused on the clerk. "I'm looking for Mr. and Mrs. Braden?" *I'm their daughter.*

"I'm afraid Mr. Braden just left to return to New York on business."

At least I caught a glimpse of you.

The clerk tried to cheer her. "But Mrs. Braden is still here with her daughter."

Justine stifled a gasp. *Daughter? Me? Will I actually see myself?*

That would be a rare experience.

"I believe I saw them go outside. The little girl is quite rambunctious and likes to run. Outside is an excellent choice."

Justine said thank you and exited the building. She looked left, then right.

And there they were. *There we are.* Mother walked slowly, holding a ruffled parasol in one hand and in the other, the hand of a three-year-old. Justine's heart beat wildly and her throat tightened. Having no memories of her time here, it was doubly odd to see that—memories or no—she *had* been here.

That's what I looked like? I'm cute. My hair is so much lighter than it is now. Justine had only seen one daguerreotype of herself as a child of three. Now, seeing her own living, moving, talking *self* was fascinating and rather disconcerting.

She walked after them, glad their rate was slowed by her own short legs, as well as the fact she kept dropping her doll.

My doll's name was Betty Ann . . .

184

She was just about to catch up with them, when she remembered meeting her 20-year-old mother in 1857 before Mavis Tyler left Piedmont. Justine had even stayed overnight and shared her mother's bedroom. Would Mother remember that meeting now in 1860? Would it matter if she did? *At the time I told her my name was Justine Braden. I can't do that now.*

The doll dropped again, causing Mother to stop and scold the young Justine—allowing the grown Justine to catch up.

"I told you to leave Betty Ann in the room. You will get in trouble if you get her dress dirty again."

The toddler threw the doll—right at Justine's feet.

"Oh my." Justine picked it up and smoothed her dress, her thoughts rushing back to the myriad of times she'd cuddled and played with Betty Ann. She spoke to the doll. "Are you hurt? You had an awful fall."

The little girl rushed forward and took the doll away. She stared at the doll's face. "I sorry. You hurt?" Then she held the doll against her shoulder, comforting her. "There, there."

"See, Jussie? It's not nice to hurt your baby," her mother said.

Jussie. Growing up I only remember Granny and Goosie calling me that.

"I be nice."

"Good." Mother sighed deeply and spoke to the woman Justine. "My husband just left. I should have let him take Jussie with him."

"It's a much prettier place to play here, than in New York," Justine said.

Mother cocked her head. "How do you know we come from New York?"

Justine shrugged. "A good guess." She wanted to introduce herself and chose a name she'd used on previous travels. "I'm Susan Miller."

Mother nodded. "Nice to meet you. I'm Mavis Braden, and this little hellion is Justine."

"Jussie," the little girl said.

Her mother looked at Justine as though studying her. "You look familiar. Have we met?"

"I don't think so." She wanted to change the subject. "May I walk with you? I only just arrived."

"Of course."

"Run, Mama?"

"Yes, you can run. But stay in sight." Jussie ran away. "Her running only provides a short respite, but a respite just the same. My lady's maid usually takes charge of her, but I sent her on an errand into Bedford."

Franny.

They began to walk. "Have you been here before?" Mother asked.

Actually . . . "I have not."

"Then let me tell you about the resort. It *does* have an interesting history."

"I'd appreciate that."

Mother moved the parasol to her left hand to better block the afternoon sun. "The springs and 2200 acres were purchased in 1796 by Dr. John Anderson. Word spread about the curative powers of the springs and people began to flock here. The Indians of the region had used the springs for centuries."

He bought the springs from the Indians?

"He built an inn here in the early 1800s, and most recently President Buchanan makes this his summer White House. Though with the election coming up who knows how that will change. A large note of significant history is that a few years ago, the president got some cable from Queen Victoria, right there in the lobby. It caused a big to-do." She sighed. "The election . . . isn't it odd there are four candidates on the Democrat side?"

Really? "That is odd." What was also odd was her mother's mention of politics.

"I've heard Noel and his friends arguing about it, but I prefer to know as little as possible."

There was the mother she knew.

"Lincoln is a Republican. He's our man. If the Democrats can't make up their mind and want three candidates, then he'll win."

"Lincoln is a good man." *Who will be assassinated in less than five years.*

"We met him once. He is an awkward but gentle giant. His features are so gaunt and serious like he's burdened from within."

And soon, from without.

"The South fears he'll take slavery away from them and if he's elected, they say they'll leave the union." She shook her head. "But that's silly. How can they leave? It makes no sense to me. But neither does slavery, so . . ."

Justine thought about the strife and fighting that would begin within a year. "A war will tear the country apart," she said.

Mother stopped walking. "Who said anything about a war?"

Justine quickly shook her head. "I've heard talk."

"Well, stop that talk. Immediately." She sighed. "Men. If women were in charge, we'd find a way to avoid the stupidity of war."

They reached a long, covered walkway leading away from the building. "Now this . . ." Mother said. "If you follow this colonnade, it will lead you across Sweet Root Road to the mineral springs. The magnesia spring supposedly helps stomach issues, and the iron spring is good for the blood. There's a sulphur spring and one for drinking. Seven all-told. They are said to have restorative powers."

"You seem skeptical."

"The restorative powers I need are not helped by a little water. I came because Noel thought it would be good for me."

"Is something . . . I don't mean to pry, but is something wrong?"

They saw that Jussie had found a little boy to play with in the piles of leaves nearby, tossing them, chasing after them, gathering them, only to repeat the process. "Would you like to sit?" Mother asked.

"Yes. Thank you." Her mother's dress took up most of the bench, leaving Justine hugging the left armrest.

"If you don't mind me commenting, I see that you've forgone your cage."

"My cage?"

Mother pressed her dress against her lap, making it rise at the sides. "Your hoop," she said. Your dress has a very simple silhouette."

What would you have thought of my bustle? "I know I'm not fashionable here, but I was traveling."

"Oh, I'm not speaking against you," Mother said. "I appreciate the functionality of your choice." She smoothed the enormity of her skirt, tucking it in on Justine's side, to give her more room. "Fashion is fickle. I both love and hate it. Why can't it be simple, like men's fashion? A pair of pants, a shirt, a jacket, and a few neckwear variations. No complications."

Justine laughed. "I can't imagine that ever happening." She remembered a quote. "A woman who reveals too much of her body, reveals too little of her mind."

Her mother was taken aback. "That's my saying! Or rather, my mother's."

Oh. My. It is!

"Where did you hear that?"

The mention of Granny gave her an out. "I think I heard it from an elderly woman. Winifred Tyler?"

"That's my mother!"

"What a small world!"

"When did you meet her?"

"I don't remember exactly, but I think it was when my parents and I were in New Hampshire."

"That's where she lived! Piedmont, New Hampshire."

"How astounding," Justine said. "It's a good saying, don't you think?"

"It is. Mama could be quite wise—when she wanted to be." She glanced at Justine. "Did you and I meet then?"

Justine felt her face grow red. "I don't think so."

Mother took care of the possibility. "I left Piedmont in fifty-seven and don't go back as often as I should. Mama enjoys seeing Jussie but doesn't always approve of my ways."

"Your ways?"

"Let's just say many of my methods — my choices — have been unconventional."

Like running off with one man, getting pregnant by his brother, and marrying a third man?

"I don't want to mislead you," she said. "My husband is a good man. Too good."

"I've never heard a man called *too* good."

"Well he is. I wish . . . "She paused and looked at Justine. "Are you married?"

"I am betrothed."

"Do you love him?"

"Of course I love him. I adore him. And he adores me."

Mother looked away. "Hmm."

"Do you love . . .?" Justine asked.

She considered this a minute, glancing toward little Jussie and the boy. Both were still playing nicely, squatted down in the grass, probably looking at bugs. "I respect Noel. I appreciate everything he's done for us."

"I know." She caught herself. "I know the type. My intended is a good man too."

"Noel . . . he saved me."

Justine's stomach flipped. To hear about her beginnings from the source would be extraordinary. "Saved you from what? Or whom?"

"From foolish folly. And from myself." She scoffed. "I'd like to blame others for my problems, but alas, all of them were my own doing."

Was I a "problem"? Justine wanted to hear more. "Since I will soon be a wife, I would appreciate any advice you'd like to share."

Mother stared across the lawn. "You are wise to marry for love. I missed my chance."

Thomas? "You loved another?"

"After the fact. After I'd shunned him and turned him away. After he died."

But Thomas didn't die!

Mother sniffed. "I only heard of his death a month ago. It's one of the reasons Noel brought me here."

"He knew about this other man?"

"Not directly. But he knew I was upset and extremely sad. He thought the resort would help me through it—whatever it was."

"I'm so sorry."

"Thomas adored me and I was too pig-headed to get off my high-horse and marry him." She chuckled. "I managed to mention pigs and horses in one sentence." She looked directly at Justine. "*And* I've shared far too many of my faults, regrets, and weaknesses. Do you always have that effect on people, Miss Miller?"

"I try to be a good listener."

"You succeed." She stood. "I really need to get Jussie back for her afternoon nap. Perhaps we'll see you again? I'd ask you to join me for dinner, but I have plans."

"Thank you for your time, Mrs. Braden."

Time. How ironic.

**

It was awkward not being a guest at the hotel while pretending to be a guest. How she'd love to have a room to sleep in. Justine had left 1879 in the evening, after a long day. She was exhausted.

The next place she could count on seeing her mother was in the dining room. But at what time? She approached the maître d'.

"Yes, miss?"

"I am joining Mrs. Braden for dinner but have forgotten the time, and she's not in her room. Could you look it up for me?"

"Certainly." He looked in his book, but his head furrowed. "I have no reservations for Braden. Perhaps it is under another name?"

She hesitated, then said, "Watkins?"

He glanced at the page, then nodded. "Here it is. Seven o'clock. A table for two. Should I make it for three?"

Now that *would be interesting.*

"Thank you, but no. Not at this time. I really would like to speak with Mrs. Braden first."

He looked wary. "Of course."

Her stomach rumbled. "Might I get a table for a late luncheon?"

His head jerked back. "Alone?"

"Well, yes."

"I'm sorry, miss, but we do not allow unaccompanied ladies in the dining room."

You'd rather see me starve? She appreciated the male of their species wanting to protect the female, but in this case, protect them from what? The *foie gras* or turtle soup?

Justine retreated to the lobby where she spotted Caesar, hard at work, carrying more luggage. She followed him up the stairs, keeping her distance. But at the top, he looked over his shoulder at her.

She stopped walking and offered him a smile.

"Can I help you, miss?"

"No, thank you. I was just . . ." she thought fast, "thinking about how strong you have to be to carry heavy baggage all day, up and down the stairs."

He set one valise down and adjusted a hat box beneath his other arm which held a carpet bag. He glanced down the hall. "Excuse me, miss, but guests are waiting."

She descended the stairs. So far she had seen three people who were no longer living. Yet she hadn't seen Lionel, the only one who still lived—and still hurt people. It was incredibly unfair.

She checked the clock in the lobby. Five after six. She needed to rest until seven. And find something to eat. Or drink.

Justine went outside and followed the crowd through the colonnade to the springs. She drank some mineral water and found it horrible. She couldn't imagine that anything that tasted so nasty could be good for her.

But on the way back to the hotel, she saw a man hawking peanuts.

Food! She rushed forward. "One please."

"That will be a nickel."

She realized she didn't have any money. "I . . . I'm sorry."

"What is your room number? I'll charge it there."

"Oh dear. I don't remember the number. But . . . Mrs. Braden's room?"

He handed her the bag and she found a bench to rest on, one that faced the front door so she would see her mother if she came out.

It was a beautiful day, the air was cool and smelled of spicy leaves and freshness. Justine loved the colors of autumn.

I'll just close my eyes a few minutes . . .

**

"Miss?" Justine startled awake, and realized she'd fallen asleep on the bench, her arm on the armrest, supporting her head. She sat up straight. "Yes?"

A middle-aged couple stood before her. The man pointed toward the west. "The sun goes down quickly at this time of year."

"The October air grows chilly," the woman said.

Justine stood, feeling achy from her odd position. "Thank you. May I ask the time?"

The man consulted his pocket watch. "Half-past eight."

"Oh dear! I'm going to miss dinner!"

She hurried toward the entrance. The chandeliers of the lobby were aglow. She spotted the same maître 'd speaking with some guests. She slid through the lobby, avoiding his gaze, and found a place to stand behind a potted palm. She could see half of the restaurant—luckily the right half.

There was a handsome man sitting with her mother. She could tell it was a much-younger Uriah—as Lionel Watkins. She had to admit he looked quite dashing. A dinner for two. Followed by . . . ?

Justine didn't want to think about it. Mother had suggested her marriage wasn't all she'd hoped it would be, but to be so easily charmed by another man—this awful man? Justine only knew a portion of what Lionel-Spencer-Uriah had done *since* this moment in time. She shuddered to think about what had led him to this point. Caesar had mentioned his ability to charm.

But was her mother so easy beguiled?

She studied Lionel and was fascinated with how he could change his appearance. She'd seen him as Uriah, with a shaved head and a slim and almost gaunt stature. She'd seen him as Lionel during the raid, with long wild hair and a full, untamed beard. Then she'd seen him as Spencer, a conservative farmer, neatly trimmed. And here he was as a younger man, suave and handsome, with his hair slicked back, sporting a trimmed mustache, wearing a three-piece suit. He checked his pocket watch with its chain looped stylishly into his vest pocket. Justine could see how women were attracted to him. He owned an air of confidence, but also a hint of the rascal Her mother had chosen such a man before, running off with Quinn Piedmont, a definite rogue.

She watched them eat and drink, speaking back and forth with purpose. Oddly she didn't see any obvious flirtation going on: no leaning in, no flirtatious laughter, no brushing of hands. Justine knew all about flirting, having learned the skill from her mother. In truth, Justine had been good at it. Tonight, her mother was not. Perhaps being married for three years had made her skills rusty. Yet illicit dalliances *did* require discretion.

"Excuse me?"

Justine looked up and saw Caesar. He had a rag in his hand.

"You hiding from someone?" he asked.

"I was just . . ." She sighed. "I wanted to speak with Mrs. Braden before she went to dinner, but now it's too late." She nodded toward the restaurant.

Caesar began dusting the leaves of the potted tree and snuck a look. "Hmm. She's with Mr. Watkins."

He did not say the name with approval.

"You know him?"

Caesar stopped wiping a leaf. "More than I should."

"Oh?"

"I didn't want to know him. Didn't mean to. But things happened and now . . . I kinda work for him."

Justine nodded at his dusting. "Don't you work for the hotel?"

"That too. But Mr. Watkins has me doing special favors."

Because he caught you stealing. "Since he's spending time with my friend . . . can you tell me about him?"

"He's good with the ladies."

"Should I warn Mrs. Braden about him?"

Caesar thought a moment, then shrugged. "Maybe she enjoys being charmed."

Knowing her mother . . . "What are his intentions?"

"That, I don't know. I don't pry. I just see what I can't help but see." With a glance toward the front desk he said, "I needs to get back to work."

"Before you go, can you tell me Mrs. Braden's room number?"

He eyed her warily. "I thought you knew her."

"I do, but since I missed dinner, I hope to catch her later this evening for a chat about old times."

"It's room 230." His gaze turned in the direction of the restaurant. "They're coming out."

She tucked further behind the plant. "I don't want her to see me. Yet."

Caesar's eyebrows rose. "To each his own." He leaned forward and whispered. "She's going upstairs. Alone."

It was a relief.

"Caesar?" a man said.

Caesar tucked the dust cloth into the planter and stepped out to answer Lionel. He took a step to the side, thankfully covering Lionel's possible view of Justine.

"I need you to do something for me."

"Of course, Mr. Watkins. Whatever you say."

Lionel led Caesar toward the stairs, talking confidentially.

Between having little in her stomach and a lot of stress, Justine felt nauseous. Yet she had to press on. She *had* to speak with her mother. If only the men would move along so she could slip upstairs.

A minute later, Caesar ascended the stairs, no doubt fulfilling his errand for Lionel.

Lionel stood at the bottom of the stairs as if he was its keeper. He eyed the ladies in the lobby, winked—more than once, and received many approving glances from the women, and wary glances from the men on their arms. He seemed to love both types of attention.

Finally, he was greeted by another gentleman and they strolled toward the entrance, deep in conversation. Justine overheard the mention of cigars.

Now was her chance.

She waited until they were out of doors then hurried to the second floor. She walked down the hall toward room 230. But then suddenly, the door opened and Caesar came out. He was holding her mother's ruby necklace—the one from Justine's painting.

"Stop!" she cried out. "Thief!"

Caesar quickly put the necklace in his pocket and rushed down the hall. Justine ran to the room and saw her mother in the doorway. "He stole your necklace! We need to—"

Mother pulled her inside—none too gently. "Hush! You have no idea what you're talking about."

"But he was holding your necklace—an expensive ruby necklace."

Mother pointed to a chair. "Sit. Now."

How many times had Justine been ordered to sit in just such a way? She sat. "I was only trying to help."

Mother pressed the palm of her hand to her forehead. "Gracious, girl. We meet one time and now you're trying to defend me against thieves?"

Justine pointed toward the door. "He had it in his hand! He was coming out of your room."

"Did you ever consider that I gave him the necklace?"

It took her a moment to remember what Caesar had told her at the stables—that the necklace was payment for passage. "I apologize. I reacted on impulse."

Mother pulled another chair close, sat and leaned toward Justine—another familiar action.

"I appreciate your sense of right and wrong, Miss Miller, and appreciate your good intentions. But . . . I am not a victim here, but rather a woman who is finally taking control of her life. I *gave* the necklace to Caesar, to give to Mr. Watkins."

He still has it. Justine pretended she didn't know. "Why would you do that?"

"As payment for passage west."

New thoughts fell into place. *Which explains why they weren't flirting at dinner.* "It's a business transaction?"

"Of a sort."

"You're not . . . involved?"

Mother scoffed. "In that way? Heavens no. I am beyond the need for dalliances."

"But you said your marriage wasn't . . ."

"Perfect? Whose is? I have been offered the choice of staying with my husband — with things as they are — or taking the biggest chance of my life and starting over out west. I choose the latter."

"And your daughter?"

"She's going with me, of course. I adore Jussie as I adored her father. Where I go, she goes."

Justine felt tears threaten. Her mother had never told Justine she loved her.

Mother touched her knee. "Have I upset you?"

"Not at all. Your love for your daughter is very sweet."

"She's the one thing I've done right." She sat back and sighed deeply. "Don't be too inspired. It's all quite selfish really. Noel is a good father and a good provider, but I want more, and so . . ." She shrugged. "I make my choice for Jussie too."

"What about your husband? Won't he miss you and Jussie? Look for you?"

"He'll miss Jussie, for certain. But me? I think he'll be relieved not to have to play the part of *husband* anymore."

It saddened Justine to realize their relationship had been that far gone. She had to remind herself that she and her mother never *did* go west. They'd stayed with Papa until he died. "When are you leaving?"

"I'm not sure. Jussie and I will return to New York tomorrow so I can pack properly."

"Will you tell your husband you're leaving?"

"I haven't decided but I believe I will leave a note."

"Doesn't he deserve more than that?"

Her mother pulled back. "Miss Miller, I don't think you know me well enough to judge me."

"Of course not. Forgive me. So when will you leave for the West?"

"I am to wait for a telegram from Mr. Watkins regarding the departure date and time."

He never contacts you. He takes your necklace and runs. "Do you trust him?"

She considered this a moment. Then, "Not really. I just met him three days ago."

"Yet you're staking your future on him?"

Mother smoothed the fabric of her skirt over her knees. "Call it instinct. He knows people, has connections. Upon his wire, we will take a train back here, meet up with him, travel to St. Louis, and then board a steamer for Kansas City."

"Do you know anyone in Kansas City?"

"Not a soul." She hesitated. "Actually, a woman back in my hometown of Piedmont has some relatives in a town called Lawrence, which I've heard isn't far. I will contact them."

Mother was going to contact Dorthea's aunt?

There was a knock on the door. It was Franny. "Jussie is asking for you, Mrs. Braden."

"I'll be right there." She moved her chair back into place. "I need to attend to my daughter in the next room. I appreciate your concern for me, Miss Miller. But rest assured all is well — or will be."

She moved toward the door, but Justine was hesitant to leave. This might be the last time she would ever see her mother.

"I need to attend to my daughter, Miss Miller. If you please?"

But I'm your daughter! And I need you to attend to me!

Reluctantly, Justine stepped into the hall. "Good evening, Mrs. Braden," she said. On impulse, she pulled her into an embrace. "God speed."

Justine ran toward the stairs, fighting back tears. She rushed through the lobby, keeping her head low, not wanting to draw attention.

She'd just gone outside when she bodily ran into someone.

"Whoa!" said the man, righting her. "What's amiss, little lady?"

Justine swiped her tears away. "Nothing. If you'll excuse me . . ."

He touched her arm with one hand, and with the other gave her a handkerchief.

She used it for her tears. "Thank you. I'm sorry for running into—" For the first time, Justine looked at his face. It was Lionel Watkins!

She must have gasped because he cocked his head, as though amused. "Have we met?"

"I don't think so." She tried to side-step around him to get to the pathway in front of the hotel.

He matched her parry. "I do believe the lady could use a chance to calm herself." He drew her arm around his and led her to a bench nearby. "Now, isn't this better?" He sat beside her. "The fresh night air is always a tonic. Take some deep breaths. In. Out."

She humored him—and actually did feel better. "Thank you, Mister . . .?"

"Watkins," he said. "Lionel Watkins, at your service. And you are?"

"Miss Miller."

He leaned back on the bench and crossed his legs as though planning to be there a while. "Look at that moon, Miss Miller. Have you ever seen one finer?"

She glanced up. "It is a fine moon."

He chuckled. "You are determined to fight the moment, aren't you?"

"I appreciate your kindness, Mr. Watkins, but I really do need to—"

"How did you come to be here, Miss Miller?"

She was taken aback by his question. Did he know about her time-traveling abilities? Surely not, and yet the way he smirked in the moonlight implied he knew secrets that even she didn't know.

"I . . . I am a guest. The same as you."

"Not the same, for I am at ease. You are on edge." He extended an arms across the back of the bench, grazing her shoulders.

She stood. "I apologize for bumping into you and I appreciate your attempt to console me."

"You needed consoling?"

"An unfortunate choice of words." She took a cleansing breath. "I was slightly upset, but now I am calm." She forced a smile. "Thank you for your gallant concern. I will bid you good evening." She walked toward the hotel. She felt goosebumps on her arms and up her spine. Was he following her? She didn't turn to find out.

As soon as she got inside, she hurried to her hiding place behind the plant. She saw him enter the hotel and look in her direction. He smiled.

Thankfully, blessedly, God took her away.

**

Justine opened her eyes and immediately fell into Harland's arms. He held her close.

"You're shaking!"

Feeling his strength, hearing his heartbeat . . . Justine began to cry.

"Oh, Jussie. What happened? You're safe. You're safe now."

He thought she'd been in danger. She'd hidden from Lionel, but he hadn't been a danger to her. Or had he?

She pulled back to see his face in the moonlight. Her first thoughts were of her mother. "I'm not afraid. I'm just spent. I saw Mother. I saw *me.*"

"I didn't know that was possible."

"Neither did I. It was the autumn before I turned three, and we were at a resort in Pennsylvania. I saw Papa too." She shivered. "Can you get me home, please?"

He led her to the surrey, and they left the cemetery. She took his hand but didn't say anything. He nodded, acknowledging her need for silence. When they got home, he helped her upstairs where Goosie took over, getting her into bed.

There was concern on her wrinkled face. "Will you tell us about it?"

"Tomorrow."

As Goosie left the room, Harland came in, and Justine spied Thomas and Dorthea in the hall.

He sat on the bed and moved a stray strand of hair away from her face. "Better?"

She nodded. "None of you have to worry about me. I'm fine. It's just a lot to manage, to comprehend."

He drew her hand to his lips. "We'll be here in the morning for you."

"I know." She touched his cheek, feeling very blessed.

CHAPTER THIRTEEN

I smell fresh bread.

Justine smiled before she even opened her eyes. She stretched and enjoyed the delicious ache of her muscles as they also awakened.

When she heard whispered voices in the hall, she called out, "I'm awake."

Her father opened the door and peered in. Dorthea was by his side. "I hope we didn't disturb you."

She pushed herself up to sitting. "Not at all. Come in." She readjusted the covers across her chest.

They stood at the foot of the bed. "Did you sleep well?" Thomas asked.

"I did. When I went to bed last night I felt like I could sleep a week."

They exchanged a look.

She had a sudden thought. "I haven't slept a week, have I?"

"No," Thomas said as he chuckled. "But it is after noon."

She'd gone to bed at eight . . . "I slept sixteen hours?"

"You must have needed it," Dorthea said.

"We're eager to hear about your travels," her father said.

Dorthea put a hand on his arms. "First things first. Are you hungry?"

Justine had only eaten a few peanuts in the past. "I'm famished."

"Goosie is eager to fill you up," Father said. "Lunch is nearly ready."

"I will be down shortly," she said.

"Would you like some help?" Dorthea asked.

She was just about to say no-thank-you, when she changed her mind. "I'd love some. I feel as weak as a kitten."

Dorthea stayed behind and helped Justine get dressed. When it was down to the final details, she asked, "Would you like to wear your gold locket or your cameo?"

Suddenly Justine remembered a detail about her time in the past. The ruby necklace.

She picked up the small portrait from her bedside table and showed it to Dorthea. "See this necklace?"

"It's very pretty."

"Mother gave it to Lionel Watkins to pay for passage out here, to Lawrence."

"Who's Lionel again?"

"Let's join the others. I have much to tell you."

When they got downstairs everyone was seated around the dining table. "I apologize for being so much trouble." She leaned the small portrait against a leg of her chair.

Harland winked at her. "I believe you're worth it."

"And it's no trouble at all," Goosie said. "I know going back exhausts you."

She didn't want them to think last night's extreme exhaustion would be a habit. "It can be."

"Let us say grace," her father said, bowing his head. "We thank You, Lord, for bringing Justine safely back to us from her travels—Your travels. Please give her great wisdom and insight to use what You have shown her, and show us how to help her in Your work. Bless this food and be with us through our day. Amen."

"Amen. Thank you for that," Justine said.

He looked at the others. "We feel so helpless when you're gone. Prayers are all we *can* do to help."

She was touched. "I appreciate each and every one."

Goosie stood at the end of the table and ladled chicken soup into bowls. The fresh bread was passed, along with butter and strawberry preserves.

They all ate a few bites and Justine's body immediately felt strengthened by the good food.

Dorthea opened the subject of the necklace. "Justine discovered something about her mother's necklace."

"Necklace?" Harland asked.

Justine leaned down to pick up the portrait, facing it outwards so they all could see. "This necklace." She passed the picture around. When it reached Thomas, his gaze lingered a bit longer than the others'.

"She was a beautiful woman," he said. He glanced at Dorthea and said, "I'm sorry. I don't—"

Dorthea waved his concern away and took her turn with the portrait. "She *was* a beautiful woman."

The picture made its way around and returned to Justine. "Goosie, remember when we were at my home in New York, Mother's lady's maid said the necklace had been lost at a spa."

"I remember."

"Yesterday's trip took me to that spa, to 1860. The Bedford Springs Resort in Pennsylvania. I saw Mother there. *I* was there, in the autumn just before my third birthday."

They all gasped at this final bit of news. She pressed their questions away—for now. "I'll get to all of that in a minute. But first, the necklace. Mother gave it to Lionel Watkins—to Uriah—to pay for passage to Kansas City."

"She never came to Kansas City," Harland said. "Did she?"

"She did not. He stole it from her by not using it for tickets. He kept it."

"Why did she want to come to Kansas City?" Goosie asked.

Again, Justine had to stop their questions from taking the story in another direction. She pointed at the picture. "Have any of you seen this necklace recently? Here in Lawrence?"

They looked dumbfounded, but then Dorthea held out her hand. "Let me see that again."

Justine handed her the portrait. She studied it a moment, then looked up. "It looks like Alva's necklace."

Yes! "Exactly," Justine said. "Alva wore it first time we met, that Sunday when we went to their house to dine after church."

Harland pointed at the portrait. "So Alva's necklace is your mother's?"

"One in the same."

"Maybe it's just similar," Thomas said.

Justine shook her head. "Alva told me that Uriah gave her that necklace. Uriah is Lionel. My mother gave it to Lionel." She spread her hands, letting the connections sink in.

Dorthea looked at the picture a long moment. "How did your mother know Uriah?"

Justine proceeded to tell the story of her adventure at the Bedford Springs Resort. She saved most of the personal details for the end.

"I spoke with Mother about you, Thomas," she said.

He set down his spoon. "Me?"

"Or rather, *she* spoke about you of her own volition. She had deep regrets about how she treated you. She said she'd missed her chance."

Dorthea looked at Thomas. "How did she treat you?"

He seemed a bit flustered by the question. He pushed his bowl toward the middle and leaned his forearms against the table. "It was a confusing time for Mavis. She'd just run off with my brother—who tried to take advantage of her."

"Sounds like Quinn," Harland said.

"She sent him away, which left her alone in New York. I came to her rescue."

"I'm sure she was appreciative," Dorthea said.

"I think she was, but—"

"She was," Justine said. "She regrets her rudeness. She said she was pig-headed and didn't appreciate your love until it was too late."

Thomas nodded slowly. "I was the victim of unrequited love."

"Perhaps in action, yes, but she *did* love you. She told me she adored you and wished she had agreed to marry you."

His forehead furrowed and he put a hand to his mouth. "She loved me?"

"Tremendously. You were her one true love. She was at the resort because she was mourning the news of your death."

He stared into the nothingness of the air. "It was wrong of me to pretend to be dead." His jaw tightened.

"You never fully explained that to me," Dorthea said.

Thomas tented his fingers and tapped them against his upper lip, deep in thought. Finally he spoke. "Nineteen years ago I discovered some evidence that my family had deceived the town of Piedmont. Committed fraud. My brother didn't want me to tell anyone, so he tried to kill me by hitting me over the head and pushing me in the river. He thought I drowned. When someone downstream saved me, I was too much of a coward to step forward and confront him. I remained dead to the world until last year." He looked at Justine, his face haggard with regret. "After I was believed dead I went back to New York and worked with the poor. In secret I kept track of you, and was reassured when I saw that that you were healthy and happy." He sighed. "I was a lowly pastor. Noel was wealthy. He gave both of you what you needed."

Justine felt bad. "Mother was wrong to choose comfort over love."

Thomas shrugged. "I was wrong to waste twenty years living in the shadows of your life — and the shadows of hers — watching but never engaging. If only I'd known how she truly felt . . . we could have been together." He pushed back his chair. "If you'll excuse me."

He exited the room and went out to the porch.

"I didn't mean to upset him," Justine said.

"Nor did I," Dorthea said. "But . . ."

"But?" Harland asked.

"You said that Thomas was the one true love of Mavis, and now I see that she was *his* one true love."

Justine panicked, not wanting to hurt their relationship. "They were only together for a short time. He's here with you now."

"But does he want to be here?" Like Thomas, Dorthea stood and left the room, escaping to the kitchen.

"I've certainly made a mess of things. I never — "

But then Thomas came in the front door, returning to the dining room. "Where's Dorthea?"

"In the kitchen," Goosie said.

He went to join her.

The remaining three remained still, eavesdropping — unsuccessfully — on their muted conversation.

Justine admired her father for not dwelling on his own troubles, but thinking about how Dorthea must feel. He was such a good man.

A few minutes later, the couple returned, holding hands. "Forgive my impulsive exit," he said. "I quickly realized how Dorthea might react." They exchanged a smile. "Mavis was not my one true love, for God has generously allowed my heart to be filled with love for Dorthea." He leaned over and they kissed.

They returned to their seats amid many happy congratulations.

"Continue your story, Jussie," Thomas said. "Was it odd seeing yourself in the past?"

She marveled at his ability to move on. "It was very odd. Having no memory of being so little was like watching myself in a dream."

"Did you talk to yourself — to the child?" Goosie asked.

"Briefly."

"Did she look at you oddly, like there was a connection?" Dorthea asked.

Hmm. "That's an interesting question, but no, she didn't." But then Justine remembered something. "But Papa did. When he was getting into the carriage, I called out to him — called out 'Papa' — and he looked at me, then touched the brim of his hat."

"As if acknowledging you?" Harland asked.

"I . . . I like to think it was so." She sighed. "Seeing him again was bittersweet. He died when I was eighteen, before I knew about you, Thomas. He was a good father. I don't mean to hurt you by saying that, but — "

"You don't," he said.

Justine set the portrait of her mother on the table. "What I found the most interesting in my travels — beyond the sentimental — was discovering that my mother was not a victim of Lionel Watkins in the sense of seduction. But she was a victim of his fraud."

Goosie held a finger near her temple. "Being unwise is better than being indiscreet." Her forehead furrowed. "Isn't it?"

Unexpectedly, Thomas drew in a breath, held it, then let it out.

"What?"

"I just realized that your mother had a history of using men to get what she wants."

This seemed a bit harsh, and yet . . .

"Forgive me," he said. "I shouldn't say such a thing."

His diplomacy helped Justine accept the truth. "Actually, there does seem to be a pattern. Think about Mother's life. When she was twenty she used Quinn to get out of Piedmont."

Thomas nodded. "She didn't care about my brother. She used him to get to New York City."

"But didn't he also use her?" Harland asked.

"He tried to," Thomas said, "but when he tried to take what he thought was due him —"

"As any man might assume from her willingness to run away with him . . ." Goosie said.

Justine didn't want to think about that. "The point is, she got to New York She got what she wanted, then discarded him."

"Quinn didn't care about her either," Thomas said. "I'm not sure my brother knew how to care for anyone. *I* loved her. I went after her and was there to help her when she had nowhere to go."

Justine continued the train of thought. "She used *you*."

His face grew pensive, then accepting. "She did. She used me — for a time. I adored her and was so happy she needed me that I didn't measure her motives. Or . . . if I did, I didn't care."

Justine extended her hand across the table. He took it. "I'm so sorry. You deserve someone who loves you with kindness and devotion." She glanced at Dorthea.

"I knew Mavis didn't love me as she should. Yet something good came from it. Something amazing and wonderful." He smiled at Justine. "You."

"Here, here!" Harland said, slapping the table for good measure.

Justine let out a happy sigh. "God is so good, bringing us together here. Now." She leaned forward. "And think of this: Mother mentioned she knew Dorthea's relatives in Lawrence. If she *had* managed to get away, she and I would have come here. Perhaps to this very house."

"Oh my," Dorthea said.

"It's as if you were destined to be here," Thomas said.

"One way or the other."

Harland laughed. "Our God is a God of details."

"He is never late and never early," Thomas added.

Goosie changed the subject. "But what about Lionel? You didn't catch him doing anything wrong."

"He stole the necklace," Harland said.

"No," Dorthea said. "Mavis willingly gave it to him. He defrauded her by keeping it for himself, but Justine didn't *see* him doing anything wrong at the hotel."

"I wish I had. The most I have against him is being disgusted by his character. He oozed charm, and dealt in inuendo and schemes. I witnessed the hold Lionel had on Caesar, but I don't think I was there for either of *them*. I . . . I was there for me." She looked at her family sitting before her. "I learned about Mother, my parents' marriage, and her choices. Not many people get such insight." She set her napkin on the table, folding and smoothing it. "In spite of our tenuous relationship in later years, I learned that when I was small Mother loved me above all others. She was never demonstrative. It wasn't her way to cuddle or coddle. But now I know she loved me and tried to do what was best for me — including staying with my father after he was injured."

"Such knowledge is a gift," Harland said.

She put a fist to her midsection. "I feel as though I've been strengthened by it."

"Perhaps you will need that strength in your other travels?" Goosie suggested.

She agreed. "God uses each step to prepare me for something yet to come."

Dorthea shivered and rubbed her arm. "Does that frighten you?"

"Very much so. But it comforts me to know that there's a purpose in everything I discover."

"That's heady stuff," Harland said.

She nodded. "For instance, I believe I just met Lionel at the beginning of his reign of evil. I believe subsequent trips will show me more about the darkness that took control of him and molded him into Uriah."

"Uriah, who is perhaps the most diabolical persona of all," Harland said.

"Why do you say that?" Thomas asked.

"Because he appears to be good and trustworthy. He wears a cloak of respectability. Evil that looks like evil is one thing, but evil that hides under the guise of good is far more sinister and dangerous."

Justine shivered.

"Don't go back again, Jussie," Dorthea said. "Sinister? Dangerous? I want you safe at home."

"I know you do," Justine said. "But I have to see this through."

Dorthea's face was pulled in serious thought. "We know the bad things Uriah has done here. You don't need to go looking into past sins."

"She's right," Thomas said. "We all know what kind of man he is."

They were missing the point. "*We* know. But no one in authority knows. There is no evidence against him, not enough to make him pay. I need to go back for Alva's sake, to keep her safe. For Virginia. For Caesar." She sighed. "This last time I thought I'd be going back to find out how he died, but God had other plans."

"You might never find that out," Dorthea said.

"*We* know," she said. "But we can't prove it."

"I don't like you going back again either," Thomas said.

"I have to. God wouldn't have started all this if there weren't evidence to be found that could bring him to justice.

He will guide me step by step and give me the knowledge I need."

Dorthea shifted in his chair. "If God wants justice, why doesn't He just strike Uriah down with His mighty hand?"

They all looked to Thomas.

"You're expecting me to explain God's actions?" He shook his head, then raised a finger and quoted the Bible, "'Thy mercy, O Lord, is in the heavens; and thy faithfulness reacheth unto the clouds. Thy righteousness is like the great mountains; thy judgments are a great deep.'" He spread his hands as though there was nothing more to say. But then he did speak. To Justine. "You're going. As often as God wishes you to go."

**

Dorthea and Justine headed out for the meeting of the ladies' church circle.

"I'm glad you're coming along," Dorthea said. "They will love meeting you."

Justine had to be honest. "I'm not going for the ladies, but for the lady. Alva. I want to hear first-hand how Uriah treated her after the funeral."

They turned onto the Benedict's block. "What are we going to do if he's hurt her?" Dorthea asked.

Justine shuddered at the thought. "I have no idea." She stopped walking. "Would you like to hear a selfish truth about today?"

"Of course."

"The truth is, I'd love to just stay home. I feel like I haven't fully moved here because I'm never *here*, I'm always in the past. I want to take long evening walks and talk about my wedding and our future. I want to play cards with you and Thomas, and laugh and make pies with Goosie . . . The only people I've really met are Virginia, Eddie Alva, Caesar, and Uriah—whose lives are all interwoven into what I'm learning in the past." She threw up her hands. "Everything is linked together but there are missing pieces. And I can't move on – I can't fully settle in – until I figure it out."

Dorthea put a comforting hand on her upper back. "I'm so sorry this burden has fallen on your shoulders. We want to help, but . . ."

"I know." And she did know they were willing, but there was little they could do. "Come now," Justine said. "Alva is waiting."

As they knocked on the door a fresh wave of sorrow sped through Justine as she remembered that Caesar wouldn't be answering. A much younger man opened the door. She wasn't surprised that Uriah had hired a replacement so quickly.

"Yes?" he said.

"We've come for Mrs. Benedict?" Dorthea said.

Suddenly, the door opened wider and Uriah stepped forward, causing the new butler to scuttle aside – with a distinct look of fear on his face.

"Good morning, ladies."

"We're here for Alva?" Dorthea said. "To take her to church circle."

He didn't respond. His eyes were locked on Justine's. And hers on him. It was disconcerting to realize she'd just seen him as Lionel. Gone was his charm and the easy mannerisms he used to lure and entertain. In their place was a sinister man with deliberate movements used to intimidate and ignite the nerves of all those in his presence. He knew what he was doing as Lionel and now, he knew what he was doing as Uriah – yet they were different objectives. So what was the all-encompassing goal that drove him? Caesar had mentioned Uriah's need for respect, but how did he gain respect by intimidation?

"Are you here for the same reason, Miss Braden?"

His question rattled her, but she quickly recovered. "Of course. I am here for Alva. I am always here for Alva." *Take that, you bully.*

Alva appeared behind her husband, as though waiting for him to make room for her to leave. She did not touch him and made no sound. She just waited. Justine thought of how *she* would act if Harland was in a doorway and she had friends outside. She would touch his arm, kiss his cheek, and brush past him with a happy, "Ta, ta! I'll be back soon!"

Uriah only turned toward his wife because he noticed the direction of Justine and Dorthea's gaze. He didn't speak to her, but stepped aside. When she passed him, she hugged the door frame so as not to touch him, as though she was reluctant to even have her skirt make contact.

The ladies drew Alva between them and hastened out to the sidewalk. Uriah did not say good-bye.

"Is he still watching?" Alva asked as they hurried down the block.

Justine glanced back. He stood at the top of the porch steps, his hands clasped in front, glaring at them. She could not stifle a shiver. "He is."

Alva grabbed her arm. "Don't look!"

Justine did more than look. She turned fully around and faced him, walking backwards. She offered him a two-fingered salute. *You will not intimidate me, Uriah Benedict.*

"No!" Alva whispered. "Don't do that!"

Justine turned forward — for her sake.

"You shouldn't taunt him," Dorthea said.

"He's a bully. Bully's respond to strength. They feed on weakness."

"You're wrong," Alva said. She walked even faster until they'd turned the corner and were out of sight of the house. Then she stopped and faced her friends. "I showed strength at the train station after we came back. He did *not* respond well. He . . ." She dissolved into tears.

The ladies comforted her and though the traffic on the residential street was light, Justine looked around for a discreet place to talk. There was a grouping of trees at the corner of a large house up ahead. She nudged Alva in that direction.

They stood behind the trees. Dorthea handed Alva a handkerchief, but Alva produced her own. "I am never without one."

A sad statement in itself. They waited until she'd composed herself.

"After Caesar's funeral Uriah pretended to be kind the rest of the day, but I knew . . . I knew it was false. It was as though he was waiting for me to give him a reason to react. I wanted to cry and grieve but I forced myself to keep it to myself." She touched Dorthea's hand. "I tried to be strong. I tried to remember how it felt to stand tall and not let him drown me."

Her shoulders were slumped, her gaze furtive, and her hands found comfort in each other. She looked broken.

"It will be all right," Dorthea said. "You can get that strength back again."

Alva shook her head, her face forlorn, making Justine wonder whether she could regain her courage. *Lord, replace her weakness with Your strength.*

"So what else did Uriah do?" Dorthea asked.

Alva nodded once, as though finding her mental place. "All day I pandered to him, asking Mrs. Russo to make his favorite meal, bringing in flowers from outside, making sure his cigars were stocked and his slippers and book were where they should be for his evening reading." She put a hand to her midsection. "My nerves were tied in knots. I could barely eat dinner. I just wanted to curl up in a corner and hide." She looked at her friends. "You have to understand that the anticipation of his wrath is just as painful *as* his wrath."

"Did he talk to you during the day?" Dorthea asked.

"Not at all—which is its own punishment. Yet it's also a mixed blessing. I tried to relish the silence—compared to him railing at me—but I knew that underneath the silence he was seething. Biding his time."

"Until . . . ?"

She leaned against a tree for support and drew two breaths before answering. "When it was finally time for bed and he retired to his room I was very relieved. That usually means that I will be allowed to sleep in my own room without fear of him coming to . . ." She glanced up, then down. Her eyes welled with tears. "Uriah doesn't care how I feel."

"Did he leave you alone that night?" Dorthea asked.

"Yes. And no." She began to pace beneath the trees. "I got ready for bed and had turned out the light and thought I was safe. Safe in body and safe to grieve. And so I began to cry for Caesar. Suddenly, the door to my room banged open, ricocheting off the wall." Her hands went to her mouth.

"Uriah."

She nodded.

"What did he do?"

She stared ahead as if seeing her words. "He stood in the doorway of my room, a silhouette against the light in the hall. He just stared at me for a very long minute. Then he walked away."

"Intimidation," Dorthea said.

"He's good at it."

"What did *you* do?" Justine asked.

"Nothing. I kept thinking he might come back and I didn't want to close my door and have him bang it open again. I slept with it open, praying for God's protection. Uriah didn't come back."

"He didn't need to," Justine said. "He had you scared. That was his goal. Is his goal."

Alva touched the tree bark, then pulled her hand away as if its texture was too rough for her. She seemed as delicate and sensitive as an open wound.

Justine made a decision. "We're not going to the circle meeting. We're going to our house."

Alva shook her head vehemently. "I need to go where I've told him I'm going."

"He doesn't need to know. We'll bring you back at the appropriate time." Justine offered Alva her arm. "Come now. You need a good cup of coffee and a piece of pie."

"Justine's right," Dorthea said. "You don't need to face a dozen church women where you'd have to put on a happy face."

Alva sighed. "You're right. I'm not up for that. Thank you."

**

Justine decided that pie and coffee should be considered a medical prescription, for after enjoying both, Alva's stress seemed to fade away. She even laughed.

During their second cup, Thomas walked in. "Well now. I thought you ladies would be at church."

"I could say the same of you," Justine teased.

"Pastor Karvins advised me to stay away when the circles meet," he said. "Too many opportunities for ladies to offer their opinions."

"You are cowards?" Dorthea said.

"I prefer to say we are wise."

Alva laughed. "I always wondered why Pastor Karvins stopped visiting our meetings."

Thomas put a finger to his lips. "Don't tell him I said anything."

"Your secret is safe with me." At the word "secret" her face clouded.

Thomas glanced at Dorthea and Justine, who each made a quick face to indicate things were not good.

"Alva, could I speak with you a moment?" Thomas said. "Being new . . . in private, if you please?"

"I . . . I suppose." Alva went with him into the parlor.

Justine put a finger to her lips. They heard voices, but could not distinguish what was said. When they heard Alva sobbing they jumped out of their chairs and rushed toward the parlor, but Thomas stopped them with a raised hand, wanting to finish his conversation. "Perhaps I could have a talk with Uriah on your behalf and —"

"No!" She looked at Dorthea and Justine, watching from the doorway. "No one can say anything to him about his actions or mine. No one! If you care for me, you must leave this be."

"You don't have to live in fear and worry," Thomas said. "You have friends who can help you."

"Who long to help you," Dorthea said.

"No. Please. Helping will hurt." Her jaw was tight. "Do. Not. Help." With that, she grabbed her hat and hurried out the door.

The three of them stood by the window. "Should we go after her?" Dorthea said.

"I don't think so," Thomas said. "I'm sorry to have interrupted and caused her to leave."

"You were just trying to help."

"What did she say to you?" Justine asked.

"She offered no details other than to say he frightens her."

"Uriah frightens *me,*" Dorthea said.

Thomas pressed his hands together. "She's balancing on a very tall fence right now. We're on one side and Uriah is on the other. If we do something wrong it could push her right into his arms."

"How do we get her to fall in our direction?" Justine asked.

Her father stared out the window and she watched the muscles in his jaw tighten. "I think the only thing that will help is for Uriah to be brought down." He turned to Justine. "The sooner you figure out the full extent of his crimes and find evidence to bring down justice against him, the sooner Alva is safe."

Dorthea stood behind Justine and took hold of her shoulders, leaning her chin against them. "Once again the burden falls on you."

"It can't be helped. I'll go. Now."

"No." Her father stopped her. "Yesterday's trip wore you out. Tomorrow is soon enough. As your father I have to insist."

"Plus, we have Virginia and Eddie coming to dinner tonight," Dorthea said.

Justine felt a wave of nerves at another looming burden. "I need to tell her that Spencer killed her father. I've put it off too long."

"Does she really need to know?" Dorthea asked.

"She does need to know because God showed me the truth." She looked to her father. "Isn't that right?"

He nodded slowly. Then he said, "The Bible says that what we learn in the dark needs to be shared in the light. Sharing truth is how we grow."

Justine sighed. "Unfortunately, there's a lot of dark to share."

CHAPTER FOURTEEN

Justine heard a buggy outside and ran to the parlor window. "They're here."

Eddie lifted Virginia to the ground. She looked very nice in a simple green dress with a lace collar. And he looked handsome in a vest and tie, with his normally unruly hair slicked down. He ushered her toward the house for dinner.

Goosie removed her apron. "Don't spy and hover, Jussie. It isn't polite."

Justine let the curtain fall as Dorthea answered their knock.

"Welcome," Dorthea said. "Come in."

Greetings were exchanged and Harland and Thomas offered them chairs in the parlor. Neither guest looked very comfortable, as if sitting in a parlor in Lawrence was foreign territory.

Perhaps it was.

Virginia kept plucking at the folds of her skirt. Her eyes flit around the room and settled on Dorthea. "You have a lovely home, Mrs. Jennings."

"Thank you," Dorthea said. "Please call me Dorthea."

"Dorthea," Virginia repeated.

Eddie's large frame looked uncomfortable in his chair. He fidgeted. "Do you all live here?"

"We do," Justine said. "Dorthea has been extremely gracious to let us stay."

"Nothing gracious about it," Dorthea said. "With my girls gone, the house needed family."

"Girls?" Virginia asked.

"My two grown daughters are off in Montana, having an adventure." She smiled at Harland. "But my boy is here and keeps me from being lonely."

"And Harland, a doctor," Virginia said. "You are very blessed to have your children doing so well."

Children! Justine looked at the others. It was clear she wasn't the only one who had just realized the talk of children might cause Virginia pain.

But Virginia didn't dwell. She turned to Eddie and smiled. "I don't know what I would have done without Eddie with me all these years. He's been my rock, seeing things I didn't want to see."

What an unusual thing to say. "What have you seen?" Justine asked.

Eddie gave Virginia a questioning look. There were obviously secrets between them. Delicate secrets.

"We can talk about it later, if you like." Justine said, even though she wanted to hear about it now.

"Thank you. You're very kind."

But still curious.

Harland took over the conversation. "I'm so glad Mr. Sutton allowed you to come to dinner."

Virginia chuckled. "He told me you'd asked his permission. But he isn't my keeper. I can come and go as I please."

"You can?" Justine asked.

"I thought you were . . . committed?" Goosie said.

"Technically," she said. "But when Mr. Sutton took the job, he realized I didn't belong at Ravenwood. He told me I could leave."

"Yet you stayed."

Virginia repeated her statement. "I can come and go as I please."

"But do you?" Thomas asked. "Come and go?"

Virginia and Eddie exchanged a look. "Not really."

"No need to," Eddie said.

"And honestly, no one ever invited us anywhere."

"Until now," Eddie added.

"When did you make the decision to stay?" Harland asked. "And why?"

Virginia smoothed her skirt over her legs and looked uncertain. Justine really wanted to hear her answer, but was afraid if she pressed, the story might never be told. And so, she waited in silence.

Virginia's hands finally stilled and she took a fresh breath. "I'll begin the story and Eddie can finish it." She looked to him for approval and he nodded. "It all started a few months after I got to Ravenwood. I received a letter from Spencer saying that the children had taken sick and died. *And* he'd sold the farm and was heading west."

"That was some letter," Harland said.

"What horrible news," Dorthea said.

"And all in one letter?" Justine asked.

"In one letter. It was the only letter he's ever sent me. Over the years I've waited to hear from him, but . . . nothing. I still find it hard to believe he just left me there."

"But he did," Eddie said.

"But he did. Of course I was devastated by the news. My babies, gone? How could that be? I wanted to go to the farm and talk to Cole and see . . . I don't know what I wanted him to see. I was so confused. My whole world had been torn apart. But the old superintendent, Mr. Roswell, he wouldn't let me leave. If I wasn't crazy before that moment, being stuck here after hearing such horrendous news . . ."

Eddie spoke up. "She couldn't go to the farm, but I could."

Virginia nodded. "Eddie went for me. But then . . ." She nodded to him. "You tell them what you found."

He sat straighter in his chair. "When I got there, no one was at the house at all. I looked in the windows and saw furniture, but no real signs of someone living there. I heard some animals so went to the barn." His eyes were on Virginia. "Ginny's brother was dead on the floor of the barn. He must have fallen from the loft."

"Another loss," Thomas said. "I am so sorry."

"We were very close," Virginia said. "I hate knowing that Cole was there through Anna and Luke's deaths, and the sale of our farm. Alone." She looked at her lap. "He died alone."

Eddie reached over and touched her arm. "I buried him in the family plot Ginny had told me about. That's where I found the graves of the children too."

Virginia drew in a sigh that was rooted in her toes. "Life as I'd known it was gone. My parents, my brother, and my children were all dead. My family home was sold without my permission. And my husband had left me in a lunatic asylum. I was broken. Why would I leave? Where would I go?"

No one had an answer for her.

The mention of Virginia's parents spurred Justine to want to share *her* news. "You have suffered so many tragedies, yet I . . ." Suddenly, she wasn't sure it was the right time. To tell her would spark more awful memories.

"Yet you . . .?"

Justine wiped a hand across her mouth. "I know who killed your father."

Virginia blinked. "Quantrill's Raiders killed him."

"Yes, but . . ." she looked to Harland for support. His nod spurred her on. "The man who actually shot him was someone you know."

She shook her head. "I saw him. I didn't know him."

"You didn't know him then, but would come to know him when . . . when you married him."

Virginia stared into the air. She took some deep breaths. "Spencer killed Papa?"

"He was going under another name then—Lionel Watkins—and of course he looked different with wild hair and a long—"

"Beard," Virginia said. She bit a fingernail, deep in thought. "If he . . .? Why would he come back into my life? Why would he want to marry me?"

"You'll have to ask him," Justine said. "Ask Uriah."

Virginia stood, then began slowly pacing between her chair and the door. The rest of them sat in silence. Justine couldn't imagine the emotions and questions careening through her mind.

"Ginny?" Eddie said.

She stopped pacing and shook her head. "So Lionel is Spencer is Uriah."

"Yes," Justine said.

She made fists at her side. "I want to talk to him. I want him to explain." She pointed toward the door. "Where does he live? I need to go see him."

Justine stood. "Not yet. We can't confront him yet."

"Uriah is dangerous," Thomas said. "We have to bide our time."

Eddie went to her. "I agree, Ginny. We can't rush ahead and—"

"Rush?" Virginia swept him away and stood defiantly near the door. "I have mourned my parents for sixteen years. I have mourned my children, my brother, and the loss of my family home. I have endured being thrown away at Ravenwood, unwanted and forgotten." She made a face, her beauty strangled by her pain. "And now I learn that an evil man who I loved, married me as a part of some sick plan? It makes no sense. I've wasted years tangled up in the vines of his scheme. I want answers. Now!"

The room reverberated with her final word.

Virginia took a breath, then looked at Eddie, then Justine, then the others. "But . . . I heard what you've all said. It's not possible to confront him, is it?"

"Not yet," Justine said. "We need proof."

"Aren't I the proof?"

Eddie led her back to her chair and sat beside her. "He deserted you. He hurt you. But—"

"That's not a crime," Goosie said.

Virginia pointed at Justine. "You say he killed my father." She paused. "How do you know that?"

I saw him? "It's complicated. I was hoping you could corroborate seeing him that night."

Virginia's shoulders stiffened. "I saw men. A man shooting. The same man riding off and saluting me. It's vivid, and yet the details aren't . . . ." She perked up. "If *you* say he was there I could lie and—"

Eddie took her arm. "No. You know you wouldn't do that."

She patted his hand. "Sometimes I wish I wasn't an honest woman."

They all jerked when there was a knock on the door. Justine answered it, and was shocked to see Alva. A disheveled Alva.

"May I come in? Please?"

Alva didn't enter the house, she fell into it. Justine caught her before she hit the floor.

Thomas and Harland were at her side in seconds and helped Alva into the parlor and onto the settee.

"Thank you, thank you," Alva murmured. Her eyes were closed as much as they were open.

Harland knelt beside her, taking her pulse. "Are you hurt?"

She shook her head. Hanks of hair had escaped her bun. She wore no hat, had no shawl. "I'm just rattled."

The door was still open. Thomas checked outside, then closed it. "Did you walk here?"

She nodded. "I ran."

Ran?

Dorthea sat beside her and took her hand. "What did he do to you?"

Alva breathed in and out with great deliberation. "He . . . we were arguing and he shoved me. . . I was at the top of the stairs. I only stumbled down halfway, but he *shoved* me."

"Like he shoved Caesar," Justine said.

Alva pushed herself upright. "He shoved Caesar down the stairs?"

Justine hadn't meant to say it aloud. "That's what we believe."

Dorthea nodded.

The ramifications of her husband's past actions in addition to his most recent violence made Alva hold herself and rock up and back. "Oh dear. Oh my. He truly wants me dead."

"We need to have Uriah arrested," Thomas said.

"Uriah?" Virginia stood. "Your husband is Uriah?"

"You know him?"

Virginia turned to Justine. "You said Uriah was my Spencer."

"Your Spencer?" Alva blinked and the two women looked at each other. "Who are you?"

She stepped forward. "My name is Virginia Meade. Spencer was my husband. I've only recently discovered that he changed his name to Uriah."

Alva shook her head, over and over. "I don't understand."

Justine knelt beside Alva's chair. "Your husband has assumed multiple identities in his life. One of them was Spencer Meade."

"My husband," Virginia repeated.

"I . . . I didn't know he was married before."

"Still is."

Alva's mouth gaped open. "What?"

"He never divorced me. He had me committed to Ravenwood and ran off."

Justine continued the story. "He took a new name and created a new identity, then came back as Uriah Benedict."

"Why would he do that?" Alva asked.

"That's what we're trying to find out," Justine said. "But at least partially — if not wholly — it's to distance himself from bad deeds."

"And crimes," Goosie added.

Alva waved her arms in front of her body, causing those who were close by to back away. "You're saying my husband is already married. He killed Caesar. And he's trying to kill me."

"Caesar?" Virginia asked. "Caesar Johnson?"

"Yes," Alva said. "He was our butler."

Virginia found her chair again. "He helped on our farm. He and his late wife lived with us. I liked him very much."

"So did I." Alva pointed at Justine. "She thinks Uriah killed him."

Virginia bit her lip. "You say he's trying to kill you?"

Alva suddenly stood. "I can't go home. Ever. I can't!"

Justine was glad she'd made the decision on her own. "No, you can't."

"You can stay here with us," Dorthea said.

Alva took a few steps. She limped.

"You hurt your ankle?" Harland asked.

She shook her head, her face tight with anger. "When I fell . . . *he* hurt my ankle. He's an evil man. He needs to pay!"

Justine was taken aback. Alva was no longer a victim. "He will pay," she said. "I promise you that."

"He's hurt too many of us," Virginia said. "We must stop him."

Alva nodded, then asked a looming question. "How?"

"Justine is handling it," Thomas said.

"She is?" Alva asked. "Why not one of you men? Uriah is strong and powerful."

Thomas stood beside Justine, showing his support. "Sometimes justice doesn't require physical, but rather, mental strength. Not brawn, but brains. Justine is the one. She will find the evidence we need — evidence that can't be refuted. And then your Uriah—"

"And my Spencer," Virginia added.

"And whatever other name he has used, will be brought before a judge in this world, and *the* Judge in the next." Thomas looked at all of them. "We promise you that."

The burden grew heavier as Justine's quest became more timely and essential.

**

Dinner was forgotten. Virginia and Eddie drove back to Ravenwood. The rest of them — including Alva — fell into bed, exhausted.

Yet Justine's sleep was furtive. Her dreams were plagued by the evil triad of Lionel, Spencer, and Uriah. Repeatedly, she forced herself awake to escape them.

But then, she was startled awake by pounding on a door — the front door. In the brief moment between asleep and awake she knew who it was.

Before retiring they'd discussed the probability that Uriah would come looking for Alva. They had a plan — one that involved physical strength. The men would handle it.

She got out of bed and checked the clock on the mantel. Midnight. Alva had come over before seven. It took Uriah five hours to come after her?

Justine tied a wrapper around her nightgown and went out to the hall. Harland and Thomas brushed past, toward the stairs.

"Stay out of sight," Harland told her.

The door to Dorthea's room opened, and Dorthea and Alva peered out. Harland pointed at them. "Stay inside!"

They took a step back, but stood in the doorway. The men hurried downstairs, their nightshirts tucked into their pants. Justine took a place in the upper hall where she could see what would happen next.

The men stood at the door. "Ready?" Thomas asked Harland as the pounding continued.

Harland detoured into the parlor and returned with the fireplace poker. He held it behind his back. "Ready."

Thomas opened the door and Uriah pushed his way in. "Where is she?" He rushed to the bottom of the stairs and yelled, "Alva? I order you to come down here! Now!"

Harland stepped between him and the stairs. "Alva is here and she's safe, but she's not coming home with you tonight."

Uriah seethed, his breathing heavy, his face splotched with red. "She's. My. Wife!"

Thomas moved beside Harland. "That, she is. But tonight she's staying with her best friend, Dorthea." He tried a smile. "The two of them had such a lovely time together, but once they got home . . ." He leaned forward confidentially. "Women need women friends." He shrugged.

Justine saw Uriah's face lose a bit of its frenzy. "Women are weak, pitiful creatures who want too much and don't do what they're told."

Really?

Thomas handled it well. "God made us different, men and women." He extended a hand toward the door. "Go home. It's late. Know that Alva is safe *here*."

The subtle emphasis on the last word was not lost on Uriah.

"What did she tell you?"

Justine wanted to step out and confront him, but the group had agreed to diffuse and delay. Justice would come later.

Uriah looked up the stairs. His face was drawn and haggard. Was he truly worried about her? He was probably *more* worried about what Alva would say about him.

A sound broke through the moment as the grandfather clock in the foyer chimed the quarter-hour. Without another word Uriah turned and walked out the open door.

Harland rushed forward and bolted it.

Justine ran downstairs, and moments later, Dorthea and Alva followed. Goosie came out from her room off the kitchen.

"You two were wonderful," Justine said. "You handled him just right."

Harland looked down and realized he was still holding the poker. He leaned it against the wall. "I'm glad we didn't have to use force."

Thomas ran a hand through his tousled hair. "I'm rather shocked he left."

Justine took his arm. "Your words were perfect. They calmed him."

Alva clutched the newel post as if needing its solidity to stand. "When I heard what he thinks of women . . ." she shook her head in disbelief. "I had no idea he thought so little of me. Of us. He hates me."

Dorthea went to comfort her. "I'm so sorry."

Thomas pointed upstairs. "Everyone get to bed. I'll sit up and watch to make sure he doesn't come back."

Alva shook her head. "I won't be able to sleep."

"Me either," Dorthea said.

Goosie walked to the kitchen. "Might as well heat up the dinner we didn't eat."

"And some coffee," Harland said.

Alva sat on the settee with Dorthea beside her. She looked up at Justine. "Please tell me about Virginia and her life with my husband."

Justine wasn't sure how that would make Alva feel better.

"Tell her everything," Dorthea said. "Just like you did with Virginia. She needs to know."

Thomas nodded. "Knowledge is power."

The long night just got longer.

Chapter Fifteen

Even though none of them had gone to bed until after two in the morning, everyone was up at seven.

Justine knew it wasn't ideal to travel into the past when she wasn't rested, but she had no choice. The clock was ticking. Uriah needed to be stopped. Swiftly and permanently.

Telling Alva about her ability to time-travel had been a risk. There had been three possible outcomes. Either she would reject the idea as ridiculous, accept the idea but be frightened by it, or accept it for what it was: a gift from God. Although skeptical at first — who wouldn't be? — Alva seemed excited about the heightened possibility of stopping Uriah. Justine was relieved, for she now had another person supporting her quest; another person who said they'd pray for her. How could such a situation be anything but positive?

With a glance in the mirror, Justine tucked a stray strand behind her ear. She noticed a crease between her eyebrows and pressed against it. "I'm looking old before my time."

So be it. She had — more important things to worry about.

Justine went downstairs and found Alva standing in the parlor, a newspaper in hand.

"Morning," Justine said.

Alva held out the paper. "Did you see this?"

On the front page of the *Lawrence Daily Journal* were ink drawings of two men. "Mayor Usher and Uriah. Why are they in the paper?"

"They're working together to develop some new area of downtown." She waved her own answer aside. "The point is, Uriah hobnobs with important men. There is no way we can win a battle against him."

Justine set the paper on a side table. "We can try." She took hold of Alva's upper arms. "We are David, setting off to beat Goliath. God worked that miracle, yes?"

"Yes . . . but none of us are King David."

"Neither was he at the time. He was a shepherd boy with a slingshot."

Alva's face lost a bit of its worry. "But . . . he had the power of God behind him."

"Exactly. Do not surrender the battle before it's even begun."

"I'll try to be brave."

"One day at a time," Justine said. *One hour, if necessary.* She retrieved Granny's shawl from the back of a chair.

"You're going now?"

"I am."

Alva pulled her into an embrace "I'm sorry you have to do this for me."

Justine pushed her back gently. "Not just for you. For Virginia, for her family, for my mother, for Caesar, and for all the other people he's hurt that we don't even know about yet."

Alva's expression was pathetic. "I know he is a difficult man, but I had no idea he was evil. At first he was utterly charming."

Justine remembered the charm of Lionel Watkins. "Uriah uses anything and everything to get what he wants. Nothing is safe from his influence."

Goosie came out of the kitchen, carrying something wrapped in cloth. "I thought you'd be heading out first thing. Here's a scone to take with you."

"You're too kind."

Goosie eyed her dress. "That's what you're wearing?"

Justine looked down at her simple tan skirt and bodice with a white collar. No bustle. One petticoat. It was more modest than the outfit she'd worn back to Bedford Springs. "Do I look all right?"

"Of course you do. I was just thinking about what people in the past will think of you, dressed so . . . plainly."

"My goal is that they accept me without question. That's why I don't want to dress up and risk standing out. I don't know how far back I'll travel but from what I know about Uriah's life, Bedford Springs was the only fancy place he lived. I think it's best to dress simply so I can blend in."

Goosie brushed her concern away. "You look lovely. Always lovely. And good." She pointed at the shawl. "I'm glad you have your granny's shawl."

Justine wrapped it around her arms. "I always feel better having something of hers along." She patted her pocket. "I've also collected a few old coins. Last trip I didn't even have a nickel." She slipped the scone in her other pocket.

"You've thought it through so thoroughly," Alva said.

"Each trip teaches me how to do it better the next time."

"How many trips have you made?"

Justine thought about it a moment. "Six from Piedmont — including a quick visit to Granny before we left, and today's trip will make the fourth from Lawrence. Ten."

Alva shook her head in amazement. "God must really trust you."

Justine felt uncomfortable with the praise. "I really trust *Him*."

Harland came down the stairs — and quickly sized up the situation. "Would you like me to take you to the cemetery and wait again?"

"No, thank you," she said. "I have the feeling I'm going to be going back multiple times this week. It's best I go by myself. You have patients." She smiled at him. "Isn't that marvelous? You have patients."

"Four, to be exact. I did promise to stop by and check on Mr. Carlsen this morning. He has a horrible cough."

She kissed his cheek. "Then we are both off and away."

Alva raised a hand. "I don't mean to sound selfish, but with you both gone . . . what do we do if Uriah comes here again? I'm sure he won't give up."

"We thought about that," Harland said. "Thomas has invited Pastor Karvins to the house for a meeting about some church repairs. A few male members of the congregation are coming too. If Uriah does show up, he won't dare make a fuss with all those witnesses."

Alva breathed deeply. "But what about after they leave?"

Goosie repeated Justine's suggestion. "One day at a time," she said. "We all need to pray that God erects a dome of protection around you, Alva."

"Thank you. That's very comforting." She looked at Justine. "Let's pray He erects one over Justine too."

Justine also found that very comforting.

**

With a prayer, Justine traced her fingers across Caesar's grave marker.

When she opened her eyes she immediately felt unbalanced. She reached for something to anchor her, and grabbed onto a railing.

On a boat.

Wooded wilderness edged the riverbank, spilling into the water with low branches and grasses. The leaves were gold and red and orange. Birds chattered at the boat's intrusion and two hawks soared overhead. She could hear and even feel the rhythmic swell of the engine, and saw steam disrupt her view of the sky.

I'm on a steamer. On a river. In autumn. But where? And when?

She spotted a couple strolling in her direction on the narrow deck. The woman held a parasol against the sun. Her skirt was wide and hooped and she wore a small brimmed bonnet with a flower marking the connecting point of each ribbon that tied beneath her chin. The man wore a long waistcoat, brocade vest, and top hat. Justine's fashion knowledge told her it was the 1860s. She was very underdressed in her simple skirt, blouse, and shawl. She stood sideways to allow them to pass, giving them a nod. The man did not tip his hat—which spoke volumes. They didn't take her for a fellow passenger.

So be it.

Once they had passed, Justine spotted another couple, talking to each other at the far end of the hall.

The man was Lionel Watkins.

She turned her back to him. If this was the trip her mother expected to take, then the year was 1860. Justine had just visited that year. She had just met Lionel at Bedford Springs. Would he remember her? Would it matter if he did?

His conversation ended, and Justine glanced down the walkway. The woman he'd been talking to approached, walking alone. She stopped near Justine. "Miss? Would you see if you could make me some tea, please? The motion of the boat is upsetting my constitution. Could you bring it to Cabin Three?"

Justine accepted the assumption that she was a servant. She bobbed a curtsy. "Of course, miss. Right away."

The young woman entered the covered portion of the ship. Justine had no idea where the kitchen was, but also made her way inside, tying Granny's shawl around her waist like an apron. They entered a narrow, open dining room. Justine approached a man wiping off the long tables and benches. "Excuse me? How do I get some tea made for a passenger?"

He gave her a once-over look, then grinned. "You new? I ain't seen you before."

"I am new." She had another question beyond tea. "Again, forgive me, but when will we get to . . . port?" Was that even the right term?

He cocked his head, looking at her warily. "We'll get to Kansas City tomorrow afternoon. You know that."

"I meant what time?"

"Due to dock at half-past two." He huffed on the back of a spoon, rubbed it against his shirt, and set it on the table. "Care to join me for dinner after? Kansas City can be a rousing place."

"Thank you, but my husband is meeting me."

His left eyebrow rose. "You have a husband?"

"I do."

"He lets you work on a steamer and be gone weeks at a time?"

It did sound odd. She thought of the only reason that seemed feasible. "He's been sick and can't work, so we need the extra income."

He flicked the cloth across the bench seats. "You's a good wife. I hope he feels better soon."

Justine relaxed. He wasn't a threat. He was a nice man. "Thank you . . .?"

"Will. And you're?"

"Susan."

He pointed with a fork. "There's a teapot in the kitchen. Tea's in a tin." He leaned forward. "Make yerself a cup. I'm not one to tell." He winked. "We'd better stop jabbering. They'll be coming in for luncheon presently. I'll be busy serving and you'll be busy cleaning cabins." He sighed. "I much prefer my task over yours."

Me too! I'm cleaning cabins? What she did for justice.

She went in the kitchen and saw two women cutting up food, and an older woman boiling something. "Hello," she said. "I'm new. A guest would like a cup of tea?"

The older woman sighed. "They's always wanting something." She pointed to a teapot. "It should still be warm. Help yerself."

Justine found a cup and saucer, poured the water, and put some loose tea in a silver infuser. She arranged a tray with a sugar bowl and a small pitcher of cream beside the cup. She added a spoon, a few crackers from a jar nearby, and a napkin. The arrangement looked quite presentable.

She took it out to the dining room and noticed the room was lined with numbered doors. She found Cabin Three and knocked.

There was a weak, "Come in."

Justine entered and saw the woman propped up in bed. With her bonnet off Justine noticed her hair was a beautiful auburn. She was very pale, her eyes closed.

"I'm so sorry to inconvenience you," she murmured.

"Not at all."

"Apparently I'm not as much of a boat person as I thought I'd be."

Justine brought the tea close. She helped the woman sit up, putting pillows behind her back. "Sugar? Cream?"

"I think it's best to keep it plain."

234

"That's probably a wise choice." Justine gave her the cup. "Is there anything else?"

The woman held the cup beneath her chin, inhaling the steamy aroma. "Could you . . . would it be possible for you to sit with me a short while?" The woman pointed at a chair.

Justine perched on the edge of the seat as she had seen her own servants do. "Take a sip, miss."

She blew on it, then sipped. Twice.

"Take a bitty bite of cracker too," Justine said. "It will settle your stomach."

She nibbled off the corner, then let out a breath. "I can already tell this will help."

Her positive attitude and sweetness made Justine like her immediately. "My name is Susan."

"My name is Helene. Helene Soames." She took another sip. "Very nice to meet you."

"And you." Justine remembered Helene speaking with Lionel. "Are you traveling with that handsome man you were speaking with?"

Helene's cheeks blushed. "I . . . no. I am traveling alone, but Mr. Watkins has taken me under his wing." She smiled. "His very handsome and charming wing."

Watch out for him! He can't be trusted! Justine tried to stay calm. "Sometimes charming men can be up to little good."

Helene's eyebrows rose. "Are you implying something about Mr. Watkins?" She pushed herself to straighter seating. "I'll have you know, Susan, that I am not as weak as I currently seem." She set her teacup on the bedside table and swung her legs over the side of the bed. "I've come all this way alone. Other than a cup of tea, I am very capable of taking care of myself. Thank you for your concern."

Justine stood. "I meant no offense. I only speak from my own experience."

Helene's body relaxed as she accepted Justine's answer. — She took the teacup again. "I am sorry to overreact. The truth is, I am very nervous about what awaits me in Kansas City. It wasn't right of me to take it out on your kind intentions."

Justine centered a vase on a nearby table, and dusted imaginary crumbs with her hand. "What brings you on this trip, Miss Soames?"

"The need for a new beginning. My parents were very ill and I've spent the past two years nursing them — sadly to no avail." She rested the teacup on her lap. "They both passed."

"I'm so sorry."

"As was I. But with them gone I realized I had put my life on hold for too long. I needed to get back to what I do best."

"Which is?"

Her expression changed to one of great joy. "I am a teacher."

"I am positive Kansas City can always use enthusiastic teachers."

"That's what I thought. Papa always wanted to go west. It was a dream of his, so I'm living it out *for* him. It turns out I have a friend who lives in Lawrence and — "

"Lawrence?"

"It's in Kansas actually, not too far from Kansas City."

"I think I've heard of it."

"I hadn't. Not until Wanda moved there and we wrote back and forth. Wanda is a childhood friend. She's the one who connected me with the principal at the school." She put a hand to her midsection. "I just realized my queasiness might not be caused by the boat at all." She let out a laugh. "Perhaps I'm just nervous about the unknown."

"You have a right to be," Justine said. "You are very brave to come all this way on your own. I commend you for it."

"You're very kind." She finished a cracker and took another sip of tea, then set the cup aside and stood. "I've kept you from your duties long enough. I do believe lunch is about to be served. Thank you, Susan, for your kindness and your willing ear."

Justine stood. "You're very welcome. If you need anything else on this trip — including a willing ear — let me know."

Upon exiting Helene's cabin, Justine saw the dining room was filling up with guests. She spotted Lionel coming out of a room. She noted the number: Fifteen.

Her immediate plans fell into place. Will had said it was time for her to clean cabins. If she could assign herself to his cabin she might be able to find her mother's necklace inside. Retrieving it would be an added bonus to the trip.

As the tables filled, she saw what looked like two servants standing at the far end. They were gathering towels over their arms and had a feather duster tucked in the waistband of their aprons.

She moved toward them and introduced herself, explaining she was new. She took up a duster and towels. A girl eyed Granny's shawl and handed her an apron. "Here."

Justine tied it over the shawl. "Where should I start?" *Please, God, please let me get Lionel's room.*

"You can help me with my rooms," said the apron girl. "You clean rooms eleven to fifteen. I'll start on the other end, and—"

Thank You, God. "I'll start on fifteen, all right?"

"Suit yerself."

The other maid grumbled. "What about helping me?"

"I'll help you tomorrow," Justine said.

The girl shrugged and they dispersed. Justine slipped into Lionel's room. It was identical to Helene's, nice but not fancy. She quickly replaced the towels by the washstand and flicked the duster here and there. She made fast work of the bed. Then she looked in the bureau drawers, pressing down on the neatly-folded clothes.

She felt it.

The necklace was wrapped in a handkerchief!

But then the handle of the door made a sound.

The door opened.

She dropped the necklace to the rug.

Caesar walked in. He looked at her, then at the necklace. "What are you doing?" He grabbed it up, then did a double-take. "You were at Bedford, hiding behind a plant. Yelling at me for stealing when I wasn't—"

The door opened again and Lionel walked in.

Justine wanted to hide under the bed. Jump out the window. Have God take her away.

He looked at Justine, then at Caesar, then at the necklace in Caesar's hands. "Stealing again, Caesar?"

"No, sir."

He glared at Justine. "So it's you doing the stealing?"

Her stomach flipped.

Lionel stepped forward and got in Caesar's face, snatching the necklace away. "Remember, I can throw you overboard any time I want and no one would miss you."

Justine hated to see the fear on Caesar's face. She stepped forward. "I'm not stealing either, sir. I was cleaning your room and a shirt was sticking out of the drawer so I opened it to make it tidy. I pulled it out to refold it and this handkerchief came out with it, and the necklace . . . it fell on the floor. I was just picking it up when your man came in. He was protecting your property, sir. Honest, I wasn't taking anything. I was just tidying up."

Suddenly Lionel blinked. He studied her. Then smiled. "Miss Miller?"

Her heart sank. How could she explain her presence here?

"Yes sir?" Maybe if she ignored their connection . . .

He tossed the necklace on the bed and strolled close, circling her like a tiger sizing up its prey. "How odd that we literally bump into each other a few weeks ago in Pennsylvania and now I find you here, in my room, nearly a thousand miles away? Are you following me?"

You have no idea. Her nerves tingled. "It *is* very odd, sir. What a coincidence." She shook her head, acting shocked. "I actually spotted you earlier and thought, what are the odds that I take a job on a steamboat where you're a passenger?" She shook her head, hoping she was convincing. "Are you enjoying your trip, sir?"

He seemed momentarily taken aback by her explanation, yet couldn't refute it. There *was* no explanation other than one beyond his comprehension. He said, "I *am* enjoying it."

It was time to get out of there. Fast. "Very good sir." She picked up the used towels and headed to the door. "Let me know if there's anything you need." She quickly left just as the other maid came out of her first cabin.

"How ya' doing?" the maid asked.

"Uh . . . I'm managing well enough."

"Move on then."

Move on. If only she could move far away from Lionel Watkins. Instead she put his used towels in a canvas bag, retrieved some new ones, and set off to clean another cabin.

**

Justine stood with the other servants, out of sight of the passengers as they ate their dessert after dinner. They chatted among themselves and a few ate this or that, taking advantage of their free minute. Justine ate a chicken drumstick — with her fingers — something she'd never done. Ever. Her lack of manners couldn't be helped as she was famished. After cleaning five cabins, she'd helped sweep the deck and had dusted pretty much everything not hidden away. She had acquired *some* physical endurance the last year, but setting the occasional table, washing dishes, helping with laundry, or making her own bed did not prepare her for a full day of labor. Goosie's scone was long gone.

Will stood beside her, his eyes on the diners, ready to hop-to it if they needed something. "Don't let anyone see you eating like that." He nodded at her greasy hands, then pointed to her chin.

She wiped it off with the edge of her apron.

"We'll eat as soon as the up-and-ups are finished. You can't wait?"

She nodded toward a few others, who were eating a roll or chicken wing. "What about them?"

When he shrugged she quickly finished the meat and tossed the bone in the rubbish bin nearby.

"Rumor is you're a good worker," Will said.

She felt an odd pride. "Thank you. I'm trying."

He looked at her, then at the direction of her gaze. "You seem mighty interested in Mr. Watkins."

Lionel was sitting at the one of the long tables, with a couple seated across from him. Helene sat beside him.

So much for Helene heeding my warning.

Will continued. "He is a handsome cuss. Even I can see that."

"He is." *Even I can see that.*

"But I figure any one of us blokes could look mighty handsome if we had the right duds."

She nodded. "Clothes do make the man."

"Aye. That's a good one. You make that up yerself?"

"I believe Mark Twain said it. Or Shakespeare or . . . I don't remember."

"Never heard of 'em."

Justine watched Lionel and Helene. He was extremely attentive, gesturing with his hands, making the other three laugh. He was a good entertainer, the sort Mother would have invited to every party to prevent dull conversation. His ease was inconsistent with the man he became. Uriah presented himself as a statue and chose his words carefully and with little inflection. The notion that he would ever — could ever or had ever — made anyone laugh was . . . laughable.

Reluctantly she admired Lionel's ability to transform himself in body and persona to another man, another *type* of man. If he'd gone on the stage, his name would have graced every marquee on Broadway.

Helene hung on his every word as though . . . he was witty like Twain or eloquent like Shakespeare. Again the comparison with Uriah popped up: Uriah witty? Uriah eloquent? Never.

Lionel looked toward Justine and she panicked. Will stepped into action, noticing his raised finger. As Will received his instructions, Lionel's eyes met Justine's.

He winked.

She shuddered.

**

Justine didn't have time to ponder Lionel or Helene, as her post-dinner evening was spent cleaning up and assisting various passengers with this and that. She was resigned to continue her surveillance the next day, when she spotted Helene heading back toward her cabin.

Helene's eyes lit up and she motioned Justine close. "Yes, Miss Soames?"

"Could you help me, please?" She pointed to the seam at her waist where her skirt connected to the bodice. "I caught the hem on something out on the deck, and when I walked away, it began to rip at the waistband. Mr. Watkins was a gem and helped get the hem loose, but the damage is done, and I need to change."

It had to be nearly ten o'clock. "So late?"

Her expression turned conspiratorial. "Lionel has asked me to meet him on the deck so we can 'ponder the sky and all the heavenlies.' Those were his exact words. I love a man who can express himself so eloquently."

The consummate actor, who knew his lines too well. "But it *is* getting late."

Helene gave her a disgusted look, making Justine know what it felt like to be her pupil. "Once again, Susan, you overstep."

"Once again, I apologize."

They went into Helene's cabin and Justine helped her change. The moony way Helene responded to Lionel made Justine wonder if she had any experience with men.

While Justine was buttoning the back of her bodice, she asked, "Did you have beaus back home, Miss Soames?"

"Not many. With my parents ill, all I could manage in my free time was reading the occasional book. *That* was my education. My only society was church on Sunday. Suitors weren't interested in the unpredictability of my situation. They wanted someone to court *now*." She looked at herself in the mirror. A strand of hair was loose.

"I'll fix that," Justine said, finding a hair pin.

Helene stopped fidgeting and studied her reflection while Justine secured the strand. She put a hand to her neck, then her cheek. "I am thirty. I've missed my best years. All my friends are married with children."

Her candor was touching. "Was that another reason to leave home?"

Her nod took Helene back to the present. She faced Justine. "I want someone to think I'm special—who makes me feel special. I want romance and love and marriage and a family. I want it *all*. Is that so wrong?"

Justine's throat tightened, realizing that Helene's desires matched her own. "It's not wrong at all."

With one last glance at her reflection, Helene went to the door. She paused with her hand on the knob. "What if I'm supposed to want something different?"

"Than a family?"

She nodded.

"I suppose if that's the case you'll get sent down a different path."

Helene smiled. "Have you ever thought that free will isn't free? That there are consequences?"

"I have. And there are. So tonight be care—"

Helene turned the knob. "Wish me luck."

She would need it. "Would you like me to come back later and help you get ready for bed?" Justine asked. *I need to see that you're all right.*

"I may be late so that won't be necessary."

Justine didn't like the mischievous glint in her eyes.

**

As it was at Bedford Springs, so it was on the steamer: Justine had no place to sleep. She sat in a chair in the shadows of a deserted deck, not wanting to be found. She was too exhausted to come up with a new story regarding why she was there.

Suddenly, her head fell off her hand and jolted her awake. She had no idea what time it was.

She walked to the railing and looked at the dark riverbank. The black water was churned up by their movement, and offered a fractured reflection of the moon. She felt the vibration of the steam engine and heard its rhythm disturbing the starry sky. She looked up to . . .

Ponder the sky and all the heavenlies.

Lionel. Helene!

She hurried along the decks to see if they were still there.

The decks were empty.

She went into the dining room. The glass sconces were turned low. She walked to Helene's room, put her ear to the door, but heard nothing. Hopefully, she was sleeping.

As Justine should be. Who knew what tomorrow would bring?

She was just about to return to her chair, when she decided to walk past Lionel's cabin. She was nearly there when she heard a stifled scream. Then scuffling. And moans of pain.

Justine softly — but incessantly — rapped on the door. "Miss Soames?" she whispered.

Nothing. Then from inside, "Yes. Please. Help!"

Justine knocked again. "Open up! Please!" She didn't know what to do. Should she get help? To knock more loudly would rouse the other passengers. Should she involve them? Or was there a way to help without — ?

The door swung open. Lionel stood before her with his shirt draped outside his trousers. His dark hair fell onto his face. "Good evening, Miss Miller. Have you come to collect Miss Soames?"

Justine rushed past him and found Helene on the floor. She was dazed and was slow to pull her dress down over her petticoats. "Help me up. Please."

Justine helped her to standing. Helene's hair was half-down, her cheeks flushed.

"Are you all right?" Justine realized her question was ludicrous. Of course she wasn't all right.

Helene leaned on her, heavily. She whispered something, but Justine couldn't hear.

"What did you say?"

Helene tried to stand more erect. She glared at Lionel. "He assaulted me."

Assault was too vague a word, but Justine didn't press. She had to get Helene back to her cabin. "Come with me."

Lionel stood nearby, watching them go. He lit up a cigar, sending acrid smoke into the air.

"How could you?" Justine hissed.

He blew out the match and shrugged. "Now I can say I've had a schoolteacher. But note this, Miss Soames, *you* have a lot to learn, and I would be happy to teach you."

Helene broke from Justine's grasp and hurled herself at him, pounding on his chest. She called him names Justine had rarely heard.

Lionel wrapped an arm around her waist and carried her bodily on his hip. He opened the cabin door and dropped her outside.

"Next?" he said, glaring at Justine.

She pointed a finger at him. "With God as my witness, you will get what's coming to you, Uriah."

His eyebrow rose, then he pushed Justine outside, and closed the door on them both.

Helene was on the floor, sobbing. Justine heard voices in a nearby cabin and needed to get out of sight. She helped Helene to her feet and led her back to her cabin, closing the door behind them.

Helene immediately fell onto her bed, turned on her side, and pulled a pillow close. She spoke unintelligible words as she cried.

Justine didn't have any experience with sobbing women. She poured a glass of water. "Here. Drink this?"

Helene leaned on her elbow and drank greedily. She handed the glass back to Justine.

"He raped me."

Justine grasped for words. "I'm so sorry."

"More than once."

What?

Helene pushed herself upright, letting her legs hang off the side of the bed. She searched for a handkerchief in her pocket, but found none. "Please?" She pointed to the bureau.

Justine found one in the top drawer. Helene wiped her eyes and nose.

"We need to tell the captain," Justine said.

Helene shook her head adamantly. "No! Please don't do that. We can't do that."

"He has to pay."

With a groan Helene stood and began pacing from the bed to the bureau and back again. "I was stupid. I flirted with him. I was flattered by him." She stopped walking to look directly at Justine. "You warned me about him."

"Can you tell me what happened?"

Helene returned to the bed, crumbling the handkerchief in her hands. "I met him at the deck and we looked at the stars and moon—just like he said. But then he wanted to walk. He was so delightful. I remember thinking what a fine gentleman he was."

"He's no gentleman."

She blew her nose again. "After a short while he said he wanted to show me a book of poems by Elizabeth Barrett Browning." She looked at Justine. "I love her *Sonnets from the Portuguese.*"

Justine had a copy. "'How do I love thee? Let me count the ways . . .'"

"Exactly," Helene said. "He knew most of it, but then neither of us could remember the rest, so he said we should go to his room and look in the book."

Smooth. Very smooth.

"We went to his cabin, and I immediately had second thoughts about going inside. So I said I'd wait for him. He teased me, made a game of it, looking both ways, putting a finger to his lips. It was rather . . . exciting. So I went in. Stupidly, I went in."

Justine didn't want to pry for more details. She got the gist of it.

But Helene continued. "We looked up the sonnet and read it together. Then he leaned over and kissed me. When I pulled back . . ." The rate of her breathing increased. "He didn't stop. The more I struggled the more he liked it. He threw me to the floor and . . ." She wrapped her arms around herself. "After the first time, I was numb and hurting. I didn't know what to do. I struggled to stand, to leave, but he threw me back down again and . . ." Her face was pathetic. "I wanted to scream as loud as I could, but he put his hand over my mouth." She touched her face. "He pressed so hard I can still feel his hand there."

Her cheek did have a red impression. "I'm so sorry." Justine wished she could think of words that would actually help.

"I'm such a fool. I enjoyed his attention. I encouraged it."

Justine needed to put a stop to her guilt. "We women are taught how to flirt. We're groomed to draw attention, and strive to encourage men's interest." Justine's ability to entice men was fine-tuned by her mother. "Interest is one thing. You did *not* ask to be raped."

This seemed to get through to her. But then Helene began crying anew. "I didn't want my first time to be like this. Now I'm ruined. He ruined me forever."

Justine's anger grew. "We need to tell the captain. We're landing in Kansas City tomorrow. He can call the police and have Lionel arrested."

Helene thought about this for the briefest moment before shaking her head. "It's his word against mine."

"I can be a witness to what I heard and how I found you."

She shivered. Her jaw tightened. "I'm starting fresh. A new town, a new job. I can't begin that new life with a trial hanging over me. A trial that will result in everyone knowing what he did to me."

Had Helene pressed charges? Or had she let Lionel off the hook? Either way, Justine couldn't interfere.

"Please don't tell anyone," Helene said. "I can't have this hanging over me. I just want to move on and forget it ever happened."

"*Can* you do that?"

Helene breathed in and out, tears flowing down her cheeks. "I don't know. I don't honestly know."

**

Helene finally slept and Justine dozed in the chair beside the bed. She awakened to the sounds of voices outside the cabin.

The clock said twenty after eight. It took Justine a moment to register whether it was morning or night.

Morning. Passengers were probably filing in for breakfast.

She gently shook Helene. "Miss, miss? It's time to get up. They're serving breakfast."

Helene opened her eyes groggily, then with a moan hugged a pillow. "I don't want to get up. Or eat. I want to stay here."

Perhaps that was the best place for her.

Helene hugged the pillow tighter. "You have been so kind to stay with me. But go now. I don't want you to get in trouble."

"I'll check back with you soon." Justine smoothed her own clothes, tidied her hair, then opened the door. No one was looking in her direction so she slipped out and hurried toward the exterior walkway.

As she turned right, she nearly ran into—

"Miss Miller," Lionel said. "We have to stop meeting like this."

She stepped away from him.

"Sleep well?" he asked with a grin.

If evasion didn't work . . . Justine stepped toward him, getting close enough to see the lines around his dark eyes. She kept her voice low but intense. "You are an evil man, Lionel Watkins. How dare you take advantage of that wonderful woman. You will pay—"

He grabbed her upper arm and dragged her to a doorway, pushing her out of sight. He leaned close. His breath was foul. "Remember what I said to Caesar when he crossed me?"

Her throat went dry.

He squeezed her arm tighter. "Do you?"

She nodded.

"Never forget that I can throw you off this boat and no one would ever know you're missing. Or care." He glanced over his shoulder. "Perhaps now would be a good —"

She pushed past him and ran down the walkway.

And back to the future.

CHAPTER SIXTEEN

After visiting the steamboat in 1860 and returning to the cemetery, Justine walked home. Her thoughts were spinning, her body was weary, and her spirit was wounded. Yet the combination fed upon itself and solidified two truths: the man who was Uriah Benedict was evil. And God wanted her to stop him.

Actually, three truths. "God will use me to stop him."

A man painting a picket fence near the street looked up, obviously overhearing her words.

"Sorry," she said.

He nodded and got another brush full of paint. "'Put on the whole armour of God, that ye may be able to stand against the wiles of the devil.'"

She stopped. "What did you say?"

He blinked. He cocked his head. "Nice day, isn't it, miss?"

She hesitated. Had he really talked about battling the devil? "It is a beautiful day," she answered.

He nodded and kept painting.

Justine walked on, smiling to herself. Once again, God had provided just what she needed, when she needed it.

By the time she got home she was energized. "Family? I'm back!"

They all came running. "You weren't gone long," Alva said.

"Actually, I was gone overnight."

"What?"

Justine didn't want the logistics of her travels to overshadow her discoveries. "Please sit." Once everyone was settled, Justine began without preamble. "Uriah is evil. Pure evil."

Harland raised a finger. "We knew that."

"You knew some of his crimes."

"You saw more?" Thomas asked.

There was no nice way to say it. "He is a rapist."

Everyone gasped — except Alva.

"Alva?" Harland said softly. "You don't seem surprised."

Her chin dropped. She looked at her lap. Her upper body folded in on itself like a wilting flower.

Justine's heart sank. Alva had told them Uriah didn't care about her feelings, but her reaction now — mirroring the body language of Helene — implied so much more.

Justine looked at Harland, trying to speak with her eyes. He nodded slightly and stood. He tapped Thomas on the shoulder and they quietly left the room.

"It's just women here now," Justine said.

Dorthea touched Alva's arm. "Has he forced . . .?"

After a pause, Alva nodded.

"He shouldn't do that," Dorthea said. "Ever."

"I know, but . . . he's my husband."

"Who is supposed to love and honor you," Dorthea said.

Justine stated the obvious, "It's not right."

"It's not," Goosie said. "I don't have to be married to know that."

Alva stopped looking at her lap. "So what am I supposed to do? Fight him off and risk more pain? Scream and have the entire household know?"

It was a good question. Although Justine and Harland had not been intimate, she knew their love-making would be . . . love making.

Alva sat up straighter. "I am not ignorant. I know it's wrong, and I wish it was different. But it . . ." Her countenance fell. "Isn't." She drew in a deep breath, as if dispelling the subject. "You said my husband raped someone in the past?"

Justine hesitated.

"Tell me the details," Alva said. "I deserve to know."

"Yes, you do." Justine needed the men to know what she'd witnessed. "May I call them back?" When Alva nodded, Justine called out to Harland and Thomas.

Harland peeked around the kitchen door.

"Come back in, please," Justine said.

They returned, warily looking at Alva. It was clear they expected her to be sobbing. "We're so sorry for what you've been through," Harland said.

Thomas nodded. "If there's anything we can do . . ."

"I'm stronger than I look." Alva raised her chin. "But not as strong as I want to be."

"We are with you," Dorthea said. "All the way."

Wherever that way would go.

Alva nodded her thanks. "Enough about me. Justine, tell us what happened in the past."

Once again, Justine was amazed at the strength of Uriah's victims. Her own courage paled when compared to that of Alva and Virginia. "I went back to 1860, and ended up on a steamboat on the Missouri River, heading to Kansas City. Lionel was there. And Caesar."

"You got to see Caesar?" Alva asked. "How was he?"

"Under Lionel's thumb."

She could only nod.

Thomas had a question. "Was it the trip you and your mother were supposed to take?"

"I have no way of knowing for certain, but it proves that he had no intention of taking us along."

"Selfishly, I'm glad for that," Thomas said. "If he had taken you away, we wouldn't be here now."

Very true.

"What did Lionel do on the boat?" Goosie asked.

"He befriended a schoolteacher who was coming to Lawrence to teach."

"Befriended?" Dorthea asked.

"Charmed. And lured her into thinking he was a gentleman."

"As Uriah charmed me into thinking the same," Alva said quietly.

"In the evening, I heard her screams and . . . I found her on the floor of Lionel's cabin, disheveled and crying. I helped her get away from him, back to her room." She let them fill in the details according to their own sensitivities.

"How horrible," Dorthea said.

"Did she report it to the captain?" Thomas asked.

"I told her to, but she wouldn't. She said it was Lionel's word against hers."

"Was she badly injured?" Harland asked.

His question brought up another. "If there had been a doctor on board, and if she'd gone to him, would he have testified on her behalf?"

Harland hesitated. "I don't know. Rape makes people squeamish."

"Squeamish?" Alva stood. Her voice turned ragged. "It hurts body and soul. It hurts!"

Justine felt tears threaten. Uriah had raped two women — and how many more?

Dorthea drew Alva back to her seat and wrapped an arm around her shoulders.

"I apologize," Harland said. "I didn't mean to upset you. *I* take it very seriously. It's just that, not all doctors do." He looked at Justine. "Honestly, even if she had reported it to the captain, he might not have done anything."

"And the reporting would have made Lionel angry," Goosie said. "He might have sought revenge."

Justine shuddered, remembering his threat to throw her overboard.

Alva composed herself, sitting upright, letting Dorthea's arm fall away. "You said the victim was a schoolteacher coming to Lawrence. What's her name?"

"Helene Soames."

Alva's face lit up. "I've met her once. She teaches at Riverside School. You need to talk to her."

"Yes, I do." She was amazed at God's provision. "I never thought it would be so easy to find her."

"Thank God for that," Goosie said.

"I do. Completely."

Alva stood, but looked tentative. "Should we go now? I could introduce you."

Justine admired — and appreciated — her offer. "Are you sure?"

Alva hesitated, then said, "We're both his victims. Perhaps we could help each other."

"That's very noble of you," Dorthea said.

Justine stood, ready to go, then felt a wave of weakness. She sat back down. "This may seem trivial, but I really need to eat something first. I haven't eaten since dinner last night."

"Breakfast today," Thomas said. "A few hours ago."

The timeline *was* hard to follow.

Goosie coaxed Justine out of her chair. "Hungry is hungry. Would you like dinner or breakfast?"

**

After having some coffee, bread, and ham, Justine was ready to meet Helene Soames.

Harland drove her and Alva to the Riverside School. Although they could have driven themselves, Justine was glad for his company as north Iowa Street was beyond her scope of knowledge.

The stone school was nearly square, fifteen or sixteen feet on either side. The windows and front door were open and they spotted children of various ages inside, huddled together, most likely working with other children in their grade level.

They spotted Helene helping some of the youngest ones.

"I never thought about school being in session," Justine said.

Harland pointed to a table with benches outside. "We can wait."

Justine was not good at waiting, but they had no choice.

They were just sitting down when Helene appeared at the door. Her auburn hair was tinged with gray—not surprising since she was nineteen years older than the last time Justine had seen her. "May I help you?"

Justine wished she'd given more thought about what to say to her. She approached with Alva at her side. Harland took up the rear. "Sorry to disturb you, Miss Soames," she said.

"Mrs. Soames."

Mrs.?

Helene looked past Justine and nodded toward Alva. "We've met, haven't we?"

Alva smiled. "We have. We both worked at booths during the harvest festival. I'm Alva Benedict."

"Yes. I remember you. You were in a church booth selling baked goods."

"That's right. And you were selling pencils as a fundraiser for the school."

Helene nodded. "It's nice to see you again." She looked at Justine and Harland. "Have we had the pleasure?"

Harland stepped forward. "We have not. I am Harland Jennings, and this is my fiancé, Justine Braden."

Justine was happy to distance herself from Susan Miller.

"So what can I help you with?" Helene asked.

Alva looked at Justine, giving her the reins. "If you have a moment, I'd like to ask you a few questions about something that happened nineteen years ago."

Helene's eyebrows rose. "That's a long time past. I arrived in Lawrence around then."

"I know."

Her eyebrows rose. "You've certainly piqued my curiosity, Miss Braden."

"I'm sorry to be so vague, but I'll explain in full when you have some time."

Helene consulted a watch that hung as a necklace. "I'm sure the children won't mind if I call for lunch a few minutes early. Wait here."

She returned to the school and cheers were heard as she announced that lunch would begin. The children rushed outside and sat in the grass, opening their tin lunch pails.

Helene shooed two boys away from the table, so the adults could sit in privacy. She was still a pretty woman, though there were lines around her eyes and mouth. She sat on one side with Alva, while Harland and Justine sat across from them.

"There now," she said. "Let's take advantage of the peace. You wanted to ask me about something that happened in the past?"

How to begin? "I realize this is out of the blue, Mrs. Soames, and may seem intrusive, but please know it's very important."

"Very," Harland said.

"It sounds ominous."

"I'm sure it does, but . . ." Justine decided to get to the point before the children demanded their teacher's attention. "The year we're interested in is 1860. I . . . I am sad to say I know what happened on aboard a steamer ship, between you and Lionel Watkins."

Her fair skin grew mottled. "I don't know what you're talking about."

Alva angled her body toward her. "We apologize for intruding on your day — on your life. And I know the subject of our inquiries is upsetting . . ."

Helene studied Alva's face, then looked to Justine and Harland in turn. "Why are you doing this? Can't you just leave well enough alone?"

"I wish we could," Justine said. "But . . ." She blurted it out. "We know the man who assaulted you."

Helene opened and closed her mouth multiple times as if fighting the words she wanted to say, against those she would say. Then she stood. "I need you to leave."

"No. Please," Justine said. "Please hear us out."

Alva extended a calming hand. "I married the man who raped you. He's done the same to me."

Helene stood in the awkward space between standing and sitting for many seconds before sitting down again. "Then I pity you."

Alva nodded. "I don't want your pity. I want justice for what he did to you, and for other crimes — so many other crimes."

Helene's breathing turned heavy. Finally she asked Alva, "Do you have children with him?"

"I do not. I want children, but not —"

Helene nodded once. "Not with him. Believe me, you are better off."

Alva was clearly caught off guard. "I suppose you're right, but—"

Helene sighed. "Forgive me. I have grown too frank for anyone's good. Your marriage is none of my business. As far as my own dealings with him, God gave me the strength to move on. I have no wish to rehash the past."

Her mention of God gave them common ground. Justine leaned on the table between them. "But *I* know that God is leading me on a quest to bring Lionel Watkins to justice. To do so, I need your help."

Helene cocked her head, then looked to Alva. "You are married to him, but your last name is Benedict, not Watkins."

"Lionel has changed his name frequently," Alva said, nodding at Justine. "First to Spencer Meade, and most recently to Uriah Benedict."

Helene sucked in a breath. "I've heard of him. That man is Lionel?"

"He is," Justine said. "He's committed many crimes under many names. It's my job to put a stop to it. To him."

Alva's voice was small. "He's tried to poison me."

"Tell her about Caesar," Harland said.

"Caesar?" Helene perked up. "He had a manservant named Caesar on the boat."

"It's the same Caesar," Alva said. "He died last week. We are nearly certain Uriah killed him."

Helene pressed a hand to her forehead as if trying to make the information stick. "How can I help you now? I didn't report his crime against me." She looked down, making a fist. "After all these years, I have nothing to offer you but a tale that he will most certainly refute. I'm very sorry."

Justine knew she was right. "As usual, there is no concrete evidence against him."

Helene glanced toward the children. Their time was short. "I only told one person about it: a young woman who helped me that night and stayed with me."

That was me!

"I tried to find her the next day, but I lost track of her on the boat. Then we landed in Kansas City and I fled, wanting to get as far away from Lionel Watkins as I could. I think her name was Susan something."

Susan Miller.

Justine felt Harland's stare. He understood the implications. The only person Helene had confided in was Justine. Who couldn't testify.

A ball flew past them as many of the children were finished eating and were playing tag and tossing a ball back and forth. Their time was up.

Justine rose. "Thank you for talking with us. I'm sorry to intrude and to bring up bad memories."

"I can see that it was necessary." Helene turned to Alva. "I'm sorry for your current pain. Get out. Get away from him any way you can."

Alva nodded. "I'm trying."

Helene walked toward the school, then turned. "How did you know about any of this? As I said, I only told one —"

Suddenly, she looked at Justine in an odd way. "You resemble that Susan woman."

Justine's stomach flipped. "I do?"

Helene shook her head. "It's been nineteen years but . . . hmm," Helene said. "How odd."

Indeed.

**

After dinner, Harland and Justine found refuge on the porch swing. As usual, he sat on the left, she on the right.

"This has become our place," Justine said, setting the swing in motion with her toe.

"What will we do when it's snowy out? Where will we go?"

She sighed deeply, but it was all for show. "I guess we'll have to cuddle in front of the fire."

"I don't think so. My mother and your father might claim that spot."

"Then we'll have to get a house of our own."

He stopped the swing. "Our own? Are you ready to get married?"

She put a hand to her heart. "I'm ready in here. But . . ."

He sighed. "You still have work to do."

She slipped a hand around his arm and leaned her chin against his shoulder. "There *will* be an end to all this. I *am* making progress."

"Mmm."

She pulled back to look at him. "I found Helene."

"Another victim who can't or won't testify against him."

She got up from the swing to face him. "What do you want me to do? I have no control over where I travel to, or when."

"I know." He patted the swing and she returned to it.

"I have to hold onto my faith that God has a reason for each trip. In the end, none of it will be without a purpose. Nothing that happens is wasted."

He raised his arm so she could slip beneath it. "Stand firm. Your work for the Lord is not in vain. Keep doing what He asks you to do."

Justine nodded against his chest and they swung up and back. Up and back.

She let herself drift with the motion and was almost asleep when he said, "After we marry . . . I will never . . ."

She wasn't sure what he was talking about.

"I will never force you."

She snuggled against him. "I know you won't." That's all that needed to be said on the subject.

But it brought to mind something else. "I detest being a witness to such wickedness. Sometimes I long to be the ignorant, naïve debutante again." She sat upright. "I was so oblivious and carefree. And now . . . I hate what I've seen."

"I wish I could travel with you, to protect you."

She liked the essence of that, yet shook her head against it. "I have God to protect me."

He looked taken aback. "Well then."

She took his hand. "I don't mean that as an insult."

He chuckled. "I know God's protection is far superior to any I could offer you." His face grew serious. "But because I love you, I hate for you to suffer or be frightened. Ever."

"I don't particularly enjoy it either. I feel so ill-equipped."

He nodded. "'Put on the whole armour of God, that ye may be able to stand against the wiles of the devil.'"

She sat upright. "Where did those words come from?"

"The Bible."

She pointed down the street. "On the way back from the cemetery I was walking past a man painting a fence and he said those exact same words. Out of nowhere. I wasn't even talking to him. He just said it."

"How did you respond?"

"I didn't. I stopped, but then he commented about the weather, as if he hadn't just talked about armor and God and the devil at all."

"I love when God does that."

Of course! "It was Him, wasn't it?"

"There is no other explanation."

"Are there more verses about armor?"

"There are, but I don't know them by heart." He stood. "Just a minute."

He went inside, returned with a Bible, and sat next to her. "I think it's in Ephesians." He searched and quickly found it. "Ephesians six . . . it's verse eleven. But it continues."

"Read it."

"'For we wrestle not against flesh and blood, but against principalities, against powers, against the rulers of the darkness of this world, against spiritual wickedness in high places.'"

"That makes me shiver."

"'Wherefore take unto you the whole armour of God, that ye may be able to withstand in the evil day, and having done all, to stand.'"

"This isn't calming me," she said.

Harland read silently ahead. "It tells you how God's equipped you. You're to wear a belt of truth and a breastplate of righteousness.'"

"I'm far from righteous."

"You have integrity and are pursuing justice with God behind you. That makes you righteous." He continued, consulting the verses. "Your feet will be fitted with shoes that help speed you on to share God's gospel of peace."

"Armor and peace? That doesn't fit."

He raised a hand, stopping her interruptions. "You will use faith as a shield to stop Satan's fiery arrows, and you'll wear the helmet of salvation and use the sword of the Spirit — which is God's Word."

She wrapped her arms around herself, staring past the porch, past the yard, past the street in front of her. "This really is a battle."

He nodded. "The final instruction is to pray for yourself and others." He closed the Bible.

"If I was overwhelmed before . . ." She shook her head. "This is more serious than I imagined, Harland. I have the feeling Uriah's sins are worse than those I've dealt with before, worse than those of Quinn Piedmont and his ancestors."

"Quinn was evil too. He tried to kill your father. His great-grandfather killed an entire family."

Justine shuddered. "Uriah has killed at least three times: Virginia's father, Caesar, and another man that Caesar told me about."

"And he raped Helene."

"And Alva," she added.

"And committed Virginia against her will."

"Yet he is revered in town. His picture is on the front page of the newspaper."

"All the more reason for him to be brought down." Harland put a hand on the Bible. "If Uriah isn't worse than Quinn, he's certainly more prolific."

"And I'm not done with him yet," she said. "There's more for me to see. Uncover."

"Is there? Perhaps you *are* done."

She shook her head with utter certainty. "I'm not done until I find proof against him." She was exhausted at the thought of it. "Tomorrow I need to go again."

"You could wait a day or two."

Justine stood. "I can't. Alva is safe here — for the moment. But time it ticking . . ." She took his hand, pulled him to standing, and wrapped her arms about him. "Pray for me, Harland. Pray I'm strong enough to fight this battle."

Or battles.

**

Justine sat at the desk in her room and took out the Ledger. She had three more life-lines to add to the list.

The first, from her mother. She carefully wrote: *Mavis Tyler Braden 1860: "A woman who reveals too much of her body, reveals too little of her mind."*

Justine smiled at the memory of Mother saying this many times as she was growing up. Justine had resented each and every time. Especially when she was sixteen and having her coming out party. The dressmaker had come to the house for a fitting of her elaborate white, custom-designed dress. While Mother and Mrs. McKenzie chatted, Justine turned down the neckline to reveal more bosom. She'd been thrilled that she actually had cleavage.

Thrilled until the women stopped talking and saw what she'd done. Mother yanked the neckline where it belonged. "Don't be cheap, Justine. A woman who reveals too much of her body, reveals too little of her mind."

At sixteen Justine didn't much care if young men cared about her mind. She just wanted their attention. But the neckline remained modest and Justine was better for it.

First, her mother, then her father's wise words: *Thomas Piedmont 1879: "God is never late and never early."* She found much comfort in God's perfection.

Now for the words of another woman.

Justine made another notation: *Helene Soames 1860: "Free will isn't free. There are consequences."*

Helene had learned this the hard way.

Justine remembered asking her father, Noel, a question about free will. "Wouldn't it be better if God just ran our lives and didn't give people choices? The world would certainly be a better place."

His answer had stayed with her all these years. He'd put a finger under her chin and had gazed into her eyes. "But what's the good of that? Choosing to do the right thing has far more value than being forced to do it."

He'd been such a good man.

Justine honored him by adding *his* life-line to the list.

CHAPTER SEVENTEEN

"Jussie?"

At the sound of her name, Justine opened her eyes.

There was a knock on her bedroom door. "Jussie?" It was Goosie.

"Yes?"

Goosie opened the door. "Breakfast is ready and—" Upon seeing her, Goosie cocked her head. "Did you sleep in that chair all night?"

Did she? Justine pushed herself erect. "I guess I did."

"Why?"

Her reasoning would sound odd. "The last two nights I slept on a bench at Bedford Springs, and in a chair on a steamboat on the Missouri River. The bed was too soft. I couldn't get comfortable."

"Nonsense." Goosie opened the curtains and the window. A morning breeze took advantage, making the curtains flutter. "You must take care of yourself." She nodded toward the bed. "After breakfast I want you to go back to *bed* and get a proper sleep."

Justine stood, causing a quilt to puddle to the floor.

Goosie picked it up and folded it. She glanced at the desk. "You wrote in the Ledger?"

"I did. Four more entries."

Goosie put the quilt in a quilt rack. "Not only are you seeking justice, but you are logging the knowledge of the ages."

"Just a few bits, here and there."

"They're important, Jussie. You're carrying on a family legacy."

She nodded and stretched. Her muscles were sore, but she didn't want to admit it. "As for going back to bed. No. I'm not doing it. I have to leave again."

"So soon? Surely God can give you a day off."

"If He wants to, He will. Until then, I need to stay on task."

Goosie picked up the skirt and blouse Justine had worn into the past the day before. She gave them a good looking at, even putting them to her nose. "Smells like river."

"I wasn't on the steamboat *that* long."

Goosie put her hands on her hips. "Long enough to sleep in a chair." She draped the clothes over her arm. "I'll wash these." She turned toward the door.

"But I was going to wear them—"

Goosie paused. "Even the past deserves a clean dress now and again." She eyed her. "And a clean body? I'll heat some water on the stove for a bath."

Actually, a bath sounded glorious. But Justine felt an urgency stirring. "I'll take one after today's trip."

Goosie sighed dramatically. "Yes, you will. Either that or we'll ask you to move out. Speaking of move . . . get a move on. I made flapjacks and they're getting cold."

**

Justine would never admit it to Goosie, but it felt good to wear a fresh skirt and blouse. Her next foray into the past would be accomplished wearing pink.

As she descended the stairs she heard voices from the dining room. And laughter. *I'm fairly sure there's no laughter where I'm going today.* She felt a twinge of envy, but quickly discarded it. She was glad for the normalcy of their lives. Even Alva seemed happy.

When she reached the bottom of the stairs, she started when she noticed a shadow coming toward the front door. *Uriah?* She relaxed when she realized the silhouette wasn't tall enough. *I'm seeing him everywhere.*

As expected, there was a knock. "I'll get it." She opened the door to find a man in uniform. "Yes?"

He held his hat in his hand. "Pardon me, miss, but my name is Officer Crandell. I'm here to see a certain Alva Benedict. If you please?"

Although his manner was polite, Justine was wary.

Thomas came to the door. "Officer?"

While he repeated his request to see Alva, Justine backed toward the dining room and made a motion for Alva to get out of sight. Out of the corner of her eye she saw the women scurry — into the kitchen.

"Why are you making this request?" Thomas asked.

The man looked rather embarrassed, but pulled a folded sheet of paper from a pocket. "This here's a warrant for her arrest."

"Arrest?" Justine said. "For what?"

The officer handed Thomas the page. "Desertion. Filed by her husband, Mr. Uriah Benedict. I'm here to take her in."

Harland joined them and they looked at the paper together. "This is highly irregular."

"That's what I —" The officer's face flushed. It was clear he didn't want to be there. "That's for the courts to decide."

It sounded like a parroted line, not his own.

"Courts?" Justine returned to the foyer. "That's absurd." *Uriah's the one who needs to be tried in court.*

The man shrugged. "I have to do what they sent me to do. You can come to the police station and argue with Chief Bonner if you want." He made a face. "Though I warn you that he and Mr. Benedict are rather chummy."

"Of course they are," Justine said, under her breath.

"What if we refuse to let you have her?" Thomas said.

Good, Thomas! "Yes," Justine said. "What if we refuse?"

The officer linked his index finger in his collar, as if it was suddenly too tight.

Justine pretended to look beyond him. "Are you alone?"

He stood taller — which wasn't very tall at all. He and Justine looked eye to eye. "There's others coming."

"That's a l—"

Thomas silenced her with a hand. It *was* probably best not to call a policeman a liar.

Thomas pointed outside. "Wait there. Harland and I will come down to the station with you."

"But the woman — ?"

"Will stay here until we speak with someone in authority. Higher authority."

Officer Crandell stepped back to the porch while the men put on their suit coats.

"*Doctor* Jennings and *Pastor* Hill will be with you in a moment," Justine said from the doorway.

His face turned ashen and he mouthed *Pastor . . .?*

It was almost comical.

If it weren't so serious.

Suddenly Alva strode out from the kitchen. "I am Alva Benedict. I will go with you to fight this absurd accusation."

"You don't have to do that," Justine said.

Alva took her hat off the coat stand. "I believe I do." She looked at Thomas and Harland. "But I *would* appreciate your company."

"Of course." To the officer Thomas said, "Would you give us a minute, please?" He closed the door. "Everyone stay here. Lock the doors. Do *not* open the door to anyone. No one leaves until we get back."

"Except me," Justine said.

"You should stay here too," Harland said.

She shook her head. "The best way I can help Alva is to get Uriah arrested. I'm going back again. Now." She was surprised when they didn't argue with her. Their faith in her was comforting, yet added to her burden. *It all depends on me.*

On Me, God whispered.

Goosie busied herself in the dining room a moment. She handed Justine some flapjacks in a napkin. "You can't get justice on an empty stomach."

Justine kissed her cheek. And Harland's. And her father's. "Go!" she said. "So I can go." To the women she said, "Pray!"

**

On the way to the cemetery Justine ate two flapjacks and put a third in her pocket. It was best to be self-sufficient in the past as much as possible.

She knelt before Caesar's grave marker and prayed for protection—and information. She traced his name. And was gone.

She was relieved to find herself somewhere familiar. She stood outside Virginia's farmhouse. The flowerbed was filled with daffodils. Out front was a wagon and a riderless horse. Anna and Luke played tag nearby.

They looked a bit older than when their mother was committed. It had been summertime during Justine's last visit. Was it the following spring?

Anna waved at her. "Hello."

Justine approached the wagon—which was filled with trunks and boxes. "Hello there." Although she knew the answer to the next question she wanted the children's point of view. "Where is your mother?"

"She's been sick a long time," Luke said. He drew on the ground with a stick.

"She doesn't want us anymore," Anna said.

Her words cut deep. "I'm sure that's not true." Justine pointed to the back of the wagon. "Where are you going?"

"Papa says we're taking a trip with some very nice people."

Virginia hadn't mentioned her family taking any trip.

"Where is your father?"

Luke pointed to the barn. "In there. With Uncle Cole."

Justine remembered that Virginia had sent Eddie to the farm after hearing about the children's deaths. He had found Cole in the barn.

Found him dead.

And the children dead and buried!

They all were alive right now, but would they soon be dead?

Yet Spencer's letter had said they'd gotten sick and died. But here they were, healthy, and on the verge of leaving on a trip.

An awful thought occurred to her. *They never were sick. Their father killed them!*

Would Spencer kill them now? Was the trip a lie?

Would Spencer be the only one leaving?

Justine didn't know what to do first. She couldn't interfere in the past, yet she couldn't watch while a father killed his children.

She knelt down to their level and motioned them close. "Do you know the place where your grandpa and grandma are buried?" She pointed towards the grove.

Luke nodded. "We used to pick flowers for them."

"When Mama was around," Anna added. "Haven't done that in a long while."

"I want you to run down there and stay. Don't come back to the house until I come get you and tell you it's safe."

Anna's forehead crumpled. "Safe?"

Justine forced a smile. "It will be all right." *Oh, Father, let it be all right!* "But you must do as I say. I promise I'll come get you."

Anna looked toward the barn. "What about Papa?"

"I'll tell your papa where you are."

They looked doubtful, but ran off toward the grove.

Justine said prayer for their safety, interrupted by shouting in the barn.

She rushed to a barn window and looked inside. At first she couldn't see anyone until their voices drew her eyes upward, to the loft.

. "Why did you sell this place?" Cole demanded.

"Because I'm done with it," Spencer yelled. "Done with all of you."

"It's not for you to sell," Cole said. "It's our family homestead. It's our legacy. It belongs to Virginia and me."

"Virginia's my wife. What's hers is mine." Spencer chuckled. "Besides, she's crazy. She's in the madhouse forever."

Cole got in Spencer's face, standing a half-head shorter and fifty pounds lighter. "She doesn't belong there, and you know it. You have to let the children and I visit. At least do that."

Suddenly Spencer took Cole by the shirt and lifted him up until they were face to face. "She's there until I say she isn't. I told you, she doesn't want to see any of you. She's too far gone." He let Cole loose and the young man stumbled to regain his footing. "I'm in charge here. I get what I want, and I want to be gone from this mediocre excuse for a farm. In case you haven't noticed, farming's not for me. Not for you either, if you're honest with yourself."

"Then why did you come here in the first place? Why did you marry Virginia?"

Spencer rolled down his shirt-sleeves. "You really want to know this? Now?"

Cole stood strong. "I do."

Spencer sighed. "I guess there's no need to keep it secret any longer. I was impressed with Virginia the first time I saw her, standing up to me by the field that night, raising her fist to me after I killed your father."

Cole took a step back. "What?"

Spencer tipped an imaginary hat then said, "Tally ho, boys!"

Cole's face was ashen. He stumbled backward. "That was you?"

"Sure was," Spencer said. "It was quite a night. *Quite* a night."

Cole fell to his knees.

Spencer used a piece of straw to pick his teeth, then made a sucking sound. "After the war and being with the James-Younger gang a while I needed to start fresh. The law was getting too close. I remembered that feisty girl who stood up to me, and your nice farm here. I knew your father was dead. Virginia would be of marrying age . . ." He shrugged. "I came back to the area, did some digging, and discovered that you and your sister were running this place alone. And not being very successful at it, neither. You needed a real man to take over." He grinned. "In every way."

"You calculating, murderous scum."

Spencer shrugged again. "That's one of the nicer names I've been called. But one name I've never been called is *fool*. You and your sister are the fools here. I cut my hair and put on a few manners and you accepted me into your lives. For the longest time I was afraid one of you would recognize me, but you never did. Truth be, I never planned to marry Virginia — just have a bit of fun with her — but when I realized I could own the farm by getting hitched I figured why not? But I never wanted them kids." He shuddered. "They are nothing but a bother."

Cole glanced outside, like he was listening for them.

Justine prayed the children would stay in the grove.

Cole's face was drawn and pitiful. "I introduced you to Virginia. Coming back from Eudora you helped me move a tree in the road. I invited you to dinner."

Spencer arched his back as if in pain. "Yeah, pulling that dead tree into the road did something nasty to my back."

"You . . .?"

"Planned it? Yes, again." He leaned down to look at Cole eye to eye. "You see how I get what I want? I'm always a step ahead of ya. Of everybody." He stood and stretched as if he hadn't a care in the world. "Cole, my boy, there is no stopping me. So get off yer knees and get yerself outta here. New owners are moving in soon."

Cole stared at the door to the barn. "I thought you were taking the kids for a visit to your family, out west."

"Out west is right. But I don't have any family." He tossed the piece of straw on the floor. "I don't need family."

Cole struggled to his feet. His shoulders were slumped in defeat. He was spent. But then —

With a scream he rushed toward Spencer.

Spencer grabbed him by the arms as if he was a pesky kid.

And tossed him off the loft.

Cold landed with an awful thud.

Justine clapped her hands over her mouth.

Spencer peered down at his victim. Blood pooled under the young man's head. "I gave you a chance to leave, you stupid chump. Your choice. What a tragic accident."

He stepped down the ladder, stepped over Cole's broken body, and headed out of the barn. Justine quickly hid behind some hay bales. *Father, what should I do? I don't want him harming the children!*

Children's voices!

"Papa!"

They ran to him from the direction of the grove.

Justine's heart pounded. Should she show herself? Jump in front of the children?

Leave it be.

Leave it be? Surely God wasn't telling her to leave it be?

Spencer grabbed Luke by the scruff of his neck. "Where ya been? Didn't I tell you to stay put?"

"The lady . . ." he said before his father shoved him away.

"The lady told us to go play by the graves," Anna said.

"What lady?"

"Mama's friend, I think."

Spencer looked around. "Where is she?"

"Papa, why are there stones with our names on them?"

Justine nearly fainted. *I'm sorry, God, but I can't just let him kill them! I have to —*

"Get in the wagon. Now. We need to go."

Go? They are going?

The children were too slow climbing into the seat so Spencer virtually tossed them onto the platform. They quickly sat, leaving room for their father.

He pointed at them. "I'll be right back. I have something to get in the house. Stay put!"

Go! Now!

Justine had one chance to stay with the children. She ran to the wagon and climbed in the back, hunkering down among the luggage, pulling a tarp over herself.

Just seconds later the front door slammed. But then she heard more than one set of feet upon the porch.

"Did you get Cole's stash of cash, Caesar?"

Caesar!

"Yessir. But won't Mr. Cole be needing — ?"

Spencer chuckled. "Mr. Cole won't be needing nothing. Ever again."

Justine heard Spencer's *oomph* as he got on a horse. Then the wagon jostled. Was Caesar going to drive the wagon?

"Where we going, Papa?" Anna asked.

"Shush."

"Is Uncle Cole coming too?"

"Quiet! Head out, Caesar."

The wagon began to move.

**

Justine had never prayed so much in her life. Her prayers alternated between prayers of thanksgiving that the children *hadn't* been killed, prayers that they *wouldn't* be killed, and prayers of sadness for Cole's death. Every time the wagon slowed, she worried this would be the place where she would be discovered or where Spencer would carry out some new form of evil. Her fears were so overwhelming that her prayers evolved into *Help us, help us, help . . .*

The wagon turned onto a rougher road. The sounds of other travelers lessened.

Caesar began to sing in a rich baritone. "'Michael row de boat ashore, Hallelujah! Michael row the boat ashore, Hallelujah!'"

The children sang along. They seemed happy enough. Justine tried to relax. As long as they were singing they were all right.

Until . . . Caesar started the third verse. "'I wonder where my mudder deh, Hallelujah! I wonder where my mudder —'"

"Stop that nonsense right now!" Spencer said. "If you can't speak proper English, I don't want to hear it."

That was the end of the singing.

A few minutes later . . .

"Slow up," Spencer said. "And you chits, not a word."

The wagon stopped. Justine heard Spencer's horse come around to the back of the wagon, where it was joined by another.

"Mornin'," a man said. "You Mr. Meade?"

"I am."

"I'm Joe Trotter." He lowered his voice. "Those the children, Mr. Meade?"

"They are."

"Nice lookin' young 'uns."

"I need the address. And the money," Spencer said.

"Whoa. Hol' up there, Mr. Meade. What's yer hurry? I got both right here, but—"

"Speed it up," Spencer said.

Trotter hesitated. "This ain't the way I do things."

"Then we're done."

"Fine!" Trotter said. "Fine, Mr. Meade. Have it your way."

Then oddly, Spencer called out to Caesar: "Sing. All of you, sing. Now!"

Caesar and the children continued the song where they'd left off.

But then there was an odd sound, a soft *whiz*. Then a *whomph*. Then . . .

"Ahh! Why'd you go and—?"

Then there was a loud thump on the ground. Groans.

Someone dismounted. Justine heard another whomph sound, and another.

And then she knew that the sounds were someone being stabbed. More than once.

Spencer killed the man? Why?

"Drive on!" Spencer called out. "I'll catch up."

The wagon began to move. Justine had to see what had happened. She lifted the top of the canvas and peered out. Spencer was digging through the pockets of the man. He found a piece of paper and stuck it in his own pocket. And some money. Then he dragged the man into the thicket at the side of the road, and rolled him into it. He slapped the man's horse, which ran through the field.

Then Spencer Meade got back on his horse and caught up with the wagon.

He even joined in for a verse of the song. "'Sinner row to save your soul, halleluiah. Sinner row to save your soul . . .'"

Such a dark, dark soul. Poor Joe Trotter.

**

The wagon stopped. Justine heard Spencer dismount. "Get down," he said.

At first she thought he meant *her*. But she felt the wagon gyrate as Caesar jumped down.

"Here's the address."

"We're gonna take 'em to this address and do what?" Caesar asked softly.

"Just let 'em off. And there's no 'we' to it. You're doing it."

"But you're their pa. Don't ya wanna say goodbye?"

Spencer's voice deepened in intensity. "Do *you* want to say goodbye? If you do, I know a fine place to dump you by the side of the road where you won't be lonely."

"I'm fine."

"I thought you'd be."

"But . . .why did you . . . do that, to the man?"

"He said my name too much."

"What?"

"Truth is, I shoulda used a different name for all this. But when I first met Trotter, I was introduced as Spencer Meade, so I had to go with that. To distance myself from them, I told him the kids' last name was Dawson, said their parents are dead. But him saying my name, over and over . . . he asked for it."

"Dawson? Their parents are dead? I don't understand."

"I've explained too much already. You don't *need* to know nothing. Go on now. There's a saloon on the west side of Topeka, the Sally-O. Meet me there with the wagon when it's done."

"Will the young'uns be alright?"

"Not my concern."

"But they're your kids. Good kids."

"I never wanted 'em. I'm doing a good thing getting 'em to someone who does. Aren't I?"

"Sure. I guess."

Thank You, God! He didn't kill them! They'll be safe!

"Go. Get it done. I'm thirsty."

Justine heard him mount his horse and ride away — without a single word to the children.

She also heard Caesar whisper from close by. "I'm so sorry, Lord. I didn't know he was gonna kill the man. Please watch over Anna and Luke. I hope they gets a good family."

A good family? As in adoption? On impulse, Justine pushed the tarp aside and sat up.

Caesar grabbed his chest and took a step back. "Miss? Miss Miller? Whatcha doing in there?"

She stood—her muscles objecting. She held out her hand. "Help me down."

The children looked back at her. "The lady! The lady!"

"Hello, there."

"We told Papa there was a lady."

"He didn't listen."

I thank God he didn't listen.

"Why are you back there?" Caesar asked. He looked behind, the way they'd come. "Did you see?"

"Heard. The man did nothing wrong."

Caesar bit a fingernail. "There's no rhyme or reason to his killing. Truth is, you don't cross the mister."

She lowered her voice, not wanting the children to hear. "Mr. Trotter wasn't crossing him. He was friendly. Talking."

"Like I said, no rhyme or reason."

Justine couldn't get the image of a dead Joe Trotter out of her mind. "Spencer pulled him into some brush in the ditch. We can't leave him there."

Caesar nodded. "I'll go back and bury him. There's a shovel in the back here."

"That would be good of you."

He cocked his head. "You musta got in, back at the house?"

"I did."

"Did you see Mr. Cole? I never told him goodbye."

It was a time to be frank. "He's dead. Spencer threw him off the loft."

A deep crease formed between Caesar's eyes. "They've been arguing something awful. And when the mister told me to pack our things—and the children's, I knew it wouldn't go over well with Mr. Cole. But killing him?" He shook his head. "No rhyme or reason." He seemed to realize time was passing.

"If I'm gonna bury . . . I'm supposed to meet Mr. Meade, and first I gotta take the young'uns to their new ma and pa."

"Adoption?"

"Yup."

"That's good. Where are you taking them?"

He pulled out the address and read it aloud. "Amos and Lar—"

He held the paper for Justine to see. "Larraine." She realized she had a treasure in her hand. "May I?"

"You coming with us?"

"Yes."

"I'd appreciate the company. You'll have to hold Luke on your lap."

"Gladly."

She stepped up to the seat, snuggled the little boy, and put her free arm around Anna. These poor children. Being tossed away as though they were worthless property.

And yet . . .

They were alive.

**

An hour later they turned onto Greenwood Street in Topeka. There was a short row of simple houses, not as nice as Dorthea's, but nicely kept. A few trees had been planted but it would be years before they provided much shade. Large trees were something Justine missed from Piedmont. New England had a hundred-year head start.

She consulted the piece of paper, then pointed to the second clapboard home on the right. "There it is."

Caesar stopped the wagon. "Looks nice enough."

"It does."

"You want to go up to the door and handle it?" he asked her.

"I don't think I should." Caesar needed to be the one. "I'm just along for the ride."

He sighed. "Not sure how they'll take to a Negro knocking at their door."

You did it the first time. You need to do it again. "Go ahead. You're bringing them two lovely children. They'll be happy to see you."

"Children they paid to take."

"Which means they really wanted them." She *could* go along as a witness. "Perhaps I will go with you."

"I'd like that." He hopped down and extended his hands to Anna. He lifted her to the ground, then got Luke. Then he helped Justine step down.

"What's here?" Anna asked Caesar.

He knelt beside her and drew Luke close. "This is your new home."

Her little forehead crumpled. "But I wanna go to *our* home."

"You know you can't, sweetie-girl. Your daddy sold the place." He nodded toward the wagon. "He's moving away."

"You'll stay?" Luke asked.

"Nope. I'm goin' with yer pa. Don't know where we'll end up, which is why you need to stay in this very nice house with—"

The door opened and a fortyish woman came out, followed by a tall man. A girl of ten stood behind them.

"Well, well," said the woman with a smile. "You must be Anna and Luke."

The children nodded.

Caesar stepped forward. "I'm Caesar and this here is . . ."

"Susan," Justine said. "We've come to see the children get settled."

The man stepped forward. "We're the Krupmans. I'm Amos, and this is my wife Larraine." He drew the little girl forward. "This is Polly. Polly meet your new brother and sister."

His use of the terms gave Justine hope the children—would be all right. They'd be part of a family.

"Luke," the man said. "Show me your things in the wagon and we can bring them inside."

Seeing little Luke spoken to with respect increased Justine's hope even more. He wasn't treated like a baby or ignored like his father had done.

Amos got Luke laughing as he took a trunk out of the wagon and carried it inside on his shoulder.

"Everyone come in and have some coffeecake."

"Coffee cake?" Justine said.

Mrs. Krupman laughed. "A cake that goes with coffee. An old German recipe." She looked down at Anna. "You like cake?"

She nodded with enthusiasm.

They went inside. The parlor was neatly appointed with two upholstered chairs, a settee, and a few other wood chairs. A shelf was filled with books. There were children's blocks on the floor, and two dolls.

Anna stared at them.

Polly stared at Anna.

The next few seconds would reveal much.

Polly picked up a fancy doll with a china head. "This is Miss Vanessa. Mama made her three dresses and two hats. And this one . . ." She picked up the baby doll. "This one is Baby Bumpkin. I've had her since I was a baby. You want to play with her?"

Anna nodded and Polly shared the doll.

Anna immediately brought it to Caesar. "Isn't she a good baby?"

"She is," Caesar said, touching the doll's head. "Just like you."

"I'm not a baby," Anna said.

"No, you're not." Caesar's voice cracked. "You're a big girl."

Luke came close and Caesar ruffled his hair. "You're a big boy too, aren't you, buddy?"

He nodded.

"Children?" Mrs. Krupman said. "Would you like to see your room? Polly, show them."

The three children noisily ran up the stairs.

Mrs. Krupman laughed. "I love the sound of children, don't you?"

Caesar was looking up the stairs, his face wistful. "You'll be good to them?"

"Of course. They will be cherished." She pointed to the parlor. "Please sit."

They did so, with Mr. Krupman joining them.

"Let me get the cake and coffee," she said.

"No, ma'am," Caesar said. "I needs to be going."

Although Justine would have loved to stay, she nodded.

"Very well then," she said. "I guess it's time to tell you how much we appreciate their family friend letting us adopt the children."

"We've always wanted more than just Polly," Mr. Krupman said. "We had the word out, saying we were kind of desperate . . ."

"Not desperate, Amos. That sounds wrong." She pressed a hand to her heart. "We just have a lot of love to spare, and we've wanted Polly to have siblings."

"You always say it better than me, Lar." He rubbed his hands on his thighs. "All this to say, when Mr. Trotter came and said there were two children in need — a boy and a girl no less — we knew God had answered our prayers."

"We're so sorry their parents died," Mrs. Krupman said. "Such a loss."

Caesar turned the brim of his hat around in his hands. "Yes'm, it was. But . . . we'd like a favor?"

"Of course."

"We think it's best if they don't talk about their lives *before* today — their ma and pa and such. They're kind of confused about things and . . ." He sighed. "We want them to start over as of right now. As Krupmans. Not dwelling on the past."

"We'll honor your request," Mrs. Krupman said. "Today we all begin fresh."

Caesar moved to the door and Justine followed. "They're really good kids," he said.

"How do you know them?" Mrs. Krupman asked.

"I worked on their family's farm," Caesar said.

They looked to Justine.

"And I know—knew—their mother well," Justine said. *If only I could stop this and bring the children to Ravenwood!*

Caesar hesitated at the door. "Just so you know . . . Luke will pretend he doesn't like green beans, but he'll eat 'em if you put some gravy on."

"I'll remember that," Mrs. Krupman said.

"And Anna?" He looked up the stairs. "She's just five, but she loves to help with chores, especially cooking."

"I'm very glad of that. Polly likes to cook too."

"They . . . they need to play more. They've been through hard times."

"Of course," she said. "There are a lot of children in our church. They will have many playmates."

"That's good, real good." Caesar's shoulders slumped and Justine felt bad for him. It was clear he loved the children. "I guess that's it, then."

"Do you want me to call them down to say goodbye?"

Caesar hesitated. "I think it's best I just go." He looked at each Krupman in turn. "God bless you for taking them in and loving them."

"God bless you for giving them up."

Caesar went out the door and made a beeline for the wagon. Justine had to run to catch up. Within seconds they were on their way.

"What are you thinking?" she asked.

"I'm thinking the children are better off."

"I'm thinking you're right."

"But . . ."

"But?"

He pulled on the reins, stopping the wagon. "Their mama is still alive. The Krupmans think she's dead, but she's not."

"Where is she?"

"At some lunatic place." He sighed deeply. "The mister told me we're gonna pretend the young'uns are dead too. He had me carve out some gravestones for 'em." She shook his head forlornly. "I just don't understand."

Justine tried to think of something positive. "At least he didn't kill the children."

Caesar looked at the clouds overhead. "There's that." Then he looked at the reins in his hand. "But now Mr. Cole is dead, and that man on the road is dead, and . . ."

Justine touched his arm. "Spencer is a very bad man. He's hurt many people."

"You don't know the half of it." Suddenly, he sat up straighter. "What if . . .? I was just thinking that I don't *need* to meet up with him. I could take this wagon and head in the opposite direction. I've had enough. I'm tired. I'm through. I don't want to be a part of his schemes anymore."

Justine was faced with a dilemma. She knew that Caesar stayed with Spencer — until his own death. Yet she longed to encourage him. What would his life have been like without the influence of Spencer — and Uriah?

"You *could* leave," she said. "Or maybe you could stay and be a good influence on him?"

Caesar scoffed. "I'm not sure that's possible."

Actually, it isn't. "Maybe . . ."

Caesar shook his head once, dispelling the idea. "Right now I need to go back to bury that poor man."

"After that?"

He didn't answer.

**

Justine expected to be whisked back to 1879 before the burying — she longed to be. She didn't want to see an innocent dead man, nor help Caesar carry him somewhere, nor hear the clods of dirt fall.

But as they neared the place where Spencer had dumped Joe Trotter, and she *wasn't* whisked back she realized God must have a reason for her to stay.

Caesar must have been thinking about Joe too. "Since the man won't have a headstone or any such thing . . . maybe we could put a piece of paper in his pocket saying who he is."

And saying who killed him.

Justine felt excitement grow. If she did this right, there would be evidence that Spencer Meade murdered Joe Trotter, evidence she could show the authorities back in 1879!

But . . . "Will paper last?"

"Last?" Caesar said. "No one's gonna dig him up. It just makes me feel better if he's got his name on him." He pointed to the back of the wagon. "We got pencil and paper in the back."

Justine's mind thought of the perfect solution. "Do you have any stoppered bottles we could put the paper in?"

"Well . . . yeah. There's some medicine and a bottle or two of whiskey."

"Perfect."

Caesar slowed the wagon. Then stopped it.

"He's over there," Justine said. "I saw Spencer roll him into the brush."

Caesar stood up in the wagon and looked in both directions. "Lucky this is an side road."

Even though there was no one in sight at the moment, the burial needed to be done quickly.

"I need the writing supplies and the bottle," she said. "I'll take care of naming him while you dig."

"Where?"

They gazed over an open field. A short distance away there were a handful of trees in a row, like those that would line a creek. "We don't want him disturbed, so not in a farmer's field or by the road. Over there?"

Caesar rubbed his mouth with the back of his hand. "I don't wanna drag him. You'll have to help me with the carrying."

Justine shuddered, but said, "I'll do whatever it takes."

Caesar got out some paper, a pencil, and rummaged around in a trunk, coming up with a bottle about three-inches long. "Laudanum," he said. "Hate to waste it, but wasting *it* is better than pouring out the whiskey. Spencer would notice if that was gone." He took a big swig, then offered it to Justine.

"No thank you. It makes me sleepy."

"That's what it's supposed to do, right?"

She emptied the bottle, shook it to release any final drops, then left the stopper off. "Go dig."

He ran across the field and she heard the sounds of shovel to earth.

Please, Father, don't let anyone see us. Let us get Mr. Trotter buried properly. And let the note still be there in the future.

She tore off a long strip of paper, and using the side of the wagon as a writing board, she wrote a note: *This is Joe Trotter. Spencer Meade killed this innocent man in the Spring of 1872. May God bless Joe Trotter's soul.* She thought about writing that Spencer Meade was now Uriah Benedict, but realized that such knowledge being buried with a man in 1872 — before Spencer was Uriah — would complicate the main fact: Spencer killed Joe. Period.

"There," she said. "That should bring Spencer down."

She rolled the strip into a tight scroll. She blew in the bottle one more time, hoping the remaining liquid wouldn't hurt the paper. Then she stoppered it closed.

Just in time, for Caesar came running back. "That's the quickest grave I've ever dug."

"You've dug others?"

He didn't answer, but looked toward Joe. "You got it ready?"

She held up the bottle.

"Let's finish this."

They went to the body. There was a lot of blood, but Justine forced herself to soldier through the horror of it. She glanced at Joe's face, the man with the happy voice who'd met them a short time ago. Did he have a wife and children?

She slipped the bottle in the pocket of his leather vest. Then Caesar took Joe under the arms and she took his feet and they staggered across the yet-to-be-planted field. She dropped his feet once, but quickly picked them up again. Her corset made it hard to breathe, but she couldn't stop.

The grave was about two-feet deep, on a high bank of the creek. They laid him in the hole. Caesar reached down and crossed Joe's hands over his chest. Then he shoveled the dirt back in place.

Anything else, Lord?

A marker. There needed to be some sort of marker, something that would last seven years, until 1879. While Caesar was filling in the grave, Justine walked to the creek and found a smooth rock. On it, she used the pencil to write: Joe Trotter 1872.

As soon as he was through with the dirt, Caesar tamped it down. His face glistened with sweat, his shirt was drenched.

She placed the rock at the head of the grave, word-side down. "To mark it," she explained.

He leaned against the shovel. "Should we say something?"

Justine was embarrassed she hadn't thought of it. She bowed her head. "Dear Father, please take Joe Trotter into your loving arms. Comfort him as a man undeserving of his fate. Bless his family — wherever they are." One more thing. "Let his death not be in vain. Let it be used to bring Uriah Benedict to justice, once and for all. Amen."

"Who's Uriah Benedict?" Caesar asked.

She didn't know what to say.

He knelt by the stream, washed his hands and face. "His name is Spencer Meade. You know that."

By the time he turned around, Justine was gone.

CHAPTER EIGHTEEN

Justine didn't walk home from the cemetery, she ran. The flood of information spurred her on. She had proof that Uriah was a murderer. She knew that Virginia's children were alive.

Did they still live with the Krupman's in Topeka?

An open carriage pulled beside her as she ran. "Miss? Are you all right?"

She stopped to grab a breath, standing tall to get air beneath her corset. Then she recognized the man in the carriage. "Mayor Usher?"

He cocked his head, as if trying to remember her. "Miss Bronson?"

"Braden. We met at Talbot's?"

"Yes. You were new in town."

"I was." She got an idea and took another deep breath. "Could I speak with you? It's very important."

"It must be, for you to be running so." He called out to his driver. "Wilson?"

The driver got off his perch and folded down the step for her. She entered the carriage and sat across from the mayor.

This was not a coincidence. It was her chance to speak to someone in authority.

But how to begin? She couldn't tell him she had witnessed Uriah's past crimes, for often she was the only witness. On her travels. Which she couldn't speak about.

The carriage pulled away. "Yes, Miss Braden? How can I help you?"

"I . . . I have evidence against a certain citizen."

"Evidence of what?"

"Murder."

The mayor jerked back. "That is a serious charge."

"It is a serious crime."

"Who was murdered?"

"Joe Trotter."

285

"I don't know him."

Here was the tricky part. "He was murdered in 1872."

He made an incredulous face. "That's a very long time ago."

"There isn't a time-restriction for convicting a killer, is there?"

"I believe you're referring to a statute of limitation, a time beyond which a crime cannot be prosecuted. And no, for murder, there is no limitation."

"Good. Then how do I proceed?"

"My, my, Miss Braden. When I got up this morning, I never expected to have a conversation about murder.

"Neither did I. I need to speak with the police."

"That would be the proper step. Would you like to go there now?"

"Please."

He told Wilson where to drive. "Would you care to tell me the name of the accused?"

She hesitated. "I'd prefer to tell the police first."

"Very well."

She hoped it would turn out *very* well indeed.

**

Justine had completely forgotten about Alva's arrest.

Thomas and Harland were at the police station. Just the people she wanted to see.

Harland kissed her cheek. "You're back already?"

"With proof," she said quietly. "I'm here to speak with the police about a murder."

"Who died?"

She shook her head. "Not now. Where is Alva?"

Thomas pointed to the back. "She's in a jail cell."

"That's ridiculous."

"Agreed," Thomas said. "We've been trying to get her released but they won't do anything until Uriah gets here."

She smiled. "I'm glad he's coming."

"Why?" Harland asked.

"Because I have proof he murdered someone."

"Murder?" An officer sitting nearby looked up from his desk. "Murder, you say?"

And here we go . . . Justine stepped forward. "I want to report a murder."

She was heartened when he stood and offered her a chair. Finally, someone to listen.

Harland and Thomas stood behind her. She appreciated their support.

The officer returned to his place and took up a pen. He was the same officer who'd come to the house. Crandell? "What is your name?"

"Justine Braden."

"What is the name of the deceased?"

"Joe Trotter."

"Joseph?"

"I don't know."

"When did he die?"

"Eighteen-seventy-two. In the spring."

He began to write it down, then looked up. "As in seven years ago?"

"Yes."

He set his pen down. "This is rather unusual."

"A murder is a crime no matter when it occurred, is it not?"

"It is, but . . ." He repeated himself. "This is rather unusual."

"I concur."

"Do you know the name of the killer?"

"I do." She fueled herself with a fresh breath. "Uriah Benedict."

His bushy eyebrows rose. He picked up a newspaper from his desk and pointed at Uriah's picture. "Mr. Benedict is a respected member of this community."

The public accolades didn't help her case. "I'm aware of that impression." She knew her words were far from passive.

The officer looked annoyed, but took out a pencil and sheet of paper and pointed to a nearby desk. "If you'll excuse me, Miss Braden. There's something I need to attend to. Please write down what you know, giving as many details as you can." He left.

"I'm being dismissed," she said. "He doesn't believe me. Or doesn't want to believe me."

"It's not just a question of belief," Harland said. "It's also a question of urgency — or lack of urgency for a murder seven years past."

She understood that. "They want a statement? I will give them one." She moved her chair to the table and began to write. Or tried to write.

"What's wrong?" Thomas asked.

"I can't write about what I saw because there's no logical explanation for how I saw it."

"Can you say where it happened?"

"I can tell them — show them — where he's buried."

"Do that," Harland said, pointing at the page.

She wrote details of the road, the field, the creek. She began to write about the bottle in his pocket, then stopped. "I can't write this part."

"What part?" Thomas asked.

She lowered her voice for their ears alone. "Caesar and I were present when Trotter was killed. We buried him. To make sure people knew who he was and who killed him, I wrote a note, rolled it up, and put it in an empty laudanum bottle in his vest pocket."

"That's smart," Harland said.

"I thought so. But I can't write that down. *I* can't know about the bottle."

"They have to discover it," Thomas said.

Justine looked at the page where she'd only written a few lines. "I have to get them to go to the gravesite. *They* need to find him."

"Is the grave still there?" Harland asked.

Waves of doubt crashed over her. What if she succeeded in getting the police to the grave and it was gone? Trotter was gone? Her credibility would be ruined. Yet without them seeing it, and discovering the bottle and the truth inside . . . *If only Caesar were alive to corroborate the murder.*

She heard the front door of the police station open and turned to see Uriah.

And Mayor Usher.

Officer Crandell returned and rushed to greet the mayor. "Mayor Usher. How can I help you today?"

He caught Justine's eye. "I gave Miss Braden a lift to the station and wanted to see how she's being treated."

Crandell's face grew mottled. "Oh. Well. She's writing down her statement."

Uriah stepped up. "I believe my issue has precedence. I'm picking up my wife."

Crandell took one step toward Uriah, then one step toward Justine, then stopped. "I'll see what I can do, Mr. Benedict."

The mayor chuckled. "We flustered the poor boy."

"A police officer shouldn't get flustered," Uriah said.

"Ease up, Benedict," the mayor said.

Justine stifled a smile.

Alva was escorted to the front. She walked by Justine without a glance before rushing into Uriah's arms. "Oh, Uriah. I'm so sorry. So sorry. Take me home."

Uriah graced her with a single hand on her back. He did not comfort her, he tolerated her. Barely.

"I'm glad you're ready to leave this nonsense behind."

"I am. Truly, I am."

They turned to leave.

Justine couldn't let them do that. She stood, nearly knocking over her chair. "Ur . . . Uriah Benedict, you are a murderer!"

He slowly turned his head to glare at her. "What did you say?"

The beating of her heart made her temples throb but she couldn't back down. "You murdered Joe Trotter. You stabbed him to death and tossed him off the side of the road."

Uriah turned around fully. "I don't know any Joe Trotter."

"You did. You killed him as though he was nothing."

"When did I do this?"

If only I didn't have to say. "In 1872."

He scoffed and nodded to the mayor. "Perhaps you shouldn't have given her a ride, Mayor. She's clearly delusional. I hear Ravenwood is good with such people." His smirk made Justine want to slap him.

Officer Crandell looked relieved when an older officer came in the room. "What's going on here?" the older man asked him.

"Mr. Benedict has come for his wife, but this woman here, has accused him of murder."

Uriah brushed a speck of dust from his hat and scoffed. "Nothing to bother about, Chief. Now if you don't mind, I want to get my wife home where she belongs."

"I'm sure you do, but just a minute, please." He scanned the room, his eyes landing on Justine. "You say there's been a murder?"

"There has." She retrieved her deposition. "Here. I wasn't through, but I've noted the location of the body."

The chief began to read the page, only to be interrupted by Uriah. "There's no need to read anything, Bonner. This woman is delusional."

Police Chief Bonner held up a hand and continued reading. "This is a serious accusation, Miss . . ."

"Braden. Justine Braden." She quickly introduced Thomas and Harland. "Murder *is* serious. Justice must be done. As I wrote, you'll find Mr. Trotter buried at that location. I would be happy to accompany you to the site."

Uriah sighed deeply. "I'm sorry you're having to waste your time with this, Chief. And you, Mayor Usher. This woman's accusation is absurd and distressing."

"It certainly is the latter," the mayor said.

Uriah seemed surprised Usher hadn't agreed with his full statement.

The Chief nodded at the page. "She gives a location of the body. I can't ignore it."

"You must ignore it," Uriah said. "Logic must prevail. One must wonder how this woman knows *I* killed a man in 1872."

The chief looked at her. "It is a good question, Miss Braden."

"Especially considering you are new in town," the mayor added .

The three men looked at her for answers. "Someone else saw the murder; witnessed it," she said.

"Who?" Uriah asked.

Justine knew her answer wouldn't go over well even before she said it. "Caesar Johnson."

Uriah rolled his eyes. "The witness to this alleged death is dead himself. Really, Miss Braden." He looked to the police chief. "Chief Bonner, will you please officially put an end to this woman's mad accusation? As the accused, I have a right to question the witness. Which I can't. Therefore . . ."

A flow of words forced their way out. "That's because you killed the witness! You pushed Caesar down the stairs before he could share details of all your crimes."

The air vibrated with her words.

"So now I've killed two people?"

"More than that, I'm sure."

"You're sure?" He actually grinned.

Justine glanced at Harland and Thomas. They looked worried. *She* was worried. "You killed Josiah Dawson too."

"Who?"

"The Dawsons owned a farm east of town."

"When was this?"

Justine wanted to find a jail cell to hide in. "August 21, 1863."

Mayor Usher raised a hand. "That's the day of the Lawrence Massacre."

"It is," Justine said. "Mr. Benedict was a member of Quantrill's raiders who rode onto the Dawson property and killed Josiah in front of his wife, causing her to have a heart attack and also die."

Uriah's jaw tightened. Was she getting to him? "Once again, I ask: how do you know? Who saw me?"

"Their daughter Virginia saw you. And her brother Cole."

"Have them come forth and make these accusations in person."

Complications came to mind: Virginia hadn't recognized Spencer as Wat, her father's murderer. Instead, she'd married him.

"Where is this Virginia?" Uriah asked.

I dug this hole . . . "You locked her away back in seventy-one."

Uriah handily changed the subject. "Miss Braden states I was involved in crimes from 1863 and 1872? That's not possible. I moved here in seventy-three." He turned to his wife. "Isn't that right, Alva?"

Alva's face was torn with conflict. "I think so."

Uriah dismissed her with a wave of annoyance. He sighed dramatically. "So. This Violet person saw me kill her father?"

"Virginia. Your wife."

He nodded. "Who is a patient at Ravenwood. Because she's crazy."

"You said she was, but she wasn't. Never was."

"Does she live there now?"

Oh dear. "She does. But . . ."

"But?"

This would not go well. "She lives there voluntarily."

Uriah spread his hands. "Which is proof she is crazy."

Justine shook her head, vehemently. "She is no such thing. She lost everything. She had nowhere to go. That's why she chose to stay."

Uriah laughed. "A woman who chooses to stay in a lunatic asylum? That proves her insanity."

"She would not be the best of witnesses, Miss Braden," the mayor said.

Uriah wasn't done poking holes in her story. "Where is her brother? Ask him to come forward and speak against me."

"Cole is dead. You killed him too. You pushed him off the loft in their barn."

"More pushing." Uriah chuckled. "Again, Miss Braden, how do you know this? Do you have another non-witness to accuse me?"

Just me.

Uriah threw his hands in the air. "Why would I kill . . . what was his name?"

"You know his name very well. He was your brother-in-law."

He studied her a moment. "Why would I kill this man?"

"Because Cole didn't want you to sell the family farm without Virginia's permission. Without *his* permission."

"What farm is this?"

"The Dawson farm, where you led the raid and killed their father."

He gave her a blank stare.

"Near Eudora."

"I assure you, I do not own a farm near Eudora."

"You don't now, because you sold it. Without consulting your wife."

He looked at Alva. "Alva, are you aware of this farm?"

Alva hugged herself and stared into the space between them. She looked scared to death. Justine knew she wouldn't be any help.

"Alva, answer me."

She shook her head. "Not that I know of."

Uriah pointed at Justine. "These accusations are beyond the bounds of bearing. You've known me for years, Mayor Usher. You too, Chief Bonner. Do I own a farm?"

"Not that I know of," the chief said.

"Not since I've known you," the mayor said.

Father, help me! The complexities of Uriah's life rushed through her mind like leaves blowing in the wind. She didn't know which one to grab, and doubted her ability to grab any at all. But she had to try. "Uriah Benedict didn't own the farm because he hasn't always been Uriah Benedict. His name before that was Spencer Meade. He married Virginia, got her property, then sold it.

"After committing her to Ravenwood," Bonner said.

Their blank faces said it all. This was not going well. Justine tried to pinpoint the one fact that would bring him down. "You were also a bank robber with the James-Younger gang, committing crimes with Frank and Jesse James. You robbed the Liberty Bank in 1866."

Uriah started to laugh, and took a seat in the foyer, crossing his legs as if he hadn't a care. He raised his hands in mock surrender. "My secret is out. Now you all know where I got my money."

Although Justine knew she was racing down a mountain with no brakes, she had to finish this. "Your . . . your name wasn't Spencer Meade then, you were called Wat. Lionel Watkins."

He counted on his fingers. "Three names? Have I any others?"

She should never have mentioned the robberies. But then Justine thought of Helene. If she mentioned her rape . . . that crime might be despicable enough for them to take notice.

"Miss Braden?" Uriah said. "Are you through falsely disparaging my character? May we move on?"

Justine's thoughts raced. Back at the school Helene had been adamant that she would never testify against Uriah. She'd moved on with her life. It would do no good to mention yet another crime that couldn't be corroborated.

But there was another crime Uriah had committed when he was Lionel . . .

Uriah pressed his hands against his thighs and stood. "Since Miss Braden is done ranting—"

"I am not done," she said. "When you were living under the name of Lionel Watkins you spent time at the Bedford Springs resort in Pennsylvania."

"Now that *is* a crime."

Officer Crandell chuckled, then covered his mouth. "Sorry."

Justine continued. "In 1860, while there, you conned my mother out of a ruby necklace. I was there with her and—"

Oops.

"I'm sorry. I prefer emeralds," he said.

Even the mayor laughed.

"You stole my mother's necklace and gave it to Alva." Justine rushed to Alva's side. "Tell them you have a ruby necklace. The one you were wearing when we went to your house for dinner."

She blinked. "Yes, I do, but . . ."

"So what if she does?" Uriah said.

Alva's eyes were full of pain. "I'm sorry, Justine."

Uriah raised a finger. "If I was at some resort as Lionel Watson—"

"Watkins."

"Lionel Watkins in 1860, and you were at the resort with your mother and were a witness to some theft? That was 19 years ago. How old were you?"

Oh dear. *Father, help me!* "My mother told me about it."

"Did she now. May we speak with her?"

Justine's throat went dry. "She died last year."

"How convenient."

"I'm sorry, Miss Braden," the mayor said. "This isn't productive."

Unfortunately, it wasn't. "I beg you, please go to the grave and see the evidence—the proof—that Uriah Benedict killed Joe Trotter."

"This has gone on long enough," Uriah said with a dismissive wave. "If you'll excuse me, I want to get my wife home."

"He's poisoning his wife!" Justine grabbed Alva's arm. "Tell them how sick you've been. Tell them about his threats, and . . ."

"Is this true, Mrs. Benedict?" Mayor Usher said.

Alva *looked* sick.

"Please, Alva," Justine said.

"I . . . I *have* been sick a lot."

Uriah threw up his hands. "Well then. A woman who feels ill is surely proof of a crime. If that were so, every household in Kansas would contain a victim and a criminal."

"It isn't proof, Miss Braden," Bonner said.

Uriah raised a hand. "*Au contraire,* Chief. My wife's illness is the ultimate proof of my criminal nature. She feels ill so it must be poison." He glared at Justine. "Were there any witnesses to this horrific act?"

Justine's heart sank. "There was."

"Pray tell us his or her name."

Her stomach turned. "Caesar Johnson."

It was over. There was no hope.

Harland stepped forward. "There is one way to prove Miss Braden's initial claim. Go out to the grave and see the evidence as she's asked. If it's not there, it's over. If it is . . . you must consider everything she has said."

"I agree with you, Dr. Jennings," Uriah said. "Let's find this grave from seven years ago. Then we can set all this nonsense aside."

Justine's initial relief faded quickly. Why was Uriah agreeable?

**

Justine was nervous as she rode in the buggy with Harland and Thomas. "Why did Uriah agree to go to the grave?"

"Not just agree to it, but encourage it," Thomas said.

"So you're worried too?" Justine ran her hands up and down her arms, suddenly cold

Harland put an arm around her shoulders. "He's a shifty man. We can't trust him."

She nodded. "He countered every crime or offense I mentioned."

"He was very smooth," Thomas said.

"As all conmen are," Harland added.

This wasn't helping. She had to focus on the task at hand. "Once they find the bottle I buried with Joe, it will do him in."

"Bottle?" her father asked.

She hadn't told him about it. "Caesar and I buried Joe, and Caesar mentioned that we needed to make sure people knew who it was. He got me a laudanum bottle from the back of the wagon and we emptied it. Then I wrote a note that said the dead man was Joe Trotter and he was murdered by Spencer Meade in 1872."

Harland sucked in a breath. "Spencer Meade."

"Yes, that's who Uriah was when he killed him."

"But he's not Spencer Meade now." Harland withdrew his arm from her shoulders. When he looked at her his face was pulled with worry. "Even though you tried to connect Lionel, Spencer, and Uriah, you really didn't."

Justine wanted to scream. "I thought about putting 'Uriah' on the note, but then I it would be unexplainable since Uriah didn't become Uriah until years later. It would make it harder to believe that Joe was killed in 1872."

They rode a moment in silence. "That was good reasoning," Thomas said.

It was little consolation. "Please help us, Lord," she whispered.

"Amen," her father said.

**

Justine's surrey led two other carriages down the side road that Justine had last traveled seven years' previous. It was little improved and was dusty and bumpy.

The road may not have changed, but the trees marking the creek had. Harland helped her down. In the second carriage were Uriah and Alva, and in the third — in the mayor's carriage — was the mayor, Chief Bonner, and Officer Crandell, carrying a shovel.

"Where now, Miss Braden?" Uriah asked.

The mayor had her deposition with him. "Says here it's down by a creek, to the south."

"That's right," she said. "Come this way."

They walked through the field, between the rows of crops, just coming up. With every step Justine prayed *Let us find him, let us find him, let us . . .*

As soon as she reached the bank she quickly looked around, trying to see anything that looked familiar. The grave had been on a high bank. And the makeshift marker. . . Hopefully animals hadn't disturbed it. Hopefully it hadn't been swept away by spring flooding.

"Where is this grave, Miss Braden?" Mayor Usher asked.

She was on the verge of panic when she spotted the stone, mostly covered by grasses. She ran to it. "Here!" She picked up the stone and turned it over. "This marks the grave."

Bonner took the stone and wiped the dirt off the back of it. "It says something on it. Barely."

"May I?" Uriah examined it. "It doesn't say anything legible." He handed it to Justine. "It's just a rock."

"It's not just a rock." She pointed at the few letters that were visible. "See? There's a distinct J and an r."

The mayor looked at it. "Perhaps."

Justine tried to keep her voice calm. At the station she'd learned that men did not react well to high emotions. "Officer Crandell? Would you dig here, please?"

He began digging, muttering under his breath about dead bodies and bones.

"Enough of the commentary, Crandell," the chief said.

"Yes, sir."

When he'd dug down about two feet, she felt panicked. Harland gave her questioning looks.

"Keep going," she said. "It's been here a long time."

Finally, Crandell brought up a shovel full of dirt that included . . . a bone. He stepped back. "Ewww."

Alva hid her face in Uriah's shoulder.

They all moved forward—except the Benedicts. Justine spotted a faint hint of panic on Uriah's face. He didn't know that Caesar had gone back and buried Joe. He'd probably come this far quite certain there was no body to find.

Crandell continued his work, but Thomas stopped him. "Careful now. This was a man who deserves our respect and care."

"Agreed," the chief said. "Here, Crandell, let me."

"Gladly."

Chief Bonner used the shovel with delicacy. When more bones appeared, he stepped into the hole and used his hands to push the dirt away. A ribcage, arms, a skull . . . and strips of decomposed fabric.

And . . . Justine pointed. "Is that a bottle?"

Bonner retrieved the bottle from beneath a flap of a decayed leather vest. Justine wanted to tell him about the note, but knew it was essential that *he* find it.

"There's something inside," he said.

Thank You, God!

He uncorked the bottle and tried to shake the note out, then tried using a finger. "My fingers are too thick. Miss Braden?"

She took the bottle and finagled the edge of the note, then the note in its entirety. She gave it to the chief, her heart pounding.

He carefully unrolled it: "'This is Joe Trotter. Spencer Meade killed this innocent man in the Spring of 1872. May God bless Joe Trotter's soul.'" He glanced at Justine, then Uriah. "The name Spencer Meade again."

"May I?" Uriah read the note, then shrugged. "Mr. Meade certainly gets around."

Her heart pounded but she remained calm. "*You* get around. For you were Spencer Meade."

Uriah flipped a hand at her. "You are delusional, Miss Braden. Your wild accusations prove nothing." He looked at the note and his face changed. Lightened. "May I see the directions that Miss Braden provided?"

The mayor handed over the page. Uriah looked at one, then the other, and as he did so Justine knew he was going to win again.

Uriah turned to the mayor. "How odd that the handwriting on Miss Braden's directions matches the handwriting on the note, which supposedly was buried with this poor man, many years ago."

Justine wanted to jump into the grave and claw the dirt down around herself.

The mayor studied the handwriting, his forehead furrowed. "How do you explain this, Miss Braden?"

"Let me see that." She needed to buy time until she could think of a plausible answer. But sure enough it was clear the same hand wrote both.

She pretended otherwise. "Yes, the penmanship is similar, as it would be for anyone who learned to write cursive using the Spencer method which is taught in virtually every school in America."

They seemed somewhat appeased.

"I have one other question before I go," Uriah said. "How did you know this grave was even here? Or that it was Joe Trotter? You clearly weren't quite sure of its location and the name on the rock is quite illegible."

I traveled through time. I saw you kill him. I helped bury him.

Alva began to fan herself. "Please, Uriah. I just want to go home." As she spoke, she gave Justine a furtive glance, as though she'd realized the truth of everything, but felt helpless and just wanted it over.

Justine felt much the same.

"I agree, wife," Uriah said. He looked at the mayor and the chief. "We are obviously through here. Can we dispense with this nonsense once and for all?"

"I believe we can," the chief said. "Forgive me for inconveniencing all of you on this wild goose chase."

Uriah took Alva back to his carriage.

And took himself away from any accountability or justice.

**

Justine was done.

She went home from Joe's grave completely spent. Her family tried to comfort her, but their words sounded hollow against the wall of her failure. She had traveled back in time and witnessed a myriad of awful deeds but had not procured one iota of justice.

All she wanted to do was sleep and forget.

She lay on her bed and faced the window. The lace curtains billowed and danced with the breeze. She stared, mesmerized, and for a few moments her thoughts settled into nothingness.

A few moments. Not nearly long enough to give her any peace.

She heard voices downstairs, but hoped they weren't conspiring to get her to come down. She didn't want to go downstairs. Ever.

Justine turned away from the window and drew a pillow to her chest, folding herself around it. "Father, what did I do wrong? What did I miss?"

There was a soft knock on her bedroom door.

"Go away, please," she said.

"No." Harland slipped inside.

She hugged the pillow harder, burying her face into its softness. "Leave me alone. I'm done in. No more."

"One thing more." He sat on the edge of the bed and stroked her hair away from her face. "There's someone here to see you."

"Not now."

"You'll want to see this person. I guarantee it."

She peeked out from the pillow. "Who is it?"

"Come down and see."

Her curiosity got the best of her and she sat up. Harland pulled her to standing, and into his arms. "Everything will be all right. I promise."

Really?

He pointed at her collar, which was askew. She looked in the mirror, fixed it, and smoothed her hair.

"You're beautiful." He held out his hand. "Come on now."

Justine had no idea who would be calling on her. She took hesitant steps, deliberately placing her foot on each stair. But as she reached the foyer and looked into the parlor, she was indeed surprised.

"Helene!" She hurried forward. "Why are you here?"

"I've changed my mind about testifying against Lionel. Against Uriah Benedict. About the rape."

Justine pulled her into an embrace. "Thank you so much."

They parted and Justine led her to a settee they shared. "What made you change your mind?"

Helene nodded toward Harland, who stood at the fireplace. "You and Dr. Jennings. And Dorthea. I honestly hadn't thought about the crime in a long time. I'd truly moved on. But . . ."

"We brought the memories back?"

"You did." She smoothed the drawstrings of her purse against her lap. "At first I resisted them. The idea of coming forward after all this time. But then . . ." She took a new breath. "I was teaching the children about the beginnings of our country, lauding the brave men and women who stood up to tyranny and the injustice of rule by a foreign king."

Justine grabbed onto a key word. "Injustice."

"Exactly. I was the victim of injustice. And because I wasn't brave and didn't come forward and accuse him then, many others have been hurt since." She shook her head once. "It's time for the truth to come out."

"That *is* extremely courageous of you," Harland said.

"And then, I saw this." She handed Justine a clipping from the *Lawrence Daily Journal* that showed the etchings of the mayor and Uriah.

"I'm familiar with the article." Justine handed it back.

"I have never met Uriah or even seen him since I arrived here. But seeing that picture in the paper — which indeed looks like an older Lionel Watkins — was the final push to make me do the right thing."

Justine was very moved, and yet . . . "Even if you recognize him, that doesn't prove his crime."

"Agreed," she said. "But this will."

She walked to the front door and opened it. "Come in."

A young man walked in.

As did justice.

CHAPTER NINETEEN

The visitor at the door shocked them. Not because they knew him, but because of his strong resemblance to someone they *did* know.

Helene went to greet him, and drew him forward. "I would like to introduce you to my son, Milton."

"Hello," the young man said.

Justine knew her mouth was agape, but couldn't stop staring. Milton was very tall with broad shoulders. His cheekbones were strong, his chin square. His eyes and hair were dark. "You look like . . ."

"His father," Helene said. "Lionel Watkins."

"Oh my," Dorthea said.

"I don't know what to say," Justine said.

Milton pulled his mother's arm through his. Her height only reached his shoulder. "I understand your reaction. Last night Mother told me the story of what happened to her before I was born." He looked down at her, his face soft with compassion. "She is very strong to endure such an assault, and very brave to carry on in a new place, alone."

"I did it for you. My boy," Helene said.

Harland raised a hand, his face bright with a revelation. "After you got to Kansas City, you found out you were with child. That is why you took the name *Mrs.* Soames."

"I thought it best. I told everyone my husband died back East. No one ever thought otherwise." She took a deep breath. "One of the benefits of starting over in a new land is that everyone you meet is also starting over. They have left their pasts behind. As did I."

Justine remembered what Helene had said at the school. "You never saw Lionel again?"

"I didn't, nor did I want to. That's one reason I was glad to travel a bit further west, to Lawrence, to get away from Kansas City. Lionel had told me that was his final destination." She smiled up at her son. "Milton is attending Kansas University here. He wants to be a doctor." She looked at Harland. "You're a doctor."

"I am."

Helene nudged Milton. "Mother told me about you, Dr. Jennings. I have questions about the process and the practice. I'd like to talk to you some time in the future."

"I would be happy to speak with you, anytime. I just opened an office downtown."

Milton beamed. "I would like to see it."

Justine was glad for the detour of conversation for it gave her a chance to gather her thoughts. "You've come forward, ready to address the crime?"

"Yes. I'm ready to confront Lionel—Uriah."

"It's the right thing to do," Milton said.

What an amazing young man. With an amazing mother.

"How do you wish to handle what comes next?" Helene asked.

They put their heads together to come up with a plan.

**

They came up with a plan.

If it worked, Uriah Benedict would be under arrest by the end of the day.

If it didn't . . . Justine had no alternative. It had to work.

The first thing they needed to do was gather the players.

Since Justine's reputation had been somewhat tarnished by her rant at the police station and the anticlimactic drama at the grave, Thomas and Harland volunteered for the following duties: Thomas would go to the Benedict's and request Uriah's presence at the Jennings' home—ostensibly so Justine could apologize. At the same time, Harland would fetch Chief Bonner to be a witness to the reunion of Uriah and his victim, Helene. Both men had already been gone thirty minutes.

Staying behind were the women of the house, with the addition of Helene and Milton.

"Will they come?" Helene asked.

Justine wanted to reassure her, but since the word of the day was *truth,* she told it. "Probably not."

"Perhaps out of curiosity," Dorthea said.

"But Thomas *is* telling Uriah you're going to apologize," Goosie said.

She shrugged. "If anything, he'll come to gloat. He thinks he's won."

Milton looked uncomfortable sitting on the hard wood chair brought in from the dining room. There was a crease between his brows. He had to be nervous. "I'm not sure there *is* any winning in all this," he said.

Helene gave him a reassuring smile. "Truth will be the winner."

He looked skeptical.

"We appreciate both of you coming here," Justine said for the third time. "We realize how difficult it must be, to disrupt your lives."

"It's time," Helene said. "I've lied every day of Milton's life, telling him that his father died." She looked at her lap. "Perhaps because I wished him dead — may God forgive me."

"I don't blame you for the lie, Mother," Milton said. "You're a survivor. You took a revolting situation and made it good — for yourself and for me."

Oh, to have such a son someday. "Soon it will all be over," Justine said.

"Speaking of *over* . . ." Helene glanced out the front window nervously. "I wish they'd just come."

"It will be all right, Mother. He can't hurt us, not when we have each other."

"And us," Dorthea said. "You have all of us to help in any way we can."

Helene nodded, though she seemed unconvinced. "When they do arrive. . . should Milton and I be out of sight?"

Justine was surprised she hadn't thought of it. "That's a good idea. We don't want Uriah to see you right away."

Goosie pointed toward the back of the house. "When we hear them coming, you can both slip into the kitchen to wait."

Helene pressed a hand to her chest. "My heart is pounding. To see him again, to finally accuse him . . ."

Justine hoped she wouldn't lose her courage and run out the back door, never to be seen again. If that happened, it would probably be easier for Justine to move away. Montana might be good.

Goosie stood. "I'll make some coffee."

As soon as she turned toward the kitchen, they heard a horse outside. Justine ran to the window. It was Harland.

"He's alone," Justine's heart sank. "Bonner didn't come with him. Our plan is ruined."

Harland came inside, his face forlorn. "Sorry. He wasn't at the station. Officer Crandell said he'd gone off somewhere, right after leaving the gravesite. He didn't know where."

Justine felt a wave of panic rise up. "But if he's not here to witness Helene confronting Uriah, then it's all for—"

"Wait!" Goosie called from the window. "He's here."

"Uriah?" Justine began to usher Helene and Milton toward the kitchen. "Go!"

"Not Uriah. The police."

Justine looked outside and saw Chief Bonner getting down from a wagon that had *Police Patrol* painted on the side. Officer Crandell stayed put. She turned to Harland. "You never spoke with him?"

"I didn't. He's come on his own." He turned to Helene and Milton. "I still think it's best if you go to the kitchen for now."

They did. There was a knock on the door.

Justine answered it. "Chief Bonner. Harland went to fetch you."

"He did? Why?"

Harland stepped forward. "We have some concrete evidence against Uriah."

"Which is?"

Harland exchanged a glance with Justine, then said. "We'll get to that. We're curious why you came on your own."

"I've come to tell you some good news."

We can use some of that. "Come in. Please." Justine showed him into the parlor.

"Afternoon," he said to those present. Harland made introductions. "This is my mother, Mrs. Jennings, and this is our dear friend, Miss Anders."

Dorthea and Goosie nodded.

"Please have a seat," Justine said.

"Hopefully, Uriah is on his way here," Harland said. "Thomas went to fetch him."

"He thinks I'm going to apologize," Justine said, "But we have a surprise for him instead."

Bonner sat in a chair near the foyer and balanced his police helmet on his knee. "You are a woman full of surprises, Miss Bra—"

They all perked up when they heard horses. Goosie went to the window. "It's them!"

Justine turned to the chief. "I wish we had time to explain more, and to hear your good news, but—"

He lifted a hand. "It can wait. Play it out, Miss Braden."

Justine's nerves stirred. *Help us, Lord. Let it all happen according to Your perfect plan.*

Thomas came inside first and held the door for Uriah—who took one look at Bonner and scowled. "What are you doing here?"

The chief fingered the six-pointed star that was pinned to his coat. "I've come to finish some business."

Uriah stood by the door and turned his ire on Justine. "Make your apologies, Miss Braden, for I have better things to do than be here."

Justine stood tall. "I plan no apologies."

Uriah blinked a few times. "Enough then. Good day." He turned to leave.

"Stay a while, Mr. Benedict," the chief said amiably. "Come in. Have a seat."

Uriah looked totally confused.

Bonner smiled. "Please. Join us."

He hesitated, but let Thomas lead him to a chair by the fireplace. Thomas placed his own chair near Bonner, moving it slightly to block easy access to the front door. Justine appreciated his forethought.

"If we can get on with it?" Uriah asked.

Bonner set his helmet on the floor beside his chair, then slapped his hands on his thighs. "I think that's exactly what we can do. The floor is yours, Miss Braden."

This is it. Father? Give me the words.

Justine stood. "We have asked you here, Mr. Benedict, to reunite you with someone from your past."

"And who might that be?" He scoffed, then looked at the chief. "Do something, Bonner. This is ridiculous."

The chief shook his head. "This isn't my show. Go on, Miss Braden."

Justine had no idea why Chief Bonner seemed to be on her side, but she was thankful for it. "I will let our guest introduce herself." She called out. "Helene? If you please?"

Helene came out of the kitchen and walked to Justine's side. For a quick moment Uriah's face looked puzzled. Then it twitched. Then held steady.

"Hello." Her voice cracked and she began again. "Hello, Lionel."

To his credit, Uriah did not react. He even looked around the room. "I'm afraid you are mistaken, ma'am. There is no Lionel here."

"But there is." She looked at the chief, as though needing his approval.

"Go ahead, ma'am."

Emboldened by his support, she began. "My name is Helene Soames. I arrived in Lawrence in 1860. I am a teacher at Riverside School, where I have worked for nineteen years."

"My mother was a teacher," Bonner said.

Uriah raised his eyebrows. "Really?"

Sergeant Bonner cleared his throat. "How can we help you, Mrs. Soames?"

"Actually, it's Miss Soames, for I never married." She paused, wringing her hands. "Why? you might ask? Because on the steamer from St. Louis to Kansas City, I was repeatedly raped by that man, sitting right there. Lionel Watkins."

Uriah huffed. "This is absurd."

Helene stepped closer, looking down at him. Her voice gained strength. "On that we can agree. Your behavior was indeed absurd. The fact you used your charm and worldly ways to make me think you were a gentleman is the essence of absurd. For you are no gentleman. You are a conniving, violent, despicable rapist." She faced the chief. "I want him arrested and tried. I will testify under oath as to his crime against me."

Bonner stroked his mustache. "I'm not sure it's that simple, ma'am. Miss. I am sorry if some man attacked you, but there is no way to prove that man was Mr. Benedict."

His words seemed to be a setback, and yet there was something in his tone that made Justine believe he was still on their side.

"Indeed, there is no proof," Uriah said.

"But there is."

"Then please, bring it forward," Bonner said.

Justine could not have scripted the line better herself. "Milton? Will you join us, please?"

Milton walked out of the kitchen, his head held high, his shoulders strong. The only evidence of nerves was a flush to his cheeks.

Justine motioned for him to stand next to Uriah's chair. "If you would, please?"

For the first time since knowing him, Justine saw a flicker of fear on Uriah's face. He stared up at Milton for a brief moment before looking away.

"Well I'll be," the chief said with a smile. "You're the spitting image."

Justine was thrilled she didn't have to say it. It *was* obvious. The only difference—besides their age —was that Milton had a head of neatly cropped black hair and Uriah's head was shaved.

Helene went to her son's side, slipping her hands around his arm. "Meet my son — our son — Milton Soames."

Suddenly, Uriah stood—revealing that they were the same height. "I will not sit here another minute and—"

Bonner also stood. "I'm afraid you're not going anywhere, Mr. Benedict. I'd like to hear your explanation."

"There's nothing to explain!" It was the first time he'd raised his voice. "I did not rape this woman."

"So you're saying you had a consensual relationship with her?" Bonner asked.

"Absolutely not," Helene said.

"I . . ." His hesitation made it clear he was pondering how to answer the chief's question. Finally, he said, "Absolutely not."

Bonner shook his head. He winked at Milton. "Consensual or no, the results are obvious."

Justine clapped her hands together. Victory was on the horizon.

The chief touched one index finger to the other. "Did you come here on a steamer in . . .?" He looked at Helene.

"Eighteen-sixty."

"Eighteen-sixty?" Bonner asked.

Uriah looked confused. "I . . . I did not."

"How did you get here?"

Justine could see the wheels of his mind turning. He obviously wasn't sure how to answer that.

"I'm from Colorado," he said.

Bonner leaned back with a sigh "No one is *from* Colorado," he said. "You land there from another place. So it is with Kansas. Where are you *from* originally?"

Uriah's jaw tightened. "Out . . . out east. I don't see how this has anything to do with —"

Justine stepped in. "He was in Pennsylvania in 1860. The same year he came west on the steamer."

"Where he raped me." Helene took a piece of paper from her pocket. "I kept my ticket." She showed it to Chief Bonner. "You can see the ship and the date. Check the manifest. You'll find my name there, and the name of Lionel Watkins."

"But I'm not Lionel Watkins!"

"Prove it," Justine said. The room went silent, and she realized the enormity of those two words.

"How can I prove who I'm not?" Uriah said. His face was flushed.

Bonner rapped a knuckle on his knee. "Can you prove your whereabouts as Uriah Benedict from 1860 to the year you came to Lawrence?"

"Eighteen-seventy-three," Justine said. "Thirteen years unaccounted for."

Uriah's eyes flit this way and that before landing on Justine with seething anger. She suffered a shiver, but pushed away her fear.

The chief leaned forward, resting his arms on his thighs. "Can anyone corroborate your identity during that time?"

His face lit up. "Caesar John—" His face fell.

Justine felt vindicated. "As you kept telling me, Caesar can't testify as he is deceased."

Uriah's dark eyes were black.

She thought of something else. "Just like Caesar isn't here to prove who you *were*, he's not here to prove who you *are*."

The room went silent a second time.

Bonner nodded at Justine, "Nice one, little lady." He noticed the newspaper on the table beside his chair. He opened it to the front page. "Nice picture."

"What?" Uriah said.

Bonner set the paper down. "Actually, I have my own copy from the station." He pulled a page from the inside of his coat. It had been torn into a smaller portion, just showing the pictures of the mayor and Uriah.

"Fine," Uriah said. "You like my picture. Can we—?"

"Actually, I just got back from showing this picture to someone else you know." He smoothed the paper against his thigh.

Uriah's large frame fidgeted in his chair. "A lot of people know me."

"But only one is your wife."

Uriah's forehead creased. "Alva's seen the article."

Bonner raised a finger. "Not that wife, your first wife. Virginia Meade."

Justine gasped. "You went to see Virginia?"

"I did." He glared at Uriah, his smile gone. "She identified this picture as her husband, Spencer Meade."

Harland pumped a fist. "Yes!"

Dorthea and Goosie embraced.

Uriah stood, and made fists at his side. "I don't have to stay here and—"

Bonner stood. "Actually, you do." He nodded toward Thomas. "Would you mind telling Officer Crandell to come in and help with this?"

Thomas left.

Bonner pulled some handcuffs from a pocket. "Spencer Meade, you are under arrest for the murder of Joe Trotter."

He bolted toward the door but Milton and Harland got hold of him. Officer Crandell came inside and with his help, the cuffs were locked around Uriah's wrists. It was very satisfying to see him in his usual stance—hands clasped in front—but with the addition of the cuffs.

"This is ridiculous," Uriah said. "You can't prove anything."

Bonner nodded, as if considering this. "Which is why I am also arresting you, Lionel Watkins, for the rape of Helene Soames."

Helene embraced Milton.

"And . . ." Chief Bonner said, "I arrest you, Uriah Benedict, for spousal desertion *and* the crime of bigamy." He shook his head. "You can't have two wives, Benedict."

Crandell led Uriah to the police wagon with Harland at his side.

The chief paused at the door to tip his hat to the happy gathering. "Well done, Miss Braden. Well done."

"What made you seek out Virginia?"

Bonner paused a moment, thinking back. "It was at the station when you first brought her up. You said that Spencer had locked her away, but you didn't say where." He grinned and held a finger by his nose. "But Benedict did. He said she was at Ravenwood and she was crazy."

Justine was incredulous. "Why didn't you call him on it?"

He tilted his head. "Didn't have much chance. Between you throwing his sins at him, and him tossing them aside . . ."

He was right. "So, out of all my ranting, you finally believed me because Uriah slipped up?"

Bonner shrugged. "I believed you before that. You were so passionate and certain, and Benedict was so slick and sure of himself." He shook his head. "I hate people like that." He shook this last away with a nod. "After finding Mr. Trotter's grave and the bottle with the name of his murderer . . . I figured that the one person who could identify Uriah Benedict as Spencer Meade was his wife — you'd said she was still there. Nice lady. Real nice lady."

"Yes, she is."

The chief looked outside. "Gotta go and get him locked up." He grinned. "I think I'll put him in the same cell his wife was in."

Yes! "Should we follow you to the station?" Justine asked.

"Should my son and I come?" Helene asked.

"There will be time enough for that. Let me get him settled in the jail. Tomorrow is soon enough." He looked at each of them in turn. "I'll make sure he pays for the pain he's caused. I promise."

When the door closed, the room breathed again.

"This started with Virginia and ends with Virginia," Justine said softly.

"God led you to her," Harland said.

"Led me every step of the way."

Dorthea clapped her hands together once. "I think it's time to celebrate!"

"I agree completely." Harland lifted Justine off the floor, spun her around, then kissed her.

**

Goosie prepared a hearty dinner and there was much rehashing of the day's events. And much praising God for bringing it all together.

At one point Milton asked, "And how do you know all these details about the past, Miss Braden?"

Everyone looked at her. Should she tell him about her gift? After a moment's hesitation, she felt no nudge to do so. "God led me to the right place at the right time." *Time.* It was almost funny.

They were getting ready to eat pie when they heard the sound of a horse out front. And hurried footsteps.

Harland ran to the window. "It's a police officer, someone we don't know."

Thomas opened the door before the officer even had a chance to knock.

He stepped inside. "Good evening. I'm Officer Wilkins. Chief Bonner sent me." He was out of breath. "Benedict got away!"

"What?"

"They were driving back to the station with Benedict and Crandell in the back, and somehow he got one hand loose from the cuffs and started beating on Crandell. The chief stopped the wagon, but then Benedict jumped out of the wagon on top of him and pounded on him. Then he got in the seat and drove off. He escaped!"

"He's free," Helene whispered.

Justine wanted to scream.

"Are the chief and Crandell all right?" Harland asked.

"Chief's face is a mess, and Crandell's bruised up pretty bad, but they'll be okay. They ran to the station and Chief sent Crandell and Benson after him. Chief's telegraphing all the law offices in the towns nearby. I was sent to tell you." He looked around the room. "Which ones are Miss Braden and Miss Soames?"

"We are," Justine said, pointing to herself and Helene.

"The chief told me to especially tell you to be careful. Everyone should stay together. I'm supposed to stay here with you, to protect you."

Justine appreciated the offer.

"What about Alva?" Dorthea said. "If he goes home . . ."

"I'll go fetch her," Harland said. He was out the door before anyone could discuss it further.

A half-hour later, he returned with Alva. She entered the parlor, her skin pale. She saw Helene and took her hands. "I am so sorry for the pain my husband caused you."

Helene looked surprised. "Thank you, but if anything I should ask your forgiveness. If I'd done something all those years ago he might have been arrested. And perhaps he wouldn't have caused harm to so many others."

They looked at each other a moment, then embraced.

The entire group had gathered. Now to wait.

**

What do you do while you wait for a madman to attack?

You try to act normal.

Which was impossible. But the people at Dorthea's house gave it their best try.

Everyone stayed close, spending time in the parlor, the kitchen, or the dining room. Harland and Milton talked medicine. Dorthea and Thomas played cards with Alva and Helene—a game devoid of any whoops of victory. Goosie explained to Officer Wilkins how to make a rhubarb pie—in too much detail.

Justine sat by the window and watched.

And prayed that God would finish His work.

Soon.

CHAPTER TWENTY

With four guests staying the night, sleeping arrangements at Dorthea's could have been difficult. But they weren't. Alva shared Dorthea's bedroom, and Helene slept in Justine's. The other two guests—Milton and Officer Wilkins—took turns standing watch. They also took turns napping on a pile of quilts Dorthea and Alva stacked on the wood floor in the parlor.

Justine couldn't sleep at all. She didn't even try.

She sat in Granny's rocker, with Granny's shawl drawn tight around her shoulders. Rocked up and back. Up and back.

"You can go to bed, Miss Braden," Wilkins whispered from his place at the window. "Milton and I have it covered."

"Thank you, but no. I started this. I need to finish it."

He nodded and moments passed when the only sounds were the ticking of the mantel clock, Milton's soft snores, and the creaking rhythm of the rocker. Her prayers found the same rhythm. *Bring him in, Lord, bring him in, Lord . . .*

Let this be over.

**

Justine was awakened by a gentle nudge. She opened her eyes to see Goosie standing before the rocker. "Sorry. I must have dozed off."

"Did you sleep here all night?"

"Sat here. Didn't sleep much." She noticed Milton was on guard at the window, and Wilkins was asleep on the makeshift bed. She hadn't been aware of the exchange at all.

She looked out the window. "The sun's coming up." The light was still dim, only hinting at the day.

"We made it through the night," Goosie said. "Praise God for that. I'm going to make coffee and oatmeal."

"Is everyone awake?"

"They are. Though I doubt anyone slept well." She left for the kitchen.

Justine pushed herself to standing and stretched. Her back and neck suffered for her awkward sleeping position.

Harland and Thomas came down the stairs and Justine put a finger to her lips, pointing at Wilkins. Harland tiptoed over and drew her into an embrace. If only she could remain in his arms, her head so snug and comfy on his shoulder . . .

"Is my mother up?" Milton whispered.

"She is. The ladies will be down presently," Thomas said.

"And then what?" Justine hadn't meant to say the words out loud. But the question remained. "Then what?"

"I don't—"

"Shh!" Suddenly, Milton leaned toward the window. "A horse. Someone on a horse."

Wilkins bolted to his feet and rushed to look outside. Harland and Thomas went to the door. Harland picked up the fireplace poker along the way. They were ready to defend the house.

Wilkins squinted and turned to the men, "Stand down. It's the chief."

"Alone?" Harland asked.

"Alone. Open up for him."

Thomas opened the door and Chief Bonner came inside. His face was swollen, and splotched with black and blue bruises. "Good," he said. "You're up."

"Are you all right?" Justine asked.

He waved the question away.

"Good news or bad?" Harland asked.

Dorthea and Helene were just coming downstairs. Goosie came out of the kitchen. He waited until everyone was present.

"It is good news *and* bad," he said. "The police wagon was found out east, near Olathe."

"Uriah abandoned it?"

"It is a rather conspicuous mode of transportation," Bonner said. "We think he ditched it and stole a fresh horse. One was reported stolen nearby." He took a deep breath. "The point is, he's gone."

"So you think." Justine wasn't convinced.

"I think it's clear he isn't coming back to Lawrence. Maybe he's heading back to where he lived with the James and Younger gang. In Missouri."

"Are they still around?"

"Some of 'em. Unfortunately." Bonner looked a little pale. "May I sit?"

"Of course." They all joined him.

He had more news. "I had an artist friend draw a sketch of Uriah from that newspaper article. He's making a wanted poster of him. I'll get the newspaper to print up a few hundred copies and get them posted everywhere in Lawrence, Eudora, Topeka, Kansas City. . . He's a unique-looking man being so tall with a shaved head. He can't easily blend in."

"Can we offer a reward?" Alva asked.

"We could, but we don't have the funds for that."

Alva sat up straighter. "I have the funds. I received an inheritance from my parents."

"I'm sorry, ma'am, but when you got married your money became your husband's. I doubt you can get to it."

"But he's abandoned me."

"Hopefully," Justine said.

"I'm sure we can get a judge to work through all that, but right now, your funds are limited."

"That's not fair," Goosie said.

Bonner shrugged. "No, it ain't."

"I'll contribute to a reward," Helene said. "One hundred dollars."

"I'll contribute too," Thomas said.

Everyone chimed in with their own contribution. Milton even offered $50.

"Well now," Bonner said. "That's very good of you folks." He looked to the ceiling, doing the math. "That's $750. Very impressive."

"Is it enough?" Justine asked.

"Billy the Kid has a $500 bounty on him and Frank and Jesse James have $5000, so $750 is a very respectable amount." He slapped his leg. "Shoot. I'll even put in fifty. And I'll talk to Mayor Usher. He was there when the truth came out about Benedict, and I'll fill him in on the rest. He might want to personally contribute or even use some city funds for it."

"Thank you," Helene said. "That's about all we can do, isn't it?"

"I believe so," Bonner said. "I've telegraphed police departments, county sheriffs, and other lawmen from here to St. Louis to the east, and as far as Salina to the west. Gave them all a description of him and noted his aliases. I asked them to pass it along from there. And I'll send them some posters too. With a little luck, soon there will be no place for him to hide." He stood to leave.

"What should we do now?" Alva said. "Should I stay here? Can I go home?"

"You are welcome to stay here," Dorthea said.

"Thank you, but I can't stay forever." She gave Bonner a pointed look. "How long should we be afraid?"

He wiped a hand over his unshaven face. "I don't rightly know."

"Till he's dead," Milton said.

Everyone was shocked, and yet Justine had had the same thought.

Bonner was at the door. "Would you like Officer Wilkins to stay?"

They all exchanged looks, then shook their heads. "That won't be necessary," Thomas said. "Though we do appreciate him staying last night."

"Glad to do it." He looked directly at Justine. "He *will* be brought to justice, Miss Braden. I know it."

"Thank you, Officer."

The men left. "The 'what now?' question remains," Harland said.

Helene touched her son on the shoulder. "In our case, the what-now involves going home and getting back to our lives."

"Really, Mother?" Milton said. "What if—?"

"Whatever *if*, we'll deal with it. Lionel Watkins has tainted our life long enough. It's time to fully move on." She expressed her thanks, said her goodbyes, and they were gone.

"I'm leaving too," Alva said.

Justine was surprised. Alva had never seemed that brave. "You can stay."

She shook her head. "Helene has inspired me. From what you've all said, Uriah has never returned to a past persona. He probably has a new name already. I don't believe he's coming back." She scoffed. "He was trying to poison me. Doesn't that prove he wants nothing to do with me?"

Dorthea put a comforting arm around her shoulders. "I'm so sorry."

Alva hesitated, then said. "I'm not. Everything that's happened has led me to this moment. And at this moment I feel stronger than I've felt in a long time — maybe ever. He wants nothing to do with me? I want nothing to do with him." She took a deep breath, then laughed. "I am free. I am finally free."

They said congratulations and shared her joy.

"Do you want me to take you home?" Harland asked.

"No. I think a morning walk is the perfect way to start my new life. Thank you all."

With their guests gone, the air of the house settled.

Goosie broke the moment. "Breakfast anyone?"

**

The conversation at breakfast was lively, but circular. Any speculation about Uriah was useless and a waste of time. He'd lived three lives without detection. As Alva had said, it was very probable he'd moved onto a fourth.

He was out of their jurisdiction and hopefully out of their lives — which was a good thing. And yet . . .

"What if he hurts someone else?" Dorthea asked.

"It's not a question of *if*," Justine said.

"I hate to bring this up," Harland said. "But if he's on the run and *will* hurt others, where is the justice? He's free."

"But so are we," Thomas said. "Alva is free of a horrible husband who wanted her dead. Helene is free to fully move

320

on with her life—and so is Milton. Virginia knows the truth about Spencer, and—"

"Ah! Wait!" Justine jumped to her feet, toppling her chair.

Harland righted her chair. "What's wrong?"

"Nothing's wrong. I'm happy!" She pressed a hand to her forehead. "I can't believe I forgot to share the most important part of my last trip."

"What?"

She couldn't stop smiling and looked around the table at each face. "Virginia's children—Anna and Luke—they are alive!"

They stared back at her in stunned silence.

"Virginia said they got sick and died," Goosie said.

"That's what Spencer wanted her to believe. But they didn't die. Spencer sold them to a family in Topeka."

"Sold?" Dorthea said.

"The family adopted them. I went with Caesar to hand them over. Joe Trotter was the man who arranged for the adoption, but Spencer killed him. Took the money." The memory flooded back. "There was no reason for him to kill Joe. Joe was giving him the money anyway."

"Maybe he didn't want a witness," Thomas said.

Probably.

"Aren't there headstones for the children at the farm? Graves?" Dorthea said.

"Fake," Justine said. "Planted there to cover up their disappearance." A sudden thought made her suck in a breath. "I tried going into the past using their headstones, but nothing happened."

"Because they aren't buried there," Harland said. "They aren't dead."

Justine laughed. "I love when things fall into place and finally make sense."

"Where's the sense in Spencer giving up his kids?" Goosie said.

Justine touched her fingers, making her point as she answered. "Caesar said Spencer hated kids. After he and Virginia had two, he wanted out. He sold the farm, killed Cole, and sold the kids. He left the area with Caesar, then came back a new man: Uriah Benedict."

"But why?" Goosie asked.

After a moment of silence, Harland had an idea. "For Alva's inheritance?"

"Maybe. Though I'm not sure he knew her before he came back."

"For prestige?" Thomas asked. "You'd mentioned he was driven by the need for respect."

"I know the real reason," Dorthea said. "He came back because he's a compulsive liar who thrives on conning people, hurting, raping and killing, and . . . because he's evil."

Justine swiped the air with a hand. "Enough about Lionel-Spencer-Uriah-whatever his name is now. The children are alive! And I know where they live."

"Lived," Harland said. "How many years ago was that?"

1872. "Seven," she said. "But they *might* still be there."

Harland stood up from the table. "Only one way to find out. Let's go pick her up."

It took Justine a moment to understand.

"I think Virginia's mourned long enough, don't you?" he said.

"We're going to get her first?" she asked. "What if they're not there?"

"If they've moved, we can find them. The point is, they are alive."

"The point is," Goosie said. "Their mother needs to know."

"Needs to see them," Dorthea said.

Now.

**

Harland and Justine drove the surrey up the drive of Ravenwood. Justine put a hand to her midsection. "I'm so excited I can barely stand it. Can't you go faster?"

Harland flicked the reins and the horses quickened, finally stopping in front of the building.

Mr. Sutton must have heard them coming, for he came outside. "My, my. You're in quite a hurry. Good morning to you both. What brings you out this fine morning?"

Harland lifted her down. "Is Virginia available for a visit?"

"Of course," he said. "She's in the garden."

They walked around the side of the building and saw Virginia and Eddie.

"You can run if you want," Harland teased.

The thought, *I would if I could,* turned into action. "I think I will." Justine lifted up her skirts and ran to the garden.

The two looked up from their work, clearly surprised.

"Gracious, Justine," Virginia said. "What's got you so excited?"

Justine pressed a hand to her chest to calm her pounding heart.

Harland caught up. "Give her a second."

Virginia smiled. "I can guess what this is about. Did Chief Bonner speak with you?"

"He did," Justine said. "Your identification of Uriah as Spencer was instrumental in getting him arrested."

"Arrested? That's good," Eddie said.

"That's very good," Virginia said. "The chief seemed pleased when he left here."

She bobbed twice on her toes. "We're not here because of that."

"Just tell her," Harland said.

Justine took Virginia's hands. "Anna and Luke. Your children are alive."

Virginia's head lurched back. "What are you talking about?"

"They didn't get sick and die. They were adopted by a couple in Topeka."

Virginia staggered and Eddie caught her. "Okay now. Let's sit." He led her to the chair under the tree.

"I'm fine, I'm fine," she said. "Please don't fuss." She touched the chair beside her and Justine sat. "My Anna? Little Luke? Are you sure about this?"

"Very sure. I know where they live—at least where they lived in 1872. The names of the couple who adopted them are Amos and Larraine Krupman."

With an intake of breath and a nod, Virginia stood. "Take me there."

**

On the way to Topeka Justine told Virginia about her husband—*all* about him.

"Why didn't you tell me this before? You said Spencer was going by another name and was married to Alva, and the policeman showed me the picture, but all the rest?" She shook her head, clearly overwhelmed.

"Perhaps I should have told you," Justine said. "But what good would it have done for you to know that your husband—under whatever name he was using at the time—was a ruthless criminal."

"You tell me because I'm *not* a delicate flower." She sat up straighter on the bench-seat of the surrey. "I *lived* through a great number of the tragedies you listed. I survived and even thrived. I deserved to know the full truth."

Justine felt the air go out of her. She put a hand on Virginia's knee. "I'm so sorry. I was protecting you when you didn't need protecting."

Virginia patted her hand. "I forgive you. Your intentions were pure."

Were they? "Thank you."

"So Spencer is on the run?" Eddie asked, from the front seat he shared with Harland.

"It appears so," Justine said.

"We hope so," Harland said over his shoulder. "The police are posting wanted posters in all directions. What can be done, is being done."

Virginia clapped her hands twice then held them out, palms up. "And so we let it go."

Justine was confused—and inspired. "You're forgiving him?"

"How can I not? 'God is the judge: he putteth down one, and setteth up another.'"

"But God let Spencer hurt you and yours," Justine said. "And so many others."

"He did. Though I'd like to understand, I know I never will. His ways are not our ways. And see the good that's coming out of it?" she said. Her eyes teared up as she looked at the fields passing by. "My children, who were dead, are brought back to me. Praise the Lord!"

Maybe it wasn't necessary to know the *why*. Maybe all she needed to know was that God was God.

And they, were not.

**

They turned onto Greenwood Street. In the past seven years the trees had grown to a nice height, creating mottled shapes of shade and sun on the road.

Justine pointed to the second house. "That's the one."

Harland pulled up and the men helped the women down. Justine started up the walk.

But Virginia held back. "The Krupmans may not be happy to see me. And the children might not recognize me at all." She extended her hands on either side. Eddie took one, and Justine the other. Harland completed the circle. Then Virginia prayed. "Lord, we thank You for this miracle. You've brought us this far. Let everything play out according to Your perfect plan."

"Amen." Apparently, a prayer was all Virginia needed, for she immediately marched up to the front door and knocked. The rest of them stood at the bottom of the porch steps.

Please, God, please . . .

The front door opened and a pretty girl of seventeen or eighteen answered. Justine recognized her as Polly, all grown up.

"May I help you?"

"Is this the Krupman's?" Virginia asked.

"It is."

"Are Anna and Luke here?"

"They are, but . . ." Polly looked wary. She turned toward the inside of the house. "Mother?"

Before Mrs. Krupman came to the door, two children peeked around Polly.

"Move back," Polly told them. "Wait for Mother."

But they didn't move back. Instead they nudged their way around her. They stared at Virginia.

"Hello, Anna. Hello, Luke. I'm —"

Anna hurled herself at Virginia, wrapping her arms around her waist. Luke joined in.

Cries of "Mama!" and "You're back!" intertwined.

Justine's throat tightened. Harland put his arm around her shoulders. "You did it," he whispered.

Mrs. Krupman came to the door. "Polly? What's going on out here?"

Virginia stepped forward. "Hello, Mrs. Krupman. My name is Virginia Meade. I am their mother."

The children ran to their other mother. "Mama, look who's come!"

Mrs. Krupman put a hand to her throat. "I see, I see. But I don't understand."

"May we come in?" Virginia asked. "There's a lot to explain."

**

They all sat around the Krupman's dining room table. Accompanying this simple act was the heady sense of family.

"When will Mr. Krupman get home from work?" Virginia asked. "I'm eager to meet him."

Her face clouded. "I'm sorry. I assumed you knew. He passed away last year of consumption."

"I'm so sorry for your loss," Virginia said.

"I miss Papa," Luke said. "He used to take me fishing."

"You like to fish?" Eddie said. "I do too." He looked at Mrs. Krupman. "Perhaps your mama would let us go fishing sometime?"

She nodded. "That would be nice."

She passed the plate of cake around. It looked delicious. "I'm very eager to hear your story, Mrs. Meade."

"Virginia. Please."

"And I am Larraine." She poured buttermilk for everyone.

"I'm not sure where to begin," Virginia said.

Justine gave her a suggestion. "Your family had a farm...?"

Justine was happy to sit back and let Virginia explain the series of events that had brought Anna and Luke into the Krupman's lives. There was no need to speak of Spencer's other crimes other than the fact he'd unfairly taken the children's mother away from them.

There were two awkward moments. The first occurred when Mrs. Krupman stared at Justine a bit too long.

She caught herself. "I'm sorry, but . . . have we met, Miss Braden?"

"I don't believe so." *When I met you I was Susan Miller.*

Larraine shooed the notion away.

The second awkward moment came when Larraine asked, "How did you know the children were here?"

Justine allowed herself a lie. "I heard it from Caesar Johnson."

Larraine's face lit up. "I remember that name. He was the one who brought the children here."

"He was." Justine wanted to move the subject along. "And now their mother has found them."

A shadow passed over Larraine's face. "They have two mothers now."

An uncomfortable tension entered the room.

"They're not leaving," Polly said emphatically. "I'm going away to school, but I can't go if you're all alone here, Mother."

"I will be all right. You *will* go to college. Your father made me promise."

"What if . . ." Virginia looked at Eddie, then at the children. "What if I moved close by so I could see the children. But they could stay here in the house with you, in the home they know."

"We'll have two mamas!" Anna said.

"None of my friends have two mamas," Luke said.

They all looked to Larraine. It was up to her.

She studied the faces of her children, then looked at Virginia. "I think that would be very nice."

May God be praised.

**

For the trip back to Ravenwood, Eddie asked to sit in the back of the surrey with Virginia. The two of them spoke in low tones and held hands.

Justine's heart swelled with happiness for them, but wished they would talk louder. When Harland began to talk she shushed him. "Shh. Listen."

A few minutes later, they heard Virginia tell Eddie, "I love you, too."

Justine looked over her shoulder and saw them kissing.

She turned forward and slipped her hand around Harland's arm. "Now, you can talk."

**

When they left Virginia and Eddie off at Ravenwood, it was confirmed. The couple was betrothed. They would have to wait for the paperwork of a divorce from Spencer, but they all agreed that no judge in the world would deny their request.

As soon as Justine and Harland got home, they told the family about Virginia's reunion with her children, and her engagement to Eddie. It felt good to share some happy news for a change. But when they started talking about what would happen next for Virginia's family, Justine stood.

"If you'll excuse me?"

"Where are you going?" Thomas asked.

"Out and away."

"Out and away where?" Dorthea asked.

She grinned at them. "None of your business." She stood before Harland and held out her hand. "Would you care to join me?"

He took her hand. "I believe I would. I've always been partial to out and away."

Justine pulled him outside, down the front walk, and onto the street. Then she began to run, forcing him to run with her.

"Where are we running to?"

"I don't know and I don't care."

He ran alongside, and she marveled at the odd joy that welled up inside her. And though it was totally improper — and all who saw her would think she had gone mad — she raised her arms to the sky as she ran.

Harland did the same — bless him.

When she reached a park near downtown she slowed, headed toward the tallest tree, and sank beneath it. Harland joined her.

"I'm not used to running."

"And yet you've run twice in one day. I love seeing you so happy."

She scooted back to lean against the trunk. "It's over, Harland. Finally over." When he hesitated in his response, she pointed at him. "Do *not* point out that we have no idea where Uriah is."

"All right, I won't."

She slapped his arm. "That doesn't matter because he's *not* here. All those who were hurt by him have found some peace and satisfaction in knowing that their pain has been acknowledged by others, and their offender accused."

"They've learned they are not alone."

His comment spurred her to take a deep breath. "I do believe I've been thinking about this wrong. Justice isn't just about getting the perpetrator convicted and punished, it's also about setting the victims free."

He scooted close and she left the stability of the tree for the stability of his shoulder. "I'm very proud of you, Jussie. God is very proud of you."

I hope so.

They sat in silence, letting the breeze waft over them. The smell of the grass made them think happy thoughts. Bird-song accompanied the special time between them.

Suddenly, a new thought spurred Justine to sit upright. "Ever since we've moved here, I've been consumed with this quest. But now that it's over . . ."

"You're asking 'what now?'" His eyes sparkled with a hopeful glint.

She nodded.

He moved to his knees and leaned forward to kiss her. Just once. "How about we plan a wedding?"

What a wonderful idea.

She tackled him to the grass and kissed him.

More than once.

Chapter Twenty-One

Two Months Later

Justine stood before the mirror in her bedroom, looking at a bride. At herself.

She almost felt detached. Surely this woman dressed in white satin and moiré, was someone else. And yet, it wasn't.

"Is something wrong?" Dorthea asked.

Goosie chimed in. "Anything you need, you ask for. Today is *your* day, Jussie. Your mother would have been so proud of you."

Maybe her mother and father's absence were at the core of her mood. From a young age Justine had been groomed to be a wife. The image of Morris Abernathy, the man her parents had chosen for her, came to mind.

And went. To be honest, she was rather annoyed that he'd interrupted a single moment of her wedding day.

Dorthea took her hand. "I know you'd love for your mother to be here, but know that I am here, as a secondary mother to you. I am very honored and grateful to have you as a daughter."

She was incredibly sweet. Justine drew her hand to her lips and kissed it. "I am the one who is honored. And there is no 'secondary' to it. You are like a mother to me and *I* am grateful."

They stood beside each other and gazed at their reflection. The high lace collar of her wedding dress topped a bodice of pleated organza. The overskirt culminated in a pleated bow at her knees, revealing a skirt made of rows and rows of alternating lace and pleats. "The dressmaker is as talented as any I would have hired in New York."

Dorthea laughed. "Why, thank you. But you helped with the ideas." Dorthea pointed at the low side bows that crowned the train. "I never would have thought of that. Or using sprigs of Lily of the Valley as a corsage and headpiece." She shook her head. "You are the essence of loveliness. Harland will swoon at the sight of you."

Justine chuckled. "A smile will suffice."

The clock on the mantel struck the half-hour.

"We need to get to the church," Goosie said. "You don't want to be late for your own wedding."

**

It was rather unusual to have her father, Thomas, walk her down the aisle, then change positions and be the officiant for their vows. Such an arrangement in New York City would have kept the gossip-vine vibrating for months, causing her mother palpitations and a good dose of hysteria. But here in Kansas, such an oddity was quickly ignored, if not embraced.

The music began. The walk was made. Justine sought Harland's eyes, and was glad he didn't swoon. As predicted, he smiled. But his eyes also filled with happy tears, causing her own to do the same. *Thank You, Lord! I am incredibly blessed.*

The vows were exchanged and the declaration made. "I now pronounce you husband and wife."

When Harland hesitated, Thomas said, "Kiss her, you fool!"

Their new life sealed with a kiss. *May there be many more.*

When they faced the congregation and walked arm in arm down the aisle, the guests did something else that would never be condoned in the city: they applauded and cheered.

**

The reception was held at Alva's home. She was the perfect hostess, as fifty guests filled her large parlor and dining room, spilling out to the wide porch and even to tables on the front lawn. Mrs. Russo outdid herself, filling a table with a three-tier wedding cake, a sheet cake, a groom's cake, and various mints, nuts, and cookies.

Justine and Harland finished their cake — Harland had enjoyed one slice of each — and pushed their plates away. Their friends and family chatted happily around them.

Justine nodded toward Virginia, Eddie, and Mrs. Krupman — Larraine — who sat together on the porch as Anna and Luke played tag in the grass with Polly. "I'm so happy to see how close they've all become. What could have been an awkward situation has been blessed."

"God arranged things perfectly," Harland said. "For Virginia to find a house to rent near Larraine . . ."

"And Eddie finding a job as a caretaker for the capital building . . ."

Harland cocked his head. "Has Virginia mentioned when their wedding will be?"

"She only says, 'as soon as possible.' They do have a lawyer working on her divorce."

"*Then* she'll be free."

"Free of her past, and free to fully love a good man."

He put his arm around Justine's waist. "As are you, wife."

She touched her head to his. "As am I."

Virginia walked toward them. "Here she comes," Justine whispered. "Will you go get her present, please?"

Harland left the table and went into the house.

Virginia kissed Justine on the cheek. "I didn't mean to chase your husband away."

"You didn't. Couldn't. He'll be right back." A moment later he returned with a package wrapped in calico. He handed it to Virginia. "For you."

"Me?" Virginia said. "It's a day for you to receive gifts."

Justine waved her comment away. "It's something I ordered ages ago, but it just came the other day. Open it."

Virginia pulled at the end of the bow and the fabric fell away. She stared at it. "*British Flowers,*" she said. "My book."

"Not *your* book exactly," Justine explained. "But *the* book, just the same." Justine had sudden doubts. "Is this the book you liked so much, back on the farm?"

Virginia stroked a hand across its front. "It is." She held it to her chest as something to be cherished. "Thank you, Justine.

This is so very kind of you." She kissed Justine's cheek a second time.

"Have a seat." Harland offered his vacated chair.

"No, no," Virginia said. "That is a seat of honor. I just came over to congratulate you both and to invite you to come visit as soon as you return from your honeymoon." She glanced at the book. I already have plans for a garden. Luke has shown interest in planting things."

"His farmer roots run deep," Harland said.

She looked in the direction of her family. "Excuse me, I want to show them the book. I'm sure the pictures will spark many ideas." She touched Justine's shoulder. "Once again, thank you."

Justine enjoyed a contented breath. "That went well."

"As all acts of kindness should go. You are a good woman, Justine Jennings."

She loved the sound of her new name. "I can't wait to see Virginia's house. How exciting for her to have her own place after so many years at Ravenwood."

"It's an exciting time for us too, my dear. Soon, we will have our own cozy cottage." He studied her eyes a moment. "I hope being a block away from Mother's isn't *too* close."

"Not at all," Justine said. "I will need her help making it a home. Such happy work: picking out furniture and linens, dishes and glassware. . ."

"Keep this up and our bank account is doomed." He pulled her close until they were nearly lip to lip. "Our *home*, Jussie," he whispered. "I can't wait."

Justine kissed him, then pulled his arm around her shoulders. She looked at the beautiful setting. The undulating shadows of the trees made designs on the gingerbread details on the roof and porch. "Speaking of houses . . . I'm glad Alva was able to stay here. She's entertaining more and is even going to have the church circles meet here. That's something Uriah would never have condoned."

They watched a man approach Alva. The smiles the two exchanged spoke volumes. It was Seth Dobbins, the nice man who'd first given Justine a ride home from Virginia's farm.

"They're getting close, aren't they?" Harland asked.

"They are."

"But she's not free to marry," he said.

"Like Virginia, she's also filed for a divorce, but that takes time."

He leaned over and kissed her. "I know how hard it is to wait. But it's very worth it."

"You make me blush, Mr. Jennings." She could hardly wait for them to be alone.

Soon, but not yet. Now it was time to enjoy the celebration. She noticed that Helene and Milton sat with Mayor Usher and his wife. Helene laughed at some joke.

"Another happy ending," she sighed. "Another victim set free."

"Milton's going to be a good doctor someday," Harland said. "He's smart and has great compassion."

"As does his mentor."

Another kiss.

"Uh-hum." Thomas stood behind them. Eddie was with him.

"Sorry," Harland said.

"Never, ever apologize for loving my daughter."

"All right. I never will." Harland kissed her again.

But Thomas didn't leave. "I have a request. *We* have a request."

"Of course."

"The toasts have been made, but we each have an announcement."

"The grass is yours." Harland tapped his fork on his glass. "Attention everyone . . . have a listen, if you will?"

Thomas nodded to Eddie. "You go first."

Eddie put his hands in his pockets, then took them out. It was clear he wasn't comfortable being the center of attention. He seemed to look for someone. Then he found her. "Ginny? Would you come here please?"

Virginia walked down the porch steps. Eddie met her halfway and made his announcement from there. "This dear woman captured my heart eight years ago. She is the strongest, bravest, kindest, and loveliest person I have ever known."

"You exaggerate," she said.

"I do not." He held her hand and got down on one knee. "I know there are things to work out, but the one thing that is certain for now and for always is that I adore you. Ginny, will you be my wife?"

Virginia held back happy tears. "Of course. Yes! I love you too."

She drew him to standing and they kissed and embraced.

The crowd clapped and called out their approval. Luke and Anna ran to their mother and the couple welcomed the two into their fold, a happy family.

When the applause died down Thomas stepped forward. "Now it's my turn. Our turn." He motioned for Dorthea to join him. He took her hand. "I am happy to announced that Dorthea has agreed to become *my* wife!" Following Eddie's lead, he embraced her and they kissed to more whoops and applause.

Harland pushed his chair back and stood. "I am *not* letting this chance go by." He pulled Justine into an embrace and a kiss.

Others followed suit—even Alva and Seth.

"There's so much to be thankful for," Justine whispered in Harland's ear.

But then she caught sight of someone standing nearby. She let go of Harland. "Chief Bonner."

He stepped forward, helmet in hand.

They'd invited him to the wedding, but he'd declined, saying he had to work. "I'm glad you made it, Chief," Harland said. "Please have a piece of cake and join us."

"Thank you, but no." He smiled. "For there is much to do. And say."

Their curiosity was piqued. "What's going on?" Justine asked.

Bonner motioned to a chair. "May I? This won't take long."

"Please. Sit."

Justine's thoughts raced ahead. It had to have something to do with Uriah. The chief's smile implied it was good news.

"I'll get right to it. You know I sent officers off to look for Benedict, got the word out to other agencies, and put up wanted posters."

"We are very appreciative," Harland said.

Justine couldn't take the suspense. "Tell us! Did you arrest him?"

Bonner drew in a deep breath, then let it out with a smile. "More than that. Uriah Benedict is dead."

"Thank you, Jesus!" Justine's outburst was loud enough for all talking to stop. She stood and pulled the chief to standing. "Everyone? May I have your attention?"

Every eye turned toward her. "Chief Bonner has just informed us that Uriah Benedict will never bother any of us, ever again."

There were gasps and cheers. Virginia and Eddie embraced, as did Alva and Seth.

Justine turned to Bonner, "Can you give all of us a few details, please?"

He faced the guests and cleared his throat. "My man — with the help of the sheriff, found Benedict up near Liberty, Missouri, living in some shacks the James-Younger gang used to hide in — shacks *he* used to hide in. He opened fire and we fired back. He was killed."

It was odd to applaud a death, but that's what everyone did.

Bonner wasn't through. He pulled an envelope out of his pocket and handed it to Justine. "As you know, there was reward money — mostly *your* money. But Officer Crandell and the others . . . they want it divided between his children. Please give this to Milton, Anna, and Luke."

Justine stared at the check, glancing at Milton and the children. "They thank you. We all thank you for finally setting us free." Impulsively, she kissed his cheek.

His face reddened. "Well now. Maybe I will get me a piece of that cake. . ." He wandered off toward the food table.

Justine sank to her chair. "It's over. Finally over."

"You did it, Jussie."

She suddenly needed a moment alone. "If you'll excuse me, just a minute?"

Justine walked quickly to the side of Alva's house, and up the driveway. She stopped at the stables where she first spoke with Caesar.

She wrapped her arms around herself, raised her face to heaven, and closed her eyes. "Thank You, God. We did it. Please let Caesar know we did it. Let all of them know that Your justice has been done."

She breathed in and out, reveling in the warmth of the sun upon her face.

The Son upon her face.

THE END

**

"Thy mercy, O LORD, is in the heavens;
and thy faithfulness reacheth unto the clouds.
Thy righteousness is like the great mountains;
thy judgments are a great deep:
O LORD, thou preservest man and beast.
How excellent is thy loving kindness, O God!
therefore the children of men put their trust
under the shadow of thy wings."
Psalm 36: 5-7

DEAR READER:

Once again Justine's journey continues in a location that means something to me personally. *Where Time Will Take Me* was set in the fictional Piedmont, New Hampshire that was inspired by the real town of Piermont. One of my ancestors, David Tyler, was one of its founders, before the Revolutionary War.

But my family didn't stay in New England. They went west and many ended up in Minnesota where my grandparents, parents, and siblings were born. Not me. I was born in Nebraska. That became home.

So why did I write about Kansas? Because in 1991 my husband and I left all of our Nebraska families behind and moved with our three kids to Kansas City. Hmm. I guess we were pioneers of a sort. Good for us.

The point to all this is that Kansas is home and so I wanted to share my slice of the world with Justine and her family. And you.

So (you might ask) why didn't I set the story in Kansas City? Why Lawrence? History, dear reader. History. Although Kansas City has lots of interesting history, Quantrill's Raid won out.

There are two photographs I want to share with you. The first (on the next page) is downtown Lawrence in 1867, just four years after much of it was burned to the ground in the raid. This is what I love about the spirit of the Midwest. We do not give up. We persevere.

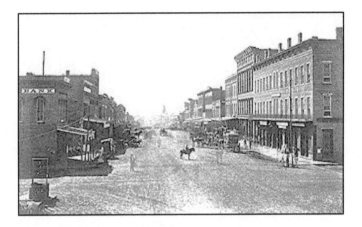

Below is another photograph of Lawrence, six years later still, in 1873 (six years before my story.) I am struck by the trees. To go from open prairie to a town with treed streets is impressive:

Now, that I've visually set the stage of the story, I'd like to share some tidbits from history that I found fascinating. Enjoy.

- **Absinthe.** This green-colored, anise-flavored type of alcohol that Uriah served was known as the Green Fairy. There were a lot of rumors about it causing hallucinations and crazed behavior, but many of those were exaggerated. But absinthe *is* strong: 110-144 proof (whiskey is 80 proof). Another issue was that the creation of this drink was not regulated so it often contained bad stuff, such as copper sulfate which turned it green. It was banned in many countries in the early 1900s. The reason for the bans is that it contains "thujone, a toxic chemical found in several edible plants including tarragon, sage, and wormwood." It's still banned in bars in the United States, but individuals can buy it in various forms. But who would want to?

- **Virginia's committal** to Ravenwood was inspired by Elizabeth Packard, who was committed to an insane asylum in 1861 for disagreeing with her minister husband about religious matters. She fell to the ground and refused to go, which inspired Virginia's reaction. Disturbingly, husbands had ultimate control over their wives. Elizabeth finally got out and spent her life working for the rights of mental patients. Here's a good book that tells her story: *The Private War of Mrs. Packard* by Barbara Sapinsley.

- **Insane asylums:** I'd like to mention a musical I was in once called *The King of Hearts*. It's about a World War I American soldier who comes upon a town of delightful villagers in France. He doesn't know that the real townspeople have all fled, and the people he meets are escaped from a nearby asylum. This gave me the idea for Ravenwood, where the patients are more eccentric than crazy.

- **Kansas University:** Harland's sisters went to Montana, to their mother's chagrin. She wanted them to go to Kansas University in Lawrence. The first class graduated in June 1873 and consisted of four students. One was a woman, Flora Richardson. She was the valedictorian. KU opened in 1866 and had had other female students, but all dropped out for various reasons. So Flora was in the first graduating class *and* was the first female graduate. When she died in 1924 her daughter said, "There has been no movement for the benefit of her community or for women and children that did not receive her ardent support. Women's suffrage, the women's rest room, the various plans to provide high school privileges for rural pupils and the farm bureau for rural women, each in their turn were things she was untiring in her efforts to secure." Five generations of Flora's descendants attended KU—the first family who's been able to boast of this accomplishment.

- **Kansas-Missouri fighting:** The people who traveled westward and ended up in Missouri and Kansas (with Kansas City straddling both states) were independent people—an admirable trait. But many came to flee from their own crimes, or because their views conflicted with established society. Those who settled in Missouri tended to have Southern roots, were often sympathetic to slavery, and had plantation-type farms. For the most part, those who settled in Kansas had Northern roots and opposed slavery. Sometimes opposing sensibilities were as close as the next farm. And so there was conflict—sometimes horrendous, violent conflict. Yet beyond the national issues—even overriding the issues of the Union and the Confederacy—was the desire and need for people to defend their families and home. The need to survive trumped everything.

- **Quantrill's Raid** was the most violent conflict between Missouri Bushwhackers and the Kansas Jayhawkers. William Quantrill was a guerilla fighter from Missouri who led a group of bandits who chased after escaped slaves and terrorized anyone who had Union sympathies. On August 23, 1863 he implemented a plan to ride from

Missouri into Kansas to attack the free-state stronghold of Lawrence. 400 men rode into Kansas before dawn. They were told to shoot any man — or boy who was big enough to hold a gun. The raiders carried American flags as cover until they got close, then held Quantrill's black flag. They killed nearly 200 men and boys, and burned Lawrence, causing $20-30 million in damages (in today's money). They rode back to Missouri and didn't lose a single man.

- Later, after being on the losing side of the war, Quantrill and his men headed down to Texas and continued to terrorize the countryside, but most broke up into smaller groups (including the James and Younger gang.) Quantrill ended up dying in Kentucky in 1865 after being shot by Union troops. He was only 27.
- Henry, the ex-slave that I mention during the raid, was based on Henry Thompson who ran from his home in Hesper toward Lawrence, to warn them of the raid. He stopped in Eudora (4 miles from his home, but still 9 miles to Lawrence.) He was totally exhausted, but spread the warning to people there.
- Jerry, another man I mention, was based on Jerry Reel, one of the men who heard Henry's warning and tried to get to Lawrence to warn the town. One man was killed when his horse reared and he broke his arm, the other was killed when his horse fell on him. No one got to Lawrence to warn anyone.
- Why didn't Lawrence fight back? Their defenses were down. They'd spent years being told that they were susceptible to an attack, and had armaments ready for such an attack. But when time passed and nothing happened . . . they let their guard down.
- The way Josiah and Susanna Dawson died during the raid is based on the actual death of Judge Louis Carpenter. When he heard the raiders come, he tried to escape outside, but they chased him. When he was caught, his wife and sister wrapped their arms around him, trying to keep him safe. The raiders tried to pull them off him, but when they wouldn't let got, they put a gun between them

and shot the judge while he was in her arms. They shot him many times.

- **The Clay-County Savings Bank Robbery:** February 13, 1866. Although there are conflicting reports of who was there, some believe this was the first bank robbery of outlaw Jesse James. It *was* the first daylight bank robbery in the country. A group of 10-12 armed men rode into town. This was not that unusual as the war had just ended. Two, wearing Union coats, went into the bank and stole nearly $60,00o in cash and bonds — nearly $1 million today. Many of the outlaws outside were recognized as Quantrill's men. One man was killed. George Wyman, a student at William Jewell College ran into the street. We don't know whether he was warning others that the bank had been robbed or trying to stop them, but he was shot dead. The robbers rode off with a posse after them, but snow quickly covered their trail. There was a $10,000 reward. No one was tried for the crime.

- **"Clothes make the man."** In Chapter 15, Justine mentions this quotation and says it's either from Shakespeare or Mark Twain. Twain published *Tom Sawyer* in 1876 so Justine would have been aware of him. He said, "Clothes make the man. Naked people have little or no influence in society." And in *Hamlet* Shakespeare writes: "For the apparrell oft proclaimes the man."

- **Mayor John Usher** is real. He served in the Indiana House and as Indiana Attorney General. He met Abraham Lincoln early in his career and was appointed President Lincoln's Secretary of the Interior. He was on the platform when Lincoln gave the Gettysburg Address, and was at his bedside when he died. After the war he was instrumental in promoting the Transcontinental Railroad from Kansas City. He served as the mayor of Lawrence for one term. He died in 1889, but his wife, Margaret, lived in their home at 1425 Tennessee (which still stands) until her death in 1911. The home is on the National Register of Historic Places and is the home of the Alpha Nu chapter of Beta Theta Pi fraternity of Kansas University. They had four sons.

- **Riverside School** at 601 N. Iowa (where Helene teaches) was the oldest school in Lawrence, dating back to 1855 – one year after Lawrence was founded. It originally was a 16′ x 18′ one-room school. Residents who lived on land with trees donated two logs each toward its building. Those who had no trees, donated money for a door and two windows. The first teacher was Allen Gentry who was paid $1 a month per student – by the parents. The timber school was replaced with a stone one in 1866 and was finally closed in 2003. Here's a picture of the new brick school in 1900:

- **Coffee Cake:** Larraine Krupman's coffee cake was a new phenomenon. The cakes originated in Germany and were more like a sweet-bread than cake. "Coffee cake" wasn't even a common term until 1879, which means I fudged by having Larraine serve it in 1872. A personal story… one of our family's favorite recipes is "Betty's Coffee Cake," named after my Aunt Betty. It has a wonderful crumbly streusel on top. Yet the grandkids never wanted to eat it. Then I figured it out: they thought there was coffee in it! Once we began calling it Cinnamon Cake, they liked it! Contact me if you want the recipe: www. nancymoser.com https://nancymoser.com/Contact.html

- The *Lawrence Daily Journal* was a real newspaper. Having Uriah's picture in it? The first photograph wasn't reproduced until March, 1880, so it wouldn't have been a photo. Before 1880 sketch artists provided the illustrations.

I could go on and on with the history. That's the challenge with writing an historical novel — the research. I'll be zipping along, writing a chapter, and then realize I need to know if the words "suitcase" or "surreal" existed in 1879 (they did not, only coming into our vocabulary in 1897 and 1937 respectively.) Or I'll have to stop to research whether Goosie could wrap a scone in waxed paper. (No. It wasn't invented until 1927!)

Beyond the historical events, finding out details about surreys and steamers, police wagons and uniforms, women's hats and corsets . . . I took a lot of detours that also led to a lot of rabbit trails where I realize two hours have passed and I've not written a word (but I have found real photographs of Lawrence or discovered that the mayor is someone with a cool history.) It's not an easy process, but it's one I choose to tackle again and again.

Next, Justine and Harland are traveling to Ireland. Remember all those ancestors listed in the Ledger? They're waiting to meet you (and me, actually!)

Thank you for your readership. It means a lot to me.

Nancy Moser

DISCUSSION QUESTIONS

- What do you think about Justine's choice to move from New Hampshire to Kansas?
- In Chapter 4, Goosie and Justine discuss their gifts. Look at Romans 12: 6-8 which lists various God-given gifts. Are you a Servant, a Perceiver, an Administrator, a Teacher, an Empathizer, a Motivator, or a Giver? (If you'd like to delve into the different pros and cons of these gifts, you might want to read *The Sister Circle Handbook* (by myself and Brenda Josee) or *Discovering Your God-Given Gifts* by Don and Katie Fortune. Hint: You probably have more than one of these gifts, but most often, one is prominent.
- In Chapter 7 Justine is about to interview people about Uriah. She has to be discreet in her questioning and prays, *Lord, help me only say what You want me to say.* Have you ever prayed such a prayer? What were the results? *Should* you pray that prayer? Often?
- In Chapter 8 Justine gets peeved at dinner because her family isn't making a bigger deal of her ability to travel through time. She admits she wants them to make a fuss — which elicits laughter. What do you think about Justine's behavior? Was she being selfish, or is her desire for a "fuss" understandable?
- In regard to Justine's gift, Dorthea says it's like any great gift — it often can be overwhelming to the family and they end up just leaving the gifted-one alone. If Justine was in your family, how would you deal with her extraordinary gift?
- In Chapter 9, Dorthea and Justine discuss time travel. Justine talks about seeing her mother at age twenty — at virtually Justine's age. "If only everyone could meet their young parents as peers, not parents, the generations would understand each other better." Think of your own parents. What would you like to know

about their younger days — before you were born? What were they like when they were young?

- In Chapter 9, Dorthea says one of the hardest things to do is to let our children go. Have you experienced this? What were the difficulties? What were the victories?
- In Chapter 9, Dorthea talks to Justine about making time to get married — as there might never be a perfect time. This bit of advice can be applied to many big decisions in life beyond marriage: having children, getting a new job, going back to school, starting a new project. Name a life decision where you made the decision to "just do it" instead of waiting for the perfect time. What were the results?
- In Chapter 10 Justine feels burdened with the responsibility God has given her. She has many unanswered questions regarding what to do with the information she's discovering. Harland tells her she's not an ordinary woman, or rather, she can do ordinary things *and* tackle the extraordinary tasks that her gift involves. Name a woman you know (perhaps yourself) who is faced with this sort of balancing act. How does she (you) balance the ordinary and the extraordinary?
- Also in Chapter 10, Virginia is faced with some hard truths, but in acknowledging her husband's sins, she is freed to love Eddie, the man who stood by her through the hard times. Has God ever placed someone in your life to help you through hard times?
- In Chapter 11, after spending time away from Uriah, Alva briefly shows a stronger side of herself to Uriah, yet she knows there needs to be a "delicacy in her strength." What do you think this means? How do you think Alva handled Uriah after this?
- In Chapter 13, Alva talks about the fear she has around Uriah. She can't eat. She just wants to curl up and hide. "You have to understand that the anticipation of his wrath is just as painful *as* his wrath." How do you handle conflict? Have you felt like Alva? How do we gain courage in the midst of fear?

- In Chapter 16 Justine is frustrated that her travels have not provided usable proof against Uriah, yet knows that nothing she discovers is wasted. Harland paraphrases I Corinthians 15: 58: "Stand firm. Let nothing move you. Always give yourselves fully to the work of the Lord, because you know that your labor in the Lord is not in vain." How has God used seemingly unimportant events or moments in your life toward a larger goal?
- In Chapter 20 Justine realizes that justice isn't just about getting the perpetrator convicted and punished, it's also about setting the victims free. Have you ever been the victim of injustice? How was it resolved? How were you set free?
- In Chapter 21 everyone finds out that Uriah is dead. They rejoice. As Christians should they rejoice?

Justine's Fashion

Bustles

Chapter 4: Justine went to her trunk and pulled out a tie-on bustle made of strips of mohair. Then one created with ruffles, and another out of wire and with intricate ties. "There's this one. Or this one. And this. And finally . . ." She tossed a fourth one onto the bed. "That one's stuffed with wood shavings. Not a favorite."

Chapter 4: The intricate lace came from Belgium, the striped overskirt was hand-embroidered. The pleated back and peplum culminated in an enormous emerald green bow, over another full-length cascade of satin pleats hanging over a two-foot train. "If I put this on without its bustle, can you adjust the back so the skirt won't drag in the muck?"

Chapter 20: The high lace collar of her wedding dress topped a bodice of pleated organza. The overskirt culminated in a pleated bow at her knees, revealing a skirt made of rows and rows of alternating lace and pleats. "The dressmaker is as talented as any I would have hired in New York."

Dorthea laughed. "Why, thank you. But you helped with the ideas." Dorthea pointed at the low side bows that crowned the train. "I never would have thought of that. Or using sprigs of Lily of the Valley as a corsage and headpiece." She shook her head. "You are the essence of loveliness. Harland will swoon at the sight of you."

Life Lines

"Sometimes silence reveals wisdom."

"We learn endurance through pain."

"Faith is like love; it has no limit."

"A woman who reveals too much of her
body, reveals too little of her mind."

"God is never late and never early."

"Free will isn't free.
There are consequences."

"Choosing to do the right thing has
far more value than being forced to do it."

My Challenge to You:
Write down Life Lines
from those you meet and love.

ABOUT THE AUTHOR

NANCY MOSER is the best-selling author of 40 novels, novellas, and children's books, including Christy Award winner *Time Lottery* and Christy finalist *Washington's Lady*. She's written eighteen historical novels including *Love of the Summerfields, Masquerade, Where Time Will Take Me,* and *Just Jane. An Unlikely Suitor* was named to Booklist's "Top 100 Romance Novels of the Decade." *The Pattern Artist* was a finalist in the Romantic Times Reviewers Choice award. Some of her contemporary novels are: *The Invitation, Solemnly Swear, The Good Nearby, John 3:16, Crossroads, The Seat Beside Me,* and the Sister Circle series. Nancy has been married for over forty years—to the same man. She and her husband have three grown children, seven grandchildren, and live in the Midwest. She's been blessed with a varied life. She's earned a degree in architecture, run a business with her husband, traveled extensively in Europe, and has performed in various theaters, symphonies, and choirs. She knits voraciously, kills all her houseplants, and can wire an electrical fixture without getting shocked. She is a fan of anything antique—humans included.

Website: www.nancymoser.com
Blogs: Author blog: www.authornancymoser.blogspot.com
History blog: www.footnotesfromhistory.blogspot.com

Find Nancy Moser here:

WHERE HOPE WILL HEAL ME

Book 3 of the Past Times Series

Coming in 2021!

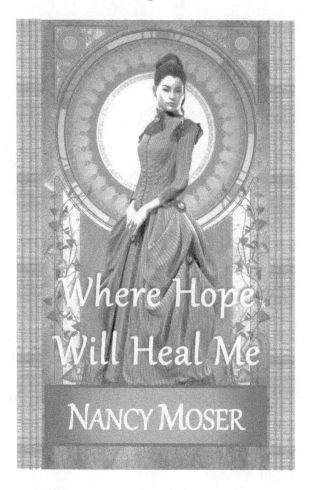

Justine and Harland begin their new life together. When tragedy strikes they feel the need to find their family roots. They head to Ireland. There, Justine explores the secrets of her own past, and discovers a way to find hope in healing.

Want more time travel?

What would you change if you could do it all over again?

The annual Time Lottery offers its winners a chance to go back into their past and make a different life choice, exploring the what-if questions that plague them.

In *Time Lottery* follow the journey of a surgeon, a socialite, and a homeless man. In *Second Time Around* watch a movie star, a contractor, and a college student accept their winnings and totally immerse themselves in their pasts, exploring what could have been. Will they choose to stay in their alternate reality==their Alternity — or will they return to life as they knew it?

What would you do?

Time Lottery **is a Christy Award winner!**

Buy on Amazon